WOMAN OF
FLAMES

Kim Stokely

Bellevue, Nebraska

Book Layout ©2013 BookDesignTemplates.com
Cover Design: Victorine Lieske

Map by Michael Weir www.patreon.com/levilagann

Woman of Flames/ Kim Stokely. -- 1st ed.
For Printed copies ISBN 10: 1492173959   ISBN 13: 9781492173953

To John
Because without your love and support, none of this would
have been possible

Although based on the Biblical account found in Judges 4 & 5, this book is a work of fiction. Every attempt was made to be historically and spiritually accurate, but some details have been altered to enhance the story. Please see the Author's Notes for more information regarding the life of Deborah.

Throughout the story, the Hebrew name for the Lord has not been spelled out in deference for the Jewish tradition. Instead, the letters YHWH are used to represent His name. The correct pronunciation is Yah-way

CAST OF CHARACTERS

+ Fictional Character

◊ Historical Person

DEBORAH'S FAMILY

◊ Deborah   *Her story is found in the 4 & 5 chapters of the Biblical book of Judges*

+ Azareel   *Father*

+ Avram   *Brother*

+ Bithia   *Stepmother*

+ Palti   *Stepbrother*

+ Nathan   *Half-brother and son of Azareel and Bithia*

+ Edin   *Nephew*

+ Rachel   *Aunt*

+ Leb   *Uncle. Married to Rachel.*

+ Adara   *Cousin*

+ Uri   *Cousin*

+ Michal   *Married to Adara*

◊ Lapidoth   *Michal's brother and an Israelite soldier*

+ Eglah   *Avram's first wife and mother of Edin*

+ Tamar   *Palti's wife.*

+ Daliyah   *Avram's second wife.*

CANAANITES

◊ Sisera   *General of the Canaanite army*

◊ Jabin   *King of the Canaanites*

+ Visnia   *Sisera's mother*

+ Miu   *Sisera's wife*

+ Zuberi   *A Canaanite high priest*

+ Ute   *Sisera's servant*

ISRAELITE ARMY

◊ Barak   *Leader of the Israelite army*

+Neriah   *A young soldier*

+ Jorim   *A soldier*

+ Deker   *A soldier*

+Judith   *Deker's wife*

OTHER IMPORTANT CHARACTERS

◊ Jael   *A Kenite orphan*

+ Seff   *A Kenite and Deborah's first love*

◊ Heber   *Seff's older brother*

+ Achida   *Seff's father*

+ Taavi   *Seff's younger brother*

+ Pallu   *Jael's uncle*

+Rivka   *Jael's aunt and Pallu's wife*

+Sanura   *Achida's Egyptian wife*

+Zahra   *Taavi's Egyptian wife*

+ Obed   *A priest*

+ Elisheba   *Obed's wife*

+ Bilah   *Deborah's friend*

+Maava   *Deborah's friend*

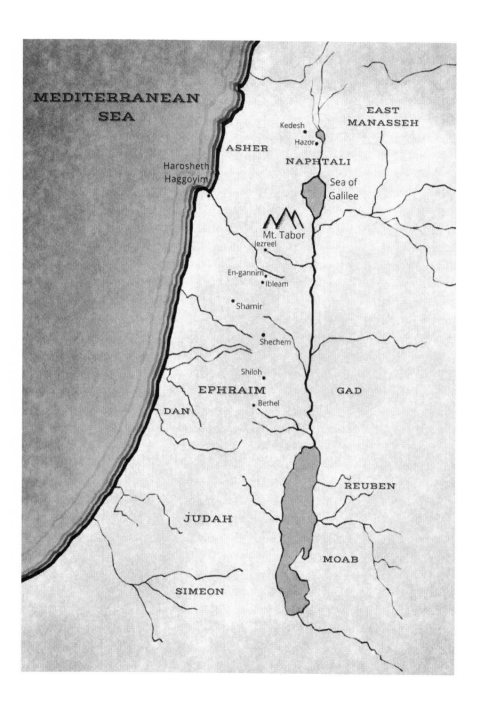

PROLOGUE

In the Hills of Ephraim

Winter-Late 12th Century B.C.

His wife's screams tore through the night and pierced Azareel's heart. He paced the floor of the mud brick house.

Omri, his brother-in-law, grabbed him by the shoulders. "It always sounds worse than it is. Let the women take care of her."

Azareel tried to break Omri's hold.

"She's already born you one son. Do not fret, my brother. She will live to bear you many children." Omri's strong hands pushed him down. "Sit."

Azareel sat on the dirt floor, resting his head in his hands. *Had the wait been this hard when Avram was born?* He had been younger then; his face not lined, his beard not peppered with gray. *Maybe the years had made him softer.*

He looked across the small fire in the center of the room to where his son lay. Avram was halfway to manhood, but still looked like a babe when he slept. The amber glow of firelight danced around the boy's head. Dark-brown curls obscured most of his face and Azareel saw that Avram sucked on a piece of hair while he dreamt.

Another cry of pain echoed through the village. Azareel knelt with his face to the ground and prayed.

Later, as the gray light of dawn filtered into the room, he heard someone approach. His older sister, Nama, carried a bundle in her arms.

"You have a daughter."

Azareel smiled. Although not the blessing a son was, he knew his wife would love a daughter. He looked at the baby in his sister's wiry arms. "She is a big girl, no?"

Nama nodded, her hazel eyes focused on the floor.

Azareel reached out and took hold of the infant. "Avram!" He called to his first born. "Come. See your new sister!"

His son scrambled to get up. "Where is Mama?"

"We will see her in a little while. Come. Look."

Seven-year-old Avram shuffled over and peeked at the red face sleeping in the blanket. "She looks funny." The boy yawned. "Can I see Mama now?"

"We will see her shortly, she needs—" Azareel halted when he looked at his sister. Nama stepped forward. She lifted her head. Tears fell from her eyes. Azareel's legs went numb. He thrust the baby back into his sister's arms. "Sarai?"

Nama shook her head. "I'm sorry, Brother. We did all we could. The child was just too big. There was too much blood."

Azareel reeled out of his sister's house. He stumbled as he ran the short distance to his own home. A blood-stained blanket smoldered in the fire outside. The acrid stench burned his nose. He stood in the doorway, his eyes struggling to see through the dim light inside. The midwife already keened softly as she prepared Sarai's body for burial.

"No!" Pushing the midwife aside, he fell at his wife's feet. He crawled to Sarai's head, then gently cradled her in his arms. He brushed her hair from her face. His fingertip traced her lips, now a light blue instead of the vibrant red he had kissed the night before. He clutched her to his chest and rocked. With his other hand he grabbed fistfuls of dirt, pouring them on his head. He tore at the neck of his woolen tunic, rending the garment down to his chest. His own keening began. Loud, guttural cries that came up from his soul. His mourning alerted the village. He heard them join in his sorrow.

Azareel stood alone in the village center, staring up at the gray sky of twilight. Hills rose gently around the cluster of sun-dried brick houses. He watched the leaves turn up their undersides from the whisper of a cold breeze, heralding the coming of the autumn rains. The wind grew stronger. Rushing down from the forested mountains and whipping up the folds of his torn and dirty robes, it blew his salt and pepper hair about his face. He didn't notice Nama had joined him until she placed the baby in his arms.

"Our cousin, Neta, will nurse her for you. The babe can live with them if you like."

Azareel looked at the sleeping infant. *Could he love this child who had taken his wife from him?* Maybe it would be best if it grew up in another's house. But the girl was also his last bond with Sarai. They had tried for so long to have another after Avram. For six years they had prayed and sacrificed. Sarai had bought herbs from the traveling merchants. They had all but given up when Sarai announced she was with child again. The whole village had celebrated. There hadn't been a new baby in more than a year.

The babe in his arms wriggled, squeaked and woke. Azareel looked down at his daughter and gasped. "Her eyes, Nama! Have you seen her eyes?"

Nama placed her hand on her niece's head. "We've asked the elders what it might mean. They do not know. We can only wait and see if they will change. They know it means something, but whether it bodes ill or not . . . ." His sister shrugged.

Azareel stared into his daughter's golden eyes. They were the color of sunlight dancing on a dark mountain stream. He felt like he could swim in them, lose himself in their peace.

The baby squirmed again, surprising Azareel with her strength. She loosed an arm from her blanket and thrust it up toward her father. The hand brushed his beard and Azareel smiled. He took the tiny fingers in his and kissed them. The baby yawned.

Azareel looked back at his sister. "Tell Neta I am grateful for her offer. The child will live with them until she is weaned."

"Brother, think carefully. What can you teach a girl? She needs to be reared with other women."

Azareel shook his head. "Our village is small. There will be other women to teach her. But I want her in my house as she grows."

They stood quietly in the courtyard. Both watched the baby as she fussed a moment, then fell back to sleep. Azareel kissed his daughter's forehead as he handed her back to Nama.

"Take her to Neta so she can be fed when she wakes."

Nama nodded and walked away. She turned back. "What is the child's name, Brother?"

Azareel thought for a moment. "Deborah. Because she has caused me pain, like the sting of the bee. But her eyes hold the promise of much sweetness, like honey. Her name is Deborah."

ON THE PLAINS OF CANAAN

Spring, Several Months Later

Sisera's breath came in hot, heaving gasps. All around the young man the sounds of battle rang; the clanging of swords, the thunder of horse's hooves. A soldier on the ground cried out in agony. Sisera stepped toward his fallen comrade. His sandaled foot lost traction on a blood-soaked stone and he crashed to the ground. His stomach lurched and heaved up bitter bile. *Please, El.* He prayed silently to his god. *Get me out of this torture!* He rolled onto his back, trying to find his courage as the battle around him quieted.

"To the King! To King Jabin!" A charioteer called as he rode by the fallen warriors of both sides.

Wiping acidic spittle from his mouth, Sisera struggled to his feet and searched through the thick smoke of battle to find the king's chariot. He stumbled forward with the other young foot soldiers, their bodies bloodied and bruised. He examined his own dark skin. Dirt clung to rivers of sweat on his arms and chest, but he saw no wounds. Ahead, the king's standard flapped in the wind. The more experienced soldiers already gathered around the iron chariot.

King Jabin shouted over the cries of the dying. "Victory is ours! Go now! Bring us the children to sacrifice to El in gratitude for our success. Take what women you want. This village is ours!"

A great roar rose from the Canaanite soldiers. Sisera watched, transfixed in mute revulsion, as mothers were dragged from their houses to be raped amid the horror of the battlefield. Other men hunted down children, binding their hands, and tying them together in a long chain. An older girl, perhaps twelve or thirteen, ran shrieking from one bald-headed soldier. She fell at Sisera's feet.

"Have mercy!" She clutched the short linen wrap that hung from his waist. Her brown eyes full of fear. "Please!"

The soldier strode like a bull toward them. His bald head and chest glistened with sweat. He grinned maliciously.

"I fancied this one, but by the look of it, boy, you've never been with a woman before. I'll show you how it's done and then you can have a turn if you like."

Sisera shook his head. The girl clung to him, pleading incoherently.

"Suit yourself." The bull-man crudely wondered aloud about Sisera's ability to perform his duties as he wrenched the girl away. The young man had to grasp his clothing to keep her from pulling it off. The soldier dragged his prize by the hair before slapping her in the face and throwing her to the ground. Sisera turned away, not wanting to see more. He called out to an officer he knew.

"General Hagai!"

The general signaled for the driver of his chariot to stop. He looked around the carnage for the source of the voice.

Sisera waved his arm. "Over here, sir!" He jogged over to the officer.

"Sisera." The general took off his leather helmet and ran a hand through his graying hair. "You survived your first battle. This will be a day you'll never forget."

Sisera dipped his head and tried to smile. "Yes, sir. Have you seen my father?"

The general wiped the sweat from his brow. "He had the left flank. They attacked first. He is probably on the other side of the village."

"Thank you, sir. I'll look over there."

The older man grinned broadly and slapped Sisera on the shoulder. "Don't hurry, boy! Enjoy yourself as I am sure your father is!" The general pushed his helmet back on his head then signaled his driver to whip his horse forward.

Sisera backtracked over the field, ignoring the cries of pain and terror around him. He had been excited before the battle. His father had raised him on tales of war and life as a soldier. Sisera longed to make his father proud. But when the time came to draw swords and fight, it had taken every ounce of courage he'd had not to run. *Why are we killing these people? What have they done to me?*

His father spoke of honor and re-taking what was rightfully Canaanite territory. But the Israelites had owned it since before Sisera was born. He could not find it in his heart to murder people who had done him no personal wrong. He had not run from the battle, but he had not fought it either. He hoped his father could forgive him.

He spotted his father's chariot standing empty next to an Israelite hut. He recognized it by the beautiful, chestnut brown horses that pulled it. Perhaps General Hagai was right, and his father was expending his bloodlust with some Israelite woman. Sisera sat on the back of the chariot to wait.

His gaze roamed over the ground in front of him, trying to make sense of the remains of the battle. Ten or twenty Israelite men lay dead nearby, their throats slashed by swords or their bodies pierced by spears and arrows. Not as many Canaanite soldiers had fallen. The chariots were sent in the first wave of battle to strike terror into the enemy's heart. As they rode into a village, the riders easily cut down the enemy soldiers. The foot soldiers were sent in next, to clean up what was left.

A frightened squeal came from a nearby hut and another girl came running toward Sisera. Her torn woolen tunic flapped open as she ran, exposing her breasts, and the blood that ran down her legs. Sisera looked up, expecting to see his father chasing the young girl but a different soldier stood laughing in the doorway. The girl tripped over a body, quickly regained her footing, and continued her escape.

"You, boy." The soldier walked toward Sisera. "What are you doing?"

"I'm waiting for my father. This is his chariot."

"Your father was Methael?"

Sisera's heart stopped beating for a moment. "You said 'was' Methael. What do you know?"

The soldier no longer smiled. "I am sorry. I saw him fall. An Israelite struck him with rock from a sling. Another took him down with a sword."

Anger coursed through Sisera's blood. "Where is he? Where did he fall?"

The soldier pointed across the field. "He's not far. I can see the bronze of his armor from here."

Sisera stood in the chariot. Now that the smoke had cleared and the sun shifted in the sky, he too, could see the glint of bronze from an officer's armor. Choking back his tears, he jumped from the chariot. He ran toward the body of his father.

It took less than a minute to reach him. A great gash marred his father's once perfect face. A gaping wound in his neck desecrated his corpse. Sisera let out a cry of rage as he lifted his father to his chest. He heard nothing now, save the sound of his blood rushing through his ears. A great roaring fury pulsed through his mind. He let out another anguished cry. An Israelite had stopped his father with a rock. Another had cut his body with a sword. Sisera wished the battle would begin again, for now the fight was personal. Now he was ready to kill.

PART ONE
The Call

1 The Hills of Ephraim

Spring-Nine Years Later

Bithia wiped the sweat off her forehead with the back of
her arm. She sat cross-legged on the dirt floor. Her
hands worked garlic and chickpeas into a thick paste.

"Deborah!" Bithia called. "For the last time, move away
from the door. You are getting sand on the leeks."

The little girl quickly scooted inside the one-room house.
"Yes, Mother Bithia." Sunlight played off her light brown curls,
while dust and sand swirled on the breeze.

The older woman shook her head. A linen wrap held her
straight black hair away from her face but a few rogue strands
broke loose and irritated her. Deborah watched her stepmother
try to brush the hair away without getting the hummus she was
making into her eyes.

Annoyed at her inability to move the hair, Bithia vented her
anger on her husband's daughter. "Why do you try and listen
to the priest? You are nothing but a stupid girl. Women are

supposed to learn how to run a household, not learn the ways of God."

Deborah bowed her head and furiously chopped the vegetables on her board. She tried to keep her tears from falling onto the leeks.

Bithia's calloused hands continued working the chickpeas and oil into a thick mush. "Answer me, Little Bee. Why do you try and hear what he's saying? Do you think God would want a stupid girl to hear his teachings?"

Deborah's lip quivered as she whispered, "I'm not stupid."

"What did you say?"

Deborah lifted her head and stared at the older woman.

Bithia shivered. "Do not look at me like that."

Deborah sighed and went back to chopping the leeks. "Why can't I learn the ways of our Lord?"

"Because you are a girl. God does not speak to women." Bithia scraped the mush off her fingers into the bowl. "It is our lot in life to serve our fathers and then our husbands. Nothing more."

Deborah brought the chopped leeks over for Bithia to inspect. The woman nodded her approval at the size of the pieces and, with a shake of her head, directed Deborah to the pot in the center of the room where a simple broth simmered. The scent of garlic and cumin rose on its steam. The little girl added her leeks, then began dicing another. She worked quietly for a few minutes before speaking again.

"What about Sarah?"

Bithia sighed. "What are you asking now, Bee?"

"Father said that God's angels spoke to Abraham's wife, Sarah, and told her she would have a son." Deborah smiled to herself. Her father had often told her that story before she went to sleep at night. He liked to remind her that her mother had been named for the much honored Sarah.

Bithia added some more spices to the hummus. "Do you think you are equal to our forefathers? Do you think you are as special as Sarah?"

Deborah almost cut her finger as she finished dicing the leek. "No. But God spoke to her and she was a woman." Once this leek had passed inspection she slipped the pieces into the broth as well. She turned back to Bithia. "And Hagar—"

The older woman slapped her thighs. "Who?"

Deborah lowered her head. "Hagar . . . Sarah's servant. God's angel spoke to her in the wilderness."

"Your father has filled your head with worthless stories, Bee. And now you pester me with your constant questions and chatter."

Deborah tried to apologize but Bithia shooed her off. "Go! Get out of here." She pointed to a small pail in the corner of the hut. "Take some bread and cheese up to your brother and Palti. And in God's mercy, don't talk anymore to me today!"

Deborah quickly grabbed the pail, then ran outside. She dare not provoke Bithia anymore. She had felt the sting of her stepmother's hand across her face before and did not desire that pain today. She slowed her step as she passed by the priest instructing a circle of young boys. Several times a year, a scribe or priest would pass through their small village. If the boys could be spared from the work in the fields, the priest was asked to instruct them in the traditions and history of the Hebrew God. The man would be fed and given a place to sleep in exchange for his teachings.

Deborah looked at the boys. Only two or three appeared interested in what the teacher was saying. The others, especially the younger boys, traced designs in the sand or stared ahead with vacant expressions. She longed to sit within the circle and learn more about their God. But Bithia was right. Girls were not permitted to be instructed. At least not in public with boys.

Deborah hurried past the circle. Once she reached the edge of their little village, she ran up the hillside to find her brothers.

The bucket of bread and cheese clunked against her leg as she reached the top of the knoll. Avram liked to take the sheep to the east side of the hills so the rising sun could warm him. The same hills would then shield him from the heat of the afternoon.

It had been cool this morning and wisps of steam rose off the grass. Deborah imagined they were the smoke of incense burned at the Tabernacle as an offering to God. Moses and the Israelites had built the tent according to God's instructions. "A map of heaven," He had called it. She would like to see it, this tent, inspired by YHWH himself.

Deborah longed to know more of YHWH . . . El-Shadai, Raphah. Even his many names fascinated her. Her father recited the stories of their ancestors to her brothers and her every night after dinner. But Deborah hungered for more. She wanted to see Him. Touch Him. Speak to Him. If only she'd been born a boy.

She made her way down one hill and up another, then scanned the landscape for her brothers and the sheep. The damp grass chilled her feet. She wished she could run home and warm them by the fire. But Bithia would not let her near until dinner. She would have to stay out with the boys. Deborah hoped Palti was not in the same mood as his mother. Her stepbrother liked to tease her and call her "wasp," saying that her voice was as painful as the sting of the insect. Her brother, Avram, used to protect. Now he spent most of his time in the fields mooning over Eglah, one of the girls from the village. Deborah sighed. She missed the way her brother used to be when he would play with her and teach her games.

She spotted the boys in the valley below and ran down to meet them. "Avram! Palti!"

Avram lifted his arm to wave to his sister. Palti turned and walked toward a small group of sheep.

Deborah put the pail she carried down at her brother's feet. "Bithia sent some bread and cheese for you."

Avram raised an eyebrow. "So early? Have you been annoying her already this morning?"

Deborah plopped herself onto the dewed grass. She pulled her knees to her chest and hid her face. "Everything I do annoys her."

Avram sat down beside his sister, gently laying his hand on her head. "She does not know what to make of you, little one. You are too smart for her."

Deborah peered up at her brother. His deep brown eyes looked kindly down at her. "That's not what she says. She says I am stupid."

Avram glanced over her head at their stepbrother. Palti stood too far away to hear Avram whisper, "You are not stupid. You frighten her because you are so smart. You don't behave like the daughters she's already raised."

"Who would want to act like them? Dumb old donkeys is what they are. Fat and ugly." They too, had tormented Deborah when they lived in her father's house. Always yelling. Teasing. Pulling her hair. Deborah was happy when Timnah and Marian had been married off to men in a neighboring village.

Avram shook his head and laughed. "There you go. You shouldn't speak like that of our sisters."

"They're not our sisters. Not really."

"They are Bithia's daughters. That makes them our family."

"They are not our father's blood." Deborah smiled mischievously. "If they were, they would have been smarter."

Avram touched his forehead to hers. "If they were our mother's daughters, they would have been pretty, like you."

Palti walked toward them. "What are you two conspiring?"

Avram tousled Deborah's golden brown curls. "Nothing, Brother. Are you hungry?"

Palti sat down by the pail and pulled out a hunk of bread. "I'm always hungry."

Deborah hazarded a glance at her stepbrother and wondered what he'd look like in a few years. Palti was thirteen and almost as tall Avram. His hair was straight and black like his mother's. His round face had lost some of its baby fat over the past months, but his tunic, which should hang loosely down to his feet, caught on his stomach, stretching the linen fabric taut. *Will his body lose some of its weight as well? Or will he always be plump?*

It was important for Deborah to know these things because she'd heard her father talking about giving her in marriage to Palti. Azareel didn't know she'd heard them when she was supposed to be sleeping. She knew that Father wanted to keep her close to him when she grew. If she married Palti, they could live in Father's house. She was only nine, but it wasn't too soon to ponder such things. Bithia's daughters had been married at twelve and fourteen. And Palti would be of marrying age at the same time she turned thirteen. She shivered at the thought.

Palti fixed her with a cold gaze. "What are you staring at, Wasp?" Bread crumbs spit from his mouth. Deborah looked away disgusted.

He picked up a pebble and threw it at her. "I asked you a question."

Avram stood. "Leave her alone."

Palti glared, but let the matter drop.

Avram reached a hand out to Deborah. "Come. You can help me tend the sheep."

Deborah jumped up willingly. She liked when her brother showed her things and allowed her to help him. Avram's hand felt strong. Deborah marveled at how her brother had grown.

His body was lean and muscular, his hair dark, a mass of curls that touched his shoulders. The stubble of a beard shaded his jaw line and chin. Her heart grew heavy at the thought of her brother married with a family of his own.

Avram took a pouch from his waist and poured a sticky substance from it into his hand. It smelled faintly of rotten eggs. Next he poured some into Deborah's palms. He explained how sheep could be bothered by gnats and other small bugs that buzzed around their ears and eyes. He moved up behind a large ewe then gently placed his hands on its head.

"We rub the oil around their face to keep the gnats away. If we don't do this, the insects can drive the sheep into a frenzy. Palti often forgets or the sheep run from him because he's too noisy."

Deborah quietly walked behind a smaller animal.

Her brother's voice coaxed her. "Gently now. Come from behind the ears at first."

Despite her caution, the sheep scampered off.

"It takes a little practice. Try again."

Deborah picked the old speckled ewe. Moving slowly, she managed to rub the oil into the animal's wool. The sheep *baa'd* loudly when Deborah was done. "She's thanking me!"

"Yes. It is a great relief when we anoint their heads." Avram poured more of the oily sap into her hands and watched her try again. Because she was small and gentle, the sheep didn't fear her. Avram finally gave her the pouch and sent her among the flock on her own while he ate and rested by the mountain stream.

I am helping. I can do something good. Bithia often made her feel unimportant or, worse, like a burden. Deborah knew she wasn't skilled at sewing like so many women in the village. Her hands were bigger than most girls, too awkward to hold a needle. She had too much energy to sit at the grinding stone and mill the barley into flour.

She followed two sheep up the side of a hill and used the last of the oil on their heads. She wiped the excess off on their wool then sat down on the grass. From up here, she could see the land stretched out for miles. Several other villages dotted the hills in the distance, along with the terraced fields of barley and wheat. Beyond the foothills, forested mountains reached toward heaven. The spring sky was pale blue. Small white clouds danced overhead. A crisp breeze carried the scent of the acacia tree blossoms.

Deborah shivered. The grass whispered as the gentle wind blew over it. Her skin tingled. The air seemed to vibrate around her. She thought she heard someone call her name.

Deborah.

When she looked down the hill, Palti and Avram still lay by the stream. She waited, but heard nothing more, only the bleating of the sheep and the soothing sound of the water running down the hill toward the valley.

That evening, Deborah ran alongside her brother as they made their way back to the village. Palti led the sheep while she and Avram followed behind, herding in any strays. It was too early in the year to leave the flock out in the fields at night. Cold spring rains could chill the shepherds so they sickened with fever. Or mud might rush down from the hills, causing the sheep to flee. Palti and Avram drove the flock to the pen beside the village with the other herds. Each family knew which sheep belonged to them just as they knew their own children.

"Deborah!"

The little girl froze at the sound of her name. Her father stood by the doorway to their home, a stern look on his face.

She wondered what she could have done wrong for her father to look so angry.

She glanced up at Avram, but received no comfort from her brother before her father called again, "Come here!"

Deborah walked slowly with her chin down. When she reached the place where Azareel stood, she didn't raise her head to meet his gaze. She felt his hand on her shoulder.

"Walk with me, little one."

Deborah swallowed with difficulty as she followed her father outside the village and up a small hill. He sat under the shade of a sycamore tree. Deborah sat beside him, peeking up through the hair covering her face. Her father looked tired and worn.

Azareel let out a long sigh. "Ah, little one. I have failed you."

Deborah shook her head. "Never, Father!"

Azareel brushed her hair away from her eyes with his calloused hand. He cupped her face with the other.

"Yes, I have. I have not raised you as a proper woman should be raised. It is causing much strife in my house." He tilted her head slightly and kissed her forehead before releasing her. "It is time you learn how to run a household."

"I try, Father. But I'm not good at such things."

Her father's voice was unyielding. "Then you will practice harder. You will learn."

"But everything I do annoys Bithia."

"No. It is that you question her about things she does not understand. No one taught her the stories of our God. That is what angers her. You must keep quiet and learn what she can teach you."

"But—"

"I will hear no argument." Azareel slapped his thigh. "You will obey me in this as you have in all things, Deborah. Bithia will need your help in the coming months and you need to learn from her."

Her father wrapped his arm around her shoulders. "She is with child. It is not an easy thing, even in the best of times, to carry a babe. And Bithia is not a young woman."

His eyes moistened with tears. He breathed deeply then smiled. "But it is a blessing from God. He will grant her strength." Azareel looked toward his daughter. "And you will help her. You will go to the well and get the day's water. Then sit and grind the barley. Whatever Bithia asks of you. And that means not speaking about God or asking her questions. Do you understand?"

Deborah couldn't talk for the lump in her throat. *Not speak about God? Could she not even think about Him anymore?*

"Do you understand?"

Deborah whispered, "Yes."

Azareel hugged her tightly. "I feel your sadness. Does it frighten you that you must grow up and become a woman?"

Deborah shook her head. "No."

Her father stroked her hair. "Then what is it?"

She pulled away from his arms. "How will I be able to stop my thoughts, Father? I think about God all the time."

Azareel's eyes sparkled. "You must not stop thinking of the Lord. You may seek Him and His will in everything you do, everything you see. But keep the thoughts to yourself." He tapped his finger gently on her head. "Talk to Him while you work and see if in the quiet, He does not answer you."

"What if He doesn't?"

Azareel pulled her to him again. "Then you will wait and ask me at night. I will still talk to you and teach you about God. But only if I hear that you are obeying Bithia during the day."

Deborah shuddered with relief. "Thank you." They sat upon the hillside, watching the sun set behind the forested mountains in the distance.

"Come. Let us see what Bithia has for our dinner tonight."

Deborah held tightly to her father's hand as they walked back toward the circle of two dozen mud brick homes that made up their village. Each hut was home to a family— grandparents, parents, children, and grandchildren. As families grew too big for one house, a room might be added on for a son and his bride. Deborah spied Avram and Palti walking to the house from the sheep pen. They made their way through the center of the village, stopping to talk to a group of men.

Father squeezed her hand. "Go. Help Bithia finish with the meal. Tell her I will be in shortly." He looked gravely down at her before setting off toward the other men. Deborah hesitated only a moment then hurried across to her home. She slowed herself at the doorway so as not to scare Bithia by barging into the hut.

A simple vegetable soup filled the home with warmth and a spicy aroma. Bithia knelt in front of the simmering pot. She looked up as Deborah stood in the doorway, her eyes narrowing. Deborah knew her stepmother questioned whether Azareel's scolding had had any effect on her.

"May I help you, Mother Bithia?"

Bithia's head tilted. "You may fetch the bread from the oven."

Deborah picked up a wooden board from one of the small niches in the wall and stepped outside. Her family shared the round brick oven with several other families, but each baker had her own mark. Deborah spotted the loaf with pinched edges that Bithia had made that morning. She slipped the wood board under the front of the loaf and gingerly pushed the rest onto the board. The round bread smelled yeasty and sweet. Her stepmother must have brushed the top with honey. Deborah brought it inside and placed it in the middle of the striped woolen blanket that lay on the floor.

"Father said to tell you he'll be in soon."

Bithia nodded. "Get some water from the cistern so that they can wash their hands."

Deborah filled a pitcher with water from the large container inside the home. Limestone gullies on the roof of the house caught the winter and spring rains, carrying them down into the large clay cistern inside the home. This water was used for cleansing their bodies and the household utensils. Water from the well outside the village was used for cooking. It remained sweet and clear, while the rainwater collected small pieces of dirt and debris on its journey to the house.

Deborah took the wine jug down from its shelf in the wall. "Would you like me to pour the wine?"

Bithia stirred the pot of soup. "You may set out the cups, but I will pour the wine when Azareel is home."

The little girl replaced the jug and set the clay cups on the blanket. She heard the raised voices of the men as they approached the hut.

"It is foolish to think of such a thing, Avram. Besides, you're not old enough to fight."

Azareel and Avram ducked their heads as they passed through the doorway. Palti followed a few steps behind.

"I am seventeen, Father." Deborah had never seen Avram so angry. "That should be old enough!"

"The age for the army is nineteen. You know that."

"But—"

"Enough!" Father waved his hand in a gesture of dismissal. "Daughter, bring the water so we can wash before the meal."

Deborah dutifully poured water into the large bowl and set it on an empty shelf. Azareel dipped his hands, rubbed them, and then rinsed them in the bowl again. Deborah brought him a small towel. Her father dried his hands and returned it to her. She repeated the ritual for Avram, Palti, and Bithia before washing her own hands. She emptied the bowl of water outside the doorway then sat down with her family. Bithia scooped the soup into wooden bowls and passed them to the men. Azareel bowed his head and gave thanks for the meal. After the prayer, he took the bread. He ripped a large piece off, using it as a ladle for his soup.

They ate in silence until Palti finally spoke. "I don't understand, Father. Who are these people attacking us?"

"They are Canaanites. King Jabin and his army. It seems the young king is restless. His father rebuilt the city of Hazor and his palace there. Jabin needs to prove his own worth now."

Avram glared at his father. "By attacking us!"

"They are not attacking us, Avram. They are attacking our neighbors to the north. Those in Nephtali and Issachar."

"But they will come here soon enough, Father. If they are not stopped."

"They have been attacking the northern tribes for ten years, and are no close to driving them out." Father's voice rose. "Besides, how do you suppose we should fight them? These Canaanites with their chariots and spears?" Azareel roughly tore another piece of bread from the loaf. "Will you take your sling shot against the mighty wheels of a chariot? The Canaanite warriors will run you down and stab you through the heart."

Avram jabbed at the vegetables in his soup with a piece of bread. "To sit and do nothing cannot be the will of God."

Azareel slashed the air with his hand. "We have no leader. There is no one to unite the tribes, and Jabin and his army are too big to fight alone."

Avram's eyes smoldered. "There must be something we can do."

"Yes. We can pray." Azareel paused and looked toward Deborah. "We all can pray to our God that He will see fit to spare us this punishment."

Deborah felt empowered by her Father's inclusion into the conversation. "May I ask a question?"

Azareel's eyes darted quickly to Bithia, who scowled slightly. "One question."

"Why are we being punished?"

Avram picked up his cup of wine and stared into the red liquid. He took a large mouthful. "Our people have turned their back on the Lord and His laws. There are many who worship at the temples of Baal and Asherah, offering sacrifices of blood and their own bodies to these foreign gods. Our God will not be mocked. He will wipe out the evil that permeates His chosen people. We must pray that we can turn His wrath away." Azareel swallowed the rest of his wine. "No more talk tonight. I want to eat in peace."

Deborah lowered her head. *How could anyone worship another god? Could an idol carved by a man create anything on its own? No!* She would do what Father asked. She would pray for God's mercy on her people. She would pray that her village, and all of Israel, would follow the Lord Almighty.

2 Hazor

The Following Day

Sisera stood facing the window, barely noticing the streets below him. Hazor, the glorious Canaanite city that the Israelite Joshua destroyed, had been rebuilt. It lacked the opulent splendor of its past, but still teemed with life and wealth. His bedroom window overlooked the two temples that guarded the city. One to Asherah, goddess of fertility and the harvest. The other to Baal, the god of the wind, storms, and seasons.

Sisera smiled to himself. He had a certain affinity for Baal, son of the great god, El. El might be the father of all the gods, but his son far outshone him. *As I have my father.* In the nine years since Methael's death, Sisera had matured greatly. As a teenager, he'd enjoyed the camaraderie of the soldiers in the field. He'd adopted their ability to rise above their emotions. He'd hardened his countenance and become seasoned in battle. As he'd proven his valor in combat, and his loyalty to the king, he'd been promoted until he now served as one of the generals of the *maryannu*, the elite corps of charioteers and guards. More and more, he found himself in the enviable position of friend, confidant, and trusted advisor to the king. At twenty-six, he had already surpassed Methael's legacy. *And I have not finished yet.*

"Master?"

Sisera turned. His Egyptian slave stood at the room's entrance. "Yes, Ute?"

"Your mother wishes to see you. She's in the garden."

Sisera studied the older man. He'd been captured during a battle with Egypt and brought to Hazor by slave traders. Forced into servitude for the duration of his life, he performed his duties without malice or hatred. Ute's dark eyes were devoid of thought, his brown arms muscled and strong. His wrinkled hands were calloused and worn from years of hard work. *He's either very good at hiding his feelings or he's a fool. I could not be a slave.*

"Sir." The slave's velvet and strangely accented voice jarred Sisera back to the present. "What should I tell your mother?"

"I will come directly. You need tell her nothing."

Ute bowed and left in one discreet move. Sisera brushed past him, walking down the stone corridor to the inner courtyard. On the battlefield, Sisera gave the orders, but his mother, Visnia, ran his household. He strode through the main foyer then out the columned entryway to the courtyard. The smell of the juniper trees floated on the afternoon breeze.

His mother sat on a large stone bench beside a tall fountain. Her slender fingers playfully splashed the water. She still looked young, having married Sisera's father when she was but twelve years old. Her black hair was braided elaborately with pearls and precious stones woven throughout. Her dress was of the softest wool and dyed deep purple. She looked up from the fountain as Sisera's footsteps crunched along the gravel pathway.

"Ah, my son. Come sit by me." She slid gracefully on the bench to allow him room. Her eyes perused his appearance as he made his way toward her. "You look well."

Sisera kissed her cheek. "As do you, Mother."

"You flatter me too much. I am old." Her black eyes sparkled with amusement, but he could see the fear behind her jest.

"Never, Mother. You are eternally young, like Asherah and Astarte."

She laughed lightly. "You play the game well." She stared at him. "I have written to King Jabin."

Sisera clenched his jaw. "What?"

The wind caught blossoms from the date trees, spiraling them to the ground in gentle circles. Visnia brushed a petal from his shoulder. "Do not get angry. We both agree it is time you marry."

He stood and paced around the fountain. "Don't you think this is something I should decide for myself?"

"Nonsense." A small, half-smile formed at the corner of her mouth. She narrowed her eyes as she looked at him. "You are too busy fighting the King's battles for him. But he and I both know it is time to start raising up a new generation of soldiers."

Sisera stopped pacing. Children. Sons. He nodded slightly. "I suppose you're right."

"Of course I am right." Her smile faded as she spoke. "We have picked a bride for you, a cousin of mine from Egypt. As my marriage to your father helped to solidify relations between our countries, so your marriage to this princess will help Jabin."

"Does this princess have a name?"

"Miu."

"Is she pretty?"

Visnia's face showed her disapproval. "What does it matter? I have not seen the girl. She is a tool for Jabin and a vessel for your children. If she does not please you, take a concubine." She pointed a finger at him. "But only after you have gotten a son by her."

Sisera turned away from her glare and focused on the fountain. The sunlight reflecting off the water burned his eyes. He closed them, but the glow from the light still bounced against his lids. "And when will the ceremony occur?" He rubbed his eyes before turning to face his mother.

"Jabin and I thought an early fall wedding, before the rains begin, would be appropriate. The girl is preparing her dowry now and should be here by summer's end. She will stay in the palace with the other virgins until the ceremony." She grinned. "Jabin plans to make your wedding part of a great celebration to Baal in hopes its consummation might bring the rains."

"So now I must not only win his battles, but sire his soldiers and convince the gods to end the drought?"

His mother stiffened. "Do not mock the King, Sisera. You will do whatever he asks, and for that, we will be rewarded."

"I know how to play the game, Mother. Do not fear." Sisera bowed and exited the courtyard without looking back.

3 The Hills of Ephraim

Spring-Five Years Later

Deborah woke before dawn. She sat up, heart hammering, eyes wide. Her younger brother, Nathan, whimpered then shifted so he lay on the warm spot left by her body. Palti lay nearby, snoring loudly.

Deborah struggled vainly to remember her dream. Nothing remained but the oppressive feeling of being pursued by something dark and evil. She thought she'd had the dream before, but since she only remembered the panic afterward, she couldn't be sure. She scooted her legs out from under the blanket and pushed herself up against the wall. Bringing her knees to her chin, she hugged her legs for comfort.

Lord, please reveal to me the meaning of this dream. What do I need to fear? Deborah prayed silently as the morning came slowly to life around her. The deep breathing of her family lightened as they came out of their slumbers. Father and Bithia slept in the opposite corner of the room. Her brother Avram and his wife Eglah slept in a nearby corner, behind a small half-wall. It offered little privacy for the young couple and their baby, but it would suffice until Palti married, and brought more children into the home.

Deborah shivered. She knew it would be time for her to marry soon. She was fourteen, and Bithia kept a close eye on her every month, waiting for the sign that her stepdaughter could carry a child. As hard as Bithia prayed for that day to come, Deborah begged the Lord to spare her. She loathed the idea of marrying Palti. Her stepbrother made a show of being kind to her when her father was present, but remained cruel and spiteful toward her when they were alone. The thought of laying with him, suffering through childbirth for a son of his; only to be set aside for another wife when father died . . . it sickened her. So far, the Lord had been merciful. If He would only stay her courses a few more months, perhaps father would give in to Palti's constant whining that he be allowed to marry Tamar. *Please Lord, let him marry her. I would rather die unmarried than to suffer at his hand for the rest of my life.*

Her father groaned from his pallet in the corner. Deborah looked over as Azareel sat up, scratching his face. "You're up early, Daughter." He rose stiffly and stretched his hands toward to ceiling. He tilted his head toward the cistern. "Pour me some water."

Deborah moved quietly to fill a bowl. Her father pulled a striped, sleeveless tunic over the plain linen dress he'd slept in, then made his way out of the hut to relieve himself. Deborah wrapped her hair in a long linen scarf and tied it behind her head. She splashed some cold water on her face and dried herself on the sleeves of her garment before Azareel returned. He rinsed his hands several times then cupped the water up to his own face, scrubbing his beard and hair. Shaking his head dry, he caught Deborah's eye.

"Come outside."

Deborah followed her father into the warm spring morning.
From the neighboring huts came sounds of other families, slowly
awakening. Deborah missed the noise of the herds. The spring
rains had ceased early this year, the grass quickly turning
brown and hard. The hired shepherds had already come and
taken the flocks into the mountains, looking for greener pas-
tures. Her father groaned and rubbed his hands. Deborah picked
up her pace to walk by his side.

"Are you well, Father?"

Azareel stretched his hands out in front of him as he walked.
"The stiffness in my joints, it is always worse in the morning."

"I could rub some linseed oil on them, when we get back to
the hut."

"You worry about me too much." His smile faded. "I want to
talk about you."

"What have I done?"

Azareel led her outside the village and up the mound used as
the threshing floor for barley and wheat. He patted the ground
next to him as he sat down. "You are not sleeping. This is not
the first time I've woken to find you already awake. And Avram
has told me he hears you call out in the night."

"What do I say?"

Her father's head shook. "No words. Just moans and cries of
fear. What are your dreams?"

Deborah's eyes filled with tears of frustration. "I can't remember. A terrible darkness. A weight, pressing down on me
until I can't breathe. But no images. Just the feeling. And the
dark."

Azareel sighed. His eyes scanned their tiny village as the sun
finally broke over the hills, blanketing the houses in its warm
glow. "You are still praying?"

"Every day."

"And who do you pray to?"

Deborah looked up, her eyes questioning. "To God."

"But which God? Have you been tempted by the others in the village? Have you been praying to Baal up in the hills?"

Deborah vehemently shook her head. "No, Father!"

Azareel placed his hand on her knee. "I did not think so, but I wanted to be sure. You have been disappearing of late, where do you go?"

Now Deborah looked away and surveyed the awakening town. She let her breath out gradually. "I try to obey you, in all things. But I cannot be satisfied with life in the village. The constant chatter of Eglah and the other girls. The older women, matchmaking and gossiping. The little ones, wanting to play; wanting to be held. I need to go . . . where I can be alone with my thoughts."

She glanced back at her father. "I go out to the hills. Where Avram used to take the sheep to graze. By the stream that flows with the winter rain. It's dry now, but I sit by it and pray. I ask God all the questions I can't ask Bithia or Eglah."

Her father's eyes looked at her kindly. "Questions you will not ask me?"

Deborah sighed. "Questions I can't ask you, Father."

Azareel nodded. A dove called to its mate from one of the olive trees nearby. Deborah shifted as her father's gaze intensified. "Go and do your work. The day promises to be hot again, and you will want to find shade later to rest." He kissed her forehead. "And to pray."

"Are you coming?"

He nodded. "I will be along shortly. I need my own time in the quiet. There will be much to do as we begin the harvest today."

Deborah walked back home. Inside, Bithia sat on the floor, stoking the fire to make it ready for cooking. Eglah changed the cloths on her son Edin in the corner, while Palti and Avram ate leftover bread. Nathan ran about them, pulling at their tunics, trying to get a morsel for himself. The men ignored the young-ster as they talked about the work to be done.

Palti shoved a thick piece of bread into his mouth. "These newcomers, what part of the harvest will they expect for their help?"

"They won't take what isn't theirs. They are Schemuel's rel-atives. I expect they'll work in his fields."

Nathan screeched as the men continued to frustrate him. Deborah cut a wedge of cheese and thrust it at her half-brother. The youngster grabbed it and ran into the corner to eat. She sliced several more pieces of cheese, laying them out on a clay plate for the others to take. She ate one herself as she listened to Avram and Palti talk.

Palti wiped the crumbs from his lips. "Our harvest will be a poor one this year. We don't need strangers coming in and tak-ing what little we have."

"They are only strangers to us," Avram said. "They are fam-ily to Schemuel. The drought is more severe in the valleys. I would not be surprised if some of our relatives come seeking refuge."

Palti choked on a morsel of bread. "Do you really think so? Where would they stay?"

Deborah answered without thinking, "With us of course."

Palti glared at her. "I wasn't asking you, Wasp."

"But it's true. Father would be obligated to house any of his family coming for refuge."

"If there's not enough food for us, he would have to send them away," Palti argued. "He isn't obligated to starve his own family for beggars."

"Deborah, Eglah," Bithia called. "Go and fetch the water."

Palti continued to glare at Deborah. She broke his gaze and took a large clay jar from its shelf. She hurried out the door without looking at him again.

Lord, forgive me . . . but I hate him! I hate the way he eats. I hate the words he speaks.

Deborah's feet stirred up small clouds of dust as she carried the empty water jug down to the well. Eglah caught up to the group of girls walking ahead of them and gossiped with her friends. She had married Avram two years ago. Their son's birth proved her fertility and secured her position in the home as a favored daughter. Deborah tried not to be jealous of Eglah's light skin and hazel eyes. It was harder not to resent her for taking away Avram's love. Avram had been Deborah's protector, her guide, throughout childhood. Now that he had his own family, Deborah felt a deep hole in her spirit.

"Sister!" Eglah called. "You look lost in thought." She giggled with her friend Sele. "Has some boy finally caught your eye?"

The sharp-faced Sele laughed loudly. "Deborah? Notice a boy? I cannot believe that day will ever come."

Deborah shifted the jug on her shoulder. "That is only because there is no boy in the village worth noticing."

"Come now," scolded Eglah. "Surely there is one that is worthy of your attention?"

Deborah grinned. "There may have been one or two who diverted my attention, but there is none who is worthy of it."

Eglah's eyes showed surprise that Deborah had even entered into the gentle teasing, then sparkled with amusement as she understood her sister-in-law's jibe at the boys in their village. The group of women around her laughed as well at Deborah's snobbery.

Deborah set her jug down to let the older women draw from the well first. She heard their tsking as they glanced her way.

She knew they thought her strange. What woman didn't want to be married and have children? What daughter would be so picky about the man she married? Her Aunt Nama shuffled over to stand near her. Nama's back was bowed in a permanent hunch, her gray hair thin and brittle.

"You should not tempt the Lord's anger, Deborah."

"How do I do that, Aunt?"

"Your jests show your contempt for who you are. You are a woman. You should be praying for God to send you a just and decent husband. Instead, you spit on the prospect of marriage."

Deborah's hands tightened into fists. "You are wrong. It is a constant prayer of mine that the Lord would send me a decent husband." She looked pointedly at Nama. "For my greatest fear is to be wed to a man I know despises me."

Nama's hazel eyes were cloudy from disease, but Deborah saw her aunt understood her meaning. *Perhaps she will talk to Father for me? Perhaps there is hope for a different husband?*

Deborah filled Nama's jug with water, then took her turn at the well. She walked home, balancing the heavy container on her shoulder. Eglah arrived at the hut first and poured her water into the pot over the fire. Deborah emptied her jug into the cistern. The rains that normally filled it had stopped months ago. Edin, her nephew, squawked loudly from his blanket. Bithia's eyes flashed in annoyance.

"He has been like this all morning. Feed him or take him outside, Eglah. I cannot bear it any longer."

Eglah picked up her son and rocked him. She glanced over at Deborah. "You'll have to do the grinding alone today. I believe he's teething and will need my comfort."

He's always teething. The boy should have the mouth of a lion by now. Deborah let out a long sigh as she hefted the stone hand-mill from its place and brought it outside the hut. She went back inside to find a basket and a clean cloth in which to put the flour. A small sack of wheat grain was all that remained from last year. Father had brought it back from the plains when he'd gone to Shiloh for the Passover. It was good that the men would begin the barley harvest today, for soon there would be no grain left.

Deborah sat cross-legged on the ground with the mill in front of her. She poured a handful of kernels into the hole in the top stone, then turned its wooden handle. The grain slipped through the hole and ground against the stone below it. The flour would fall on the cloth she laid below the mill. The job was easier with two women, one to grind and one to pour, but Deborah didn't mind doing it alone. It meant she could be quiet.

She paused to pour more grain in the top hole. Looking out over the village she saw the men heading out to begin the barley harvest. Their wives and daughters brought out their own mills to start the day's grinding. She waved in greeting to her neighbors before returning to her work. Her thoughts drifted with the circular movement of her arms and the steady rhythm of the stones.

She thought about life in the village. It moved at a constant pace, too. The passing of time marked by the drama of the fields. It was by the harvest that the people lived . . . or died. The rains came in the winter, when the fields were plowed and sowed with seed. For only four months could her village rely on water flowing to their crops. The barley and wheat were planted first. Lentils, cucumbers, garlic, and sesame came in the late winter and early spring months. Then they prayed. Some to YHWH, some to foreign gods. They prayed for protection from the locusts, the animals, the birds and the sun.

Deborah stretched her arms and stood to loosen the stiffness in her legs. She watched the men on the hills, harvesting the barley. Their backs bent as they brought the sickle to the stalks and cut them down. These dry spring and summer months were the time to reap the barley and wheat. The grapes would be harvested later in the summer. The last of the crops to ripen were the olives, gathered in the fall. When the rains came, the process would be repeated again for another year.

Deborah returned to finish grinding the flour. For her, time moved slowly. The monotonous pace of the fields, the ritual movements of sowing, reaping, grinding . . . these were tasks that no longer required thought. As the years progressed, the rhythm of the harvest had become ingrained into her, as it did with all the villagers; a matter of necessity, of survival. The repetition was a source of comfort to her this morning, an escape from the dreams that plagued her sleep and warned of some impending danger. *As long as a new crop waits to be harvested, life cannot change too drastically, can it?*

"Is the flour ready yet?

Deborah looked up to see Eglah standing in the doorway. "What?"

"Bithia is like a bear this morning. She's waiting for the flour to make the bread. If she does not get it soon, she's going to tear off someone's head."

Deborah gathered the flour she'd ground and handed it up to her sister-in-law. "Here. I was almost finished. That should be enough."

Eglah took the cloth of flour into the hut while Deborah collected the remaining grain back into its sack. She brushed her hands on her tunic. *Bithia will only become angrier if she thinks I'm daydreaming.* Deborah brought the mill back inside.

Bithia sat, pounding dough with her fists. Sweat beaded on her forehead. "Go to the vineyard and prune back the vines." She lifted her head, gesturing toward Nathan. "Bring him with you. Keep him out until the sun is high overhead. Then you can take some wine and bread up to the men in the fields."

"Yes, Mother Bithia." Deborah reached her hand out to her brother. "Let's go to the hills." Nathan gratefully took her hand but wrenched it away when he got outside. "Wait for me, you little imp!"

Her brother laughed and scurried even faster across the village center. Deborah rolled her eyes and hurried after him. She let him run ahead, but kept a careful watch on the youngster. She picked up pebbles along the way. When they reached the vineyard, she gave him a handful then pointed to two young boys on the edge of the plants. "Do you see Reb and Machau? Take these pebbles and use them to scare away the birds. But if you leave the vineyard, I'll find you and make you eat the pebbles yourself, do you understand?"

Wide-eyed, Nathan nodded and took the stones. He ran off to join the other boys. Deborah made sure he stayed in the area before turning down the nearest row of grape plants and beginning her work. The tops of the vines had to be pruned back to allow the sun to reach below and ripen the fruit. Rotting leaves near the ground also had to be trimmed.

Deborah worked hard by herself for much of the morning. She welcomed the distraction when several other girls from the village came up to tend the vines. Most were younger and went along a different row of plants to gossip, but two saw Deborah working alone and came alongside her. The rest of the morning passed quickly as they drew their knives across the vines and talked. Bracha and Mava, both fourteen, told her about the strangers that had come to live with Schemuel.

"The father is Schemuel's brother-in-law. He looked for him at the Passover." Mava said. "He's brought his wife and sons up from Jezreel."

"What are they like?" asked Deborah.

Mava wiped the sweat that sought to drip into her deep brown eyes. Her dark hair shimmered with cinnamon-red highlights in the sunshine. "The wife is ill. My mother says she has the look of death about her."

Bracha stood an inch or so taller than Deborah, but carried much more weight than both her friends. Her round face brightened with a large smile, and her cheeks dimpled as she nudged Deborah with her shoulder. "But the sons! I saw them when they came into the village. They are like gods!"

Deborah stood and arched her spine, then wiped her forehead with the back of her arm. "You think every boy is handsome."

Mava nodded. "But this time, she's right. There are three of them. The younger one is just a boy. But the older two, their skin is light, like honey. Their hair is the color of wheat and full of curls."

Deborah's eyebrows furrowed. "Aren't you promised to Micha? Why do you know so much about Schemuel's nephews?"

Mava sighed. "I am not married yet . . . ."

Bracha sat down between them. "It is a sin to even think about Schemuel's nephews, Mava. You're not free to make another choice." She glanced up. "But we are. I'll take the older one. Deborah, you can have the younger."

Deborah laughed. "I'm not sure I trust your opinion of men. I'll wait to make a decision until I meet them."

Nathan scampered down the row of plants, his face streaked with mud.

"Where have you been, little imp?" asked Deborah.

"With Reb." He pointed at an olive grove near the edge of the vineyard. "Up there."

Deborah checked the position of the sun. It stood overhead. She pocketed her knife in a small leather pouch at her side and glanced at her brother. His eyes looked heavy. Running about

the vineyard in the heat had tired him. He would sleep this afternoon. That should make Bithia happy.

Deborah said good-bye to her friends, then took Nathan by
the hand. By the time they reached the edge of the village he
whined to be carried. Deborah's own arms and back ached, but
she knew Bithia would be angry if the boy came home cranky.

She knelt down in front of him. "Climb on my back." The
toddler wrapped his arms around her neck. Deborah stood up.
He giggled as he nestled his head against her.

"Donkey!"

"I'm not your donkey. Don't think I'm going to be your slave
for the rest of my life."

Nathan's chubby legs slapped into her ribs. "Mine! Mine!"

She shifted the boy so he sat more comfortably on her back
as she walked toward home. "No. Not yours." *I'll have to serve
someone soon. But who?*

Returning to the house, Deborah paused for a drink, then
picked up the bread and wine to bring to her father. The sun's
heat made the walk up to the fields seem longer than usual.
Small beads of sweat dripped down the back of her neck by the
time she reached the men.

"Ah, daughter. It is a relief to see you." Azareel straightened
up from his work.

Deborah saw the look of pain that crossed her father's eyes.
He is getting too old to be working the fields.

Azareel raised an arm toward his sons. "Avram! Palti! Come
take your rest."

Deborah handed the pouch of watered wine to her father. He
took a long drink. Sighing with satisfaction, he wiped his hand
across his mouth. "Two loaves of bread? Does Bithia think we
are starving?"

"She wants to make sure you are fed, Father."

Azareel took one of the loaves as Palti and Avram came alongside them. "Take the other loaf and bring it to Schemuel in his field."

A look of disbelief flashed in Palti's eyes. "What?"

Azareel handed the bread to his stepson. "One loaf is enough for us. I am an old man, and do not need much."

Palti ripped the loaf in half. "But I need food."

Azareel glared at him. "And you have it. You have a mother and two sisters now who cook for you. What does Schemuel have? His wife is dead. His sister is dying. His young niece will not think to make him bread to help him through the harvest day." He took another gulp of wine then handed it Avram. "I would hope for the same kindness if I were in need." He held out his hand and Palti passed him the remaining loaf. Azareel took a small piece and gave the rest to Avram. He turned back to Deborah. "Take the bread to Schemuel. Ask if there is anything else you can bring them."

"Yes, Father."

The three men headed up toward a small grove of trees. They would eat and rest awaiting the cooler temperatures of the late afternoon.

Deborah carried the bread along the terraced hillside until she came to Schemuel's fields. He sat along the edge of the barley next to another man. The two looked worn.

"Good day, Schemuel," called Deborah.

Schemuel raised a hand to shade his eyes. "Who is there?"

She approached the men and squatted in front of them. "It is Deborah bat Azareel." She held the bread out. "My father sends his greeting and says his wife has made too much food for him this day. He asked me to bring the extra to you."

Schemuel ran a hand through his shoulder-length hair. Deborah saw the pride in his eyes. She quickly added, "Perhaps you and your family could help make sure we do not waste the food the Lord has provided."

Schemuel smiled and took the loaf. "I would not want to cause your father's house to fall into sin. We will be glad to eat what the Lord has given." He passed the bread to the man sitting next to him.

Deborah watched the older man tear a small piece from the loaf. His beard and hair were gray, but his face and hands were not as deeply lined as she thought they'd be. He gave the bread back to Schemuel. "Here you go, Brother."

"Deborah, this is my brother-in-law, Achida. He has come to live in our village." Schemuel turned back to Achida. "Call your sons. They can share in this blessing."

The older man walked up the hill to where three figures still toiled. Deborah rose as well. "Is there anything else you need? Do you have any wine or water to drink?"

"You are kind. There is a sack of watered wine in my house. Would it trouble you to fetch it for me?"

Deborah groaned inwardly. *Another trek there and back up the hills.* She gave no indication of her frustration to Schemuel. "It would be no trouble at all."

A boy of about her age ran up to them. "Is there really food, Uncle?" Schemuel held up the bread. The boy grinned. He took the loaf and hurried to meet his brothers. Deborah gasped softly as the others approached. They did indeed seem like gods. Or at least angels. They had taken off their outer robes and wrapped their cloaks around their waists. The muscles in their arms and legs were well defined. Even dripping with perspiration, the sun shone off their golden hair. The air sang with their laughter as they took the bread from their younger brother. Deborah lowered her eyes when they looked her way, but still watched them discreetly.

"Uncle!" The taller man called out, "To whom do we owe this bounty?"

Schemuel stood. "Deborah, these are my nephews." He pointed to each, starting with the eldest. "Heber, Seff and Taavi." Deborah judged them to be about twenty, seventeen and thirteen-years-old.

Heber took a step toward her. "Does this generous neighbor have a face?"

Deborah willed her heart to slow its beating before she looked up. Her gaze shifted from Heber to Seff. Both were handsome. *Oh Bracha, I'll take whichever one you don't want!* She smiled at the boldness of her thought.

"Ah, Seff," Heber's eyes twinkled with mirth. "I told you there would be much beauty in these hills."

Deborah felt heat rush to her cheeks. She dropped her gaze so they wouldn't see her embarrassment. Another voice spoke.

"You were right, Brother. But I fear you have caused this doe to flee from us." He came closer. Deborah caught the musky scent of his exertion. She breathed in deeply. Gathering her courage, she raised her head.

Seff took in a sharp breath. "Your eyes . . . I've never seen any like them."

Heber strode forward and pushed his brother away. "Let me see." She looked at him. Heber nodded slowly. "Lovely."

Deborah flushed again and spoke to Schemuel. "I . . . I will go fetch the wine."

The older man frowned at his nephews then turned back to her. "Thank you."

Deborah hurried away from the men. Her heart beat like a drum in her chest. A voice called down to her.

"Wait!" Seff followed her down the hill. He stopped only feet from her side. She resisted the urge to reach out and run her hand across his face to brush a curl from his eye.

Seff handed a leather flask to her, then took another from around his neck. "Would you be kind enough to fill these with water on your way back?"

Her voice betrayed her and she could only nod in response. A smile lit across Seff's face. "Not only beautiful, but generous as well. Thank you, Deborah." He passed the other flask to her, their hands touching briefly. "I will be waiting for your return."

Deborah stood transfixed until Seff disappeared over the hill crest, then she ran down toward the village, her feet barely touching the ground beneath. At the base of the hill, she threw herself down on the ground and tried to catch her breath. Above, the sky shone the most beautiful color blue she'd ever seen. She clutched the water flasks to her chest as laughter bubbled up from inside her. She pictured his eyes, his smile. The fullness of his lips. She brushed the hand that had touched his across her face. *Oh Lord! Truly, he is the most perfect of men!*

She sat up and composed herself. He was thirsty and had asked her to bring him water. She would fulfill his desire quickly, so he would see how responsible she could be. It took only a moment to fill the flasks from the well. Deborah was already racing back up the hillside when she remembered the wine Schemuel had requested. She turned and hurried to his house.

A young girl of about eight sat outside the doorway. Tears streaked her cheeks.

"What's the matter, little one?" Deborah asked as she approached.

The girl sat in front of a hand-mill, her golden curls circled madly about her head. "I can't mill the grain. I've tried all morning, and mother is too sick to help. They'll be angry when they come home and nothing has been prepared."

Deborah knelt. "What's your name?"

The little girl's eyes were the same deep green as her brothers'. "Leah."

"Leah, I've just come from your father and your brothers. They asked me to bring them some wine. Would you show me where it is?"

The girl nodded and brought Deborah into the dark hut. A woman lay in the corner, asleep. Her breath came in deep rasping gasps, like the sound of dead leaves being carried on the wind.

Leah pointed at the sleeping woman as she walked by. "That's my mother. I'm supposed to take care of her, as well." Leah took a large skin of wine from a cubby in the wall. "Here."

Deborah brushed the hair from Leah's face. "You have a lot of work to do, but rest for a moment with your mother while I bring the wine to your father."

The little girl looked up at her with worry.

"Don't fret. I'll be gone for just a few minutes then I'll come and help you grind the grain and make the bread. But first, we will find something to make for their dinner tonight."

Leah's eyes sparkled. "Really?"

Deborah scanned the hut's contents. She spotted dates and raisins. "We can make them some cakes." She looked at Leah. "Do you have any lentils and garlic?"

Leah nodded.

"You gather those things up for me. Then rest with your mother until I get back."

"Thank you.

The flasks and wine skin sloshed loudly as Deborah flew back up the hillside. She slowed down at the crest so she could catch her breath, and straighten her head wrap.

Schemuel and his family lay clustered around a tree, asleep. Deborah lay the wine down by his feet then walked to the other side of the tree where Seff and Heber sat with their backs propped against the trunk, their eyes closed. She put Heber's flask by his feet, but stepped lightly to Seff's side and placed his next to him. His eyes came open. He reached out to grab her arm before she could move away. A rush of heat coursed through her body, starting from where his hand held her arm.

"Thank you, Deborah," he whispered.

"You are welcome."

His hand ran lightly down her to her wrist. "Will you sit with me?"

Deborah shook her head. It was difficult to breathe around him. "No, my lord. It would not be right."

Seff held her hand. "Why not?"

She tried to pull away before she totally lost control of her feelings, but Seff held her hand tight. She couldn't remember why she shouldn't sit among a group of unmarried men, but she knew it would be wrong. An image of Azareel and Avram's angry faces flashed across her mind. "My father and brother would not like it." She tried again to free her hand. "Please."

Seff kissed her hand and let it go. "Then I will lay here and dream about you. I will pretend that you sit beside me, with your head on my shoulder."

Deborah stepped away; not taking her gaze from the young man in front her. He leaned back against the tree and sighed deeply. "Your eyes will haunt my thoughts."

For the next week Deborah woke early, not from nightmares, but from excitement. Schemuel's hut stood within sight of the well. Seff had, on several occasions, found an excuse to stand outside while Deborah drew her water. When she glimpsed his way he would smile, like they shared a secret between them. Her heart would skip a beat, and it would be a moment before she could breathe. Her friend Bracha was mad with jealousy because neither Seff nor Heber had even glanced her way.

"I don't know what he sees in you, anyway," Bracha complained as they made their way down to the well. "I'm ready to be betrothed. You're still a girl."

Deborah scowled at her. "He doesn't know that. Besides, I can be betrothed without starting my courses. I just have to wait to be married."

"But I'm older! Why doesn't he notice me?"

Deborah shook her head. "I don't know. Love is a strange thing."

"Love?" Bracha laughed. "Who said anything about love?" She glanced at Deborah and lowered her voice. "He has not spoken to you of a betrothal already, has he?"

"Of course not. We've only known each other for a week. We have barely even spoken." Deborah blushed. "I just know how I feel. Whenever I see him."

Bracha smiled. "All the girls in the village feel that way when they see him!"

Deborah frowned when she arrived at the well and saw no sign of Seff. She let the other women draw their water before her, hoping he might appear before she had to leave. She wasn't disappointed. He walked toward the well as she pulled her jar up from its depths.

"Good morning, Deborah."

She nearly lost her grip on the jug. Seff reached across to help her right it. Deborah dropped her gaze. "Thank you."

"You are welcome."

She held the jar tightly to keep her hands from shaking. Stepping down from the well, she turned back. "Good day, my lord."

"That's all you have for me today?" Seff walked toward her. "May I not talk with you?"

Deborah surveyed the village. Most of the other women were back in their homes. Eglah was still visible in the distance. "I should go. It wouldn't be right to be seen with you alone."

Seff let out a laugh. "We are not alone. Everyone in the village is watching us. Can't you feel their eyes?"

Deborah knew the women watched from their doorways, hidden in the darkness of their houses.

Seff grabbed the jar from her hands. "Let me carry this for a while. Surely they will not say anything if my hands do not touch you."

Deborah tried to take it back. "Please. You will get me into trouble."

Seff relinquished the water. "Then I will walk at a respectable distance from you. I only want to speak with you a moment."

She adjusted the jar on her shoulder. "What about?"

"The end of the harvest is today. I am told there is a festival when all the barley has been threshed."

Deborah nodded. "It will be next month. When the full moon shines."

"I am told there will be music and dancing. Is that true?"

"Oh, yes! Everyone comes. Before sundown, the boys have races and other games. After dark, we light a huge fire out near threshing floor. The women all dance in a circle around it."

Seff stopped walking. "Will you dance?"

Deborah slowed her pace and turned to him. "All the girls dance."

His green eyes studied her face. "Where I come from, when there is a festival, the girls let their hair down so it flies freely as they dance."

Deborah gasped. "That is not the custom here."

Seff frowned slightly. "A pity. I would like to see your hair uncovered, flowing about you."

Deborah's pulse quickened. She took a step backward. "I. . . I need to get home. Bithia will be wondering where I am."

Seff smiled at her embarrassment. "Then I will say goodbye. I will look forward to seeing you at the festival." He bowed slightly before walking away.

Deborah hurried home. Her sister-in-law raised an eyebrow as Deborah ran into the hut. They both glanced at Bithia, but she was too busy chopping leeks to notice them. Edin slept on his pallet so Eglah picked up the hand mill and called out over her shoulder, "You get the grain."

Deborah poured out her water and grabbed the grain sack. Picking up a cloth, she followed Eglah outside. Eglah placed the mill away from the doorway and pulled Deborah down to sit by her. "What did he say to you?"

Deborah poured the grain. "He asked me about the festival."

"Is that all?"

"Yes."

Eglah turned the crank on the mill. "You need to be more cautious."

"All we did was talk."

"It does not matter. You know what your father wants from you." Eglah turned the stone faster. "He won't approve of this stranger."

Deborah groaned. She sat up straight and poured more grain into the mill. "Then I will talk to Father. I will make him see that Seff is an honorable man."

The scraping of the grinding stone slowed as Eglah looked up. "I've heard things about him."

"What things?"

Eglah lowered her head. "He's from the city. And a Kenite. They worship other gods."

"I don't believe you. Who told you this?"

"Avram. He's spoken to our cousin Omar. Omar says Seff and Heber both bragged of going to a temple of Asherah. Of the things they did with the priestess there."

Deborah paled. Her stomach rolled. "It's not true."

"Why would Omar lie?"

"He's jealous, because all the girls are talking about how handsome Seff and Heber are. He's jealous and he's making up lies."

Eglah stopped turning the stone. "Omar is already betrothed. He has no reason to lie."

Deborah sat back on her heels. "Seff may have been brought up in the city, but he's here now. He will learn about our God. He will change."

"Men like him do not change. He does not have to." Eglah stared at her. "You haven't told him you love him, have you?"

"No!" Deborah shook her head. "Of course not."

"You are young, little sister. I know I've teased you about love, but this is serious."

"I'm not stupid."

"All I'm saying is, be careful. I see the way you look at him. More, I see the way he looks at you. He is used to the ways of the city, where a girl's virtue is taken and no one thinks twice." Eglah leaned closer and whispered, "It is a game to him. Don't let yourself be fooled into thinking otherwise."

Deborah couldn't look at her sister-in-law. She poured more grain into the mill. Her mind went round and round with questions as she watched the kernels being ground between the stones. *Was it just a game? Does Seff care nothing for me?*

The girls finished grinding the flour and Bithia found other chores for them to do until the sun's heat grew unbearable. Deborah spent the afternoon on the hillside by the dry river bed. She tried to pray, but Seff's face kept intruding on her devotions. *Lord, why would you give me these feelings if they weren't good? Please Lord, help me to know your will.* She drifted off to sleep, thinking of the way Seff had smiled at her that morning, when he'd spoken of her dancing with her hair uncovered.

She walked along a sparkling river, wearing a long white robe. She had never worn anything as soft against her skin. Softer than the wool of a baby lamb. Like the petals of the roses that grew wild along the forest's edge. She squinted as she looked above at the sun. A shadow seemed to melt away from its golden light and move toward her. A voice called, "Deborah." It rang like music to her ears. Strong and powerful, like the call of the ram's horn—the shofar, but also sweet and gentle, like a harp's note. She stepped toward the shadow, longing to reach out and be held by whatever being called to her.

"Deborah!" *This time the voice called out in warning. She stopped moving and looked down. She stood in the river, the water flowed about her ankles. She tried to step out of the current, but a torrent of water rushed toward her, forcing her away from the shore. She struggled in vain to keep her head up and breathe in air. The water pushed her down, enveloping her in darkness.*

"Deborah!"

She sat up, confused, gasping for air. The sun hung low in the horizon, casting hues of pink and orange across the sky. She rubbed her back, trying to loosen the stiffness that had settled while she'd slept.

"Deborah!"

She spotted Avram at the base of the hillside and waved. "I'm coming!"

He waited for her to make her way down. "I am sorry," she called as she drew closer to him. "I fell asleep. I had the strangest dream—"

Avram interrupted her. "You left Bithia and Eglah to do all the afternoon's work. You told no one where you were going."

Deborah stood still. "Father knows this is where I go when I need to think."

Her brother grabbed her by the arm and yanked her toward him. "Father knew, but Eglah didn't. She's been worried sick all afternoon."

Deborah tried to pull her arm away but Avram held her too tight. "I don't understand."

"She thought you'd run off to see Seff."

"What?" Avram dragged her alongside him as he walked toward the village. Deborah's own anger boiled up inside her. "Does she have so little faith in me, to think I'd dishonor my father that way? And you? You thought so, too."

Avram stopped walking and spun his sister around to face him. He grabbed her shoulders. "Listen to me. Whatever is going on between you and this man stops now."

Tears of frustration and pain fell from her eyes as her brother's fingers dug into her skin. "Nothing is going on! We spoke today, that's all!"

"You will not speak to him again, do you understand?"

"But I—"

"And he will speak no more to you."

Deborah struggled to be released from Avram's grasp. "Why are you doing this? I have done nothing wrong!"

"And I will see to it that it stays that way." His gaze softened as he watched her cry. He loosened his grip and brushed her tears with one hand. "I'm sorry, little sister. I was worried for your safety. We will not speak of this to Father. You'll have to face Bithia's anger for making her do your share of the work, but you are used to that." He pulled her into his arms. "You're young yet. You don't understand the ways of men. I don't want to see you get hurt."

Deborah wiped her tears on his robe. *You're the one who hurt me. Seff has never been anything but kind.*

Avram kissed the top of her head. "Come. Father will wonder what's keeping us."

Deborah fought to contain the conflicting emotions welling up within her. She had never been so angry at her brother, but then, he had never hurt her before. She longed to tell him about her dream, but couldn't. He had been too mean to her. Her thoughts raged within her, out of control, full of fury. She balled her hands into fists and hit them against her legs as she walked. *What is happening to me?* She needed to talk to someone, but there was no one who would understand. She jumped when Avram touched her shoulder.

"Go home." His eyes were like iron. "There is something I need to do first."

Deborah's stomach fluttered. "What?"

"Go home, Deborah."

She forced her legs to move, but watched to see where Avram headed.

"Go!" He turned, and strode toward Schemuel's house.

"Avram! Please don't—"

Anger radiated from her brother's face. His voice was quiet, but she could hear him from where she stood. "Whatever is going on between you will stop tonight. I will see to that. Go home, Deborah."

A hand seemed to grip her stomach; twisting, churning, pummeling it. Her eyes filled again with tears at this new humiliation. *Seff will never speak to me again. No man will after this. I'm not a child!*

Azareel looked up and wiped a drop of lentil soup from his beard when she entered the hut. "Where have you been, Daughter?"

"Yes," Bithia spat. "I called for you! I had to go to the well myself this afternoon. The weight of the water has left my back in such pain." She let out an exaggerated groan. "Where did you run off to?"

Deborah bowed her head and willed herself not to cry. "I am sorry. I fell asleep, up on the hill."

Palti snorted and rolled his eyes. His smirk told her he believed she'd been with Seff as well. She bit her lip. *You have no right to judge me. I've seen you with Tamar. Talking to her by the woods. Making friends with her brother so you can be close to her. You've done more than Seff has ever done.*

"Are you feeling well? Azareel nodded toward her customary place at the blanket. "Sit down and eat."

Deborah shook her head. "I'm not hungry."

"You can sit down with us while we eat, then," said Bithia. "And when the meal is over, you will do the cleaning."

Deborah didn't move.

Bithia clapped her hands as if trying to wake Deborah from a dream. "Did you hear me?"

"I heard you."

"Then sit down!"

Deborah shuffled over and sat by Nathan. Her little brother happily slurped at his soup, oblivious to the tension surrounding him. She toyed with a piece of bread, dipping it in the bowl in front of her but not eating.

"Where is Avram?" asked Azareel.

Deborah's shoulders tightened. "I'm not sure. He told me to go ahead of him."

Azareel stood and walked to the doorway. "Ah, here he comes."

Avram entered and placed his hand on his father's shoulder. "Sorry. My sandal came loose. I stopped to fix it."

Palti let out a short, choking cough, but said nothing.

Deborah tried unsuccessfully to read Avram's thoughts. *What did you do? What did Seff say?*

Avram ignored her questioning glances and sat by Eglah, giving her a kiss on the cheek. "I'm famished. Is anything left?"

Eglah served him fresh soup from the pot over the fire, and gave him a piece of bread. Avram tucked into the meal with eagerness.

Deborah listened in frustration as he and father spoke of the harvest and the drought. She wanted to run screaming from the room, but instead pulled at a thread in the blanket in front of her as her irritation grew. The walls of the already overcrowded house seemed to lean in closer to her, making the room even smaller. Next to her, Nathan slurped his soup even louder.

Deborah slapped her hand on the ground in front of her half-brother. "For mercy sake, will you stop making that noise?"

The boy's lower lip trembled. His face reddened as he prepared to bellow. Deborah closed her eyes while Bithia ranted at her and Nathan screamed. It would do no good to argue. She sat with her head in her hands and waited for the tirade to be over. When Bithia finished yelling, Deborah stood. "I don't feel well. I'm going to sit outside by the door. I'll do the evening chores," she added before Bithia could start in on her again. "Once everyone is done with their meal, call me."

The evening air relieved some of the tension in her shoulders and neck. She rubbed her temples with her fingertips, trying to stop the pounding in her head. Never had a day seemed so long. Never had she wanted one to end as badly as she desired this day to be over. Eglah came out a short time later. She knelt beside Deborah.

"I'm sorry. I didn't know where you were. I thought—"

Deborah looked up. "I know what you thought." She stood. "Is the meal done? May I clean up now?"

Eglah rose. "Please don't be angry. I only did what I thought was best."

"Is the meal done?"

Eglah nodded.

"Then I must go in and do my work."

She finished the evening chores under the watchful glances of Avram and her father, thankful when Azareel finally snuffed the oil lamp and stirred out the fire. She lay awake in the darkness and prayed.

4 Hazor

A Week Later

Sisera and his shield bearer held onto the sides of the chariot as his driver whipped the horses to go faster. The sun glinted off the bronze armor and helmets of the charioteers surrounding him. The hooves and iron wheels thundered in a mighty chorus across the valley toward the city in front of them. He smiled. He loved this part of the battle. The power of the chariots, the feel of the wind on his face. This felt pure. No blood, no smoke to burn his eyes. Just the unending possibilities of the upcoming combat.

Of course, there was something to be said for the heat of battle, he mused. The thrill of the hunt; the exhaustion of a well-fought confrontation and the glory of victory. In the thirteen years he'd served King Jabin, he'd learned to love every aspect of the military life. If he could spend every day out on the battlefield, he'd be a happy man.

The horses raced up the small mount to the walled city. Foot soldiers heaved a battering ram, splintering the wooden gate just as Sisera's chariot crested the hill. The soldiers cleared the debris and Sisera waved his men inside with the chariots taking position around the outside of the wall to prevent anyone escaping.

The general entered the city and watched as his men quickly conquered the rag-tag resistance the Israelites had sent out. Old men and young boys fell under the swords of the Canaanites. Sisera surveyed the carnage and frowned. One of the Israelite boys lay groaning in the dirt. Sisera jumped from his chariot and knelt by the boy. He brushed a lock of hair from the child's face.

"What is your name?"

The child's eyes widened in fear as he drew in a halting breath.

Sisera took off his helmet and leaned closer to the boy. "Don't fear, child. I can help you. Tell me what your name is."

A tremor ran through his body. "Dan."

"Dan. Where are your fighting men?"

The boy turned his head away and took another painful breath. Sisera pushed his hand into the wound in the child's stomach. Dan cried out, his legs convulsing in agony.

Sisera whispered into his ear. "Tell me where your soldiers are hiding, or I will see to it you will not die, but suffer much more than you are now."

The general removed his hand and waited as the boy's spasms relaxed. Dan's pale face looked up at him, sweat beaded on his brow. "A raid . . . of the merchant route."

Sisera swore under his breath. He stood and kicked the boy in frustration. Turning to his spearman in the chariot he ordered, "Kill him." He addressed the rest of the soldiers. "The men we seek are not here. But we will make them pay for their failure to protect the city. Search every house, every hole, every cistern. Find every survivor. Every last woman, child, infant. I want them dead." Sisera's eyes blazed with anger. "Dash their heads on the rocks. Throw the babies from the walls. Annihilate the entire village!" The soldiers caught his thirst for blood and eagerly searched the streets to fulfill their general's demands. Sisera signaled his driver to take him out of the city. They pulled up to another member of the *maryannu*.

"I have ordered the men to destroy the city and those who remain. I leave the rest to you."

The officer took off his helmet. "What will you do?"

"I want to take twenty chariots out to the pass. The mercenaries we seek were not inside the walls. I will lead a reconnaissance mission; see if we spot them along the southern route."

"The King is expecting us back tonight."

"We won't be far behind. But it will improve his mood greatly if we can bring him a prisoner or two."

The other officer nodded and put his helmet back on after wiping his brow. "You're right about that. May the gods give you luck to find the others."

Sisera called to the group of charioteers who guarded the southeastern edge of the city. "You! Follow me! We are going hunting in the pass!" A cheer rose from the men as the chariots sped down the mount and out onto the open plains once again. A great cloud of dirt followed behind them, like the thunderheads of a storm.

Sisera jumped from his chariot and strode toward the palace entrance. He chuckled under his breath remembering how timid he'd been the first time he'd come before the king thirteen years ago. The palace had seemed huge to him then. It remained the largest building in Hazor, but Sisera had been to the southern city of Ugarit and seen its palace. He'd seen the great pyramids of Egypt. Jabin's home paled in comparison. Still, it spoke of the king's love of fine construction and good taste. Exquisite mosaics decorated the entrance. Marble tile and columns reflected the torches that illuminated his path to the King's throne room. A general murmur of conversation drifted down the hallway. Sisera frowned. He'd hoped to hear the sounds of drinking and revelry. If the king was in a subdued mood, it could mean he was angry with the way Sisera had led the attack. He brushed the dirt from his arms and armor before stepping into the doorway. He stood until the king noticed him, and then bowed slightly at the waist, waiting for permission to enter the room.

King Jabin stood, his purple robe shimmering in the torch light. He waved the general forward. "Sisera! Finally." The king's dark eyes focused on him intently. "I trust you bring me good news?"

Sisera strode between the tables on either side of the room where noblemen reclined and ate. He approached the king's table at the far end of the room and bowed again. "The men we sought were not in the city, my lord."

A small tremor seemed to run down the king's body, from his bronze face to his sandaled feet. "What?"

"I had our army destroy the village completely. Everything but the livestock has been killed and burned to serve as a warning for others who seek to go against us."

Jabin ran a hand through his black hair then turned away. He clapped his hands twice and a servant rushed forward to fill his goblet with wine. Jabin drained the cup before turning back. "But the rebels? They got away?"

Sisera smiled crookedly. "No, my lord."

The king's eyes narrowed. "What are you saying?"

"I did not want to disappoint you, so I took a small contingent out to the pass where I suspected they were hiding. We routed them out."

"Are they dead?"

Sisera nodded. "Most. I lined the road back to Hazor with their heads."

"Ha!" Jabin grinned. "That will show them. What did you do with the rest?"

"They are in the prison. I left ten alive."

Jabin sat down. "For what purpose?"

"I am sure they know of other pockets of rebellion. I think they may be persuaded to give up that information."

"You think you can break them?"

Sisera shrugged. "If not, we will have them followed when we release them. Any town they seek refuge from will be searched. We will put an end to any more uprisings."

The king nodded. He summoned a servant with a wave of his hand. "Fetch the general some water so he can wash. Then bring him food and wine."

Sisera bowed. "Thank you, my lord."

Jabin raised his hands. "More wine for everyone. Now we can celebrate, for my friend has once again brought me victory!"

The roomful of advisors and noblemen cheered and lifted their goblets in a toast to the general. Sisera accepted their praise, but took note of their thinly disguised animosity toward him. Younger nobles and princes envied his favored position with the king while the older men resented his influence in matters of state. He didn't mind their coldness. The only friendships he cultivated were those that could bring him more power, and he already had Jabin's. What did he need of these sycophants and fools?

5 The Hills of Ephraim

Three Weeks Later

Deborah had not spoken to Seff since the month before at the well. He no longer stood outside his home, waiting for her. Her mood turned gray, unlike the relentless sun and heat of the summer. She talked little and ate less. She overheard Bithia explain to her father, "Truly, there's nothing to worry about. All girls go through this. It will be her time soon, and then she will be back to normal."

I'll never be who I was before. Everything has changed. She no longer revered Avram as she had done in the past. She had a newfound sympathy for Palti. *If he truly loves Tamar, no wonder he hates me, the only obstacle to his happiness.* And for the first time in her life, Deborah was angry with God. *Why have you done this? Why did you even bring Seff here?* It was God's fault she felt so terrible.

On the afternoon of the harvest festival, the entire village gathered at the threshing floor to celebrate and give thanks to

God. The drought had caused a smaller harvest than the year before, but the people were grateful they had something. The elders led them in prayer and offered a sacrifice on an altar of stone. After this, the men spent the afternoon in various competitions while the women looked on and cheered. Games of skill were also played. Two sheep were roasted over an open pit, and the women brought barley and honey cakes to be shared. Deborah tried to catch of glimpse of Seff throughout the day but Avram kept sending her on various errands.

"Father forgot his walking stick. Fetch it for him." Or, "Edin needs to be washed, take him home and bathe him."

Deborah carried her nephew on her hip and headed to the village as dusk fell. She cleaned Edin quickly, then walked back to the threshing mound. Even though the sun sat behind the hills, heat still radiated from the ground. The breeze that blew from the southeast did not bring cooler air, but hot, dry winds from the desert. Deborah looked enviously at Edin's naked chest and wished she didn't have to wear her linen dress and tunic. The cloth stuck to the sweat on her body and irritated her skin. Lost in thought, she turned sharply around the last house of the village and ran directly into Taavi, Seff's younger brother.

Taavi stumbled back. "Watch where you're going!"

Deborah clutched her nephew tighter to her chest so he wouldn't fall. "You are as much to blame as I!"

A gentle laugh rang out behind Taavi. "She's right." Seff reached a hand out to help his brother up, then looked at Deborah. "Are you hurt?"

She shook her head. Like a deer caught in the sights of an archer, her heart pounded wildly, but her body froze in panic.

His eyes sparkled in the last of the day's light. "I know I'm forbidden to talk to you, but are you forbidden to talk to me as well?"

She nodded.

Keeping his eyes on Deborah, Seff commanded, "Taavi, fetch the wine our uncle wanted."

"But he told us-"

"Go!"

The boy muttered to himself but obeyed his brother. Seff took a step closer to Deborah. "I have missed seeing you at the well." His eyes searched her face. "Did you miss me?"

She nodded again.

His smile increased his beauty. "I'm glad." He let his eyes roam over her body. No one had ever looked at her the way Seff did at this moment. Deborah shuddered even as a bead of sweat trickled down the back of her neck.

"Your brother thinks you're still a child, too young to think for yourself." His eyes came back to her face. Deborah was mesmerized by their deep green color. "Are you?"

She shook her head.

"And yet . . . ." Seff sighed. "Still you do not speak to me. Do you do everything your brother tells you?"

She was surprised to hear herself answer, "No."

"I am glad." Seff stepped directly in front of her. Leaning down he whispered, "Tonight when you dance, remember that I will be watching only you." His warm breath smelled of sweet wine. It tickled her neck, sending tiny shivers throughout her body. He ran his hand across her cheek. "Now go, before you get into trouble."

Deborah walked back to the festival. She fought her desire to run, and instead moved slowly across the dirt path, swaying her hips as she'd seen Eglah do. She kissed her nephew's head and laid her cheek against his soft hair, wishing it were Seff's. Up ahead, a bonfire now burned bright orange against the gray sky of twilight. Villagers reclined on the ground around it.

Deborah found Eglah and handed Edin to her. "I'm going to find Mava and Bracha."

"Don't stray too far. Avram is worried."

Deborah scowled. "Does he have another errand for me to run? Or will he let me enjoy some time with my friends?"

Eglah pursed her lips. "Don't leave the bonfire. I'll tell Avram where you've gone."

Deborah spun on her heels and hurried away. It didn't take long for her to pick out Mava's copper hair among a group of other young girls.

Mava called to her. "Come by Bracha and me!"

Deborah sighed as she sat down.

Bracha's pudgy lips pouted. "What's wrong? Still mooning over Seff?"

Deborah glowered at her friend in the golden light of the fire. "I'm not mooning. I'm angry with my brother. He won't let me grow up. He still thinks I'm a child."

"Well, be glad he thinks so." Mava tossed her hair over her shoulder. "Or you'd be married off to Palti already."

Deborah plucked the brittle grass at her feet. "You're right. Either way, my life is not my own." She threw a handful of grass into the air and watched as the breeze whipped it up, whirling it in small circles until it spun down to the ground. "Sometimes I wish God had made me a man. Then my choices would be my own."

Bracha shook her head. "Not me. I wouldn't want all that responsibility."

Mava smirked. "It isn't like this everywhere, you know."

"What do you mean?" Deborah asked.

Mava leaned in closer to her friends so she could speak in a whisper. "Heber has told me all about the city. The women there have more say in who they marry and what they do."

Bracha breathed in sharply. "All women?"

"No. But the Canaanite women and those from Egypt. The royalty still have to follow protocol and such. But the common girls, like us, they can see who they like. Men and women often go to festivals together. They dance together." Her voice grew even softer and she smiled mischievously. "They even kiss before they're married. Often." All three girls giggled.

"Wait," Deborah's eyebrows furrowed. "When did Heber tell you this?"

Mava sat up and glanced around them, then leaned back to her friends. "I've been meeting with him at night, when everyone is asleep."

"Mava!" Bracha gasped.

"We only talk," insisted Mava. "And sometimes hold hands. He's a good man."

"But you're betrothed," Deborah said.

"Yes, but I'm betrothed to a man I don't even know, from a different village. That is not the life I want."

"What are you going to do?" Bracha asked.

"Heber has told me he wants to leave here and go to Jezreel. He said he would take me with him, if I wanted to go."

Deborah looked at her friend, stunned. "You wouldn't, would you?"

Mava leaned back to rest on her elbows. "I don't know. At least it would be my choice, and no one else's."

The sound of a lively melody played on a wooden flute interrupted their conversation. It was soon accompanied by a tambourine. A shout rose up from the crowd and they all began to sing. After several songs, the women stood and joined hands up on the hill around the bonfire. Deborah spotted Eglah and Bithia across the flames, laughing and singing with the women near them. They moved to the rhythm of the tambourine, which started slow, but soon sped up. Deborah danced with abandon as she spun around the fire with her arms raised. *Avram can keep Seff from speaking to me, but he can't keep him from looking at me. I will dance for Seff tonight!* She threw her head back and laughed at the thought. The tambourine pound out a beat, going faster and faster. Deborah breathed in the smoky air, trying to catch her breath. When the song finished, she and her friends fell to the ground, exhausted.

A sack of watered wine made its way around the circle. The girls each took a long sip to quench their thirst. Deborah lay on her back, watching the smoke drift up toward the stars.

Mava stood. "I have to go."

"Where?" asked Bracha.

Mava smiled. "I already told you."

Bracha's brown eyes widened. "But everyone is awake!"

Mava shrugged. "Yes, but father will be drunk by now and mother will be asleep before long. They won't miss me until the morning. I'll see you tomorrow."

Bracha lay down beside Deborah. "Maybe we should tell someone."

"Let her do what she wants."

"But she could get into trouble. I don't trust Heber."

Deborah sat up. "You're just jealous because he doesn't care for you. Mava says he's a good man. Let them alone."

Bracha rose to face her friend. "Your eyes are blinded by your feelings for Seff." She pointed a finger at Deborah. "Your brother is right to keep you from him. Heber is filling Mava's head with sinful thoughts. Who knows where it will lead?"

Guilt pierced Deborah's conscience, but she ignored it. "If he loves her and wants to marry her, what's wrong with that?"

"And take her away from her family? To a city of Gentiles? Think about what you're saying."

Deborah whispered forcefully, "They are going to marry her off to someone in a different village anyway. It's the same thing."

"It is not, and you know it. Think, Deborah. It's not right what he's doing."

Deborah stood. "Why do you, and my brother, and everyone else in this village, have to think the worst of them? I choose to believe they're good. Goodnight, Bracha." Deborah strode down the hill. She shivered when she reached the bottom of the mound, the air cooler away from the fire. She walked through the crowd hoping to see Seff. Instead, Palti found her.

"Avram sent me to find you."

"What for?"

"He thinks you should go home now."

Deborah frowned. "But I'm not tired."

Palti shrugged. "I'm just telling you what he said. Father was there as well. He agreed."

Deborah snorted in frustration. "Fine. Goodnight, Brother."

Palti smiled crookedly. "Goodnight."

She refrained from slapping him and made her way through the crowd. It wasn't difficult to find the path back to the village as the full moon illuminated the darkened fields with a silver light. A shadow separated itself from a sycamore tree and blocked her way.

"There you are," said the black shape. "Your brother said he could get you to meet me."

"Seff?"

He stepped out of the shadow. "Of course. Didn't you know?"

Deborah shook her head. "No. Palti said Avram wanted me to go home."

Seff chuckled. "Would you have come if he told you the truth?"

"I . . . I don't know."

Seff reached out and took her hand. His voice floated through the darkness. "Will you come now?"

"Where?"

"Just walk with me." He led her away from the path. "Come."

He chatted as they walked, telling her about a man he'd met who told the future by looking at the stars. He told her of his life before they'd come to her village. "We were metal workers. But the drought caused the caravans to take the roads nearer the coast. No one came into our city anymore to trade. Then King Jabin and his army started to attack around us. Father said it wouldn't be long before they reached our city."

"Is the drought worse in the valleys?"

Seff nodded as they continued to walk. "Much worse. The farmers haven't had a decent crop in three years. Most of the nomads have taken their sheep and cattle so there's no meat." He took a pouch from his shoulder and drank. He offered it to Deborah. Taking a sip, she was surprised to taste the rich flavor of undiluted wine. She coughed as it burned her throat.

Seff teased her. "You're not used to real wine, are you?"

"Not that strong. No."

"Try it again. It won't burn so much this time."

Deborah took another drink. The wine spread its warmth through her body. Seff drew her beside him. Once again, his proximity seemed to affect her ability to breathe. She pushed him away. She hadn't realized how far they'd walked, until she saw the edge of the forest up ahead. "I should go home. Avram will be looking for me."

Seff kissed the top of her head. "Don't worry. Palti will think of something to tell him. I want to show you something."

He led her to the woods. Deborah stopped. She rarely ventured into the forest, frightened by her brother's tales of mountain lions and wild boars.

Seff pulled her in. "It's perfectly safe. There is a path here."

"Where are we going?"

He helped her over a fallen log. "You will see."

Even with the bright glow of the full moon, Deborah had difficulty distinguishing the path through the growing denseness of the trees. Small branches reached out and snagged her tunic. Rocks on the ground tore at her feet. A strong odor of dirt and decay hung in the air. Even the forest was dying from the lack of rain. Halfway up the mount, Deborah realized the only sounds she heard were the snapping of dry twigs, and her own breathing. No insects chirped in the trees. No owls called. The darkness crept in around her. As Seff guided her further up the forested hillside, a sense of panic rose within her. *It's the dark from my dreams. It's the thing I can't remember when I wake. It's here in the forest.* She wrenched her hand out of Seff's. "I want to go home!"

His voice was gentle, but tinged with frustration. "What is wrong?"

"I dreamed of this place."

"What?"

"There is something here, in the darkness. I've dreamt of it. I know I have."

"Tell me more." He placed his hands on her face then brushed them down until he held her shoulders. "What do you dream?"

Deborah shuddered under his touch. "Please . . . there is a presence in the darkness. A power."

His grip tightened. "She calls to you! Don't you see?" She had no time to ask Seff what he meant before he leaned down and kissed her on the mouth. A great swell of energy rushed throughout her body. She tried to catch her breath when his lips finally released hers. Seff cupped her face with his hands. "I knew you were meant to come here. As young as you are." He took her hand and pulled her up the hill. "It's not far now. Just up ahead."

Deborah looked up the path. The soft glow of firelight flickered ahead. Faint voices and smoke drifted down the hillside with the breeze. They came to the top of the rise and stood at the edge of a clearing. A circle of torches illuminated the packed ground in front of them, in the center stood a large pole, about ten feet in height. Next to it, a group of men prostrated themselves around a stone altar, praying. Three older girls wove through the torches in a kind of unaccompanied dance. Deborah recognized one of them from the village. Outside of the circle, Deborah could see the forms of several couples including Heber and Mava. They sat talking, but others were lying down, their limbs entangled with each other.

Deborah drew away from Seff. "What is this place?"

"It is holy ground. A place to worship Baal and his consort, Asherah."

"Oh no." Her stomach heaved in revulsion. "No."

Seff knelt in front of her, pulling her to him, so his head rested on her chest. "Your heart beats so fast. There's nothing to be frightened of, little doe. I would never hurt you."

Her body betrayed the cry of her mind to run away. Instead, her limbs melted against him. Her hands reached out and ran through the thick mass of hair that crowned his head.

Seff groaned at her touch. "I knew you were different. From the moment I saw you. Your eyes . . . full of wisdom beyond your years." He pulled her down so she knelt with him. He took the scarf from her head then brushed his hands through her long brown curls. "You were meant for me, Deborah. I feel a power within you. I know you are destined for more than being some fool's wife in this forgotten village." He tangled his hands in her hair and kissed her roughly.

Her mind screamed at her to stop but her body responded to every touch of Seff's hands and lips. When he drew away from her, she came back to him for more. She clutched at his garment, as if trying to keep from drowning in a raging current. She kissed his hair, his cheeks, his lips.

"Come." Seff stood, pulling her up with him. "Come into the center and pray to Asherah. Let her bless our union."

Deborah allowed herself to follow him into the circle of torches. A soft hum filled her head, like a swarm of bees. Her skin shivered with gooseflesh, even though the air hung heavy and warm. No darkness surrounded her, but she felt the oppressive weight from her nightmare press down on her chest.

The pole stood before her. It had been carved to resemble the shape of a woman with broad, rounded hips and full breasts. Seff sank down to his knees. He tried to pull Deborah beside him, but she resisted. A voice spoke over the noise in her head. **Choose, Deborah. Choose this day whom you will serve**. The droning in her mind increased. A myriad of voices spoke from within its hum. *To us, Deborah! To us! Feel the pleasure of the flesh. A life without sacrifice is yours! Bow down to us!*

Deborah cried out. She yanked her hand from Seff's. Her mind filled with conflicting images and emotions. Passionate couplings . . . herself, wild-eyed and ranting. A wedding feast, the villagers dancing around the veiled bride . . . Avram, wearing funeral garb, crying . . . a battlefield, strewn with blood.

She struggled to make sense of everything she saw and heard. Her eyes stared ahead in horror toward the idol. A low moan rose from her throat. She saw the things around her clearly, but in her mind, the random pictures kept flashing.

"Deborah?" Seff stood. "What is it? What's wrong?"

The praying men also got up while the others outside the circle came forward.

"It's a vision!" cried one man. "Asherah is speaking to her."

Seff reached out. "Deborah?"

"Do not touch her!" Heber ran to Seff and pulled him back. Mava stood behind them, gripping the base of a torch. The women who had been dancing now fell to the ground, praising Asherah for her oracle. Seff fought against his brother, but Heber locked his arms around his chest, keeping him from Deborah.

She stood, wanting to run away, but unable to move. The buzzing grew louder. Another wave of images assaulted her. A man, beautiful and tall. His head shaved, but for a long, black braid. A golden collar around his neck. His hands, red with blood . . . **Hear, Oh Israel, the Lord your God, the Lord is One**. A temple with white stone steps. Another man, covered in silk robes and jewels, reaching out to her. Taking her hand, he led her to the edge of the temple platform. Below, hundreds of people cried out and bowed to them. The voices spoke out of the hum again— *To us, Deborah! Power . . . wealth . . . all you desire is yours! Bow down to us! Worship us!* They rose to such a cacophony she thought her head would surely explode. Then the other voice commanded. **Choose**.

And all went silent.

Deborah stumbled out of the circle. She dropped to her knees. Crawling, gasping for air, she vomited, then collapsed on her back. The others cautiously stepped toward her. Seff broke free of Heber's hold and fell at her side. Deborah rolled away from him. "Don't touch me!"

Seff's head snapped back, as if he'd been slapped. "What? What did you see?"

Deborah shook her head as she slid further away. "I don't know. Too many things."

Heber stood over her. "Tell us."

Deborah looked at the faces gathered around her. Their eyes were filled with anticipation and something else. *Hunger? Yes.* They stared at her like a lioness stalks its prey, ready to pounce and tear her to shreds. She struggled to feet. "No!" She pushed past the on-lookers and into the circle. "I don't want it. I've never wanted anything but the God of my fathers. I sought Him. I never wanted you!"

Heber jerked her away from the pole. He slapped her cheek. "How dare you speak like that to Asherah."

Tears sprang to her eyes from the sting of his hand, but it only fueled her anger. "I care nothing for your god." She spit in his face.

Heber threw her to the ground. "Do you want to bring the wrath of Asherah down on us? You will beg her forgiveness! Do you understand?"

"Never! I will give her nothing!"

The hungry eyes around her filled with rage. They murmured among themselves. "She must be punished . . . a sacrifice . . . she should be killed."

Seff fought through the crowd. His eyes alone were afraid. "I'm sorry, Deborah. I'm sorry."

Heber thrust him away. "Be quiet, Brother. If she defies Asherah, she must pay the price."

Mava came around behind Deborah and yanked her up, gripping her arms as if holding her prisoner. "Run!" She whispered in Deborah's ear then pushed her toward the woods.

Deborah fled past the torches and into the forest. The others followed in pursuit. She could not out run them for long. They were bigger and stronger, but they had also been drinking much more than she had. Deborah followed no path, rushing madly down the hillside then up another. She broke free of the forest and out onto an open meadow. She screamed as Heber sprinted out of the trees, tackling her.

"Let me go!" She kicked and writhed underneath him, trying to crawl free.

Heber flipped her onto her back, straddling her body, pinning her arms to the ground. He panted heavily into her face, his sour breath turned her stomach.

"Asherah has spoken to you. Come back to the circle and worship her."

Deborah wept as she struggled under his weight. "No!"

"Then you will die!"

Deborah stopped fighting. "You can't kill me. My family will miss me. Palti knows I was with Seff. They'll know what you've done."

Heber dropped his head down and spoke softly in her ear. "I'm so sorry Azareel, but we never saw her." He gripped her arms tighter causing her to cry out. "My brother was with me on the hill. He waited for Deborah, but she never came. She must have been attacked by some wild beast." He lifted his face so he could look into her eyes. "Will you come back with me now? And pray to Asherah?"

Deborah shook her head. "I can't."

Heber wrapped his hands around her neck. "A pity, I think Seff was right. You are filled with divine power." He squeezed his hands together. "It will be a waste to snuff it out." In the moonlight she saw his eyes fill with madness as he tightened his grip around her throat.

She clutched his arms, trying to pull them away, even as the last of her breath escaped her lungs. She scratched at his face, his neck, to no avail. Her arms dropped to the ground as a bright light flashed around the edge of her vision.

And then she was free.

She thought at first that she must have died. Heber's weight was off her and she seemed to float. But then her lungs heaved. Fresh air stung as it filled them again. She gasped and rolled to her knees. Two men fought a few feet from her. She heard the heavy pounding of fists against skin.

Seff's voice called out, "Run, Deborah!"

She crawled toward him, but he stopped her. "No! I can't hold him much longer, and the others will find us soon. Go!"

Deborah pushed herself up. She only staggered a few steps before she fell.

Heber's voice growled from the shadows, "You will pay for this, Brother."

Deborah struggled again to her feet. This time she managed to lope across the open meadow. Behind her, the sounds of the fight lessened, but other voices called out. Her legs cramped and her lungs burned, but she forced herself to run faster. She found herself sobbing through the pain as she pressed on. *Oh Lord! Help me!*

"There she is . . . Look, over that way!"

Fear propelled her forward. She could just make out the edge of more woods ahead, then a dark cloud floated in front of the moon, obscuring most of its light. The steady rush of footsteps behind her faltered, her pursuers losing sight of her in the blackness. Deborah cried in relief and continued toward the forest. She soon lost the sound of her hunters in the thick trees. She slowed her pace, treading with care through the branches and undergrowth. She thought about hiding until morning, but feared the others might find her while she rested. *I must keep going. I must find my way home.*

She staggered through the forest for hours. Her feet and legs bled from the scratches of stones. Her arms bore the slashes from tree branches. She stumbled out into a clearing and lay on her back on the dry grass. The sky still shone with many stars, but the moon hung well past its zenith. *I can't go any further, Lord.* Her breath came in short, gasping sobs. *Please . . . help me. Please.* She heard a sound and rolled to her side to investigate. A small fire burned about a hundred feet from where she lay. She would have sworn it had not been there a moment ago.

Beside it sat a man. Deborah's heart froze in panic. *I've run straight to one of them.* Her fears alleviated when the figure raised his head. She could see by the firelight that this was an older man, about her father's age.

"Well, well." His voice sounded soft and raspy. Like the wind when it caresses the trees. It calmed Deborah's fears, filling her with a sense of peace. "You are a long way from home, are you not?"

Deborah could only nod.

"Would you like some water?"

She nodded again and forced herself to sit up. Every muscle in her body screamed in pain. She moaned as she doubled over.

"Sit, sit." He waved his arms. "I will bring it to you." The old man picked up a full skin and brought it to her. Her shoulder twitched when he placed his arm around her, but his soothing voice relaxed her again. "There now. Do not worry. Drink up and I will take you home."

Deborah drank deeply from the skin. The water tasted sweet and cold, as if it had just been pulled from a mountain lake.

"Be careful not to drink too fast. You may give yourself a cramp."

Deborah paused for a moment then drank again. "Thank you."

"You are welcome." In the dark, Deborah couldn't discern the color of his eyes, but they looked at her warmly. His face was lined, but handsome. He wore no beard and his hair was cut short. He smiled. "Now, how about something to eat?"

"No, thank you."

The man frowned. "No? Are you sure?" He gestured behind him. "I have plenty, and you need your strength."

Deborah looked over to the fire. A full loaf of bread sat beside a bowl of pomegranates and dates. The old man's eyes danced in the light of the flames. "Come. Eat." He placed his arms under her, lifting her as if she were a babe. He carried her over to the food then gently set her down. "This looks good, no?" He offered her the bread.

The loaf felt warm in her hands. Deborah ripped herself off a large piece. She said a prayer of thanks before taking a bite. It melted in her mouth. Never had she tasted anything so good. Buttery and warm, as if made with the finest flour and honey. She took another mouthful.

"I knew you were hungry." He picked up a date. "Here. Have one of these."

She marveled at the fruit in her hand. "How did you get this? They won't be in season for months."

The old man grinned. "I have my ways."

She bit into the fruit, reveling in its flavor, succulent and sweet. After she finished it, she licked her fingers.

"You may have another, if you like."

Deborah reached into the bowl and took another. She jumped when an owl screeched in the woods, thinking at first that Heber had found her again.

Her benefactor surveyed her. "You are safe here. No one will harm you while you are with me."

Deborah eyed him while she ate the second date. His shoulders were broad and strong, not stooped like most of the older men she knew. The way he had picked her up and carried her to the fire had shown great strength. And yet he didn't appear threatening. Again, she licked her fingers, savoring every bit of the date's flavor. "My name is Deborah."

The old man nodded.

"May I know your name? So I may thank you properly?"

He gazed up at the stars for a moment. "You may call me Remiel."

"Thank you, Remiel, for sharing your food with me. Truly, I have never tasted anything as good."

"I trust it has revived you?"

"My spirits, yes. I don't know about my body yet."

He held out his hand. "It is time."

Deborah shuddered. His voice rang with an authority she'd not heard before, and for a moment, she feared him. Then he softened his countenance.

"Come."

Deborah put her hand in his and he raised her to her feet. Heat pulsated from his palm up her arm, spreading warmth and strength throughout her body. Her muscles still ached, but not to the extent they had before she'd eaten. "Don't you need to pack up your food?"

Remiel shook his head. "No."

"But—"

"Follow me."

He led her through the woods, finding a path that Deborah couldn't see. Branches no longer tore at her arms and tunic. She rarely stepped on rocks or sticks. Her body moved on its own, drawn somehow by Remiel, though he didn't touch her as they made their way through the trees. They came out of the forest and walked up a large hill. The sun broke the horizon behind them. Feathered clouds glowed pink and purple across the sky. Remiel pointed to the distance.

"Do you see? That hill over there, with the olive trees on top?"

Deborah nodded.

"From its crest you will see your village."

"Aren't you coming with me? So my father can properly thank you?"

"No."

The sun rose higher behind him. Deborah walked down the hill a few steps so she could see his face without squinting.

"You will return to your village, but not to the life you knew."

Deborah's heart pounded at his voice. It no longer sounded like a soft breeze. Now it surged with power and energy. Like a stream when it flows down a mountain with the winter snow melt. The brilliant light of the morning sun seemed to fade as a new radiance glowed around the figure in front of her. She fell to her knees.

"Do not be afraid, Deborah. The Lord is merciful. You have been tested, and although you faltered, you showed yourself faithful. You have asked for a life of service to Him, and tonight, you glimpsed some of what is to come."

The figure stepped toward her. "If you choose to follow the Lord, you must first go to Shiloh and offer a guilt offering at the Tabernacle. Until you have made this sacrifice, His voice will be silent. Use this time to prepare yourself, with fasting and prayer, for the Lord will grant you a mighty gift. One that will cause great love and great envy in those around you, for the Lord will be with you, as He has been with no other woman."

The light around the figure blazed brighter. Deborah lifted her hands to cover her eyes. When she looked back, Remiel was gone.

Deborah sat back on her feet, still in a kneeling position. She fought to release the tightness in her chest, then took a deep breath and looked for some sign that what she'd seen was real. *Surely the blazing light scorched the grass?* She crawled forward, but saw no burns on the ground. Around her, birds sang out their morning songs, while the roar of Remiel's voice faded from her within her head.

Father! I must go and tell Azareel what has happened! She jumped up and raced toward home. From the grove of olive trees Remiel had shown her, she could see her village a short distance away. The town sat unusually quiet. *The festival!*

There will be little work done today after last night's celebra-tions. She stopped herself from running directly down into the village, and instead circled around until she could approach it from the side her house stood. *I want to tell Azareel first what has happened!* With a final burst of energy, Deborah sprinted the last hundred feet to her home.

"Father," she called as she ran through the doorway. She squinted in the dim light, trying to see where her father stood. A small figure approached her.

"Whore!" Bithia slapped Deborah across the face with such force, it knocked the young girl off her feet. For the second time that morning, Deborah found herself on her knees, this time in pain. Her hands flew to her cheek. Bithia stalked over, pulling Deborah's head up by the hair. Deborah let out a yelp of pain.

"Where have you been?" Her stepmother's spittle sprayed her face. Bithia slapped her again. "The dishonor you have brought to your father." Another slap.

Eglah pulled Bithia away, while Edin and Nathan cried from the corner of the room. "Stop! We've got to tell Avram and Az-areel she's back! We may be able to avert a scandal!"

Bithia's ranting ceased. "You are right. They must be stopped!" She ran from the house.

Deborah sobbed on the floor. The excitement from her vision lost now amid the realization of how things appeared. She had been away from home the whole night. Alone. *Who knows what Palti told them?*

Eglah went to the boys in the corner and quieted them down before returning to sit by her sister-in-law. She placed an arm around Deborah's shoulder, but didn't speak.

Avram entered the house first. He strode over to the two girls. Pushing Eglah aside, he grabbed Deborah by her shoul-ders and pulled her up. "I told you to stay away from him." Her head rocked as he shook her. "You are ruined. Do you understand? No man will have you now."

"I wasn't with him!"

Avram shook her harder. "Don't lie! Palti saw you together!"

Deborah broke free of her brother's grip. "Palti knows nothing but his own desire to be rid of me!"

Her stepbrother came through the doorway, followed by Azareel and Bithia. "I saw you walk with him to the forest. Don't deny it."

"Enough!" Azareel cried. His voice sounded tired. Deborah could see the anguish in his eyes. She ran to him, falling prostrate at his feet.

"Father, please. You have to believe me when I tell you. I have not been with Seff this whole night."

Her father lifted her head so she looked into his face. "But you were with him. Were you not?"

She nodded.

From behind her, Avram let out a groan. Palti smiled. "I told you so."

Deborah's hatred for her stepbrother flowed from her. "I'm sure you did. After you tricked me into going to him."

Palti's eyes flashed in anger. "Liar."

Bithia stepped forward to strike her again, but Azareel stopped her hand. "I will hear what my daughter has to say."

Bithia struggled against him. "You cannot believe her?"

Azareel let go of her. "I have heard everyone else's opinion this morning." He let out a long sigh. "I will hear my daughter's story now."

Deborah sat up and breathed deeply. She struggled to stop her tears. "Thank you, Father." Avram growled as he paced the room, but Azareel stood still while she spoke. She told of meeting Seff on the pathway back to the village. Palti again denied her accusation that he'd arranged their meeting, but Azareel quieted him down with a wave of his hand.

"Let her speak. You will have your turn later, if you desire."

"It is true, Father," Deborah continued. "I did not seek to find Seff last night. But I do admit I walked with him once we met."

Avram groaned, but didn't speak. Deborah lowered her head. "I am sorry to have disobeyed you, Brother. And if I have brought dishonor on you Father, by my actions, I beg your forgiveness."

Azareel still did not move. "This walking. Where did you go?"

Deborah told him of the clearing on the hill, of the people worshipping Baal and Asherah. The voices she'd heard and the visions she'd seen.

Azareel interrupted her. "These people you saw. In the visions. Did you know them?"

Deborah searched her memory. "Only some of them. I saw a wedding, here in the village, but the bride's face was covered. I saw Avram in sack cloth, crying at a grave, but I don't know whose. The man at the temple, I don't know. Nor the man in silk robes. They were visions from Asherah, I think."

Azareel nodded. "Go on."

"I ran. Heber and the others wanted me to bow to Asherah, and I wouldn't. I told them I serve only the God of Abraham. There were so many of them and they were angry with me. I ran into the forest and got lost."

Azareel rubbed his beard. "You got lost?"

"Look! Look at the cuts on my arms, Father. The branches scratched me. The rocks cut my feet. It was dark. I couldn't see where to go."

Azareel took her arm to survey her wounds. "It took you all night to find your way home?"

"Yes, but there is more, Father."

He arched his eyebrows. "More? You have more I must struggle to believe?"

"This may be the hardest part of all, Father." She told him of Remiel and of all the angel had said before leaving her on the hillside.

Bithia laughed derisively. "You cannot be serious? You fell asleep and dreamed this miracle. Or else you are lying to keep from being beaten."

Deborah sat up on her knees. "Father, I swear to you on my life, I saw and heard these things. All I have said is true."

Azareel's dark eyes stared into hers. "Daughter, tell me the truth. Are you still a maid?"

Deborah grabbed his hands. "Yes, Father. I have been with no man."

Azareel lifted his head and walked away from her. He waved Avram to his side. Heads bowed, they talked quietly, so as not to be overheard. After several minutes Azareel approached Deborah.

"What you have told me is too hard to accept, and yet, I know you believe it. Perhaps Bithia is right, and you only dreamt these things." He raised a hand to stop Deborah from speaking. "But we will act as if the things you saw were real. For now. We will go to Shiloh after next week, once the barley has been properly stored. There you will sacrifice a sin offering. Until then, you will remain in the house." He looked to the rest of the family. "We will tell those who ask that she is ill. That she caught a chill at the threshing festival and needs to remain inside."

Azareel turned to Palti. "As for you, whether you set a trap for my daughter or no, you did nothing to stop her from going with this man. Your disregard for her honor and mine proves to me that you are not the man I want for her husband." Palti tried to sputter an excuse, but Azareel's cold stare silenced him. "You are no longer my son. I allow you to stay only for the sake of your mother. But from this day forth, you will receive no blessing from me." Bithia let out a cry and ran forward. Azareel pushed her away. "I will talk to Tamar's family and see if a marriage can be arranged. Avram and I will help you build a house. As soon as it is ready, you can take your bride in it and live there. Do you understand?"

Palti nodded while Bithia wept softly.

Azareel turned to Eglah. "Find cloth for my daughter to wrap her head. Then go fetch water so she may clean herself."

Voices raised in anger could be heard approaching from outside. Eglah hurried to Deborah with a piece of linen while Avram went to the doorway. Several men stood silhouetted against the morning sun.

"Avram!" called one man. "Is your sister home?"

Avram blocked the entrance with his body, allowing Deborah time to wrap her hair up in the cloth. "Of course she is, Simon. What is wrong?"

From behind, other voices called out. "We told you Simon. Our children have nothing to do with Mava."

Avram stepped through the doorway. Azareel motioned for the rest of the family to stay inside before following his son. They obeyed, but moved to the center of the room where they could see the activity outside. Deborah recognized Mava's father, Simon; behind him stood Schemuel and Achida. Azareel crossed his arms. "What is this all about?"

"Mava is gone." Simon's shoulders stooped. He dragged his hand down his long, gray beard. "She never returned home last night after the festival." His face reddened with anger as he shook a finger at Achida. "I know his son had something to do with it!"

Azareel placed a hand on Simon's shoulder. "What has this to do with my Deborah?"

Achida stepped forward. His face showed little worry as he spoke. "The fool heard gossip at the well that Mava and your daughter were meeting secretly with my sons last night. I told him it was a thoughtless rumor."

Mava's father stepped away from Azareel and grabbed Achida's tunic. "If so, where are your sons?"

Achida glared at Simon. His eyes cold and hard as metal. He brushed Simon's hands away. "They went hunting last night. After the festival."

"You lie!"

Azareel restrained the older man from accosting Achida again. He turned his friend to face him. "Deborah is home with us. Whatever happened, she is not with your daughter."

Simon bowed his head and sighed. "I am sorry, Azareel. When my wife came back from the well and told me what she had heard . . . we asked others if they saw Deborah this morning and none had."

Avram stepped forward. "My sister is ill. She caught a chill in the night and needs to rest."

Simon nodded and took a deep breath. "I am sorry. When she wakes, please ask if she knows where Mava might have gone."

Azareel patted Simon's shoulders. "I will. If Mava does not return soon, I and my sons will help you look for her."

"Thank you, my friend." Simon cast another glance at Achida and walked away. Schemuel and Achida turned to go.

Azareel called to them. "One moment, please."

The men turned back. "What is it, friend?" asked Schemuel.

Deborah's father and brother both stepped forward. Azareel straightened his back so he stood almost as tall as Achida.

"Avram has already told your son to stay away from our Deborah. He did not."

Achida's shoulders stiffened. "Seff is a good man."

Azareel took a step toward the men. "My house serves the God of Abraham, the God of Isaac and the God of Jacob. Your son tried to lead my daughter into idolatry."

"My family is of the Kenite tribe, descendants of your Prophet Moses' father-in-law." Achida raised his arms in a gesture of openness. "We respect your God. Our people intermarry. That is how my sister came to be Schemuel's wife." He placed a hand on his brother-in-law's arm.

Deborah's father drew himself up even straighter. He spoke with authority. "My daughter will not marry anyone who does not bear the mark of the Lord's covenant. She will marry no man who does not follow the laws of the God of Israel." Azareel pointed his finger at the men. "Tell your son to stay away from Deborah. If he does not, I will call the elders together and I will charge him with blasphemy. He has spoken to my daughter and others about his love of idols. He could be stoned."

The wind caught Azareel's tunic as he turned away from the men and strode into the house. Avram followed close behind.

6 Hazor

One Week Later

"Congratulations, General!" Jabin called as Sisera stood before the King's table. Jabin lifted his goblet. "Your wife has borne you another son?"

"Yes, my lord." His heart swelled with pride. The offerings his wife and mother made to the gods had again given him a healthy boy child. "Another warrior for Canaan."

"I drink to his health, my friend." The king grinned over the rim of his cup. "May the gods keep blessing your bed."

Sisera bowed as he backed away from the table. He turned to search the great hall for an open seat.

Jabin frowned. "Lotan, move. The general must have a place near the king."

With that, a middle-aged man stood, nodding graciously towards Jabin. "Of course, my lord." Sisera did not fail to catch the look of hatred Lotan cast his way before the older noble walked to the back of the room to sit in a less distinguished place at the table. Sisera reclined next to a man he didn't know. Dressed in a fine woolen robe woven through with gold thread, the stranger appeared to be of at least twenty years in age.

"This is our friend, Khali," called Jabin. "He is a prince of Megiddo."

Sisera took the goblet of wine a servant offered him. "How do you find our city?"

Khali smiled. His jeweled hand tapped the rim of his cup. "I am impressed. It is full of much beauty."

"I am glad you think so." Sisera tore off a piece of bread. "What business brings a prince of Megiddo to Hazor?"

"Only friendship, General. The desire to keep good relations between our two cities." The prince picked up a handful of almonds from the platter in front of him and popped one into his mouth.

"Tell him why else you came," Jabin said from his raised dais. "I think you'll find the general an eager listener."

The dark prince crunched another almond. He scrutinized Sisera before he spoke. "My father and I believe now is the time for the Canaanites to reestablish their superiority in the land."

Sisera leaned toward the handsome man. "How do you propose we do that?"

Khali glanced at the king, then back to Sisera. "Our armies need to be brought up from the south to patrol the northern passes and the merchant routes. We no longer fear Egyptian raids. It has been over twelve years since they've attacked. Our treaties are secure. We need to push the Semites back into the hills and assert our position as rulers of the plains and coastal roads."

Sisera raised his glass to the young man. He took a long drink before turning to the king. "He is echoing what I have told your Majesty."

"Yes," called an older nobleman from across the room. "We all know your thoughts, General. But to act now would be foolish."

"You want Jabin to wait for what, Nahab?" Sisera slammed down his goblet. "Always with you and your friends it is 'Wait. Wait for a better time.' I say there is no better time. The Israelites have been quiet for years. They have no set leader, only rogue bands of mercenaries. If we could arrange a coalition between the kings of Megiddo, Carmel, and the coast cities, we could easily vanquish all foreigners in our land."

Nahab stood, his face red with anger. "It is not cowardice to wait. We need a sign, an omen from El that now is the time to move. Without that-"

"Make sacrifices and ask the oracles. I know that the gods will bless our efforts."

King Jabin clapped his hands. "Enough! I have already called for a sacrifice. We will consult the priests for the best time to hold a festival and seek the answers we need." He nodded toward a servant in the corner. "Bring in some musicians. Let us have songs and dancing."

The tension in the room lessened only slightly as the dancers sought to divert the men from their anger. Sisera leaned back on his elbows to watch the movements of the veiled women. He felt someone's eyes on him and glanced toward the king. *Now is the time, my lord. The time to act!* Jabin lifted his goblet in a silent toast to his friend. Sisera lifted his cup in return.

7 The Hills of Ephraim

The Following Day

The early morning sun crested the hills, bathing the surrounding landscape in warm, peach-colored light.

Deborah and her family gathered near the entrance to their house. She wore a long, plain linen dress with a sleeveless blue tunic over it and a linen belt wrapped around her waist. Her father and Palti wore dark brown cloaks over their shifts. They were dressed for traveling. Azareel had not forgiven his stepson for allowing Deborah to walk with Seff, but he did not feel confident in his strength alone to get them safely to Shiloh.

Azareel placed a hand on Avram's shoulder. "We should be back before the Sabbath. God keep you safe while I am gone."

Avram bowed his head. "And may the Lord bless your travels and bring you safely home."

Azareel patted his son's arm then turned away. "Come Deborah. Palti. It is time to go."

Avram did not return Deborah's tentative smile as she passed him in the doorway. She swallowed hard. She knew he didn't believe her story. No one in the family did. Avram and father had both been beside themselves with worry when she insisted on fasting until she'd offered her sacrifice at the Tabernacle. She'd had no food in two weeks. Although a little light-headed, she had no fear of being too weary to travel to Shiloh. *It is the Lord's will. He will sustain me.*

Neighbors called out blessings for a safe journey as they made their way out of the village. Azareel had told the elders that they traveled to Shiloh to give an offering of Thanksgiving, now that Deborah was well again and Tamar's family had accepted Palti's offer of marriage. The betrothal ceremony would be when Palti returned from the Tabernacle.

Deborah caught up to her father. "I remember when you allowed me to come to with you to the Tabernacle for the Passover. What was it? Two springs ago?"

Azareel looked straight ahead. "It seems longer."

Deborah heard the weariness in his voice. "Father, I know you doubt what I have said. But you will see. The angel promised I would receive the Lord's gift if I went to Shiloh." Azareel's face hardened as he focused on the path up the hill. She sighed. "You will see, Father."

Deborah kept stride with Azareel as long as she could, but soon fell a few steps behind him and Palti. Her heart beat fast, not only from exertion, but from excitement and fear. She'd hardly slept the night before, wondering what would happen in Shiloh. *Will there be more visions? Will I hear your voice, Lord?* She did not relish seeing more visions like the ones she experienced with Seff, but if that's what the Lord required, so be it. She had spent the weeks praying to have the courage to accept this holy task. She knew she could refuse it. If she didn't make the journey to Shiloh, life would go on as it always had.

But she realized that Remiel had been right. She could never return to life she'd known before, not after all she had seen. She must go on and fulfill the Lord's will.

By mid-morning they reached the main road and mingled with the other travelers to the low country. Peddlers pushed carts filled with leather goods and pottery. Several priests traveled with their young scribes or servants to help them. A small caravan of Egyptian merchants made their way along the road. They dressed in white linen, loosely fitted about one shoulder, then flowing down to their thighs. The sheer material hid little of the body underneath. Deborah kept her eyes averted from them, but couldn't resist walking close to their donkeys so she could smell the exotic spices and rare perfumes they carried.

"It's spikenard."

Deborah looked up to see a tall young man walking beside her. The sun shimmered off his black hair. He smiled down at her. "The fragrance you smell. It's spikenard, one of the rarest spices in the land." His deep voice was strangely accented, but Deborah could easily understand him.

"It's beautiful."

The trader patted his donkey on the rump, but kept his gaze on Deborah. "Yes."

"Daughter," Azareel called.

Deborah hurried to his side.

Azareel turned his hard eyes to her. "Stay by me."

"Yes, Father."

"When we reach Shiloh, we will buy a veil so you will not walk uncovered."

She bowed her head. "Yes, Father."

They reached Shiloh by the early afternoon. Deborah followed Palti and her father through the crowded streets. Shiloh was a bustling town of several hundred people. Many had settled here because of its proximity to the Tabernacle. Traders and merchants took up residence, taking advantage of the eternal influx of pilgrims and visitors to the holiest of Hebrew sites. The town sat far enough from the coast to avoid raids by Egyptian armies but not far enough in the hills to make travel uncomfortable. The land belonged to the tribe of Ephraim, as Deborah's village did, but foreigners and Canaanites also settled in the area. Deborah marveled at the many robes made of deep purple cloth, the colored beads that hung from posts in the stalls, and the fine pottery that lined the shops. Her stomach growled at the aroma of roasting meat and spices. Azareel stopped in the entrance of one of the store fronts.

"Wait here. I will see if my sister's husband is inside." Palti wandered over to one of the merchants to look at some beads, but Deborah stayed just outside the doorway. She heard her father call out a greeting and smiled at her uncle's enthusiastic response. She had met Leb only once, when the whole family had traveled to Shiloh for the Passover. She remembered him as a kind, jovial man with a round face and a quick smile.

"Brother!" Leb exclaimed. "What brings you here?" Azareel spoke low, Deborah couldn't hear his answer. Her father soon walked out of the shop with Leb following close behind. Her uncle struggled to untie a leather apron from his rotund midsection. He threw the apron at a young man behind him. "Uri finish the order for Levi. Then close the shop and come home. We must celebrate!"

Azareel looked uncomfortable at Leb's fussing. "Please, Brother. Go to no trouble."

Leb clapped him soundly on the back. "Nonsense! We seldom have company. Rachel will be so pleased." He glanced up as Palti walked toward them. "You brought your son with you? How wonderful." He gave Palti a slap on the shoulder.

Azareel nodded toward Deborah. "And my daughter."

Leb swung around to look at her. He lifted his eyebrows. "This is little Deborah?"

Deborah smiled shyly. "Yes, Uncle."

He placed a hand on her shoulder and shook his head. "It can't be. You were as small and gangly as a newborn lamb last I saw you. Now look at you!" His eyes surveyed her. "You are a beautiful young woman." Deborah felt heat rush to her cheeks as Leb turned to Azareel. "Is she betrothed yet?"

Azareel's face hardened slightly. "Not yet."

Leb grinned. "Ahh, we will have to change that!" The portly man turned and scurried down the street. "Come! Rachel was speaking of you just last night. She will be so pleased to see you! Come!"

They wove their way through the streets toward the northern corner of the city. Here the buildings stood close together, many sharing walls. Rugs and colored cloth hung over the sides of the rooftops. Children played in the alleys while women sat in doorways sewing or carding wool. They called out to each other as they worked, sharing the news about their families and neighbors. As Deborah and her family turned the corner onto another street, an older woman with no teeth called out from one house.

"Leb! Is there trouble?"

The stout man slowed his pace. "No, Batya. Rachel's brother from the hill country has come."

Batya smiled her toothless grin and waved as the group strode by. Deborah recognized the doorway to her uncle's house. She had been here once before, and remembered being awed by its size. Although she had grown, it still impressed her. A front room, twice the size of her father's house, opened to a rectangular courtyard. A sheltered storage area lay off to one side and a set of stairs opposite led up to the roof. Leb rushed through the door.

"Rachel! Guess who is here?"

His wife knelt by a small stove, her graying hair swept up in a bun on top of her head. Her brown eyes lit up with joy when she saw her brother enter. She lifted herself off the floor with a groan, then ran to hug Azareel.

"Brother! I thought of you only yesterday. Didn't I, Leb?" She glanced at her husband, but didn't wait for him to answer. "I said, 'I think there is news from Azareel. I can't shake him from my mind.' And here you are." She took Azareel's face in her bony hands. "What news is there, Brother? Is there trouble?"

Azareel took her hands in his and kissed them. "No . . . no trouble."

Rachel tilted her head as she stared into his eyes. She caught sight of Deborah and Palti in the doorway. She turned back to her brother. "We will talk later. Now who are these that lurk outside my door?"

"I'm Palti, Aunt." He embraced her. "Don't you recognize me?"

"You cannot be Palti." She pushed him away so she could look him over. "Palti was always chubby and short. You are tall and lean!"

Deborah laughed silently while Palti squirmed at the reminder of his former awkwardness. Leb reached over to pull her forward. "You think Palti has grown? Look at our little Deborah!"

Rachel let out a small gasp. "Not this young woman? Can it be so long since we've seen you?" Deborah nodded and gave her aunt a hug.

Leb led Azareel toward the center of the room. He spoke over his shoulder to his wife. "I told Uri to close the shop early and come for dinner. He'll fetch Adara along the way." He and Azareel sat down on a striped rug. Leb motioned for Palti to join them.

Rachel frowned. "That will never do. Adara will be making her own supper soon." She grabbed Deborah's hand. "Come. We will go tell her ourselves. Maybe we will stop on the way home and buy a salted fish to put in the stew I'm making."

Deborah's aunt hurried to a niche in the wall and picked up a clay pot. Lifting its lid, she took out several coins. "We won't be long." She took Deborah's hand again, pulling her out into the street. "You remember Adara, don't you?"

Deborah nodded. Her cousin had been newly married when they'd first met. Her husband, Michal was a robust man in his twenties. He'd towered over little Adara, who'd been just fourteen.

"She has a son of her own now. A beautiful boy."

Deborah struggled to keep up with her aunt. "Is Uri married now too?"

Rachel's eyebrow's lifted. "From your mouth to God's ears. No, he's having too much fun with his drunken friends to settle down."

Rachel stopped to let Deborah catch up to her. The older woman then turned and sped down a narrow ally. "This is her street."

Adara beamed when she saw her mother and Deborah in the doorway. She agreed to bring what bread she'd made that day to share at her mother's house. "I'll put on some honey cakes as well."

Rachel and Deborah didn't stay long before setting off for the market to buy the fish and a new skin of wine. That done, they headed home to finish preparing the night's special dinner. Rachel eyed the men closely when she entered the front room of the house. "Did you have a good talk?"

Azareel glanced at the floor, but Leb focused his attention on Deborah. "Yes, Wife."

It was obvious Leb knew some of what had happened over the past month. Deborah wondered how much her father had said, but since he would not look at her, she couldn't read his eyes. The men soon left the women to get the meal ready, while they sat in the small courtyard at the back of the house and drank the wine Rachel had bought.

Deborah enjoyed the loud laughter and lively conversation at dinner that night. The men discussed and argued about everything. Adara's son, Josiah, nestled at her breast, while Rachel fussed about, refilling cups and plates.

"Cousin," Uri called to Deborah. "You're not eating. Aren't you well?"

She stole a fleeting look toward her father, but he turned away from her. "I am fine."

Uri chuckled. "You can't be well if you're not eating! What's wrong?"

Deborah longed to know how much her father would approve of her saying, but he gave no clue. An awkward silence ensued as the family all turned to wait on her answer. Leb finally came to her rescue.

"She is fasting, Uri. Something that would benefit you, one of these days."

Uri scrunched his face. "Fasting? Why in the world would you do that?"

"That's between her and the Lord," Leb answered. "As for me, I would like to have another helping!"

A hearty shout of approval went around the room. Deborah sighed with relief that the interest was now off of her. She helped Rachel serve more food, then sat down in the corner to watch the mayhem. Her concentration was broken when she heard her name spoken by Adara.

"Is Deborah betrothed, Uncle?"

Azareel shook his head. "Not yet. I thought to inquire of my family here, to see if they might know of a suitable husband."

Deborah felt the blood drain from her face. The room seemed to rock, as if it sat on water.

Uri surveyed her. "I have a few friends she might do for."

"One of your friends?" Leb snorted. "I think we can do better than that."

Adara patted her baby on the back. "You don't look well, Cousin."

Deborah took a deep breath. "I think the long journey has tired me more than I thought. And the smell of food." She stood. "Perhaps I'll sit in the courtyard." She hurried out into the cool night air.

It took a moment for her chest to loosen so she could breathe again. *A husband, here? Why? Do the others at home know of my night in the woods? Do they think I'm not pure? Or maybe father thinks I'm insane, talking of angels and visions?*

"Cousin?" Adara placed her hand on Deborah's shoulder. "Did you not know of your father's plan?"

Deborah shook her head, afraid if she spoke, her voice would break.

"I could tell by your reaction." Adara guided her over to a stone bench. "At least you had some warning. I came home one day from the well to find Michal standing in the courtyard. The first time I met him was at our betrothal ceremony." She gave Deborah's hand a gentle squeeze.

"It's just . . . ." Deborah sighed heavily. "Father always said he wanted me to live near him. Now he wants to send me away."

"Did you argue?"

"Not exactly." A breeze caressed her face, chilling the tears that rolled down her cheeks. "So much has changed."

"What happened?"

Deborah wiped her face. "Too much." She glanced at the stars overhead. "I will know tomorrow, after I make my sacrifice."

Adara furrowed her eyebrows. "Know what?"

"If everything that happened is true." She smiled at Adara's confused expression. "It is too hard to explain tonight. I will know more tomorrow."

"I thought maybe you were in love with someone already."

Deborah lowered her chin and whispered, "I did love someone."

Curiosity lit her cousin's eyes. "And?"

"He's gone." Deborah bit her lip to keep from crying again. No one had heard from Seff, Heber or Mava since the night of the threshing festival. "I don't think I'll ever see him again."

"Do you want to tell me about it?"

Deborah shook her head. "No. I have other things to think about now. It's best he's gone and out of my thoughts."

Adara shrugged. "Well, if you need to talk to someone, come find me." She patted Deborah's hand. "And for whatever its worth, it's not so bad. Being married." Adara stood. "I'm sure my father and yours will find you a decent man."

"Thank you." *But what man wants a girl who sees visions and talks with angels?*

A gray and white feather fluttered down from the cheap wooden cage Deborah carried. The two turtledoves inside cooed nervously. Deborah avoided looking at them. Azareel had bought a pair each for her and Palti to offer at the Tabernacle. She shuddered at the thought of the priest killing these delicate creatures and tried to push the image from her mind, instead quickening her steps to catch up to her father, Palti, and Leb.

They left the walled city then headed down to the valley where the Tabernacle stood. Deborah marveled at the sight. From the rise of the hill she spied the huge structure. Curtains made of fine linen separated the Tabernacle from the surrounding land. The courtyard they created stood a hundred and fifty by seventy-five feet. Inside the space, Deborah could make out a smaller tent. The morning sun gleamed off the golden columns that supported it. This was the Tabernacle. Inside was the Holy of Holies, where the Ark of the Covenant sat. The throne of God. A shiver passed through her body. *I'm afraid, Lord. And tired. Please give me the strength I need to do this thing you ask.*

They walked in silence out to the holy site. Azareel brought Palti forward to the curtained outer gate first. Leb placed a hand on Deborah's shoulder. "I need to speak with you." He led her away from the small crowd gathered by the entryway.

Deborah looked up at her uncle. His eyes searched her face. "Your father has told me of your visions." He tightened his grip. "Tell me. Are they true?"

"Yes, Uncle."

His eyes glinted with intensity. "You are not making up tales? To cover your sin?"

"No!" Deborah twisted her body to try and make him loosen his hold but Leb grabbed her other shoulder.

"Then why the sin offering? What did you do?"

Deborah's eyes watered. "I walked on unholy ground. I went within the circle of the idols. I was tempted, Uncle, to bow down to another god."

"That is all?"

She shook her head. "I disobeyed Avram and Azareel. I walked with a man."

"What else did you do with him?"

Deborah's faced flushed with her guilt. "We kissed. No more."

Leb's eyes bore into hers, his voice quiet, but severe. "Are you sure? He did no more?"

"Nothing. There was desire, Uncle. Nothing more." Leb released her. She wiped her cheeks dry.

Her uncle chewed on his lower lip before turning back to her, glowering. "Do you know the anguish you have caused your father?"

Deborah fought against her tears. "But why? If he would only believe me, he would be proud. The angel said I was chosen by God!"

Leb's hand rocked against her face. "Stop! Do not blaspheme!"

The birds squawked loudly as Deborah lost her grip on the cage. It dropped to the ground. She fell to her knees to pick it up before the doves could escape through the now open door. She hugged the cage to her chest and lifted her gaze to her uncle. "Why does no one believe me?"

His red face glared down at her. "Listen to me. Make this sacrifice and repent of this folly. When it is done, speak no more of these . . . visions, to anyone. Do you understand?"

Deborah's breath caught in her throat.

Leb stepped toward her. "Do you understand?"

Deborah struggled against her fear and spoke with strength gained by the days of fasting and prayer. "I will do whatever the Lord commands of me. No matter what the cost."

Her uncle looked to strike her again but stopped his hand, his eyes locked onto hers. He lowered his arm. "You truly believe the Lord has spoken to you?"

She nodded.

Leb's face showed his confusion. "But why? Why would He choose a woman? No . . . a girl?"

"Because I asked. All my life, I have prayed that God would reveal himself to me." She rose to her feet. "Please, Uncle. Take me to the priest. Let me receive the gift the angel spoke of." *Before I become too scared.*

Leb took her arm, gently this time, and led her back to the gateway. Only a few pilgrims stood ahead of them. Deborah could see inside the courtyard. Halfway between the entryway and the actual Tabernacle stood the smoking bronze altar. The sunlight shone so brightly off it, she had to shield her eyes. Palti walked to the priest and handed over his cage. Deborah saw the priest grab one of the birds and wrench its head from its body. Her stomach lurched as he sprinkled the sides of the altar with the dove's blood. She turned away, swallowing the bile that rose to her throat. Looking back, she saw the priest kill the second bird and throw it onto the fire. The others in line presented themselves to a different priest to have skin conditions examined.

The white robed priest by the altar motioned Deborah forward. The pounding of her heart reverberated through her head as she walked toward him. The sweet odor of the burning sacrifices drifted on the breeze. The smoke swirled around the priest, obscuring him momentarily in a cloud of gray. He stepped forward and held out his hands.

"Why do you make this sacrifice?"

Deborah stared at the young priest. His black hair and beard stood out in contrast to the gleaming white robe and turban he wore. His dark eyes bore into hers.

"Daughter, why do you make this sacrifice?"

She handed the cage to him. "To atone for my sins."

His eyebrows rose slightly. "Kneel then, and confess to the Lord. May the blood of your sacrifice wash away the guilt of your sins."

Deborah knelt as the priest took out the first bird, its frightened squawking cut off sharply as he twisted its neck. She closed her eyes and bowed her head. *Forgive me Lord, for my sins. I repent of my desire for Seff. Forgive me for disobeying Father and Avram, and your commands. Forgive me for going up to the high place. For daring to approach the pole of Asherah.* Deborah's heart pounded within her, her breath came in rapid gasps. *Accept my sacrifice, O God of my fathers. Forgive me.*

Deborah prostrated herself on the ground, her arms stretched out toward the altar, her face pressed against the dirt. A thunderous wind seemed to whirl around her, inside her. A voice spoke from within her.

I am the Lord your God. Do not worship any other gods besides me.

Deborah's fists pounded at the ground. *Forgive me! Please, Lord! Forgive me! I love you! I give my life to you. Whatever you ask of me, I will do!* The wind grew louder and a bright light, full of warmth, enveloped her.

Deborah, you will speak the words I give you. You will lead my people back to me. You will know me as no other woman has. Behold!

A great hand wrenched her spirit from her chest. She floated, apart from herself. Up, up, up toward the heavens. Then her spirit swooped down like a bird caught on the wind. She followed the current up to the highest mountain and watched the sunrise, casting hues of the boldest purple and red over snow covered peaks. Next she soared above a crystal blue ocean, the waves pounding white foam against the shore. A meadow, ablaze with the colors of wildflowers; a waterfall, towering hundreds of feet high amid the densest jungle she had ever seen. All the while voices sang out in her head, "Holy, holy, holy is the Lord Almighty! The whole earth is filled with His glory!" The mighty chorus vibrated throughout her body as she experienced one marvel after another. Finally her spirit cried out, *Stop, Lord! It is too beautiful. It is too much! You are too big for me!*

Tell them, Deborah. Speak of my glory!

Deborah lifted herself to her knees and threw her arms in the air. Tears of joy streaked her dirt stained face.

"Great is the Lord and worthy of all praise! He has created all things! The mountains sing out His power and majesty! The waves crash and speak of His everlasting glory! I will sing of the Lord! I will tell of His unending mercy and love for His servant!"

Deborah stood, still enraptured by all she had seen and by God's spirit moving within her. "Oh, Israel! Can you not see how my heart breaks for you? I call to you, and yet you turn away. You chase false gods; you give your praise to stone and wood. Do you think I do not see? Do you think I do not hear?"

Anger filled her and she ripped her robe as if in mourning. "Hear O Israel, the Lord our God calls to you! You must love the Lord your God with all your heart, with all your mind with all your strength. I have chosen you out of all the people of the earth to be mine. I have led you out of bondage and into this land and yet you do not love me. Like a wife caught in adultery, I have seen your sin. I know your lies. I have stopped the rain so that you might see your betrayal and turn back to me!"

The priests gathered around her. Azareel reached out for her but Leb stopped him. They watched transfixed as Deborah continued to prophesize. She whirled around to face the priests.

"Her eyes!" one gasped.

"They blaze like fire!"

Deborah confronted the holy men. "Do not think that you are above the sins of the people, for I have seen how you have corrupted my ceremonies. You think to dishonor me like Nadab and Abihu, the sons of Aaron. But I will not be mocked! Repent! You have eaten the choice meat of the sacrifice instead of burning it as an offering to me. You say to yourselves 'our God will not see our folly.' But I have seen it and my anger burns against you."

The priests dropped to their knees and Deborah turned to the people in the courtyard. Her voice resonated with power, even as her muscles trembled with exertion, as if she ran a great distance. "Repent, all of you! For the Lord our God longs to restore the rain and cause our harvests to overflow the granaries. He longs to crush the heads of those who oppress us and give us peace and rest. Seek Him! Follow His commandments. Fear Him and He will restore you."

Deborah collapsed on the ground.

"Daughter?" Azareel ran to her. He lifted her head. "Deborah?"

She struggled to open her eyes, her father brushed her face with his hand and kissed her cheek. "Forgive me, Deborah. I believe you. I believe."

She closed her eyes and drifted into welcome darkness.

8 The Hills of Ephraim

Fall, One Year Later

Deborah ran up the path leading away from the road. "Come, Uncle. This is the way to my village."

Leb and Rachel puffed slowly up behind her. "Calm down," Leb called. "We will be there by afternoon."

He couldn't see her pout behind the veil that covered her face. She waited at the top of the hill for them to catch up. "I'm sorry. I am excited to see my father again."

Rachel smiled. "We know you are. I am sorry that we're so slow." She patted her husband on the back. "But you will have plenty of time to help your family prepare for the wedding."

Deborah nodded. She hadn't seen her family in over a year. She'd stayed in Shiloh to be near the temple and the priests. In the month of Elul, God had laid it on her heart to call for a three-day period of fasting and prayer before the celebration of the Feast of the Tabernacles in the fall. Priests and scribes were sent throughout Israel to tell the nation about the new prophet and God's will. People from all the tribes heeded God's call, and when the time for the festival came, thousands of pilgrims journeyed to Shiloh to pray. When the three days ended, God opened the heavens and the long-awaited rain fell throughout the winter planting season. The resulting harvest had been the best in years. Deborah's position as a prophet of YHWH had been firmly established. She returned now to her home to celebrate the wedding of her brother Palti to Tamar.

Deborah tried not to run ahead of her relatives as they plodded along the narrow dirt path that wound through the hills of Ephraim. By the ninth hour of the day they reached the crest of a large hill and she could see her village in the distance. Tears of joy spilled down her cheeks. "Look! There it is!"

They made their way swiftly. Even Leb seemed to find energy with the thought of a place to sit out of the sun, and a cool drink of water or milk. As they approached the village from the south side, Deborah's eyes searched the various houses. *It all seems smaller, like a dream.* Several old men sat on the ground in the shade of one of the houses. Deborah recognized her friend Bracha's father.

"Good day, Levi!"

He shaded his eyes. "Good day. Do I know you?"

Deborah had forgotten the veil and new clothes she wore. "It's me. Deborah bat Azareel."

Levi stood. "Ah, Deborah! Home for your brother's wedding, no?" He poked the other men with his foot. "It is the prophet," he whispered. "Stand up, you fools."

Deborah frowned beneath her veil. "Don't stand, friends. I am only Deborah."

The men shuffled to their feet anyway. Levi bowed slightly. "We heard how the Lord speaks through you. Many of us were at the festival and heard you speak ourselves."

Another of the men also bowed. "You are not the same girl. You have spoken to YHWH, blessed be His name."

The others echoed, "Blessed be His name."

Deborah swallowed the lump in her throat. She didn't know what she'd expected when she returned home, but it wasn't this. Leb touched her shoulder.

"Are you well, Niece?" he asked.

"Yes." She turned to the men. "I hope to see you at the celebration. I must go to my father now."

The men nodded. She felt their eyes on her as she walked through the town. She didn't call out to anyone else on the way. She turned the corner and saw a little boy sitting in the doorway to her old home, his blue tunic barely touching his knees.

"Nathan? Is that you?" Deborah couldn't believe how big her brother had grown.

Nathan jumped up and took a step toward her. He peered intently at her face. Deborah realized he was trying to see through the veil. She lifted the filmy material over her head.

Nathan grinned. "Father!" He called back into the house. "She's here!"

Deborah fell to her knees and opened her arms to receive her brother's excited greeting. She kissed his curly brown hair and held him close. "Nathan! You're so big now! Such a help you must be to our father!"

Nathan snuggled against her shoulder. "I missed you."

"I missed you, too." She stood as the rest of her family came from the house; Palti, tall and proud, his straight black hair blowing in the wind; Avram, strong and serious, his brown eyes momentarily flashing his happiness at seeing his sister. Eglah stood beside him, holding their son, Edin, now a toddler. Bithia made her way out next, her back bent from age, followed by Azareel. Deborah could not stop her tears when she saw her father. His hair and beard now almost pure white. She fell at his feet.

"Father, I am home."

He reached down and put his hands on top of her head. "Rise, Daughter, joy of my heart. You are chosen of God and bless our home by your visit." He raised her to her feet and they all entered the small house.

Azareel motioned to Eglah as the family sat down on the rugs in the center of the room. "Bring milk for our guests. They have traveled far today."

Deborah moved as if to help, but Azareel stopped her. "Sit." Deborah bowed her head and obeyed. Rachel and Leb both groaned, their muscles popping loudly as they sat.

"It was a good day for traveling," Rachel said. "A gentle breeze eased the heat."

Leb chuckled. "Deborah would have flown here if she could. She has been so excited to see you all again."

Eglah set three mugs of milk before them. Deborah smiled. "Thank you, Sister."

Eglah bowed slightly. "You are welcome."

"I've brought gifts for you all." Deborah shifted the satchel on her shoulder and opened it. Nathan squealed with excitement.

Azareel looked gravely at Leb and Rachel. "You should not have brought anything. It is enough that you keep Deborah in your home."

Rachel opened her mouth as if to speak. Leb reached out and put his hand on her knee. "It is our honor to have Deborah live with us, Brother. God has blessed us through her." He gestured to the satchel. "And these gifts are not from us. Deborah bought them with her own money."

Azareel exchanged anxious glances with Leb and Avram. "What money does Deborah have?"

Leb nodded toward her. "Tell him."

"After the feast of the Tabernacles, people began to leave gifts outside our door. Some left them with the priests."

A low groan escaped Azareel's throat. "Charity?" He stood and paced around the group. "Do they think I am too poor to take proper care of my daughter?"

Leb's cheeks flushed with anger as he rose to face Azareel. "Do you think we'd treat our niece so ill?" He pointed to Deborah. "They bring her gifts to honor her! It is a sacrifice they are glad to give to God's own servant! Even the very priests of the Tabernacle have given her offerings!"

Azareel stood frozen, disbelief in his eyes. "Truly?"

Rachel nodded. "Truly, Brother."

He stared at his daughter. "The priests . . . have given you gifts?"

"Yes, Father." Deborah lifted her arms. "These robes were from the priests. The women who serve them gave me the veil and headdress I wear."

Azareel tugged on his beard and shook his head. He walked slowly to his seat on the rug and sat down. Deborah looked around the circle of her family. She saw the mixture of awe and fear in their eyes. *They don't see their sister or their daughter anymore. They see the prophet.*

She fought back her tears. "Rachel has also taught me to twine the wicks for the lamps Leb makes."

Leb clapped his hands as he sat back down. "Ah! Such a blessing that is! Rachel's hands are no longer able to do the fine work, and Adara is so busy with her little one."

Rachel beamed. "And another one is on the way! It should be here by spring."

"Congratulations." Azareel smiled. "You must take our blessings back with you."

"I will, Brother." Some of the tension in the family released as the adults all added their blessings.

Leb grinned. "And next year, before the Passover, Uri will marry, God willing. You must travel to Shiloh and celebrate with us."

"Do you think you will come, Father?" Deborah asked. "It would be such a comfort to know when I will see you again."

"God willing, I will come."

"And you, Avram? Will you come?"

Avram shook his head. "I don't think so." He took Eglah's hand. "My wife will have just delivered our own baby by then."

Another round of congratulations and blessings were said by all. Deborah hurried over to embrace her sister-in-law. "I'm so happy for you!"

"Thank you, Sister."

Deborah sat back by her satchel. She looked to Azareel. "May I give you my gifts, Father?"

Azareel nodded.

She pulled out a beautiful white woolen shawl with deep blue stripes. Long tassels hung from the ends. She knelt before Azareel. "For you. A prayer shawl made by the women who serve the priests."

A collective sigh of admiration rose from the circle. Azareel hesitantly reached out and touched the cloth with his fingertips. His eyes filled with tears. "It is so soft."

"Take it, Father." She lifted it up to him. "It's yours." She unfolded the shawl and placed it around his shoulders. "There. You look like one of the elders at the Tabernacle."

He took her face in his hands. "Thank you, Daughter. I have never received so fine a gift."

Deborah grinned and returned to her bag. She passed out her other presents. To Avram she gave another prayer shawl, though not as fine as Azareel's. A new wool tunic for Bithia.

Bracelets of beautiful beads for Eglah. To Nathan, she gave a bag of wooden marbles. Finally, she turned to Palti.

"For you, for your wedding tomorrow." She pulled a cap from her bag. Golden thread wove around it in an intricate geometric design. Colored beads sparkled in the light from the door. "The bridegroom must be properly attired when he knocks for his bride."

Palti's face paled. He shook his head. "I . . . cannot. Not after all I did to you."

Deborah held out the cap. "It is all forgiven, Brother. Everything happened as God ordained. Please. Take the gift and wear it proudly tomorrow for your bride."

He took the cap from her hands. "Thank you. Sister."

They spent the rest of the evening discussing the plans for the wedding and the preparations that would have to be done the following day. It was well past sunset before they all settled onto their pallets to sleep. Deborah lay awake in the dark with Nathan snuggled next to her. She listened to the sounds of her family as they slept. As she recognized each individual's breathing, whether gentle whisper or heavy snore, she offered up a prayer of blessing.

Many hours passed before Deborah finally dozed off. She slept fitfully. Her dreams filled with images from the night of the threshing festival the year before. Heber stood over her, his eyes manic and full of anger. She tried to scream, but had no breath. Seff and Mava appeared behind Heber, pulling him away. The three fought as Deborah watched, unable to move. A great wind swirled around her, pushing her away from the fight. She woke herself up, struggling against the force of the storm. She did not fall back asleep until almost dawn, and when she did, the dream repeated itself.

In the morning, Deborah insisted on going with Eglah to fetch the water. She no longer wore her veil. She was home with family and friends she'd known all her life, she felt no need to hide her face here. The women gathered around her excitedly as she approached the well.

"Your clothes!" several exclaimed. "Where did you get such a fine garment?"

Deborah lowered her eyes. "It was a gift."

"From an admirer?" joked an older woman.

"No." Deborah shook her head. "The priests gave it to me."

A general murmur of awe went through the women. A stern faced woman raised her eyebrows. "The priests? Why?"

Deborah shrugged, but then lifted her head proudly. "They said it was an honor to give a gift to a prophet of God."

The woman pushed a gray hair from her eyes. "Prophet? You?"

Deborah's aunt Nama hobbled forward. "Hush, Mara. Why must you seek to make trouble?"

Mara glared at her. "What trouble? I just want to know why we should believe she's a prophet. She's Deborah. The bee. Always causing her mother worry, as I remember."

"That's not true." Nama pointed her finger. "She was a good girl."

Mara snorted. "Oh yes, we all know how good she was. Talking with that Kenite boy. Alone."

The women around the well muttered to each other as the spark of last year's gossip re-ignited. Nama and Eglah stepped to either side of Deborah, as if guarding her.

"What girl hasn't talked with a boy she fancies?" asked Eglah. "There was no indiscretion."

Deborah put a hand on her aunt's shoulder. "I know what I have seen. I know what God has said to me. More importantly, He knows."

Mara and several other women collected their water and walked away, but most waited to hear more from the prophet.

"Deborah!" A voice called. "Deborah!"

She stood on her toes to see over the heads around her. "Bracha!"

Her old friend made her way through the crowd. Still plump, with a delightful round face and small full lips, Bracha had changed little over the past year. Deborah embraced her. "How have you been?

Bracha pulled away and smiled broadly. "I am betrothed."

"To whom?"

"My cousin, Chasid. In Bethel."

"I am so happy for you!"

"The wedding will be in the spring." Bracha's smile grew hesitant. "Maybe you would bless us by attending?"

Deborah grabbed her hands. "I will do everything in my power to be here. I would be honored to walk you to your bridegroom's house."

Bracha squealed as she hugged her again. "Oh, how I've missed you!"

The women interrupted their reunion with more questions for Deborah. "What was life like in Shiloh?" "Will God again send the rains?" Deborah answered them all as best she could.

Nama asked, "When will the Lord deliver us from our enemies?"

A hush fell over the women. Deborah lowered her head and waited for the affirmation of the spirit within her, before she spoke. When she lifted her gaze, several women gasped.

"Your eyes," whispered Bracha. She turned to the women next to her. "Do you see how they . . . they seem to burn?"

Deborah ignored the murmurings around her, her voice clear and authoritative. "The Lord is slow to anger and His mercy is everlasting. But we have turned our back on Him and all He has done for us. The tribes of the North give themselves over to their lusts in the temples of Astarte and Asherah. The plains and the South pray to Baal for rain to sustain their crops. God will not be mocked. Until we cry out as one, He will not purge the land of our enemies."

As always, when she finished speaking what the Lord put on her heart, Deborah felt weakened. She took a deep breath to regain her composure. The women sensed her fatigue and they soon broke up their discussion to start the day's work. Several touched Deborah as they passed by, as if convincing themselves she was still the same person. Deborah stopped Bracha before she left.

"I didn't see Mava. Did she never return?"

Bracha shook her head. "Neither did Heber or Seff. Their father left soon after you did with his youngest son and daughter. He left his wife here to die with Schemuel."

Deborah shivered.

Bracha whispered to her. "There was talk. Before the news came from the Tabernacle. They said that you and Mava had run off to worship at the Canaanite temples." Bracha's eyes searched hers. "Did you see Mava that night?"

"Yes," Deborah said in a hushed voice. She told her what happened at the high place and how Mava had helped her escape from Heber. "But I didn't see her again after that. Maybe she went with Heber after all."

Bracha nodded. "Perhaps they feared what would happen if you told, so they fled?"

"Maybe." A heaviness settled within Deborah's spirit. She tried to brush it off with a smile. "We will talk again. At the wedding."

Bracha grinned. "It will be like old times."

"Yes." Deborah sighed as she turned to go. *But things will never be the same. Is that what I am to learn while I'm here, Lord?*

Deborah gathered with the other girls of the village in the late afternoon to help adorn Tamar for the coming of her bridegroom. Tamar's younger sister and cousin took turns brushing her hair. They poured scented oil on it until it shone. Friends rubbed her arms and shoulders with fine perfume, bought years ago and saved for this occasion. When the anointing was completed, Tamar's dress was carried over the heads of the women and draped over her head. Its deep rust color accented her dark skin and eyes. A beaded sash cinched in the waist. Many women brought bracelets and necklaces for the bride to borrow for the ceremony. Tamar soon looked like a queen.

Deborah stepped forward. "Tamar. Tonight you become my sister. I would be honored if you would wear this gift I brought for you." She held out her hands and presented Tamar with a veil made from the sheerest Egyptian gauze. Trimmed with gold thread and semi-precious stones, it sparkled in the candlelight. The women murmured with approval.

"Oh, Sister! It's beautiful!" Tamar exclaimed.

Deborah smiled. "It pales next to you on this night."

The girls around her laughed and agreed. Tamar's mother and aunts paraded the headdress Tamar would wear for the ceremony. The hat stood high, covered in rows of white and brown beads. From the sides, more beads draped down in long, flowing ribbons. The women clapped with excitement as they placed it on the bride's head. Then they draped Deborah's veil over the top, the shimmering gauze flowed past Tamar's shoulders. Sighing, the women stepped back to admire their work.

Loud shouts could be heard from outside. Someone played a flute and many voices sang.

"He's here!" cried several girls by the door. "Your bride-groom is here!"

The women stood on either side of Tamar and helped her to stand. Her mother lifted the veil and kissed her daughter on each cheek. "May the Lord bless you, my daughter." She wiped a tear from her eye.

The voice of Tamar's father could be heard. "Who is it that approaches?"

"Greetings, Bechor! I, Avram bar Azareel bar Juha bring my brother, Palti bar Mayir bar Lazar. Let him call for his bride."

The women inside held their breath and waited. Three loud knocks broke the silence. Cheers rose from the crowd both in-side, and outside, of the house. The younger girls opened the door. Another joyful cry rose from the revelers behind Avram and Palti. The groom wore Azareel's best white linen robe, a sash of striped wool tied around his waist. The cap Deborah had given him shone like the crown of a king.

Palti held out his hand. "I have come for my beloved, Tamar. Come home with me and be my wife."

The women made a path in the center of the room for the bride to walk through. Avram stepped forward. "Sister, may this day bring you blessings. May you increase to thousands upon thousands; may your children possess the gates of their enemies." He embraced Tamar lightly then stepped aside. Palti took her hand and together they walked out the door and under the canopy held by the men of the village. Torches lit the evening sky so that it seemed the sun still shone. A flute and tambourine struck up a festive melody. The crowd danced and sang their way across the village to Azareel's house.

A larger canopy had been set up between Azareel's home and the house they'd built for Palti. Underneath, Azareel and

Bithia stood ready to welcome the wedding guests. Baskets of raisin and barley cakes sat waiting to be consumed. Two large jars of wine, dried fruit and a small lamb would also be served. Palti and Tamar paused as the men fixed their canopy into the ground, just outside of the larger tent.

Azareel approached the couple as the people gathered around in a circle. Tamar's father also came forward.

Bechor took the couple's hands in his own. "I give you, this night, my daughter. May she be a blessing to you as she has been to her mother and me. May your house be filled with bread, children and peace."

He let go of their hands and took the veil from Tamar's head. He passed the veil to Deborah's father. Placing it so it draped around Palti's shoulders, Azareel proclaimed, "The government shall be upon his shoulders. May you rule your wife in strength and love." The on-lookers cried out their blessings as Palti and Tamar sat under the canopy. The musicians played again and Deborah's family set about serving the guests.

Deborah marveled at the sight before her. *I saw this in my vision, on the high place, with Seff!* She shuddered. *What of the other vision? The one of Avram, in mourning?* She gazed at the faces around her. Azareel and Leb poured the wine for their neighbors. Bithia, Eglah and Rachel served the food. Nathan and Edin ran about the crowd, playing with their friends. *One of these will be dead. But who? And how long will it be until the vision comes to pass?*

The festivities lasted throughout the next day and a half. In Shiloh, Deborah had known the wedding feasts to go on for a week. But here in the hills, where the people were poorer and the land needed to be worked daily, celebrations were shorter. Palti and Tamar had withdrawn into their home late on the first evening. They didn't emerge again until called forth by the elders on the second night. The younger men made crude comments as the couple sat down to eat while the elders entered the house to examine the bedclothes. Once Azareel, Avram and Bechor had seen the evidence of Tamar's virginity, the marriage became official. Another night of drinking and singing ensued before the celebration ended at day break the following morning.

Deborah sank to her pallet on the floor of the house. Azareel and Bithia already slept in the far corner with Nathan and Edin curled up beside them. Avram and Eglah soon entered and went to their own corner to rest. Deborah fell to sleep as the sun rose, bathing the house in deep gold. She dreamt she wandered at night in a dense wood. A voice like rushing water called to her.

"Come, Deborah. Come and see."

She stood in the clearing where she'd met Remiel. She knew it was his voice that spoke. An unseen force tugged at her, pulling her up and over the forest. She floated above the trees, her skin a silvery color in the light of a full moon. She came to a meadow and her body descended until she could see figures before her. Heber stood in the center of a crowd, his arms spread wide, his face a mask of pain, an unholy scream coming from his mouth. The sound chilled Deborah's blood.

"It is time, Deborah," said the voice of Remiel. "Look and know."

Deborah searched the crowd in the meadow. She could recognize none of the faces around her. "Where is Seff? Where is Mava?"

"Look and know."

Again, Heber cried out, drawing Deborah's gaze to him. This time, she saw his tunic. Dark stains marred the once plain fabric. Fear gripped her chest. She looked at his hands. They were wet, the moonlight shimmering off whatever covered them.

"Remiel? Where is Seff?"

"Look and know."

She saw Seff then, illuminated in the soft glow of the moon. His body lay behind Heber, crumpled in a heap. She knelt beside him. His eyes stared vacantly up at the sky. A river of blood flowed down his white cheek. Deborah's mind screamed in grief, but before she could force the sound up from her soul, Remiel touched her shoulder. A shock shuddered through her, then peace.

"There is more the servant must see."

The scene around her shifted. Now she floated above the high place. Inside the circle of torches three men stood over the body of a woman. Deborah knew without looking closer who lay on the ground. Her grief rose again, threatening to consume her. "Why? Oh, Lord! Why?" The men backed away and Deborah could clearly see Mava's violated body, her eyes holding no life, her blood spilling from the wound in her throat.

Remiel's voice poured over her like a raging river. "The evil one sought to stop you. When he could not, he took their lives instead. Know that he is searching for a way to prevent you from serving the Lord. Be strong and courageous. Find strength in the Lord, even in your pain."

He touched her again and now she stood beside a cave, its entrance covered by a large boulder. "Bring peace to her family, Deborah. Let them know where she lies."

Deborah screamed as hands pulled at her. She was sure the evil that had murdered Seff and Mava had followed her into her dream and sought to kill her, too. She thrashed and fought and cried out to the Lord.

"Deborah! Daughter!"

Azareel's voice woke her from her sleep. She clutched at his tunic, too terrified to let go.

"Deborah?" Her father's eyes were filled with worry.

She buried her face against his chest, gulping the air around her. She breathed in his scent, comforted by the familiar smell of sweat and wool. He wrapped his arms around her and held her close until she stopped sobbing. Slowly she lifted her head to look around her. The rest of the family stared in mute fascination. She wiped her face on her father's tunic then pushed herself up.

"I must go to Schemuel and Simon. I must tell them what happened to their children."

9 Hazor

The Following Spring

Sisera slipped into his decorative armor. His personal slave, Iabi, had polished it so that the stream of sunlight from the window gleamed off the silver scales. Iabi handed him his helmet.

"Is my family ready?"

Iabi bowed. "I believe so, my lord."

"Good. Let's get this over with." Sisera stuck the helmet under his arm and strode out of his bedchamber down the stone hallway to the inner foyer of his home. Miu stood with his son, Khenti, by her side. Khenti stood nearly up to Miu's hip already. The four-year-old wore a fine white linen tunic with a gold-braided belt at his waist. A servant girl held his younger brother, E-Saum. Miu's white dress draped to her ankles. She wore an elaborately jeweled collar. The black hair of her wig was woven into hundreds of small braids, colored beads dangled from the end of each one.

Sisera smiled broadly. "Ah, my family. You do me proud."

Miu bowed her head. "Thank you, Husband."

He looked beyond her as Visnia appeared down the hallway. "Mother. I'm glad you felt well enough to join us."

Visnia laughed. "I should say the same to you, my son." Her eyes narrowed. "I was not out until the cock crowed, drinking with the king."

Sisera stiffened. "The king drinks, Mother. I do not."

Visnia stepped around Miu and brushed her son's face with her hand. "I'm glad to hear it." She wore a simple deep maroon, floor-length dress. Her black hair lay coiled around her head, adorned with beads and jewels. "What did you learn last night, while the king drank and you did not?"

Sisera grinned at her, then turned to his wife. "The king will make me general over all the army today. Nine hundred chariots, fifty thousand men at my command."

Miu lowered her dark brown eyes. "That is wonderful news, my lord."

He ignored her reaction, knowing it stemmed from her desire that he be home more, instead of on the battlefield. *But that is the last thing I desire.* He reached out to tweak the chin of his eldest son. "Yes, it is wonderful news. The king has already begun building us a palace in Harosheth. From there, I will lead all the army against our enemies and drive them from our land."

Khenti looked up to his father with awe. "Will we live in a palace?"

Sisera widened his own eyes. "Yes, almost as grand as the king's. And you will get to visit the sea."

The boy giggled with excitement. Visnia stepped to his side, whispering in his ear. "And what of the sacrifice today? Will the oracle declare this to the people?"

Sisera inclined his head in affirmation. "The priests will do what the king desires. Do not fear." He clapped his hands. "Now, let us join the king as he makes his way to the temple. I can hear the trumpets now." Khenti skipped out ahead with Visnia and the servant girl following behind. Sisera grabbed Miu's arm tightly and snarled. "Look happy, Wife. Jabin wants only gaiety and amusement today. Your sour countenance may spoil his mood."

Miu lifted her chin and grimaced. "I am happy, my husband, for your success."

He tightened his grip and pulled her along as he strode outside. "You must do better, my pet."

Her sneer softened into a gentle smile. "How is this, my lord?"

"Better." He let go of her arm and took her hand as they stepped out into the street. They caught up to Visnia and Khenti. "I must go to the palace and lead the king to the temple. After the sacrifice, the queen has invited you both to a banquet. I will see you back home."

"When?" asked Miu.

He raised an eyebrow. "When the king no longer desires my company." He brushed her cheek with his lips. "Be good, Wife. What you do reflects on me." He patted Khenti and E-Saum on the head then made his way through the throng of people to the palace.

Soldiers carried the king's banners ahead of Sisera, clearing the mob from the street so the chariots could easily pass. Sisera marveled at the crowd. *Offer them free food and drink and every peasant from here to Kedesh comes into the city.* Jabin had declared a three-day festival culminating in the sacrifice of ten oxen. One would be given to the priests at the temple, four would be served to the dignitaries at the palace, and the other five would be given to the people. Sisera shook his head, imagining the chaos. *They'll kill each other for a morsel of meat.*

The chariot stopped at the limestone steps of the temple to Baal. Sisera stepped down from the chariot and waited for Jabin. The king wore deep purple robes trimmed with gold. Bright rubies and sapphires glittered from his crown. Jabin took hold of the rope binding the first bull and pulled it up a side ramp. A slave followed, coaxing the animal with a many-tailed whip. The animal's horns had been blunted then capped with gold, a precaution in case it went mad in the crowd. Sisera and several other officials walked behind them.

At the top of the ramp, the King gave the rope to a servant then turned to the crowd. "People of Hazor! Hear me! Today we make this offering to Baal and ask that he bless our land with rain, and our fields with crops. We will ask the priests to read the signs of the gods and tell us of the future."

The crowd let out a cry of affirmation.

"Canaanites! Bow now and worship Baal! Ask for his blessings!"

A dark-skinned priest stepped forward. He had tattoos about the face. He lifted his hands so the blade of his sword shone in the sunlight. Again the people cheered. The priest led the ox into the temple.

Jabin raised his arms to the sky. "Pray! Pray that the gods will reveal their will to us!"

The people knelt down in the streets and called out in prayer. Sisera followed Jabin into the temple. The tattooed man led the ox up another ramp, to a stone altar where two more robed priests waited. Behind them stood the statue of a man with a bull's head, seated on a throne. Sisera and the others knelt before the altar. The animal bellowed as one priest pulled the ox's head back by the horns. The priest with the sword swiped his blade across the beast's throat. Blood sprayed the holy men as they twisted the ox onto the floor. They positioned the wound over a trough, allowing the blood to flow out before the altar.

After the blood drained, the priests sliced the beast open, pulling out the internal organs and putting them on a golden platter. They placed the offering on the altar and cut the entrails open to read the messages from the gods. The three men conferred together. The one who had slain the ox seemed troubled as he poked at the bloody offering. He argued with the other priests.

Finally one lifted the platter over his head. "King Jabin, Baal has spoken."

Jabin glared at the agitated priest before turning to the one holding the offering. "I trust all is well?"

"Of course, my king." The robed priest smiled graciously. "Baal has confirmed your desire."

Jabin stood. "Let us tell the people." He touched Sisera's shoulder to signal he should stand. "Come, General. It is time to announce your promotion." The three men headed out to the temple balcony. The King stood between the priest and Sisera. The priest stepped forward.

"People of Canaan, Baal has spoken!" The crowd roared its approval. "He has called on his servant, Sisera, to lead our army to battle! Baal has foreseen our victory over those who tried to hold us captive. We have broken their chains, now Baal demands we crush them completely! Only then will he release the rains to feed our land."

The crowd's shouts rose to a frenzy. Jabin stepped forward with Sisera, lifting their arms in the air. "I will obey the gods! I declare this day that General Sisera will be the commander over all of the armies of Canaan. Second only to me, he will wield power over the land and destroy our enemies!" The throng shouted their praises to the king and his commander. When the noise diminished, Jabin signaled for the other oxen to be brought up the ramp.

"My people!" He called out to them. "Tonight you will feast as kings. The meat of these animals will be roasted throughout the city so that all may enjoy the bounty of the gods." Jabin turned and re-entered the temple as the crowd's shouts peaked again. The priest who had killed the ox approached the king and bowed.

"My lord, please. I must speak to you."

Jabin stopped. Sisera saw the king's nostrils flare, but his countenance remained otherwise composed. "What is it priest?"

The man bowed low. "Sire, there was another omen in the offering."

The king turned to the robed priest with the platter. "Odji, did you see more?"

Odji looked between the king and the younger priest before inclining his head to one side. "Perhaps, my lord, but it does not conflict with the approval of your plans."

The king frowned and turned to the tattooed priest. "What did you see?"

"Baal has sent a warning, my king."

"A warning?"

The priest nodded. "Yes. There is a new leader being raised from your enemies. Strong in power and in the ability to unite them."

Sisera stepped toward them. "A leader you say?"

The priest glanced toward the general. "A great leader. Filled with the power of their god."

Sisera grinned. "That will only make the battle more interesting." He turned to the king. "Do not worry, my lord. Whoever this leader is, I will destroy him before he can unite the Israelites against us."

10 Shiloh

The Following Day

The weeks following Deborah's visit home were not peaceful. Often she woke with a scream on her lips, the vision of Seff's body still in her mind. Her prayers were chaotic, filled with sadness and fear. With the advent of the winter months, she lost any sense of calm, becoming overwhelmed with the knowledge that something evil pursued her. Whatever had haunted her dreams in childhood crept back into her life now. Oppressive. Dark. Invisible. Always lurking.

Deborah kept inside, forgoing walks to Leb's shop or Adara's house for the safety of home. She spent hours in the courtyard and on the roof of Leb's house praying; begging the Lord to keep her from sin, to keep the evil from finding her. As the seasons progressed, she realized that even with her hours of prayer, the Lord had not spoken to her since her dream. By the time the trees began to bud again with new life in spring, she despaired that she may never hear His voice again.

Leb scooped up the thick barley stew on his plate with a piece of bread. His eyebrows furrowed. "You pick at your food, Deborah. What is wrong?"

She ran a crust of bread through the stew in front of her, but didn't lift it to her mouth. "Nothing. I'm fine."

Rachel glared at her, then Leb. "She's not fine. You see how she doesn't eat. She's been like this for days. Weeks! Only you've all been too busy with Uri's betrothal to notice."

Deborah's cheeks flushed with the heat of embarrassment. She'd tried to hide her anxiety from her family, not wanting to admit her weakness to them. "I'm fine. I'm just not hungry tonight."

Rachel snorted softly. "You weren't hungry this morning either. Or last night. It has been days since I have seen you eat more than a morsel of cheese or scrap of bread."

"She hasn't been herself since Palti's wedding," noted Uri. He spooned another helping of stew onto his plate, then pointed to Deborah with the ladle. "Do you miss your family?"

"No." Deborah shook her head. She lifted the crust and took a bite. It turned to dirt in her mouth. She resisted the urge to spit it out and forced herself to chew. The wad of food stuck in her throat so she nearly gagged. She took a sip of milk to push it down. When it finally sank to her stomach, she glared at the others. "See? I'm eating."

Leb lifted his hand to stop Rachel from speaking. "Yes. I see." His eyes darkened as he watched Deborah pick up another piece of bread and push it around her plate. "I see."

Rachel grunted while she stabbed her stew. Uri glanced around at his family. He took a large mouthful of food then spoke to Leb. "There's been another raid, outside of Jezreel."

Leb frowned. "Where did you hear this?"

"Michal. He had some business at the city gate this morning."

"Was the attack south of the city?"

Uri shook his head. "No. The Canaanites are still concentrated on the northern tribes. They have a new general. Sisera is his name."

A cold finger ran down Deborah's back, making her shiver.

"Niece?" Leb asked. "Are you well."

She couldn't shake the icy hand now tightening around her heart. "I don't know. I heard that name and I'm afraid."

Uri took a sip of from his cup. "What name? Sisera?"

Deborah trembled again as a series of visions assaulted her mind. Hundreds of chariots storming across the plains. Villages burning. Women screaming. Through it all, Deborah could sense something watching, approving of the massacre. She cried out, seeking to free herself of the premonition.

Leb held her shoulders. "What did you see?"

"He will move south. This Sisera. He wants to destroy us all."

Uri's eyes lit up with anticipation. "When?"

"I don't know." A warmth flooded her body, followed by a gentle voice in her head.

I will not fight for Israel, until my people cry out to me. The famine; the raids; all will worsen before I will save my people.

The relief she felt at hearing the Lord's voice did little to calm her anxiety. Deborah shuddered and reached out for Leb. "God has spoken."

Her uncle's grip tightened on her arm. "We will go to the Tabernacle tomorrow. You can speak to the priests."

Deborah's heart skipped a beat. She knew she must tell of this new vision, but fear threatened to engulf her. She stood up. "I must go and pray. See if the Lord wishes to reveal any more before tomorrow." She ran up the steps to the roof of the house. The pale light of the waning moon barely illuminated her way.

Leaning against the ledge, she sought to catch her breath. *Oh Lord, help me! I'm afraid to leave the house. What if what I've seen is wrong? What if something happens on the way to the Tabernacle? What if . . . what if . . .* The thoughts swirled in her head like a whirlpool. She pushed one question down, only to have another swirl up to the top.

A touch on her shoulder made her jump. Her uncle steadied her before she lost her balance and fell over the edge of the roof. "Deborah. It is time to rest. Come inside now."

She fought to keep the panic she felt from exploding forth. "I'll be down shortly."

She could see his eyes search her face in the dim light of the oil lamp he carried. "It is late. You need to sleep."

A small laugh escaped her throat. *Sleep? I haven't slept in days.* "Yes, Uncle."

Deborah allowed Leb to lead her down the stairs to the house below. Someone had set out her bedroll and blanket. Her uncle kissed her on the forehead.

"Goodnight, my child."

"Goodnight, Uncle." Deborah sat on her pallet and watched Leb retire to the other room where he slept with Rachel and Uri. She had the small storage room to herself. Instead of lying down, she pushed her back up against the wall and hugged her knees to her chest. She prayed for hours until she noticed the gray light of dawn in the courtyard, then she lay down. She kept her eyes open a crack, watching the house come to life.

Rachel rose first, wrapping her braided hair up in linen then pulling a brown tunic over her shift. After she got the fire started, she headed out to the well to get the water. A wave of guilt passed over Deborah. She knew her aunt could use help at the well, but now that Deborah rested, she felt unable to make her body move. Leb and Uri got up when Rachel returned with the water.

"I hate to wake her," murmured Leb. "She went to bed so late."

"It is time," said Rachel. "You must go to the Tabernacle with her, and there is still work to be done at the shop."

"Yes, yes." Leb shuffled over to the entrance to her room. Deborah shut her eyes completely. "It is morning, Niece."

Deborah stretched her arms over her head.

He smiled down at her. "Come get some bread before we leave."

Deborah reluctantly made herself rise. She rinsed her face with water from the cistern and washed her hands. She took the cup of milk Uri offered, but refused any food. "I'll eat when I return from the Tabernacle." Rachel clucked her disapproval, but otherwise kept silent. Deborah prepared herself to deliver God's word to the priests by putting on her finest robe and veil. But when the time came to leave the house, she couldn't summon up the courage to step outside. Leb walked a few paces ahead of her. Deborah held onto the door frame.

"What is wrong? Another vision?"

She shook her head. Her knuckles white on the threshold. "I can't," she gasped.

Leb placed his hand on hers. "You must."

Deborah looked up at him through her veil. "You go."

"But you are the Lord's prophet."

Her body trembled as if a cold wind blew around her. "You tell the priests what I told you last night."

Leb pulled back her veil and held her face. "Stop this! I do not know what you fear, but you must conquer it."

"I am trying, Uncle."

He stared at her. His normally kind face, severe. "No. You have given yourself over to it. You have allowed it to cripple you. It stops now." He took her hands. "I will be with you. God is with you. You have nothing to fear."

Her eyes filled with tears. "Please, Uncle—"

"No more." He replaced her veil and took her arm. "We leave now." He forced her out of the doorway and into the street. Deborah's leaden feet shuffled beside his. A few neighbors gathered in the alley.

"It is good to see you, Deborah! We haven't seen much of you lately."

"Is there news, Leb?"

Leb pulled her along, compelling her to move faster. "She's had another vision. We go to see the priests."

A small crowd followed behind them as Deborah and her uncle made their way through the city. His hand held her arm in a vice, willing her to stay by his side. Her fingers dug into her palms, her hands curled into tight fists at her side.

"Don't fear," he whispered. "I am here. Nothing will harm you."

The walk to the Tabernacle seemed to take hours, although it stood only a mile or so from the city gate. When they arrived, Leb spoke to one of the priests in the courtyard. He led them outside the linen walls to a large tent.

"Wait here," a turbaned man ordered. A few moments later, an old man came out. His gray hair and beard flowed like thick flax from his head. When he smiled at Deborah, his hazel eyes twinkled.

"My child, we have not seen you for some time." He reached out to grasp her hands. "I trust you have been well?"

The warmth of the priest's hands spread throughout Deborah's body. The tension she'd been holding released. Leb struggled to keep her upright but she crumbled to her knees. The crowd that had followed them from Shiloh gasped as the old priest knelt in front of her. He took hold of her shoulders.

"Child! What is wrong? What has God shown you?"

Deborah bowed her head. "Oh, Phinehas. God has turned His face away from us. The crops will fail this year. The Canaanites will come further south. I have seen death, from hunger and from the soldiers."

The priest moaned. "Is there nothing we can do?"

Deborah shook her head. "God will fight for us only when the people call out for Him."

"Then we will pray and fast again." The old man sat back. "We will send the message out."

Deborah clutched her hands together as she rocked on her heels. "No, Phinehas. God has shown me their hearts. They will not turn until there is nowhere else for them to go. But so many will die before then!"

The priest watched her. He took her hands again in his. "But He will save his people? Eventually?"

Deborah took comfort in the old man's touch. "Yes. He will not leave us to perish completely."

The high priest stood to address the group. "Go! Prepare yourself for a time of fasting and prayer. In three days I will sacrifice an ox for our sins and seek to turn the Lord's face back to us."

The crowd left murmuring among themselves. Deborah knew her vision would be spread throughout the city by the afternoon. Phinehas turned back to her. "You will come for the ceremony, Prophet? You will pray for us while I make the sacrifice?"

The heavy weight of her anxiety pressed down on her chest. She was glad she wore the veil so he wouldn't see the fear in her eyes. "Yes. I will come."

The old man smiled. "Good. Pray for us, Prophet. Perhaps God will change His will for us yet."

Deborah nodded, but knew it would do no good. YHWH's will had been clear. The Israelites would be punished harshly for their refusal to follow His commands.

"You said you would eat when you returned," complained Rachel.

Deborah thrust the bread back into her aunt's hand. "But the priest has called for us to fast."

Rachel waved the bread at her niece. "And what will the priest say when you collapse from hunger?"

"Three more days. Then I will eat." Deborah's mood had lightened with the prospect of having a reason not to eat. It would save her the trouble of forcing food down. The fact that she would not have to go any further than the well for the next three days also relieved her anxiety. "I'll be on the roof, making wicks. Call me if you need help with supper."

"What's the use?" Rachel threw the offered bread back into a basket as she turned away from her niece.

Deborah spent the rest of the afternoon taking the threads of flax she'd spun and twining them together into wicks. She prayed as she worked. In the daylight, her prayers tended to be more meditative. But as dusk approached, apprehension crept back into her mind.

A cry of despair sliced through her thoughts like a sword. At first, Deborah thought it had been her own voice, but when it came again, she recognized it as Rachel's. Deborah flew down the steps and found her aunt on her knees, clutching Leb's tunic. Behind them stood Michal, Adara and Uri. Adara wore a black shawl over her head and shoulders. Michal's tunic was torn at the neck. Their son, Josiah, buried his head into his mother's chest.

"No, no, no." Rachel rocked back and forth. "They can't leave. They cannot go to Shamir!"

Michal stepped forward. "We must, Mother Rachel. If I don't go, my family will lose their land."

Rachel stood, her eyes rabid with panic, her face covered in tears. "Yes and why is that? Because your brother was killed by the Canaanites? What makes you think they will not do the same to you?"

Michal's face was set. "Jesse fought against them. He joined the soldiers. I will be a farmer, Rachel. I will not fight."

Rachel reached for her son-in-law, but Leb held her back. "And what do you know of farming, Michal? You? A candle-maker?"

Leb shook Rachel by the shoulders. "Enough!" He shook her again. "Enough. It is his duty as the eldest remaining son. He must go back to his father's house or else the land will be for-feit. His mother will be destitute."

Rachel's chest heaved as she tried to breath. "What about Lapidoth? Why can he not have the inheritance?"

Michal lifted his chin. "My younger brother has also joined the army."

Rachel groaned. "You take my daughter to Shamir. To the plains. Only miles from Jezreel, where the Canaanites pillage and burn." Her voice rose. "How long do you think it will be before they attack Shamir? What will happen to Adara when you are dead and your land taken by the Canaanites?"

"Mother." Adara pleaded. "God will protect us."

Rachel's face reddened. "No, He won't." She spied Deborah at the base of the steps and pointed. "Did you not hear? The prophet said God has abandoned us!" Rachel shrieked. "There is only death on the plains!"

Josiah cried at his grandmother's ranting. Leb put one arm around his wife and waved the others away. "Go now. I will calm her down. We will talk tomorrow about your plans."

Adara looked wounded. "Please, Father—"

Leb waved again. "Go."

Michal took Josiah in his arms and put his hand on Adara's shoulder. "I am sorry. But I must go home."

Rachel wailed and sank to the floor. Leb knelt by her side as Adara and Michal left the house. Uri walked over to Deborah. He sighed deeply before speaking. "Michal received word of his father's death this morning. I think you heard the rest."

Deborah nodded. "When will they leave?"

Uri shrugged. "As soon as they can. There isn't much here for them to pack. Father will buy them a donkey to carry their belongings to Shamir." His eyes surveyed hers. "How long will it be? Before the Canaanites move south?"

Deborah stared at her aunt, grieving on the floor, then looked up at her cousin and whispered, "Not long."

Dust and smoke swirled about the brazen altar. A gray cloud climbed from the fire up toward heaven. Deborah knelt inside the curtained courtyard of the Tabernacle. Rachel knelt beside her, along with the women who served the priests. Outside the linen walls, the people of Shiloh gathered for the solemn sacrifice. The elders of Shiloh led an ox through the crowd, then between the columns of the gateway. Its pitiful bellow caused Deborah's stomach to turn.

The high priest stood beside the altar, his ceremonial robes adding authority to a face already etched with wisdom. On top of his pristine blue robe he wore a golden ephod. Over this was a breastplate fixed with twelve precious gemstones to represent the twelve tribes of Israel. Sapphires, rubies, amethyst and emeralds reflected the sunlight, seeming to radiate light from Phinehas's heart. Along the bottom of his robe jingled golden bells fixed between embroidered pomegranates.

As the men drew the ox nearer, Phinehas called out in a loud voice, "Our God has spoken." The old man raised his hands up. "The Lord rebukes his people for their sin. We have not trusted in the God of our Fathers to bring rain. We have not kept ourselves from idols. We have chased after foreign gods and the Lord has turned his face from us."

The elders brought the animal next to the north side of the altar. The crowd outside of the courtyard fell to their knees and cried out to the Lord.

The High Priest continued, "YHWH! We call on you now. We beg your acceptance of this animal's blood as atonement for our guilt. We admit our sin to you. Forgive us and return your favor to us."

Deborah bent forward, placing her hands on the ground and resting her head on them. She couldn't bear to watch the innocent animal's slaughter.

Look, Deborah. Look at the suffering. The beast dies for your sins as well as Israel's.

Deborah sat up. The animal let out a mournful sound. *My sin, Lord? What have I done? I've put myself in isolation, all to keep myself from transgression.* The ox bellowed again as two men pulled its head back.

No. You have allowed evil to overwhelm you. You have lived in fear, rather than in my peace. You believed the evil to be greater than I am.

The Lord's rebuke stung her as sharply as the dagger held across the beast's throat. *I am sorry, Lord. I am sorry I have failed you. Forgive me.*

The dagger cut off the ox's frightened cry. The priests serving Phinehas stepped forward to collect its blood. Deborah's vision swam and she leaned forward, clutching her stomach. *Do not let this beast's suffering be in vain, Lord. Please say you forgive me.*

Admit your sin, Deborah.

She prostrated herself on the ground. *It is true. I was afraid. Afraid of the evil that killed Seff and Mava. It sought me, and killed them instead. It's my fault they died.*

The thoughts of the Lord swirled through her mind, like the smoke of the altar caught on the wind. **There is evil all over our land. It seeks to destroy any hope. That is why it attacks you. You give the people hope. But I am stronger than any power in heaven or on earth.**

Her heart beat faster as God's spirit spoke to her, pressing her to confess all the fears that had sought to keep her from serving Him. *Do my visions cause things to happen? I saw Palti's wedding, and it came to pass. Did I make it happen? Because I dreamed Avram would grieve, will someone die?*

The Lord's voice grew in power within her, seeming to echo inside her mind. **Are you God? Do you speak and make the sun shine? Do you tell the rain where to fall and where to stay dry? Does the wind blow at your command or the lightning strike where you will?**

No! Of course not!

Then do not think you control what I have allowed you to see. You are my servant. My voice to the people. But you have no power over your visions.

Deborah shuddered in relief. It's not my fault. Her stomach tightened in another knot. *What if I fail? What if your people never listen to my warnings?*

That is not your failure. It is theirs. Their hearts are hard.

What if I do something to bring shame to my family or to your name?

Seek me with all your heart, all your soul, and all your strength. If you do this, you will be free from shame and you will have my forgiveness when you ask for it.

A great weight lifted from Deborah's back as she let go of the fear that had oppressed her for the past months. Her heart sang out to God in praise, even as those around her cried out to Him for forgiveness. *Great is the Lord, and full of mercy. From everlasting to everlasting, His power is never ending. He watches over His servant, even the lowliest of bondservants, and He pours out His grace and His love. Great is the Lord and worthy of all praise!*

She raised her head and watched as the priests sprinkled the ox's blood on the sides of the altar. Phinehas's voice rose and he instructed the people to follow the Lord's commands. "Listen to the words of the Lord. 'Do not worship any other gods besides me. Do not make idols of any kind."

Deborah interceded on the people's behalf as Phinehas recited the Lord's commandments. *Soften their hearts, Lord. Bring them back to you. Remove the temptations of the Canaanites and their gods.*

Phinehas spoke of the Lord's great power. He reminded the people of how the Lord led them out of bondage in Egypt to this land. He told them about Joshua and the battle of Jericho, and all the while Deborah prayed. When at last the animal's body had been skinned and its entrails cleaned, the priests prepared to burn the remains on the brazen altar. Deborah had lowered her head as she continued to pray, but raised it when she heard the jingling bells of the high priest's robe draw nearer. She could clearly see the words inscribed on the gold medallion he wore on his forehead. Phinehas had told her they read, *Set Apart as Holy to the Lord.*

The old man's eyes searched her face. "Have you heard the Lord's voice, Prophet?"

Deborah nodded. "But He has revealed nothing about the coming trials."

The high priest frowned. "I go now to seek the Lord within the Tabernacle. Pray that I might hear his wisdom, Prophet. That I might discern His will for our people."

"I will."

"Pray that He will turn his anger from us and grant us His favor."

Deborah read the worry behind the priest's eyes. "If all of Israel had a heart such as yours, Phinehas, I know the Lord would grant that prayer."

Phinehas drew himself up then strode toward the Tabernacle as the priests placed the offering onto the brazen altar. The meat sizzled on the fire and the wind carried the sweet aroma of roasting meat up toward heaven. Deborah again prostrated herself.

Hear the prayers of this good man, Lord. His heart is truly yours and he longs to lead your people. Speak to him. Give him courage to face whatever trials you may send.

God's voice burst through her thoughts, intense and commanding. **I will not turn my anger from my people. The rains will not come this year. The land will not bear fruit. Like a sickle to the grain, I will cut down my people until their hearts cry out in earnest to me.**

Part Two

Refiner's Fire

1 Harosheth

The Following Spring

"We were pleased to receive your message, my lord," Sisera called as ten chariots clattered through the gates. Jabin's came to a stop directly in front of the general. He reached out to rub a horse's nose. "To what do we owe this honor?"

Sisera noted the shadows under the king's eyes as his friend dismounted from the chariot. A servant ran up and removed a dust-covered cape from Jabin's shoulders, while another immediately replaced it with a fine, golden-threaded robe.

Sisera bowed and presented the rest of his family and servants for the king's perusal. He could sense Jabin's frustrations with the formalities of the visit. His mother, Visnia, must have felt the tension as well. She gestured toward the house.

"Please, come into the banquet hall. Dinner will be ready shortly."

Jabin stood back. "I'm afraid I have some business to discuss with the General before I can relax."

Sisera nodded to his servant. "Prepare the King's room and bring fresh water so he can wash." He turned to Jabin. "Send Iabi when you are ready for me, my lord. I await your command."

Visnia stepped forward to address the others in the king's entourage. "Friends, let me escort you to the banquet hall where you can wait for the king. Our servants will bring you wine to refresh you after your journey."

Jabin paced the room as Sisera entered. "What's wrong, my King?"

"What's wrong? Have you not been outside these palace walls? Have you not seen the fields?"

Sisera shook his head. "I know the rains were sparse this year—"

Jabin threw up his hands. "Sparse? They were non-existent! It has been over four years since we've had a decent season of rain. We are facing famine." He strode toward Sisera. "We make war against the Israelites, but we will be putting down our own rebellion if the people do not get food soon."

Sisera frowned. "Is there no one to barter with?"

"The kings are coming here, all of them, in two weeks, to discuss the situation. But my spies tell me the famine is throughout the cities of Canaan."

Sisera clapped his hands. Iabi stepped forward. "Pour us some wine." He turned to Jabin. "Sit. Rest."

Jabin took a goblet from the servant then walked out to the courtyard. He sat on a stone bench, placing the cup by his side. He put his head in his hands. The general came up beside him. "What else troubles you?"

Jabin looked up from between his finger. "You know me well, my friend."

Sisera shrugged. "It has been many years." He took a sip of wine. "There is more on your mind than the famine."

The king drained his cup. "There has been an oracle, another message from the gods, about a leader from our enemies."

Sisera saw the deep lines of worry on the king's forehead. "What did the gods say?"

Jabin thrust out his chin. "Shaul, king of Megiddo, sent me the news." He looked out over the gardens. "I am sure he keeps the details to himself so he can be the one to tell the others." He shook his head. "Such a game we all play."

The general put a hand on the king's shoulder. "Come with me to the banquet hall. I have plenty of wine, and several beautiful dancers, to help you forget your troubles for tonight."

"It will take more than wine and women to make this go away."

Sisera put his foot on the stone bench and leaned in toward Jabin. "You underestimate me, my lord. I have not spent the winter months in idleness." He pointed to the courtyard with a sweeping gesture. "You have given me much, and I am always at work, thinking of ways to give you more in return." He turned back to Jabin. "Whatever the news is from the other kings, I can readjust my plans accordingly."

"Do you fear nothing, Sisera?"

He chuckled softly. "Nothing, my lord."

"My friend, I knew when I came here you would put my mind at ease." He stood and grasped the general's shoulders. "I've missed having you in Hazor."

"Be at peace. Once I have heard from the other nobles, I will devise a plan to end your worries." He placed a comforting hand on Jabin's back. "You also, have nothing to fear."

2 Shiloh

A Week Later

As Passover approached, Deborah frequently sat on the roof of Leb's house, scanning the city streets for signs of Azareel. Uri's wedding was to take place four days before the festival, in hopes that relatives would make the journey for both the wedding, and to celebrate the feast of Passover at the Tabernacle, as required by the law. Each morning, Deborah prayed her father would be well enough to make the journey. She spent as much time on the roof as she could, working with the flax, hoping to catch a glimpse of him walking toward the house. Two days ago, Adara and Michal arrived with Josiah and their new baby, Hannah. Rachel's quick laugh and sparkle returned as soon as she held her granddaughter. Leb's brothers, sisters and cousins followed soon after. But no Azareel.

The next day she sat on the roof with Adara and several other young relatives. Deborah had no idea of all their names. So many kept coming and going throughout the day, helping

Rachel to prepare for the wedding. Bread and cakes baked non-stop in the oven downstairs and in the homes of other family members. Nuts were spiced and roasted. The various ways to flavor the meat to be served was a subject of argument. The younger women took refuge on the roof when the evening sun stood low and pink on the horizon.

"I pity poor Katriel," Adara said. "Having to marry my brother."

"Why?" asked a chubby girl of about twelve. "He's handsome. He'll own Leb's shop someday. He's a fine catch."

"But he snores like a lion! And his breath always smells of onions!"

The women laughed. An older girl with dark braids spoke next. "And what of Michal? What are his faults?"

Adara smiled angelically. "My husband? Why, he has no faults."

A murmur of disbelief ran among the girls. "Come now, Cousin. Surely he isn't perfect."

"I have heard her mention." Deborah giggled. "On several occasions, that he becomes quite . . . fragrant? After eating her lentil soup."

The girls laughed loudly, Adara hardest of all. "It's true! I won't even sleep with him after we have lentils!"

They continued talking in this lighthearted manner until someone called out, "New guests are arriving. Does anyone recognize them?"

They crowded around the ledge to see the street below. Deborah's heart soared. "Father! Avram!" She waved down to them. "Azareel!" The two men looked round until they spotted her on the roof. Her father lifted his arm in greeting. A heaviness settled into Deborah's spirit. She maneuvered her way out of the group and hurried down the stairs to welcome her family. "Leb! Rachel! Avram and Azareel are here!" She pushed her way through the relatives to the entrance of the house. "Father!" She ran into his arms. "I am so glad to see you!"

He hugged her, patting her head gently. "You are taller, Daughter."

She smiled up at him. His eyes seemed sad. New wrinkles furrowed his skin. Her smile faded. "What has happened?"

Azareel looked to his son. Avram opened his arms to receive his sister's embrace. He held her tightly, as if afraid she would disappear. Deborah's spirit grew heavier. She pushed him away.

"What's wrong?"

Avram lowered his head. "Eglah is dead."

Deborah reached her hand out. Azareel took her arm to steady her. "What? How?"

Her brother swallowed before speaking. "The baby came early. With much blood." He shook his head. "There was nothing I could do." He looked down at his sister, his eyes filled with tears. "There was so much blood." He bit his lip and turned away. He straightened his shoulders. "But I do not come to grieve. I have another son. And Uri is to be married. There is much to be thankful for."

Deborah wiped the sweat from her forehead with the back of her arm. She paused from carding flax, and stretched her back. The mid-morning sun beat down on the roof where she sat, but she did not consider going down into the shade of the house. Too many people. Too much celebration. She sighed, pulling the flax back and forth between the boards. Loose bits of straw fell to the ground as she worked the linen fibers into a mass on the boards of nails. She picked out the linen fluff and placed it into a basket at her feet to be spun later. She gathered up more tow, the fibers left when the flax was made into thread. The tow often contained bits of straw and so was considered too course to make linen for fine clothes. Deborah carded and spun it into a thicker thread that she then wove into the wicks for the oil lamps Leb made. The process was long and tedious, but Deborah enjoyed the mindless repetition. It quieted her spirit and gave her time to pray.

Lord, hear my prayer. Speak to me, Lord. I feel alone, even among all these people. Be with my brother, Avram. Ease his grief. Bless Edin and the new baby, keep them safe. Help them to grow strong.

"You are deep in thought, Sister."

Deborah looked up to see Avram at the top of the stairs. She shaded her face with her hand. "What brings you up to the roof in the middle of the day?"

Avram shrugged. "I thought to ask you the same thing."

"The flax needs to be carded. I'll lose several days with the wedding and festivals. If I wait too long, it will rot."

Avram walked over to the edge of the roof, looking out at the city. "Shiloh is a busy place."

Deborah nodded, but said nothing. She pulled more fluff from her card and set it aside.

Avram sat across from her. "Do you ever miss our village?"

She grabbed another handful of tow to card. "Every day."

"Why?" Her brother stared at her. "When there is so much here?"

Deborah thrust the carding boards together then brushed the right one through the left. "I miss you. And father. Nathan and Edin. I miss the hills."

Avram watched her work. He picked up a loose piece of straw, twirling it in his fingers. "What is it like? How does God speak to you?"

She rested her hands on her knees. "I hear Him in different ways. Sometimes, I hear His voice and it is like a mighty wind surging through my body. Most times, I feel a peace as I meditate on his law or I pray. And I know He is with me." Deborah lowered her gaze, focusing on the cards of flax. "The worst are the visions and the dreams. Even the good ones. They're so powerful. I get lost in them and it frightens me." She sensed Avram's indecision. She remained quiet. He would speak when he was ready.

"Did you know Eglah would die?"

Deborah placed her hand on her brother's knee. "No. I knew only that you would grieve."

His eyes searched hers. "Would you have told me, if you had seen it was her?"

His pain was palpable. She longed to give him some peace. "Would you have wanted to know?"

"To lose her as we lost our mother—"Avram let out a sound— half sob, half sigh. "I miss her."

Deborah put the carding boards aside then wrapped her arms around her brother. It felt strange. He had always been her protector. Now, she comforted him. Avram wept as Deborah held him and rubbed his back. He sighed deeply, his breath ragged, then pulled away from her.

"Ah, my sister. I have missed you as well. You were always a blessing to me."

Deborah chuckled. "Your memories deceive you, Brother. I was a bother to everyone. Especially Palti and Bithia."

"To them, maybe. To me, a blessing." He ran his hand over his face, removing the evidence of his grief. "Now, tell me. Why do you hide up here?"

She reached for the flax at her side. Avram stopped her. "What is it, Little Sister? You can't confide in me anymore?"

Deborah's own emotions lay just under the surface, bubbling like a pot of soup left to simmer. She stared at her fingers.

Avram placed a hand on her shoulder. "You eased my pain. Let me help you with your burden."

She took a deep breath. "It is foolish."

"What is?"

Her gaze flickered up to his face before settling back on her hands. "The girl Uri is to marry. She's fourteen."

Avram paused. "And?"

Deborah swallowed past the lump in her throat. "I will be seventeen when the rains come this year." She looked up at her brother. "And there is no betrothal. No one has even come to Leb to question him about me."

Avram glanced away.

Deborah's fists pounded the packed grass of the roof. "See. Even you don't believe I am to marry."

"I didn't say that!"

"You don't have to. Your face tells me everything. What man would want me? To have to compete with God?"

Avram held her face in his hands. "Surely, God will provide for you. You have no need for clothing or food."

Deborah pulled away. "But there are other needs, Avram." She crossed her arms in front of her chest, holding herself tightly, trying to keep her frustration from raging out. "I know I am blessed. I delight in the role God has given me. And yet, lately . . . I long for a companion. Someone to share some of my responsibilities. Someone to care for me."

"Perhaps . . . ." Avram put his hand on her knee. "It is time for you to come back to our village? Father and I would care for you."

Deborah shut her eyes. "You have your own families to worry about." She smiled weakly.

"But you should be home," Avram insisted. "With us. If none of this had happened, you would still be living in our village."

"In my own home. With my own family. I would be someone else's burden. Not yours." Deborah covered his hand with her own. "No, Brother. I am only being selfish. Thinking of what I lack, instead of all God has blessed me with." She lifted his hand to her face and rested her cheek against it. "God will reveal His plan to me as He sees fit. And right now, I know I can best serve Him here." She kissed his hand before setting it down again. "Now go down with the others. I must get this flax carded, and you must leave soon with Uri to fetch his bride. It will be a long walk to Arumah."

Avram leaned forward and kissed her lightly on the cheek. "I will pray for you, sister. That God will give you the desires of your heart."

He made his way down the narrow stairs to the house below. Deborah shut her eyes. A lone tear dropped from her eyelash. She let her breath out slowly, then picked up the carding boards once again.

The frantic activity of the previous days increased that night with the arrival of the wedding procession. Uri and his bride set their canopy outside in the street. Relatives from all over the lower hill country had followed the procession to Leb's house to celebrate. Deborah, Adara, Rachel and the other women set out the food and wine for the company to feast on, after the the formalities of the ceremony had been performed.

At first, Deborah felt overwhelmed by the noise of the guests. It seemed like a hundred people or more milled about the house. They sat on the floor, out in the courtyard, up on the roof, overflowing into the street. Many were relatives of Leb's she had never met. She tried to melt herself into the corners of rooms to stay out of their way. As the days wore on, she grew more at ease. She realized, to her surprise, that many of them feared her as well. "That's the prophet!" She overheard more than once, as people stole secretive glances in her direction.

In the evening, Deborah enjoyed dancing with the other women, or sitting around the fire, as the old men told stories of Moses and Joshua. But her favorite pastime was to sit by Adara and her cousins, listening to the gossip about the people gathered around them.

"Who is my brother speaking to?" she asked her cousin on the third night.

Adara scanned the crowd until she spied Avram. Her eyebrows lifted and she grinned. "That is Daliyah. I wondered when she'd find him."

"Why? Who is she?"

Adara leaned in closer. "She's been a widow for about six months. She is my cousin on my father's side. Married less than two years before her husband dropped dead. But he was much older than her."

"How sad."

Adara shrugged. "I think it was the Lord's blessing. He was terrible to her. He would beat her over the smallest thing."

"How awful!"

"Not every husband is as good as Michal or my father." Adara's eyes held Deborah's in a frank stare. "My uncle married Daliyah off so he could use her bridal price to pay off debts and buy a piece of land." She shook her head. "She was treated worse than a slave, if you ask me." They watched as Daliyah offered to fill Avram's cup with more wine.

"It would be a good match for them both." said Adara. "She had no children and she has a good heart. At least her husband didn't beat that out of her. Avram needs someone to care for his sons and is a patient man." Adara smiled again. "Yes. Perhaps I will talk to Michal. He might be able to speak a few kind words about my cousin to your brother."

Deborah put her hand on Adara's arm. "Remember. Avram deeply loved Eglah. He may not be ready to marry again so soon."

Adara snorted softly through the hard line of her lips. "A man does not always marry for love, Cousin. There is desire, and then there is need. Avram needs someone to take care of his children, and to take care of him in bed. At his age, love plays little part in marriage. It is lust and necessity."

Heat rushed to Deborah's face and she quickly turned her head so her cousin wouldn't see her blush.

Adara giggled at her embarrassment. "You will see, Deborah. Someday it will be your turn under the canopy."

For a moment, Deborah's heart stopped beating at the weight of her sadness. *No, Cousin. I have seen no husband in my future.* She swallowed the lump in her throat. "Perhaps. Someday." She stood and wandered back into the house to see if Rachel needed help with anything.

3 Harosheth

The Following Evening

Sisera had informed his mother of the coming summit of
noblemen. He knew Visnia would have everything prepared to accommodate the kings. Miu could not be trusted to meet his high standards. He kept Jabin diverted with
hunting parties during the day, and fine drink and women at
night. By the end of the two weeks, as Jabin had said, ten kings
and several tribal chieftains sat around the large banquet hall.
The low tables overflowed with stuffed quails and platters of
fish. The aroma of turmeric and garlic hung in the air. As the
men finished their meal, their voices rose with discontent at the
predicament they found themselves in.

Torches hung along the stone walls, illuminating the group
of frustrated leaders. A heavy set man with long, dark hair
stood in the center of the room. His robe of cream wool showed
him to be one of the chiefs, not a nobleman. His body quaked as

he spoke. "There is nothing in Sarid! The little that managed to sprout in the spring has been destroyed by hail."

Another man stood up. "It's the same in Dor. Our people are starving." He turned to Jabin. "The kings must do something." Others around the table murmured their agreement.

Sisera clapped his hands. Servants set about refilling wine goblets as the noblemen settled back around the table.

Jabin rose to his feet. "My honored guests, I have heard your plight. Is there anyone who knows where there is grain to be found?"

The raven haired king beside Jabin spoke. "I have sent emissaries to Pharaoh in Egypt."

Jabin sat down. "And what was his answer, Aza?"

The lines on Aza's face seemed to deepen as he spoke. "There is grain in Egypt, but the price will be high. Pharaoh will bleed our coffers dry before he agrees to send us help."

A low grumbling ran through the room. Khali, the prince from Megiddo, stood. "Our spies tell us that the Israelite lands in the south have food. Three years ago they had an abundant harvest. This year, the drought affected them as well, but still they will reap grain. Not much, but at least what grew was not destroyed by hail."

Sisera's eyes narrowed as he smiled. "That is good news."

Khali's father, Shaul, put a hand on his son's wrist. The prince leaned down to hear what the king whispered. He straightened up. "My father wonders, do you think you are strong enough to move south, General? Your attacks have been concentrated in the northern cities until now."

Sisera ran a finger around the rim of his goblet. "My men are ready. I am ready."

A fierce cry rose from the men. The chieftain who had spoken first jumped to his feet. "My men desire to serve with you,

Sisera. They are weary of waiting, and long to destroy those that have taken our land!"

"Yes, General," called another chief. "I have men who are willing to join the fight. Let us restore our honor and wipe out the Israelite infection on our land."

"We will line the roads to Hazor and Megiddo with their heads!"

"Rip the babies from their mother's womb and feed them to Moloch!"

Soon all the leaders were caught up in the frenzy to spill Israelite blood. The king from Megiddo clapped his hands then put a hand on his son's wrist, pulling him down to sit. The king rose. Tall and clean shaven, Shaul gave off an air of superiority over the noblemen around him. "General. I have brought my servant, Zuberi, to speak with you. He is a high priest at the temple of Baal. Trained in Egypt, he has much knowledge of spiritual omens." He touched the shoulder of the man to his left. "Tell the general what the oracle has said, Zuberi."

The priest got to his feet. Taller than Shaul, his cream and gold linen robe contrasted sharply with his brown skin and bald head. The tattoos that decorated his face gave him a menacing look, even though he smiled at the others in the room. "My lords, there have been several signs over the past year. All pointing to the same thing. And just last month, one of the priestesses received another revelation."

Sisera watched the priest intently. "What did she say?"

"There is a leader rising from the Israelites."

"I know that already, Priest." Sisera scowled. "Did the oracle say anything more specific?"

Zuberi's gaze burned as he spoke to Sisera. "He will come from the south. The power of their god will be in him. If this man is not stopped, their god will use him to unite the Israelites and they will defeat us."

The general rose, his hands open at his sides. "My lords, there you have it. Confirmation from our gods that we need to turn our armies south. We will come down on the Israelites like locusts, harvesting what crops they have, and bringing them back to our own people." His lips rose in a sly half-grin. "While we are there, I am certain our gods will set the Hebrew chieftain in our path. We will destroy him, before he can unite our enemies."

Jabin stood. "I have faith that Sisera can deliver all he has promised. The captured grain will be stored at Megiddo and Hazor. The people can come to the cities and receive rations that will see them through this season. Who here agrees?"

The consensus around the table was in Sisera's favor. A few grumbled about the danger in relying on raids to feed the people, but since they offered no other solution, the plan was accepted.

Shaul stood again. "I have one demand."

The room quieted as all eyes focused on the king from Megiddo. "I want Zuberi to accompany you on your raids south."

Sisera frowned. "It will be a military campaign. Not a place for a priest."

"Nevertheless. Zuberi will go with you, to consult the signs. He will be the one to seek out the leader we fear."

The others nodded. Jabin faced Shaul. "Although I have complete trust that Sisera would uncover the man on his own, I accept this compromise. Is there any here who does not?"

The gaze of all the nobles shifted about the room. None raised any objections to the plan laid before them.

Sisera rose to stand by his friend. "I too, accept the will of my lord. I will call the army together and we will set out within six weeks. This will ensure the crops will be ready to harvest." He lifted his cup to the nobles. "To our victory!"

The men raised their goblets. "Victory!"

4 Shiloh

Two Days Later

It seemed that new people arrived to the festivities every evening as others left to visit nearby family and prepare for the Passover and the Feast of Unleavened bread. Deborah worked at finishing a barley soup at dusk on the fourth night when another large group entered the house. The family and remaining guests rested in the back rooms or milled about the courtyard waiting for the celebrations to resume after sundown. Deborah tucked a curl back under her head wrap then turned to see who entered.

A boisterous crowd of eight men stood in the doorway. Deborah shuddered. The men weren't dressed like wedding guests. Their hair and beards were long and untamed. Their sunburned skin and tattered clothing told of days spent away from any town. Deborah took a step back, wishing she were carving meat with a sharp knife, instead of stirring soup with a wooden spoon. "Can I help you?"

One of the tallest men, obviously their leader, stepped away from the group. His hazel eyes were light, and reddish curls framed his face. "I am looking for the house of Leb, the lamp maker. Is this it?"

Deborah nodded.

He turned to his companions with his arms raised in a kind of salute. "I told you I could find it!" A murmur of relief and laughter ran through the group. The red-haired man spoke again. "I am Lapidoth, brother to Leb's son-in-law." He scrutinized her. "You are not Adara."

"No." Deborah shook her head. "I'm her cousin."

"Lapidoth?" Michal entered from the courtyard.

"Brother!" Lapidoth strode forward then pulled Michal into a strong embrace.

Michal pushed him away. "What are you doing here?"

His brother shrugged. "We thought to spend the Passover with you in Shamir. When we arrived, your neighbors told us where you'd gone." He held his arms out. "And here we are."

Leb and Uri came into the room. Leb looked at the ragged men. "Is there a problem, Michal?"

Lapidoth raised his eyebrows. "Is there, Brother?"

Michal's face grew hard. "This is a wedding celebration. You and your . . . men . . . are not dressed properly for the occasion."

His brother's head tilted to one side. "If you could show us to some water, we would be glad to make ourselves presentable." He gestured to his men. "We haven't had much access to civilization lately."

Deborah's skin prickled with goose bumps in the silence of the room. Leb and Michal stood side-by-side, their shoulders tense. Behind them, Uri eyed the newcomers with barely concealed enthusiasm. He'd grown up on stories of Joshua and

Caleb fighting the enemies of Israel. Deborah knew he longed to prove himself on the battlefield.

Finally Uri stepped forward with a broad smile. "Of course! Welcome!" He turned to Deborah. "Wake up my wife and mother and then fetch some water from the well for our guests." He placed a hand on Lapidoth's shoulder. "Please, come outside into the courtyard and take your rest. We will be eating short-ly."

Lapidoth smiled but gave his brother a cold stare. "Thank you. My men and I have traveled a long way and are grateful to your hospitality."

Deborah hurried to the roof to wake Katriel and Rachel. Adara sat in a shaded corner, nursing her baby. "Who has come? I heard voices."

"It's your brother-in-law and some of his friends."

Adara's face whitened. "Lapidoth?"

Deborah nodded. "Michal seems angry. Why?"

"Lapidoth hasn't been home since his father's death. He runs with that gang of mercenaries and soldiers, conducting raids on the Canaanites."

Rachel sat up. "Are we in danger? Will they follow him here?"

"No. If they seek them anywhere, it's in the northern hills. That's where they normally hide." She looked at the women around her. "But they are rough men. I would be careful around them."

Katriel whimpered softly. Deborah patted her arm. "Don't worry. Stay by Uri's side and you'll be safe."

Rachel lifted her eyebrows. "And what of you, Niece? You must stay by your father's side tonight. Or Avram's. Under-stood?"

Deborah nodded and hurried to the well.

The celebrations that night overflowed Leb's house and poured into the street. A fire had been lit between the houses. The men of Shiloh gathered around it. Lapidoth and his soldiers commanded most of the guests' attention. They told of their battles, giving their opinions as to the strength of the Canaanite army.

"How can we fight against the chariots?" asked one of the older townsmen. "We cannot come against them on the open plains."

Lapidoth's eyes flashed with passion, his hand clenched in a fist. "If we do not come against them as one, we will soon be forced out of the plains entirely and up into the hills."

Azareel grinned. "And what is wrong with the hills? I have lived there all my life."

"But the Lord gave us all of Canaan." Deborah recognized the speaker as one of Lapidoth's men, but didn't know the lanky man's name. "It's time we take back what is ours!"

Deborah could see how the soldiers' talk excited the younger men in the gathering. Their faces glowed in the firelight with enthusiasm. The older men sat back, some in quiet amusement, others in anger, at the idea of waging war. Most of the women sat inside, discussing the various gossip of the city. Some, like Deborah, stood around the edges of the fire, listening and watching the newcomers with nervous fascination.

"Nathan is right." Lapidoth leaned forward, seeming to look every man in the eye as he spoke. "It is God's will that we inhabit this land. He commanded Joshua to take it. We have given it up too easily." A cheer rose up from the younger men.

Uri held up an empty pitcher. "We need some more wine to fuel our debate."

One of the mercenaries grabbed it and made his way through the crowd. Deborah stopped him. "I know where the wine is. I'll fill that for you."

The man smiled. His dark eyes looked black in the dim light. "Thank you. I'll wait here."

Deborah stepped into the house and searched for her aunt. She found Rachel sitting in the courtyard among a group of women. "Aunt, Uri has asked for more wine."

Rachel's lips pursed together in a small frown. "I knew this would happen. The boy has no sense." She placed a hand on Deborah's shoulder, guiding her away from the other women. "Refill the jug, but water down the wine. We do not want them getting drunk this early in the evening."

Deborah did as her aunt ordered. She brought the refilled jug outside. The soldier stood where she had left him. He took the pitcher from her hands.

"You are very kind." His dark eyes watched her intently. "We haven't had such good food and drink in a long time."

"My uncle feels blessed to celebrate the marriage of his only son. It has made him quite generous."

The man nodded. Although he'd freshened up with the water Deborah had provided earlier, and trimmed his beard, he had left his black hair long. It hung down to his shoulders. "I am-"

"Abiel! Pass the wine this way." Another of the soldiers called out. "You can't keep it all to yourself!"

A roar of laughter went up as Abiel passed the jug to the nearest man. He turned back to Deborah with a shy smile. "Well, now you know my name. I'm Abiel. May I know yours?"

Deborah lowered her gaze. "I am Leb's niece."

He chuckled softly. "I know who you are, but what is your name?"

She could feel the blood rush to her cheeks and hoped he wouldn't see her blush in the dim light. "Deborah."

Abiel gestured to the group sitting around the fire. "And which one of these fine men is your husband."

She shook her head. "None."

Abiel took a step closer. "You are not married?"

Deborah looked up, startled to see him so near. She could see the weathered skin on his cheeks and the red rash on his newly shaved neck.

"You're not married?" He asked again.

"No."

"Surely you are promised to someone?"

Deborah took a step back. "No."

"Daughter!" Azareel called to her.

"Excuse me." Deborah bowed her head to Abiel then ran over to where her father sat. He took her hand.

"Go into the house. Stay with the women. This is not a place for you."

"Yes, Father."

As she turned to go, she heard Uri's voice rising up from the crowd. "The prophet has said that the Canaanites will soon come south. Have you seen signs of them advancing our way?"

Lapidoth frowned. "They struggle with us in the north, protecting their precious cities of Hazor and Megiddo. And they are weakened by the drought." He shook his head. "They won't come south anytime soon."

"But the prophet-"said another man.

"Your prophet is wrong." Lapidoth took a large swallow from his goblet.

Deborah spoke without thinking. "I am not."

A hush fell about the men from the city as they turned their focus to her. Lapidoth and his men laughed quietly.

"What did you say?" asked Lapidoth.

Deborah squared her shoulders. "I am not wrong."

The red-haired man looked around at the others. "I don't understand."

Her voice rang out across the now silent gathering. "I am the prophet. And I am not wrong."

Lapidoth stared at her with disbelief. "You?"

"Do you not think God would choose a woman to speak His will?"

"A woman? Maybe." Lapidoth chuckled. "Not a child."

Someone touched her shoulder. She turned to find Azareel beside her. "Do not waste your time arguing with him. He is too drunk to listen to reason. Go inside."

Lapidoth stood. "I am sober. I am just not foolish enough to believe the ranting of young girl."

Deborah jerked away from Azareel's touch, but made no move toward the house. Instead, she took a step toward Lapidoth. The men closest to her shifted to give her more space.

The air around her seemed to crackle with energy. She narrowed her eyes to see the soldier before her more clearly. "You know nothing of the Lord's will. You fight against the Canaanites in vain." Her voice grew stronger. "They are the rod of discipline the Lord will use to correct His people. Until the Israelites repent of their idolatry and wickedness, nothing you do will stop them, because you do it without God's help. The Canaanites will come south. Sooner than you believe, Lapidoth."

She held his gaze a moment longer before turning on her heels. She pushed her way through the crowd of women who had gathered to watch the argument. Adara hurried toward her.

"Are you well?"

Deborah shook her head. She rubbed her chest, trying to loosen the tightness around her heart. "I need to be alone."

Adara frowned. "I don't think there is any place here, Cousin. Perhaps up on the roof?"

Deborah hurried up the stairs. Glancing around she saw Adara had been right. A large number of people congregated, even on the rooftop. Deborah ignored their curious stares and found a corner where she could sit alone. Insufferable man. So confident in his own power. She shivered as her anger faded. *I know what I have seen, Lord. Help me to be strong in the face of those who doubt.*

The celebration of Uri's wedding lasted another night before the preparations for Passover and the Feast of Unleavened bread began. Leb's house remained crowded with guests. Azareel and Avram; Adara and her family; Lapidoth and his men; all looked forward to observing the holy week in Shiloh. The Passover lamb had been chosen before Uri's wedding and kept in a small pen in the courtyard during the festivities. Deborah knew she shouldn't get attached to the animal, but every day she found herself feeding it from her palm and rubbing its soft wool.

On the fourteenth day of the month of Nissan, the men took the lamb out to the Tabernacle to slaughter it. The women stayed behind, cleaning through the cupboards and all the storage jars, making sure that no yeast or leavened bread remained in the house. Rachel swept the floors of all the rooms, so that not even a trace of leaven could be found to defile her home. When the men arrived home at sunset with the carcass, it was set out in the courtyard to roast over a spit. Josiah, as the youngest male, looked forward to his role in the evening ceremony.

The smell of the roasted meat wafted into the house from the courtyard. Deborah and Katriel ground horseradish and mixed it with bitter herbs. These were the only spices permitted at the Passover meal. Rachel made several loaves of matzo, or unleavened bread, while Adara kept Josiah out of the way. When the meat was ready, Leb sat down with Josiah on his right side. Michal, Lapidoth and his men sat next to them along one side of the room. Uri sat on his father's left, followed by Azareel, Avram and the women. The large front room had barely enough space to accommodate them all.

Leb waited until everyone was seated then poured a cup of wine. Gesturing, he commanded them all to stand. He lifted his cup to heaven. "Blessed are Thou, O Lord our God, King of the universe, Who createst the fruit of the vine. Blessed art Thou, O Lord our God, Who has chosen us for Thy service from among the nations." Leb sat down and drank from his cup. The others sat and waited for Rachel to pour their wine. Once everyone had been served, Josiah beamed up at his grandfather.

"Now?"

Leb nodded solemnly.

The boy spoke out in a strong voice. "What is the meaning of this ceremony? Why is tonight different than any other night?"

"It is the celebration of the Lord's Passover," answered his grandfather. "For He passed over the homes of the Israelites in Egypt. And though He killed the first born of the Egyptians, He spared our families and did not destroy us."

The family and their guests lowered their heads as Leb finished with a final prayer. "Blessed art Thou, O Lord our God, King of the universe, Who has kept us in life, Who has preserved us, and has enabled us to reach this season."

As one, they answered "Amen."

After the ritual of the meal had been performed, the atmosphere in the room relaxed. Deborah found herself in a pleasant conversation with one of the men from Lapidoth's group. His light brown hair stood wildly about his head, even though he and the other men had shaved their beards and trimmed their hair for the wedding.

The young man passed a basket of matzo to Deborah. "My name is Neriah." His brown eyes looked at her shyly from under his bushy brows. She and Neriah sat across from each other at the far end of the room. Although she was older than Katriel, she was also unmarried, so she sat in the last seat in the row. Deborah deduced Neriah to be the youngest man among his friends, since he too, sat on the end.

"I am Deborah." She smiled at him and ripped off a piece of the flat bread before handing the basket to Katriel.

"Is it true?" Neriah asked.

Deborah nibbled at her bread. "Is what true?"

He leaned forward. "Have you heard the voice of God?"

Deborah looked quickly at the others around her. She was not eager to be the center of attention, but the others seemed interested in their own conversations. "Yes. It's true."

Neriah sat up and watched her with awe. She smiled at his fascination. "I am not Moses."

The young man's eyes cleared, as if he'd been lost in thought. "What?"

Deborah chuckled under her breath. "You look at me like you expect me to start speaking to a burning bush or bring the walls of the house down."

He dropped his gaze. "Sorry."

She laughed again. "It's fine. I know I intimidate people, but I am really nothing special."

He looked up. "Nothing special? But God speaks to you!"

"It is only because I prayed to serve him. My heart yearned for Him even as a child. I am a servant, nothing more."

Neriah's brown eyes still looked at her with wonder. "How long have you heard his voice?"

Deborah thought for a moment. "For almost four years." She tried shifting the conversation away from herself. "Where are you from?"

"Kedesh."

"Where's that?"

"In the hills north of Hazor."

"How long have you been a soldier?"

Neriah sat up, puffing his chest out slightly. "Two years. As soon as I was able to go to war."

"Then you are only twenty-one?"

Neriah nodded. "But I have seen much in that time."

Deborah frowned. "What about your family? Do you see them?"

His face hardened. "My parents died when I was young. I had two older brothers. One still tries to farm his land near Hazor. One was killed by the Canaanites."

"I'm sorry." Her heart went out to this young man who seemed to have so much innocence in him, even though he'd experienced so much death.

Neriah shrugged. "It is the way things are. I am honored to fight for God and my people. It gives me a reason to go on."

Deborah felt someone's gaze on her. Lapidoth sat at the opposite end of the room, watching her. She had the odd sensation that even over the din of the other voices, he had been listening to her conversation with Neriah. When he realized Deborah watched him, he didn't lower his eyes. Instead, he seemed to examine her closer. At first she was taken aback by the boldness of his stare, but then decided to return his scrutiny.

She knew he was younger than Michal's thirty years, but Deborah didn't think it was by more than a year or two. He had trimmed his beard and hair. Unlike Neriah, his red hair sat tamely on his head, and his beard was neat against his chin. Michal spoke to his brother and Lapidoth turned his focus to the conversation next to him, but not without nodding slightly to Deborah.

Once everyone had eaten their full, Abiel pulled a small harp from his belongings. He played softly as the women cleared away the remains of the meal. It gladdened Deborah's heart to see Michal and Lapidoth laughing together. The bonds of family run deep. Too deep for old hurts to keep them apart. She hummed along to Abiel's tune, her voice lifting up with words of praise as she and Katriel rinsed the dishes in the courtyard. Her soul rejoiced within her. Those she loved the most surrounded her. Although the Lord had promised the worsening famine and Canaanite attacks, the trouble seemed to be well off in the distant future. For now, she could relax and enjoy her family. She continued her singing as she finished with the dishes and re-entered the house. The men sat silent, watching her.

Deborah looked furtively around. "I'm sorry. I didn't mean to sing so loud." She lowered her head. "Forgive me."

Azareel smiled up at her. "We are not angry, Daughter." His eyes glistened in the lamplight. "I have missed your singing."

Deborah brought the dishes over to Rachel to be put away. Leb laughed and clapped his hands together. "When she isn't praying, the prophet is singing to herself. Always I hear humming as she does her work. It is such a blessing."

They all turned expectantly toward her as Abiel strummed another tune. She blushed at their attention. "Please, everyone sing."

Abiel lifted his strong tenor voice to hers, and soon the others joined in. Abiel's dark eyes sparkled as he played his harp. The room filled with the sounds of laughter and song. Only Lapidoth, Deborah noticed, sat back in the shadows, watching her.

Deborah went to bed that night still singing to herself. She curled up in a far corner next to Azareel and Avram. The rest of Leb's family slept around the main room, except for Uri and Katriel who had taken possession of Deborah's little storage room. It was the only area that offered any privacy for the newlyweds. Lapidoth and his men slept in the courtyard. Tomorrow they would all go to the Tabernacle to watch the priests make the offering that marked the first day of the Feast of Unleavened Bread. No work could be done. It was a Sabbath day. A day of rest. She took pleasure in the thought of sitting at home, listening to Azareel tell her stories of their forefathers. She drifted off to sleep to images of Moses parting the Red Sea.

Deborah stood on an open plain. She had never left the hill country of Ephraim so the flatness of the land seemed strange to her. "There's nothing to hold up the sky!" It was absurd of her to fear the lack of hills, but still she couldn't shake the feeling of dread. "No, I will not be afraid again. YHWH is greater than anything on earth."

Remiel stood before her, his face shining. "Good, Prophet. You will need your courage to face what is next."

Deborah knelt. "What? What is coming?"

The angel moved toward her, his feet gliding over the dry ground but stirring no dust. "Whom do you serve, Deborah?"

"I serve the God of Abraham, Isaac and Jacob. El-Shaddai."

"All those who serve Him will be tested. All will have to pass through fire. Are you ready?"

Deborah shivered. "I will do my best to serve Him with my whole heart, soul, mind and strength."

Remiel nodded in approval. "Prepare yourself."

"How?"

"With prayer. Meditate on the goodness of God, so when the time comes you will remember, and hold fast to his promises."

"What must I do?"

"You must travel to Shamir with your cousin Adara. Remain there until the time of testing."

"How long will that be? What will happen?"

The light surrounding the angel's face grew brighter, consuming him in a brilliant flash. His voice reverberated within her head as she woke from the dream. "Wait on the Lord, Deborah. Call on His name and He will give you strength."

5 Shamir

Six Weeks Later

Two hundred chariots bore down on the city, dust swirling around them like a great brown cloud. As they rode closer, Sisera held up his hand and called for the *maryannu* to halt. He inspected the land surrounding the city. An ember of anger, deep within his stomach, threatened to ignite.

He got down from his chariot and strode over to what had been a field of grain. He picked up a forgotten stalk and crushed it in his fist. "Where is the wheat?" Several officers came to stand by him. They too surveyed the countryside. "Can anyone tell me how they knew we were coming? How they could have harvested so much before we arrived?"

My plan was perfect! His nine hundred chariots were divided into raiding parties. Four small armies spread out across the southern lands, forcing the Israelites to harvest their grain for the Canaanites. He had timed the raids before the crops were completely ripe, counting on that fact to keep the Israelites from hoarding the grain for themselves. *And now, here is a city that has done just that.*

Sisera inspected the horizon. Along the eastern edge of the city, several large fields of wheat still stood. Their stalks moved in the wind like waves on the water. Sisera mounted his chariot then drove over to the foot soldiers and prisoners who marched behind. "Harvest what is left," he called to the officers. "I want this done before the sun is overhead." The general pulled his chariot around to the closest flank of the *maryannu*. "Pinon and Iram, you and your men follow me. I want to know how these wretches knew of our plan."

Sisera's army poured into Shamir like a tidal wave. The people of the village, armed with pitchforks and wooden spears, swarmed into the streets to meet the advancing soldiers. A few dropped their weapons when they saw the steel blades and arrows of the Canaanites. An uneasy truce settled over the mob as Sisera led his chariot into an open area to address the crowd.

The chariot horses snorted and stomped their hooves. The General glared at the people around him. Young men, their chins barely covered with stubble, elbowed their way to the front of the mob. A group of older men, with gray hair and long beards, congregated together. Sisera ignored the younger men; his army would take care of any foolish attacks. Instead, he focused on the elders. "What spy told you we were coming? Bring him to me."

One of the gray haired men stepped forward, his brown eyes clouded with age. "There is no spy, General." His rich voice rang with authority. He gestured to the poorly armed townsmen. "You can see, we are not ready for a battle."

"A good story, old man, but someone warned you of our plan. Who?" Sisera nodded to a foot soldier who then thrust his sword through an elderly woman leaning on a crutch at the front of the crowd. Her body fell as the soldier pulled his weapon from her stomach He grabbed a young boy and held the bloody sword to his throat. Someone cried out from one of the nearby houses.

"Bring me the spy or the child dies."

A man pushed past the mob into the clearing. "Please! There is no spy!" Several others tried to pull him back. The elder spokesman stepped toward him.

"Jesse, say nothing."

The younger man tore away from the hands that held him, his eyes pleading. "Don't hurt my son."

"Jesse," spat the elder, "enough!" He put his hand on the younger man's shoulder.

"Let him speak." Sisera ordered.

"No." The old man's clouded eyes brightened with his anger. The father wept. "There is no spy . . . ."

Sisera waved his hand toward the gray haired man. Two soldiers drew their swords and held them at his throat. The other elders moved as a group to intercede, but stopped when all the guards unsheathed their weapons and pointed them at the crowd.

Sisera stepped down from his chariot. He walked toward the sobbing father. "Explain how you knew we were coming." He nodded to the soldier who held the man's son. The youngster whimpered as his captor pressed his sword against the boy's neck.

Jesse fell to his knees. "Please! I beg you!" He reached out to Sisera. "Do not kill my son!" His arms dropped to his sides. "It was the prophet." The men around him cried out. Several rushed past the soldiers to strike him. With another nod from the General, foot soldiers pulled the father up and carried him to Sisera.

The General leaned closer to the man and spoke in a whisper. "This prophet. Where can I find him?"

Helplessness filled the man's eyes. "I don't know."

Sisera looked at the boy. The guard who held him tightened his grip. The boy screamed.

The father would have collapsed to the ground if the soldiers didn't hold him up. "I swear to you. I don't know where she is!"

"She?" Sisera stood up. He scrutinized the broken man before him. "Some kind of oracle? Where can I find her?" Jesse shook his head. Sisera turned to the people. "Tell me where this priestess is, or I will kill every child in this town."

The Israelite men gripped their crude weapons tighter, their dark eyes filled with anger and fear. Each looked to a neighbor, as if trying to will another man to make the first move against their invaders.

"Do not be fools." The general strode around the open area. "My men are far better armed than you and well trained for battle." He spread his arms out at his side. "Tell me where this woman is, and no one else need lose their life."

A voice called from outside the crowd. "Here."

Sisera looked up, but couldn't see the source of the voice. The mob behind him seemed agitated, as if they fought against some unseen force. He climbed into his chariot. A figure made its way through the throng, although the people tried to hold the person back. When she finally broke free, the general laughed. "This is your prophet?"

A young woman, no more than a girl really, stood before him. Dressed in a simple brown woolen shift, her hair in a braid and wrapped in light blue cloth, she drew herself up and met Sisera's gaze. He looked at the faces in the crowd. Whatever this was, it wasn't a trick. The people were genuinely upset that the girl had come forward. He narrowed his eyes to study her. "What is your name?"

"I am Deborah bat Azareel."

Sisera smirked. "And you're a prophet, are you?"

"As God wills it, He has given me visions. He has given me words to speak."

"Tell me, Prophet. How did your God warn you of our coming?"

Apprehension flickered across her face. "A dream."

Sisera raised an eyebrow. "Tell it to me."

She closed her eyes for a moment then looked up. "I saw the fields of wheat, ready for harvest. A great swarm of locusts darkened the horizon. As they descended on the wheat, I saw their heads bore the faces of men. They devoured the grain and left nothing behind. The people were left to starve. Then I saw the wheat, tall and strong again. The villagers harvested it while the black cloud of locusts gathered on the horizon. When the plague arrived, nothing remained in the fields for them to eat. The locusts invaded the town and began to eat the people."

Her voice broke. She took a deep breath. "Then the locusts set the village on fire and burned it to the ground." The girl shook her head, as if trying to erase the image from her mind. "Finally I saw the fields a third time, ripe for harvest. The villagers took half the grain and hid it as the locusts gathered. When the plague came, they ate the wheat in the fields, but left the villagers alone."

She looked up at Sisera. "I warned the town of your coming. I told the younger women to hide in the hills. God had shown me our only hope of survival was to give half the harvest to you, and ration the other half for ourselves." She took a step toward his chariot. "Please. This way we all survive one more year of the drought. Do not destroy these people for what I told them to do."

"You warned the other women to flee. Why did you stay?" The general let out a cynical laugh. "Another dream?"

She glanced toward the boy with the sword at his throat, then at the elders. "I knew I would be needed."

Sisera's eyes narrowed as he surveyed the crowd. It would be an evenly matched fight, here in the streets of the town. He and his soldiers maneuvered more easily in the open fields. *We would still crush them. But we would lose men, probably quite a few, if we fought to find the rest of the harvest. And we have more towns to conquer.* Sisera kept his anger hidden. He would not show his enemies any of his doubt. *We have three full wagons. Surely the King will be satisfied with that.* He turned his gaze to the girl. *Especially if I bring him a different prize. Maybe not the Israelite leader, but certainly an impressive addition to the temple.*

"You may keep the rest of the harvest." The villagers called out praises to their god and to the girl. Sisera pointed to her. "In exchange for your prophet." He gestured and two foot soldiers grabbed the girl by her arms. The crowd cried out and started forward, but the soldiers raised their swords. "It is her for the grain. If you do not like the agreement, we will kill her now in retribution. It is your choice."

The girl's face whitened, but she called out in a strong voice, "Do nothing! God will protect me!"

The people backed away. Sisera looked to the guards. "Take her and put her with the other prisoners. Make sure she's tied to the front of the line so I can find her again. They all look the same." The two men dragged the girl through the crowd. Sisera addressed the other soldiers. "Take what food you can find in this hole and meet back at camp." He signaled to his driver. The chariot sped forward sending villagers fleeing out of its way.

The hemp rope bit into Deborah's wrists each time the soldier who held the other end pulled it taut. He seemed to do it often, just to watch her grimace in pain. She vowed silently that she wouldn't cry out. She concentrated on the droplets of blood dripping down her arms and tried not to pay attention to the soldier or her thirst. The smell of sweat hung heavy in the stagnant air.

She led a chain of about sixty women, most of them younger than herself. A line of men walked beside them; captives from the raids the general and his army had conducted over the past week. All of them bound to be sold as slaves in the markets of Hazor and Megiddo. The soldier ahead yanked the rope again. Deborah lost her balance. Without her hands to break her fall she landed on her chest, scrapping her face on the hard ground. Her captor laughed as the next three prisoners also fell.

"Get up!" The soldier's sandaled foot kicked Deborah's ribs. She let out a cry before she clamped her lips shut and struggled to rise. His light brown eyes filled with amusement as he watched her efforts. "It's not time to rest yet." He pushed her forward. "Keep moving!"

She glared at the man as she straightened herself up then spit the dirt out of her mouth. With no beard to hide his face, Deborah could see a deep scar along one cheek. He watched her with eyes filled with loathing and lusting. She dropped her gaze. *Help me Lord. I don't know your plan. All I know is I'm scared. Be with me. Let me know you're near.* She heard no answer, but a cool breeze offered her some slight relief from the heat of the day, giving her some peace.

They walked for hours, finally stopping by a river as the sun set on the horizon. A great wail went up when the soldiers dragged the captive men off to the far side of the camp. Separated from their fathers, brothers and husbands, many of the women shrieked in despair or fought against the soldiers that surrounded them. The Canaanites only laughed and pushed them away like flies. Deborah was forced to sit as the others in line fell to the ground in tears or exhaustion. Two older women wept next to her. A girl of about twelve sat stoically next in line. Her black hair lay unbound and uncovered around her face. A lone tear tracked down the dirt on her cheek.

"What's your name?" Deborah asked.

The girl blinked then focused her eyes. "Jael."

"Was your father one of the men taken away?"

Jael shook her head. "No. My brother." She looked up at Deborah with large dark eyes. "My father is dead."

Deborah swallowed a lump in her throat. "I'm sorry."

The girl stared ahead, her expression devoid of emotion. "My mother, too. They killed them."

Deborah scooted her body as close to the girl as she could without pulling on the two women tied between them. "Who killed them?"

"The soldiers. They came into our house. Father hid me under the blankets so they didn't see me. They put a spear through him. It pinned him to the ground." The little girl's eyes clouded over for a moment, as if she were puzzled about something. "The soldier was mad that he couldn't get his spear back. He pulled and yanked on it, but he couldn't get it out of my father."

Deborah's heart broke for the girl. Jael's eyes cleared. "They dragged my mother outside. I heard her scream. My sister too. Then they stopped."

Deborah stared at the girl, trying to think of a way to comfort her. "Would you like to put your head in my lap?"

Jael seemed confused at first but then nodded. She lay down on the grass with her head on Deborah's legs. "My mother would let me do this when I couldn't sleep."

Deborah used her bound hands to stroke the girl's hair as best she could. "I never knew my mother, but I always wished someone would do this for me."

"My mother is dead," said Jael. "They cut her chest. I saw the blood. My brother tried to make me look the other way, but I wanted to see."

"How old is your brother?"

"He's thirteen. He hid in the blankets with me, but when they took our mother, he cried out. That's when the soldiers found us." She snuggled into Deborah's lap. Soon the girl's breathing grew deeper. Within a few minutes she snored lightly in exhaustion.

Deborah leaned down to kiss the girl's head. "I'm sorry, little one, for all your pain. But the Lord is with us. He has not forsaken us." She lifted her eyes up to the hills behind them and prayed.

The man from the chariot found her at dusk. Jael still lay sleeping, while Deborah sang softly.

"A prophet and a singer? What else can you do?"

Deborah stopped. He stood over her. He had changed clothes since she'd seen him last. He wore a clean robe of deep blue. A golden collar decorated the neck. Without his helmet on, Deborah saw his head was shaved but for a long, black braid. Her mind flashed back to the night she'd been on the high place with Seff. *It's the man from my vision!* She tried not to let her surprise show on her face, but she could see the man sensed some change in her.

He called to a nearby foot soldier. "Cut her ropes, bring her to me. I will be in the priest's tent." He strode away.

The soldier who'd held the rope throughout the day drew his sword. Stepping behind Deborah, he jerked her hands up. The rapid movement woke Jael. The young girl's eyes widened with fear at the sight of the sword over Deborah's head. The women around them cried out, but Deborah remained silent. The soldier laughed as he sliced her bonds. Once she was separated from the other women, he pulled her up against his chest.

"I guess the general fancies you." His putrid breath made Deborah gag. She turned her head. He grabbed her braid, forcing her to face him. "Think you're too good for me?" Deborah shut her eyes. He pulled her away from the other women, while calling over his shoulder, "Keep an eye on them. We don't want any running off."

The guard led her through the camp. Several hundred soldiers set up tents and made small fires as night fell. They stopped their work as Deborah passed. She could feel their eyes on her. She worried not only for her safety, but that of Jael and the other women. She didn't know the rules of the Canaanite army. Perhaps they could have their pick of the prisoners. Deborah prayed not. The smell of baking bread caused her stomach to growl loudly. The soldier chuckled under his breath.

"If you're lucky, maybe the general will feed you first, but I wouldn't count on it."

Four large tents stood in the center of the camp. The soldier dragged her to one. Larger than the mud brick home she'd grown up in, the tent was made of a heavy striped cloth. He drew aside the door flap and pushed Deborah inside. Several torches illuminated the opulent surroundings. The sides of the tent shimmered with golden thread woven in intricate patterns. Thick wool rugs covered the ground. Pillows lay around a low table made of dark wood. A smoke haze and the spicy odor of incense permeated the room. A quiet hum filled her mind, like the drone of bees. In the far corner stood an altar with the statue of a bull-headed man on it. She shuddered and turned her head away.

The man from the chariot rose from the table. "Here she is, Zuberi."

A larger man, also bald but with no braid, handed the General a goblet before turning to face Deborah. His brown skin shone with a thin sheen of sweat. He wore only a floor length skirt of cream linen. A golden sash held it at his waist. His torso and arms bore intricate markings made from henna and scarring. Dark tattoos decorated his face as well. Around his wrists were gold bracelets inlaid with sapphires and rubies. He surveyed Deborah from where he stood.

The man looked skeptical. "This is the prophet?"

"That's what she told me. The people were ready to fight for her." The general eyed her a moment, then took a sip from his cup. Deborah could see he appreciated the taste of whatever the priest had given him. "She told me the dream she had, warning of our approach." He gestured with his cup. "Tell him the dream."

The soldier shoved her forward. She stumbled, but didn't fall. Looking down at the floor, Deborah recounted her vision to the priest. There was silence when she finished. She kept her focus on the woolen rug at her feet, but sensed the large man approaching her.

"She seems homely. And young." The priest circled around, inspecting her.

"She is older than most of the captives, but younger than twenty years, I think."

The large man stopped at her side. "How old are you?"

"When the rains come, I will be seventeen."

The priest grunted in response. "Take the cloth from her head."

The soldier tore the linen from her head and threw it to the ground.

"Now the hair," ordered Zuberi. "Girl, undo your braid."

Deborah's hands trembled as she loosed her hair. The priest took a handful and rubbed it with his fingers. "With some water, she could clean up. The hair is thick, and has some curl. Jabin will like that." He lifted her chin. "Let's see the face." Deborah kept her gaze cast downward. "She is not as bad as I first thought. Look at me."

Deborah fought the panic rising in her chest. She looked up. The bald man gasped. "Why did you not mention her golden eyes, Sisera?"

"I did not notice them. She stood too far away." Sisera approached her.

Deborah's blood chilled. *Sisera! Destroyer of towns. Monster!* She tried to keep her emotions from betraying her, but knew they would read her fear.

The general searched her eyes. "Do you think they are a sign?"

The priest nodded. "Definitely." The humming in Deborah's head grew louder as Zuberi stepped closer. She could smell the wine on his breath. "How much power do you possess? Do you even know?"

Deborah swallowed and tried to speak calmly. "I have only the power my God chooses to give me."

Zuberi studied her for a moment then shook his head. "No. I think you have more. If you were willing to open yourself to it." The priest went over to the table in the opposite corner from the idol. He took a small vial and placed a few drops of liquid from it into a goblet made of silver. Then he filled the cup with wine. Walking back to her, he swallowed a large mouthful. The hum in Deborah's head increased. The priest turned to Sisera. "Wine mixed with a few drops of poppy juice." He drank again. "It has remarkable power. It can open the mind to all kinds of influences." Zuberi held the goblet out to her. "Drink."

The liquid the goblet contained frightened Deborah more than anything she had faced before. She backed away. The guard grabbed her shoulders and pushed her toward the priest. Zuberi lifted the cup to her mouth. "Drink."

She fixed her lips shut and ducked her chin down to her chest. The soldier tried to wrench her head back up, but the priest stopped him. He handed the goblet to Sisera. "There are other means of persuasion." He circled around her again while the guard held her still. "You see, Sisera. If we force the fluid down her, we may get some results, but not the best. We have to make her want to take it, for the drug to have the most influence."

"How do you propose to do that?"

The large man drew a dagger from the sash at his waist. The guard yanked her hair away so her throat lay exposed then clamped her arms behind her in a vice-like grip. Zuberi placed the tip on her neck. "Do you fear death?" Deborah's body stiffened as she prepared to feel the blade cut through her skin. The priest pressed harder on the dagger. "Drink or die."

"My God will save me," Deborah said through clenched teeth. "And if he doesn't, that is His will."

The priest drew the blade lightly across her throat. She flinched at the bolt of sharp, intense pain. A thin stream of blood ran down her neck.

"Drink."

Deborah groaned.

"Your power as a prophet will make a worthy sacrifice to El." He placed the knife at her chest. "I will cut your heart out and place it on his altar. I'm sure he would be pleased."

Deborah closed her eyes. *Please God, I'm not afraid to die. But I do fear pain. Make it quick. Please.*

Zuberi pulled the knife away, wiped the blood off on her tunic then placed it back at his waist. "I didn't think that would work, but it was the easiest to try." He crossed his arms as he studied her. Zuberi's gaze wandered over her body, from her toes to her head. "What do you think, Sisera? Is she still a virgin?"

"At sixteen? I doubt it. These Hebrews marry young." Sisera set the goblets on the table behind him.

The priest reached out and grabbed Deborah's hips. His hands stroked her intimately. Deborah tried to move away, but the guard held her still. "She hasn't had children. That's certain."

Deborah's stomach rolled. She fought to swallow the vomit that rose in her throat.

Zuberi laughed. "See her fear, Sisera? She is a virgin." He caressed her face. "What do you say now? If I tell you I will give you to Sisera for the night?" He took her from the soldier and thrust her toward the general, who caught her in his arms. "Go ahead, take her."

Deborah punched at Sisera's chest, but could get no power behind her attack because he held her too close. He pulled the hair away from her face, staring down at her with such lust, her breath froze in her lungs.

Zuberi whispered in her ear. "What do you say now? Will you drink, or do I let the general take you here. While I watch?"

Deborah cried out in frustration, twisting and turning her body but unable to loosen the general's hold.

The priest's breath blew hot against her neck. "What will your God do if we take your purity from you? Now will you drink?"

Deborah ceased her fighting. The priest had given her an escape. She turned her head so she faced the tattooed man. "God would take His power from me. I would be nothing. Of no use to Him, or you."

Zuberi's eyes showed doubt, then fear. "You could be lying. Your God might leave you, but others might be able to speak to you." He shook his head. "I'm sorry Sisera, but she is right. We cannot risk it."

Sisera turned her so she faced the priest. He placed his arms around hers and held her tightly, her back pressed against his chest. The blood from her neck itched as it dried. She tried to scratch it on her shoulder, but only succeeded in opening the wound again.

Zuberi poured himself another goblet of wine, this time without the added drug from the vial. He drank as he walked over to the statue on the altar. He stared at the idol then drained his cup. Throwing it to the ground he grasped the sides of the altar and bowed his head. The droning grew louder still in Deborah's mind. She could hear voices speaking, but not in a language she understood. Zuberi pushed himself upright and turned to her with a smile.

"I have been going about this all wrong, Sisera. Our young prophet does not fear for herself. Her faith is too strong." He approached Deborah slowly, reaching out to run a hand down her cheek. She shivered at his touch. He looked up to the general. "Was she brought in with anyone? A sister or brother perhaps?"

Sisera shook his head. "No. But there was a girl she seemed to care for. The little one slept in her lap while she sang."

Zuberi's grin widened. "Guard, you know this girl?"

The soldier nodded.

"Bring her here."

Deborah's legs buckled under her. Sisera's arms kept her from sinking to the floor. The priest watched her as one might study a bug crawling on their arm. "You see how she faints?" He gestured to the general. "Let her sit. Then she can drink whenever she is ready."

Sisera sat her next to the table with the goblet. Deborah stared at it with mute revulsion. *Lord, help me! I do not know what this wine will do, but I fear it. I beg you, take these voices from my head! Tell me what to do!* She fell across the table and covered her head with her arms, trying to block out the voices that now swirled in and around her thoughts in constant conversation.

The priest knelt by her, crooning softly. "Do not fear it. I promise, the wine won't hurt you. I only need to know your powers." He pushed the goblet nearer to her. Deborah took the cup. His gloating look of victory disappeared when she threw the wine in his face.

She screamed at the droning in her head as much as to the priest. "I will serve no God but the Lord of Abraham, Isaac and Jacob!"

Zuberi's slap propelled her onto the table. He clapped his hands as he stood. Two women came out from behind the curtained back of the tent. "Bring me water and a towel." He wiped the wine from his cheeks and glared down at Deborah. "That was foolish. I have been patient until now." He stopped to rinse his hands and face with the water a servant brought him. He removed his stained linen covering and put on the robe the other servant carried. It was made of many colored panels of wool. He secured it with the same golden sash he'd worn before.

The soldier returned, dragging Jael by the hair. He threw her to the ground. She immediately scrambled to her feet and tried to flee the tent. The guard pinned her arms while she kicked his legs.

Zuberi's smile sent a chill through Deborah's blood. "Bring her to the table."

The guard carried Jael to the table then forced her to sit across from Deborah. The priest gestured to one of the servants who then brought him the goblet. Jael squirmed against her captor. Deborah reached across the table to comfort the girl, but Sisera pulled her back. Zuberi took his time refilling the cup. He handed it to Sisera then turned to the guard. "Hold out the child's hand, so it sits on the table."

The soldier did as he was ordered. Zuberi drew his knife from his belt while he watched Deborah. "You will not drink to save yourself. What about this little girl?"

Deborah felt the room sway as the blood ran from her head. *Lord, what do I do? What do I do?*

"Hold the girl," ordered Zuberi. The soldier tightened his grip on Jael's arm and she cried out. The priest held his knife over her hand. Deborah saw his eyes flicker with malice then he plunged the blade into Jael's palm. Deborah screamed as the child shrieked in agony. Zuberi twisted his knife before pulling it out. "Do I do it again? This time removing a finger?"

Please, God! Help us!

Save her, Deborah. As I will save you.

Zuberi raised his knife again.

"Stop!" Deborah begged, reaching out to stay his hand. "Don't hurt her anymore." Her voice broke. "I will drink it."

The priest pulled his hand from hers. "Give it to her."

Sisera held the goblet in front of Deborah. She looked at Jael who sat quaking, blood pouring from the hole in her palm. Deborah took the cup and drank a mouthful of the cloying liquid.

Zuberi tipped the goblet to her lips again. "More. You must drink all of it."

She took a deep breath, then drained the cup in several large gulps. She gagged as her stomach rebelled against the wine.

Zuberi sat next to her. "Relax, breathe deeply and the nausea will fade."

Deborah gasped for air before her chest finally loosened and she could take a decent breath. Her stomach slowed its churning. She glanced at Jael then back to Zuberi. "Let her go. I've done what you asked."

The priest's large hands brushed her hair from her face. "Yes, you have. But I do not think we'll let this little one go just yet. In case you decide to be uncooperative later." He turned to the guard. "Bind her hands and feet, but leave her in the corner so that our prophet can see her and be reminded of what will happen if she does not comply." He frowned at the girl. "And do something about the blood. She's dripping on my rugs."

Deborah blinked her eyes. Her vision blurred. The soldier dragged Jael into the corner as the whole room ebbed and swayed.

"You see, Sisera? It is already taking effect." Zuberi waved a hand toward the general. "Sit and relax. She should be no problem now."

Beads of sweat formed along Deborah's brow. "What's happening to me?"

Zuberi patted her leg. "Do not worry. The effects are temporary." He took a sip from his own wine, then sat back on a pillow as if relaxing with friends. "What is your name?"

"Deborah, daughter of Azareel."

"Tell me, Deborah. When did you first know you had this power?"

She rubbed her face, trying to stop the numbness that tingled around her lips and cheeks. "I always knew God, even when I was a child." Deborah wiped the sweat from her forehead. "But He spoke to me first at the high place with Seff."

Zuberi's eye's glistened with interest. "Who is Seff?"

"A boy." She ran a hand through her hair. "I loved him."

"Where is he now?"

She shook her head, trying to fend off the effects of the drug.

"Does he live in the village? Where the general found you?"

Deborah shook her head again. "No. He's dead." She ran her hands across her face. "He died a long time ago."

The priest sipped his wine. "And the high place? What is that?"

"A place to worship Baal and Asherah." She shuddered at the memory. A prickling sensation ran through her body. "There were other voices then, too."

The priest leaned forward. "You hear voices. Now?"

"Yes." She put her hands over her ears. "I wish they would be quiet! But they keep getting louder." A spasm of pain clenched her stomach as the room pitched and rolled. Her mind struggled to hold on to reality, but the opiate in the wine distorted everything around her.

"What are they saying?" asked Zuberi. "These voices?"

Deborah cried out when she looked at him.

His face transformed as she watched him, as if he pulled off a mask. Underneath hid a hideous lizard with yellow eyes.

"What do you see?" Zuberi's voice hissed.

Deborah tried to back away from the monster.

Sisera grabbed her shoulders to stop her from escaping. "Tell us what you see."

Tell him! A voice inside her head shrieked. High and grating, she knew it was the lizard who spoke to her mind.

"I see what you really are," she told the priest. "You think you control the demon, but he controls you."

Zuberi's face solidified momentarily before pulling back to reveal the lizard again. "What do you mean?"

"I see him, he lives in you. The demon you serve. He feeds off of you." She shook her head, not only in an attempt to focus her vision, but to try and make sense of the voices in her head.

He is weak, Deborah. He is a fool. You are the one with power. If you served us, we could give you anything you desired. Images filled her mind. The night of the threshing festival, so many years ago. Seff kissing her. Deborah groaned at the heat surging through her body as she remembered the passion she felt for her first love.

Sisera tightened his grip on her shoulders. "What is happening?"

"I think she's having a vision. Wait. The gods will reveal it."

Deborah saw her father, in a beautiful wool tunic. She wore a fine linen robe. They stood before a table filled with food. No soup in sight, only platters of roasted meat and fish. Pitchers of wine. *Not only for you, but those you love. What has your God given you? Only suffering and pain.*

She fought against the desires of her heart. "No!"

"What are you seeing?" Zuberi took her face in his hands. "What are they telling you?"

A dark shadow flowed out of the priest's mouth and spilled onto the ground beside her. A low rumble, like the sound of distant thunder, filled her mind. *You will bow to us, Deborah. We know you. You are not strong enough to resist us.*

Deborah thrashed against Sisera and the priest. "God help me."

The black puddle at her feet bubbled. A thick tendril coiled upward like a giant serpent. *I will help you. I will give you more power than your god ever has, if only you bow to me.*

Wild with anger and fear, she kicked at the priest until he was forced to back away from her. "O God, where are you?" She wrenched herself from Sisera's grasp and stood to face the inky figure before her. "I will not serve you!"

Sisera rose to grab her, but Zuberi stopped him. "No! Wait." The priest's eyes flashed with heated desire. "Our gods call to her."

The ebony serpent lunged toward her. Deborah's body shuddered as the dark, malevolent spirit entered her. Where God's presence brought only peace and lightness, this spirit filled her with fear and rage. God's voice prompted her thoughts, but

never overpowered her. This took control of her mind, forcing
Deborah down into some black pit while it spoke through her.

Sisera stood transfixed at the sight of the girl. Her whole
body shook. Her golden eyes rolled back so only the whites
showed. She flung her arms out to the side and screamed.

Then she went silent, save for her panting breath. She
writhed slowly, seductively, before her eyes refocused on the
priest.

What is this? Sisera struggled to comprehend what he wit-
nessed.

"Stupid fool!" The girl's mouth moved, but it was not her
voice that called to Zuberi. Instead someone, *or something*,
spoke through her. The timbre was deeper. Older. The creature
in front of Sisera pointed to the priest. "You have no understanding of what power is. This girl is filled with it, while you
play at tricks and illusions to deceive those more ignorant than
you." She stepped toward the priest, her hips swaying, the
movement fluid, like a serpent. "Do you not realize that she is
the one the oracle spoke of? She is the tool the God of the Israelites will use to bring about your destruction."

Zuberi stared at the figure in front of him. "Should we kill
her? Bring her as a sacrifice to the temple?"

The being stopped, as if considering the idea. "That is one
option, but I think we can do better." She reached out to caress
the priest's chest, her fingertips tracing the lines of his tattoos.
"She may be turned to our side. She has great strength, but
there is a weakness." The creature cackled. "She loves too well."

The figure smiled sensually as she turned to Sisera. "It would
depend on you. If you can seduce her and win the girl's heart,
we could control her." She walked over to the general. "It would
have to be subtle, for she will be wary of any tricks. But if you

could convince her of your love, she would follow you." The creature's face contorted, as if it tried to smile, but was unfamiliar with how its muscles worked. "We could thwart the great Lord's plan. We could use His own servant to bring about the annihilation of His chosen people!"

Sisera cringed at the figure in front of him. She, *it*, stroked his face. Its fingers were cold. Ice. Its breath foul as death.

"Do not fail us, Sisera. If you succeed, the girl will unite the land into one kingdom. Jabin may be called 'King,' but it would be in name only. She would hold all the power. And you, as her consort, would control her." The creature addressed Zuberi. "As for you, Priest. We will see that she does not forget you. You would share in her prestige. The benefits would be great—"

It stepped back abruptly, its eyes focused on something behind Zuberi. The creature snarled, "You are too late, servant of the Most High. She is ours now."

Sisera looked behind him. "Who does it speak to?"

Zuberi's gaze darted around the tent. "I do not know."

A gurgling sound rose from the figure's throat. It thrashed about before pointing to something Sisera could not see. It roared, its voice filling Sisera's head like a thunderclap. "She is *ours*, not yours, Remiel! You cannot free her from us!"

The general and Zuberi backed away. Sisera could only imagine his face mirrored the confusion and fear he read on the priest's, as the girl continued to flail.

The creature shrieked, the scream of an animal falling, tumbling from a great height to its death below. The cry cut off sharply.

The girl stood in the center of the tent, trembling. She panted wildly. She glanced between Sisera and Zuberi, her expression one of innocence. Bewilderment.

The priest studied her a moment then asked, "Who are you?"

"I . . . I am Deborah bat Azareel." She looked around the tent as if trying to orient herself. Her gaze fell on Jael, cowering in the corner. "Do not hurt the child. I will drink from the cup."

Sisera stepped toward her. "You drank already."

"I did?" She looked up at him, her golden eyes wide with fear.

Without knowing why, he cupped her face in his hands. "Do you not remember?

"No," she whispered, before collapsing on the ground at his feet.

6 The Plains of Shamir

The Following Day

Sisera led the chariots out on another raid the following morning, but his mind drifted from the task at hand back to the young woman in the priest's tent. She'd fainted, lifeless at his feet, after the spirit had spoken through her. Sisera thought she might have died, but Zuberi assured him she merely slept.

Her face consumed his every thought. The look in her eyes, the instant before she fainted. Pure innocence. Whatever had possessed her, the being that wanted Sisera to seduce her, the thing that reeked of foulness and decay, that spirit had fled. The girl. Deborah. The girl was left. At the moment before she fell, she had been only a frightened child; her eyes wide, confused.

Why does she haunt me? I have had more beautiful women than this. Younger, older. She is nothing special.

And yet her face appeared again.

Sisera roared in frustration as his chariot raced into another village. He drew his sword and cut down whatever enemy happened across his path. His blade found every mark and still it did nothing to quench the fire burning within his chest. His ferocity fueled his men. They too set upon the helpless Israelites as hungry lions on fresh meat. The battle quickly ended. The Canaanites took possession of whatever remained in the town. If it could be sold or harvested, the men filled their wagons with it. They burned the houses and raped the women. The children they left to die by the fires or starvation. The whole expedition ended by early afternoon. Sisera started toward camp. He would see the girl again. He would begin the plans Zuberi had made for them the night before. Maybe then he could rid his mind of her face.

Deborah woke slowly from her dreamless sleep. She thought she rested on her pallet in Adara's house, but soon felt smooth, cool linen on her feet, not the course wool of her blanket. She opened her eyes, confused. Rolling to her side, she saw a young girl staring at her. Memories rushed through Deborah's mind, images from the night before.

"Jael?"

The child's eyes widened.

"Are you well?"

The girl nodded.

Deborah tried to sit up, but her head swam so she lay back down. She looked toward Jael. "Last night. Did they . . . were you hurt?"

Jael held out her bound hands. One showed a large, bloody wound. Deborah cringed. "I'm sorry. I'm sorry they did that to you because of me." She turned on her back and rubbed her temples. "Did they do anything else?"

Jael shook her head.

Deborah sighed. "Good." She ran a hand over her face. Her head throbbed. Her mouth felt inflamed and parched. A black cloud obscured her memory. She rolled back toward the girl. "Were you here the whole night?"

Again, the girl nodded.

Deborah gently touched Jael's leg. "Please. Tell me. What happened to me? What did they do to me?"

Jael's eyes darted around the tent. She shifted her body so she lay next to Deborah. "They made you drink something that made you . . . ."

"Made me what?" Deborah whispered.

"Someone else. At first the priest was excited, but then he seemed scared."

"Why?"

"I don't know. You spoke different. You touched him."

Deborah's heart fluttered in fear. "Touched him? How?"

"You stroked his chest."

Deborah swallowed hard. "Is that all?"

Jael nodded.

"What did I say?"

"I couldn't hear it all-"

A deep voice called from somewhere in the tent. "Ah, you're awake." Jael moved away, her eyes wide with fear. The large priest soon stood over Deborah, still wearing the robe from the night before. He thrust a goblet at her. "Here." Deborah turned her head. "It is water. Nothing else. It will ease the headache you undoubtedly have from the wine."

Deborah struggled to sit up. She held her head for a moment before taking the cup. It looked like water. She sniffed the liquid. No odor. Her tongue seemed swollen inside her mouth and she longed to quench her thirst. She looked up at the priest.

"Drink it."

She took a swallow. The cool liquid soothed her throat and cracked lips. She drank the rest.

"Would you like more?"

She held the goblet up. "Please."

Zuberi clapped his hands. A young man, dressed only in a short linen tunic, approached. He took the goblet from Deborah then left, returning a moment later with more water.

"Thank you," she said as she took the cup. This time she saved some for Jael and handed it to the girl. Jael quickly finished the water. The priest hovered near them. "What are you going to do with us?" Deborah asked.

"I have plans for you, Prophet. Don't fear."

"But the girl. Why not let her go?"

"The girl is useful to me."

Deborah shivered at Zuberi's smile and tried to steady her voice. "She won't be if you allow her wound to fester."

The priest tilted his head in agreement. "I have salves that will help her heal."

"Then, for mercy's sake, give them to her."

He brushed his hand across Deborah's face. "As long as you cooperate, I assure you, the girl will be cared for."

Deborah shuddered, but nodded at the dark man's bargain.

He stared at her as if in deep concentration. "What do you recall from last night?"

She searched through her memory. "Everything until I drank the wine. Then it's black." She looked up. "Did I fall asleep?"

The priest chuckled. "Not right away. But do not worry, your purity is safe. Your God should still speak to you."

Heat rose to her cheeks and she turned away from him.

"Embarrassed, Prophet? Don't be. I am used to being blunt with those who serve at the temple."

She lifted her head. "But I don't serve at your temple."

Zuberi played with a strand of her hair. "You may yet be persuaded." He glanced toward Jael, who pushed herself away from him.

Deborah swatted his hand from her head. "Please. May I have linen to wrap my hair?"

"No, I do not think so." The priest's eyes twinkled, as if he'd thought of some private joke. "In fact, I think you should be rid of all your clothes."

Deborah crossed her arms, hugged herself tightly, and swallowed her tears.

Zuberi considered her for a moment. "A prophet with your power needs to wear something more special than course wool and cheap linen." Deborah cringed as he touched her head again. "You need to be bathed and perfumed. Dressed in fine robes and gold."

"I won't do it."

"Oh, I think you will. Do not forget about the girl." His eyes glinted as he looked toward Jael.

Deborah's stomach contracted as if she'd been punched. *Please God, get me out of here.*

Zuberi walked away from her. "Don't worry, Prophet. I'm not totally immune to your prudishness. I'll have my slave girls take you to the river." He poured two goblets of wine. "I would not presume to make you suffer the humiliation of having the men watch you bathe; unless of course, you force me to require the guards to bring you to the river." He held out one of the goblets. "Have some wine. It will make the process a little more tolerable." He paused for moment when Deborah refused to drink. "It is free of the poppy juice. You have my word."

Deborah knew she had little choice in the matter. Even if it were drugged, she'd drink it to spare Jael anymore torture. She took the cup and sipped. It was undiluted, but not drugged. At least not with what he'd given her before.

Zuberi watched her take another drink. "You can trust me, Prophet. I am only seeking your well-being." He drank from his own goblet. "I have already sent to Jezreel for suitable clothing. We cannot present you to Jabin, looking like you do."

Jabin? The king? A chill ran through Deborah's body. "How long will it take? To go to Hazor?"

"It depends." He took a sip of wine and held it in his mouth before swallowing. "If we stay with the army, it will take us about six days. We may decide to bring you on ahead. In a chariot, with a small contingent, the journey should take only three."

Deborah bit her lip and forced back her tears. She could not show any more fear to this man. He only fed off it. "I don't know why you bother. I will not serve at your temple. Not even to save the girl's life." Jael let out a soft moan, but Deborah did not look at her, afraid her resolve would fail.

The priest raised an eyebrow. "No? We shall see. I will have many more tools of persuasion in Hazor." He swept away from her and strode toward the back of the tent. Placing his goblet down, he clapped his hands. Four female servants entered from behind a curtain. "Take the older girl down to the river and bathe her. Wash her hair with the lavender oil and henna. When she is thoroughly clean, bring her to Sisera's tent and anoint her with oil and perfume. I want her looking like a noblewoman when you are through."

He turned back to Deborah. "I would drink all of that wine if I were you. I want you submissive during this little ritual. There will be guards posted nearby, so don't try to escape."

Deborah glared at him. "You gave your word. No men would be present."

"My eunuchs will hold a curtain for your privacy. The real men won't see anything, unless you misbehave."

Deborah lowered her head as Zuberi continued to bark out orders. *Lord, I need you! Please, rescue me now.* She continued to pray while the servants made preparations to take her to the river. Two large black men entered the tent. She had never seen skin so dark. One carried poles and a length of cloth. The eunuchs. They towered over Zuberi, their bald heads glistening with sweat. The priest pointed to Deborah and one of the giants came toward her. He held out his hand. Deborah sat frozen in fear.

The eunuch thrust his hand at her again as he said something in a different language. Deborah put her hand in his and he pulled her up. It surprised her that his palm felt dry, since the rest of the man's skin shimmered with a light sheen of perspiration. He towed her outside, followed by the servants. Deborah squinted in the bright sunshine. Her head resumed its pounding. When they reached the river bank, the eunuch waited for the other man to set up the poles. Once the curtain was up, her captor grabbed hold of the neck of her tunic, tearing it in half. Deborah screamed and tried to hold the front of her garment closed, but the giant slapped her then ripped the cloth from her body. Deborah fell to her knees, her arms trying futilely to cover her breasts. The eunuch backed away. The four women pulled her into the river. As the cold water shocked her warm skin, Deborah closed her eyes and prayed for deliverance.

Sisera pushed his chariot horses to the brink of exhaustion, but made it back to the camp well before sunset. A wind blew from the west, bringing cooler air from the sea. He took a deep breath before stepping down from his chariot. The scent of cooking fires woke his hunger, but he determined to find the girl first and hopefully put her out of his mind. He jogged to his tent and pushed the flap aside.

The two eunuchs flanked either side of the room, their eyes fixed straight ahead. The girl sat on the floor behind a low table, her head bowed. Two women sat next to her, rubbing her arms with oil. The rich scent of amber stirred his pulse. Another servant combed the girl's hair. It flowed over her shoulders and down her back. Dark brown curls with deep golden tones that caught the light. Sisera turned his gaze to the servants. "Leave us."

The three women stood and hurried past the general. He grabbed one by the arm. "Give us a few minutes, then bring food and wine."

The servant bowed. "Yes, my lord."

Sisera stepped inside and let the flap close. He looked to the eunuchs. "You. Wait outside the doorway."

The men left. The girl remained on the floor, her face hidden by her hair. The general swallowed. *Why is this so difficult? I've seduced any number of women in my life. Why is she different?* He knew it wasn't because the spirit, god, whatever had possessed her, had demanded it. He could easily pretend the role of lover. He did it whenever he slept with his own wife.

I want her to love me.

The thought surprised him. He took a step toward the girl, but stopped when he noticed her tremble. *Why? Why do I desire her? Above any other?* He knew when that need had come to him— when she'd looked at him before fainting. In that moment, she'd been open and vulnerable. She had desired him. Not as a lover, but as a protector. She had forgotten he was her captor and saw him instead as someone to shield her from whatever had invaded her soul. *And now, here I am, plotting to allow that spirit to use her for my gain.* He growled in frustration while pacing to the curtained section of his tent. Peering over his shoulder he saw the girl did not move.

In his private room, he stripped off his armor and bloody clothes. A bowl of water sat on a small table. Sisera used his tunic to wash the battle from his body. Naked, he approached the idol of Baal that stood on an altar in the corner of his room. *Help me, lord. Talk to your goddesses. Speak to Astarte, to Asherah. Free me from this desire and let me be the ruler I know I am destined to be.* His mood lightened after his prayer. A new sense of direction filled his spirit. *She is no more than a tool, not a girl at all. She is my path to ultimate power.* He smiled at the thought and thanked the gods for their gift of wisdom. He dressed himself in a modest floor length robe and tied the sash firmly about his waist before approaching the girl again.

"Deborah?"

The girl did not lift her head. He poured two cups of water then sat down on the opposite side of the table. "I don't know what you expect to happen tonight, but do not fear me. I have no plans to force myself on you."

She spoke so softly, he had to lean closer to hear her. "Then why am I here? Why did the priest dress me this way?"

"Did he not explain? You are to be presented to the King in a few days. In our culture, the dress you are wearing is appropriate for a woman held in esteem. Your peasant's garb would have made you seem unworthy of the King's attention." Sisera reached out and tucked a lock of hair behind her ear so he could observe her face. "We saw your power last night. We want to honor you, as best we can."

Deborah pulled her head away from his touch. She lifted her chin and looked at him.

Sisera's breath caught in his chest. *By god, those eyes! A man could drown in their depth. Haunted, yet strong. Help me, Baal, to resist her.*

"Why now?" she asked.

Sisera shook his head. "What?"

"Why must I be dressed like this now? It will be days before I see your king."

"I suppose Zuberi wanted you to get used to how they feel. We know this will be a change for you but our desire is to make you happy."

Her eyes flashed in defiance. "Then let me go home. That would make me happy."

He shrugged. "I am sorry. I can't do that. Zuberi has plans for you."

"What plans?"

"You should not concern yourself with them tonight."

Her eyes darkened as she glared at him. "Do not be so sure. I will never serve your gods. I'd rather die."

Sisera stared at the girl, impressed by her courage but knowing such strength would be futile against Zuberi.

A puzzled look crossed her face. "What do you know, General?"

He frowned. "I know you will wish you were dead. But there will be nothing you can do to stop Zuberi." Sisera sipped from his cup. "As gifted as you are, you are still a woman. You cannot win in a battle of strength against King Jabin and the priest."

"But I will not serve!" Deborah stood. "I won't speak any words to honor your gods." She paced angrily. "Nor can they force me to perform any ritual to glorify them."

Sisera watched her, his pity mixing with desire. Zuberi had done his job well. A necklace of turquoise stones hung at her throat. The dress she wore was cut deeply down her chest. A golden rope tied below her breasts accentuated her figure. The cream sheer fabric streamed to the floor. Shimmering Egyptian gauze flowed from her back to golden bracelets on her wrists.

The effect was stunning as the light from the torches in his tent glistened off the metallic threads in the garment.

She stopped pacing to glare at him. "Why do you look at me that way?"

"Because you are beautiful."

She let out her breath with a sound of defiance. "Do not seek to flatter me, General. I am not so easily swayed."

He stood and approached her. "It is not flattery. I speak the truth."

Deborah backed away. "I saw something else in your eyes, a sadness. You know what the priest plans to do with me, don't you?"

Sisera nodded, but said nothing.

Her face softened. "Please, General. Tell me something of what is to come."

I can deny those eyes nothing. "It will only cause you grief. Why not live a few more days in ignorance?"

"Because the pain I envision may be worse than what is to come." She walked away in agitation. "For years now, God has shown me what He intends to do before He does it. I find strength in knowledge." She spun back to him and knelt. "Please, General." Her voice broke. "What will happen in Hazor?"

His emotions warred within him. His duty to follow Zuberi's plan conflicted with his own to desire to possess the girl. He steeled himself but melted as he looked into Deborah's eyes. "The priest will present you to King Jabin. Then he will consult the oracles at the temple of Baal. When the time is right, probably within the month, Jabin will take your virginity on the altar."

Deborah's cheeks paled. She took a ragged breath.

Sisera cupped her face with his hand. Again, she shrank from his touch. He shook his head. "You cannot fight them. As powerful as you are spiritually, you will be helpless against them. It won't be a battle of wills, but of strength."

Her shoulders had slumped while he spoke to her, but now she straightened herself up, though she still knelt. Sisera admired her bravery.

Deborah's eyes searched his. "Why would they do this thing? What purpose does it serve your gods?"

"Zuberi believes that Baal will be pleased by the powerful offering and release the rains next planting season."

To his surprise, the girl laughed. "But Baal didn't stop the rains. YHWH did."

"What?"

Deborah stood, eyes gleaming as though on fire. "My God stopped the rain because His people are stubborn and unfaithful."

Her enthusiasm enthralled him. "How do you know this?"

"When His people fasted with me and prayed four years ago, God opened the heavens. But they are stiff-necked and fickle. As soon as we were blessed with a bountiful harvest, they forgot the Lord and chased after Baal and Asherah and Molech." She paced about the room, the bracelets sparkling as she gestured with her arms. She turned back to Sisera. "If the rains come, before I am given to Jabin, would they still do this thing?"

Sisera frowned. "The season for rain is over. There will be no more until the winter."

"If you told the priest that YHWH stopped the rain, that He would open the flood gates of heaven to save me, would Zuberi change his plan?"

"You can't do that. It is impossible."

Deborah's face lit up, like that of a child who had been given a great gift. "Nothing is impossible with my God. He turned the Nile to blood. He parted the Red Sea. He made the walls of Jericho crumble and the sun stop in the sky. He will cause the rain to fall to save his servant."

Sisera stepped toward her. "Your faith is commendable, but not practical." He reached out and held her shoulders. "There is nothing you can do, Deborah."

"I can pray," she said boldly. "And fast. I will leave the rest up to God."

This isn't going as I'd planned. She should be turning to me for solace, not her god. She twisted away from him, but he grabbed her arm. "Zuberi will not allow it."

Her eyes bored into his, as if she looked into his soul. "You fear him."

Sisera scoffed. "I fear no man."

Still those eyes searched him. "You fear your gods, then?"

"I fear nothing."

Small lines creased her forehead. "Nothing?"

He pulled her into his chest. "Nothing."

The girl breathed in sharply, her muscles taut under his grasp. Unlike his wife's soft body, Deborah's was hard and strong. Her eyes shone with emotion. Sisera ran his free hand through her hair and down her back. She shivered under his touch, *with apprehension or yearning?* He couldn't tell. When he spoke again, his voice was thick with desire. "I only fear what they will do to you."

"Why? What does it matter?"

She cried out when he tightened his grip on her arm. He breathed rapidly. He tried to control the anger welling up inside, but found it impossible to hold down. "I don't know why it matters." His fingers dug into her flesh. "What spell have you put on me, Prophet?"

Her voice trembled. "I have cast no spell."

His arms crushed her against his chest, his hand grabbed her hair and turned her face toward his. "But you must have. I have thought of nothing but your eyes. I think of Jabin taking you and my blood rages. I want no man to touch you." He kissed her forehead. "None but me." His lips pressed along her neck.

She writhed in his grasp, fighting to free herself. His arms held her caged against his body. "Do not resist, Prophet. Give yourself to me. I can save you from the priest. Even from the king." He forced his mouth to hers, relishing the fullness of her lips. He pulled away, staring into the girl's eyes. "Anything you desire, I could give to you."

"Nothing you could give me would be worth betraying my God."

He brushed the tears that spilled down her cheek with his fingertips. "Are you certain? Gold? Jewels? Power? What is it you desire? You need but name it."

Sisera could see the struggle that warred within her. It stirred his passion for her even more. He pulled her in and kissed her again. Deborah's body trembled under his touch.

"Please," she whispered. "You said you wouldn't."

Her denial enraged him. His fingers bruised her arms as he shook her. "Yes, I did. And why should it matter if I keep my word to you?" He flung her away. She stumbled and fell to the floor. "Do you know how many women I have taken, with their permission, or not?"

Deborah stared up at him. "But you won't . . . take me. Not now."

"I won't?"

She shook her head. Her hair lay disheveled about her shoulders, her face flushed. Sisera breathed deeply. The scent of her. The perfume. Her apprehension. Her power. It threatened to overwhelm him. He took a step toward her. *You mustn't take her now. Wait. Wait until Jabin has had her, then she will come to you of her own accord. You will rule her with desire, not with fear.*

"My lord?"

Two servant girls stood at the entrance to the tent. One carried a tray of food, the other, a pitcher. Sisera composed himself. "Put it down on the table then leave us."

The girls hurried to finish their task. Sisera lowered his hand to Deborah. "Come, Prophet. You may pray later, when you are alone. But there will be no fasting. You must eat."

She took his hand cautiously, but allowed him to pull her up and lead her to the table. He sat opposite her, then poured a goblet of wine for each of them. He drank his down and poured himself another. "Drink, Prophet. Drink and eat." He pushed a plate of meat toward her. "Talk to me. Tell me a story of your god, to take my mind off your eyes."

Deborah bowed her head. "Many years ago, before our Father Abraham had spoken to the Lord, there lived a man named Noah."

Sisera sipped the wine and let her voice wash over him like a gentle rain. *I will follow Zuberi's plan. I will deny myself of this girl until she has fulfilled the priest's purpose. But then, she will be mine.*

7 The Plains of Shamir

Later That Night

One of the eunuchs escorted Deborah to another tent after her dinner with Sisera. She stepped inside. Two of the women who had dressed her lounged in the corner. Several others slept on woolen rugs. The eunuch shoved her further into the tent then exited. Deborah waited a moment before peering outside. The large man lay across the tent entrance. He grabbed her leg and pushed her back. The women in the corner glared at her before continuing their conversation.

Smoke from a cooking fire clouded the air. The lingering scent of roasted meat made Deborah's stomach grumble. She had eaten little in Sisera's tent, convinced that through prayer and fasting the Lord would free her from the fate the priest laid out for her. Deborah surveyed the dimly lit room. Smaller than Zuberi or Sisera's tent, it housed six women including herself. As her eyes adjusted to the light, she caught sight of a figure huddled at the back wall.

"Jael?"

The girl lifted her head in response, but didn't speak. Deborah knelt by her. "Are you well?"

Jael nodded. "Are you?"

One of the women from the corner snickered as they both glanced at Deborah. She could tell by their looks they thought she'd slept with the general. She folded her knees to her chest, praying she wouldn't blush, but feeling the heat rush to her cheeks.

Jael's large eyes looked worried. "Did they hurt you?"

Deborah shook her head.

The girl stroked Deborah's arm, where small bruises, the size of a man's fingertips, showed the evidence of Sisera's anger. "He did hurt you."

"Not in the way that you think." *How do I explain how I feel? I loathe the man. I hate what I know he's done to others. And yet . . . I'm not afraid of him. Not like the priest.* She groaned as she tried to make sense of her thoughts. *He is a man of such great power, and yet, he fears me.* Deborah let that thought settle in her mind for a moment. *He fears and desires me.* She shuddered at the emotions that ran through her. Pride, power and ambition warred for possession of her until Deborah forced them aside. *Lord, do not let me be swayed by the craving for riches and prestige. Being your servant is the highest honor I could have. Knowing you as I do is the greatest reward. Help me Lord, to be free of this place. Free of this man and his gods.*

"Deborah? What is wrong? What did he do to you?"

Deborah trembled. "Nothing. Yet." She shifted so she sat next to Jael. "I'm cold. Would you lean over and warm me?"

Jael laid her head on Deborah's shoulder. "I saw the priest throw your clothes on the fire. Is he going to make you sleep in this dress?"

"Apparently." Deborah's teeth chattered slightly. "Grab us one of those blankets."

"The others wouldn't let me have one. They pushed me away."

Deborah lifted her eyebrows. "Did they?"

The girl nodded.

Deborah walked over to where the two servants sat. Their eyes flashed, but they did nothing as Deborah bent to pick up a blanket. When she stood again, she glared at the women. "I am to be presented to your king. As a woman of honor, not as a slave." She gestured to Jael. "That girl is my servant. You will treat her with all courtesy when I am gone. If not, I will tell Sisera that I am unhappy with your service to me, and I am sure that won't be pleasant for you." Their lips pressed into hard lines, but they said nothing. Deborah walked back to Jael and spread the blanket over them both. She put an arm around the girl's shoulder.

"You're not really my servant," she whispered. "I only told them that so they'd treat you better."

"What am I, exactly?"

Deborah pulled the girl closer. "You are my friend."

They sat quietly until the other women snuffed out the oil lamps and dampened the cooking fire before lying down to sleep. Jael's body tensed under Deborah's arm.

"What is wrong?"

"I don't like the dark." Jael's voice cracked. "I cannot stop the memories when it's dark."

"Try and think of happier things," whispered Deborah. "Tell me about your family. To what tribe do you belong?"

"My family isn't Hebrew. We're Kenite."

"I thought the Canaanites only attacked the people of Israel." She felt the girl's head shake.

"We lived among the people of Manasseh. I guess that's why they attacked us."

"Do you have other family? Someone you can go to when we get out of here?

Jael hesitated. "I have several uncles in Jezreel. Maybe I could live with one of them."

Deborah patted the girl's arm. "I have faith, little one. God will get us out of here. And when he does, I will see you safely to Jezreel. To your family." The girl shook with quiet sobs. "I promise you. God will free us."

Deborah stroked Jael's hair and sang quietly until the girl's shaking ceased. As soon as she was convinced Jael slept, she laid the girl down and covered her with the blanket. The dress Deborah wore did little to keep her warm in the cool night air, but she was too agitated to sleep anyway. She shivered as she knelt on the woolen rugs. *Lord, help me. Help us. If I must go to Hazor, please send the rains and save me from King Jabin. Do not let your servant be used in such a disgusting ritual. Do not let me be used to honor foreign gods. For you alone are God. You alone are the most high.* She leaned forward with her arms stretched out on the floor. *Forgive my sin, Lord. Forgive me for being tempted by Sisera. For craving, even for a moment, more than what you have given me.* On and on she prayed, fighting sleep and calling on the Lord.

Deborah.

Your servant is here.

Arise.

Deborah stood.

Take off your necklace and lay it beside one of the sleeping women.

She obeyed.

Do you see the embers of the fire?

Deborah walked toward the glowing wood.

Pick up a stick and carry it to the back of the tent.

She marveled as her hand went into the embers that she felt
no pain. Her fingers did not burn. She brought the stick to the
back of the tent.

Lay it down, so it touches the fabric.

Deborah placed the stick in the corner so it smoldered
against two panels. A breeze blew through the tent, igniting the
glowing wood into a flame. She watched, mesmerized, as the
hungry fire lapped up the walls filling the room with thick,
black smoke.

**Down on your knees, Deborah. Crawl to the girl and
wake her.**

Deborah placed her hand on Jael's mouth then shook her
awake. Even through the smoke, Deborah could see the girl's
frightened eyes. She tried not to yell, but had to speak loudly to
be heard over the roar of the flames. "The Lord is with us. Follow me to safety."

Jael nodded.

**Stay down, Deborah. Crawl under the tent and head
for the southern hills. Do not stand until I tell you.**

Deborah yanked on the bottom of the tent until she had a
big enough space for them to crawl through. She pushed Jael
through first then dug her way out. Jael stood up but Deborah
grabbed her hand and jerked her down. "We mustn't stand! Not
until I tell you!"

The fire swept up to the roof of the tent. The other women
woke as burning fabric fell in on them. One servant, engulfed in
flames, ran shrieking out into the camp. Deborah watched in
horror as the woman danced in agony while the flames consumed her. The wind whipped up, carrying blazing embers
across to the tents next to it. A few sparks traveled on the
breeze to the makeshift corral. The horses panicked as the wood
caught on fire. Soldiers woke, bleary eyed and confused. Some

ran to the river to fill buckets with water to try and stop the inferno. Some darted about, evading the crush of horse's hooves. Others simply ran in panic.

Deborah and Jael crept along the ground while soldiers dashed around them, oblivious to their presence. The horses narrowly missed them, stepping over their heads and legs, but never treading on the women. The stones on the ground cut their palms and knees, but otherwise they remained unharmed. Smoke blew around the camp, covering it in a dark cloud and obscuring the light of the moon. A cry caused Deborah to freeze in panic.

"Deborah!"

It was Sisera. She turned back to see the general running about the tent, trying to step into the flames.

Do not look back. Keep moving.

"Deborah!" Sisera called to the men around him. "We must save the prophet!"

Deborah pulled her gaze away and crawled faster. Jael struggled to keep up beside her. They were well away from the panic of the camp when the Lord spoke again.

Arise, Deborah. Head to the southern hills. Run!

"Now, Jael!" Deborah pulled the girl to her feet. "Follow me."

Behind them, the cries from the fire still drifted on the wind. Though the smell of smoke followed them, they had lost its inky covering. Deborah feared being sighted in the moonlight as they sprinted toward the refuge of the hills.

Jael stumbled and lay gasping on the dusty ground. Deborah crouched by her. "Come, little one. We must keep going."

Jael rolled over and retched. "I can't." She wheezed then coughed up a wad of phlegm. "My chest hurts."

Deborah rubbed the girl's back. "It's from the smoke. Just breathe easy, you'll feel better." She tried not to panic at their lack of progress. It would do no good to have the girl freeze up entirely. Deborah's eyes gazed at the hills looming in the distance. *We have a long way to go before the sun rises and we're found.* She estimated they had a good two hours before daybreak. Maybe three if there were clouds. "Can you stand?"

Jael groaned, but got to her feet. Deborah put her arm under the girl's for support. "We'll walk for a while. But we need to keep moving."

Jael dragged a foot forward as an answer.

"Good girl," soothed Deborah, her own body beginning to rebel at being to forced walk again. "Slow and steady. Here we go." She continued to murmur encouragements to Jael as they made their way toward the hills.

The hours passed swiftly even as the hills appeared to move farther away. Finally, as dark clouds drifted across the fading glow of the moon, the ground turned steeper. In the dim light, Deborah couldn't find a path up into the hills. The two girls stumbled and groped their way along, fighting exhaustion. Jael fell further behind.

Deborah stopped moving when she heard the girl cry out. "Jael?"

The trickling sound of falling pebbles was the only answer. Deborah's blood pounded in her ears. "Are you hurt?"

Silence.

Deborah slid herself downward. *I couldn't have gotten that far ahead of her. Could the girl have rolled down the hill? It's not that steep, is it?* "Jael?"

Rough hands grabbed her from behind and pulled her up. One covered her mouth before she could make a noise. She found her cheek pressed up against the beard of a very large man. "Make one sound, whore, and I will snap your neck. Understand?"

Deborah could not move her head much, but the small nod she gave him must have been a satisfactory answer. Soft grunts and squeaks told her that Jael was another man's prisoner somewhere nearby. Her captor spun her around. Muscular and tall, Deborah knew she could not escape him. His eyes leered at her.

"Some kind of priestess, are you? A prostitute for your god?"

"No."

The sharp sting of his hand across her face made Deborah's eyes water. She dropped to her knees, the man stood over her. "I didn't say you could speak."

He shoved a leather strap in her mouth and tied it behind her head. Next he pulled her hands in front of her. "What do we have here?" He yanked her arms up to examine the gold bracelets around her wrists. He ripped them off then pushed her back to the ground. He put the bracelets into a pouch at his side before tying her hands with another leather strap. He tugged her up against his chest when he was done. "I don't want to hear any of your heathen prayers while we walk."

Heathen prayers? Who is this man?

She spied Jael several yards ahead, being carried like a sack of grain over another man's shoulders. Her own captor dragged her behind him like a man leading a stubborn donkey. As the incline grew steeper, Deborah fought to keep her balance on the rocky terrain. Sunlight broke through the deep gray of dawn as they made their way up the hill. They came to a plateau and Deborah collapsed in fatigue. The man stepped into the entrance of a cave.

"Barak! We have visitors."

"Bring them inside."

Jael's captor carried her into the dark opening. Deborah's assailant kicked her. "Get up!"

Deborah got to her knees, but teetered to one side. The man grabbed the strap tied to her hands and jerked her to her feet. She fell against his chest. He put an arm around her waist and pulled her into the cave. The narrow entrance turned a corner. Deborah found herself in a large room lit by a fire. Several men sat along the back of the cave. One stood, his face hidden by shadows.

"Women, Jorim? Where did you find them?"

Deborah's guard shoved her forward, but held her shoulders so she wouldn't fall. "I wouldn't exactly call them women." He gestured to Jael with his head. "That one is just a girl. A slave it looks like." The rough hands dug into Deborah's shoulders as he shook her. "This one looks to be a whore. A temple prostitute, maybe."

Deborah flailed against her captor, trying to explain who she was, but the leather strap kept her from making any intelligible words. Her hair covered her face so the men couldn't see her desperation.

"Deker and I spotted them running across the plain, away from the fire. We caught them on the hill."

For a moment the only sounds Deborah heard were that of her heavy panting and her heart pounding in her chest.

The man in the shadows spoke again. "Put the young one down here. If she's a slave, she's probably Hebrew and not to be harmed. She may be able to tell us about the army we've been tracking."

Deborah's captor pulled her head back so his cheek rested against her forehead. "And this one?" Her hair still covered her face, but the way she stood allowed the men to take full view of her provocative dress, made even more revealing by the hard journey.

The man in the shadows chuckled. "Take the whore to the men. They deserve a little recreation."

Deborah screamed, but all that escaped her raw throat was a desperate whimper.

The large man holding her laughed. "I thought you'd be used to men by now. Of course, your Canaanite soldiers aren't as hairy as we Israelites, are they?" To make his point he ran his beard roughly across her face and neck. Deborah kicked and flailed as best she could, but the man was unfazed. She caught sight of Jael as they put the girl down on the ground. *Help me!* Deborah pleaded with her eyes. *Help me, Jael!*

The man dragged her down a short tunnel then thrust her into the center of a bigger cave. She only had a moment to look around. More than a dozen men lay on the ground. Some slept while others stretched and yawned as they woke. More figures sat along the curved walls. Torches around the room cast odd shadows, like black demons dancing on the walls. The air was thick with the musky scent of the men and the smoke of the torches.

Her captor spun her around, pressing her against his chest. "Me first."

The other men stirred around them. "What do you have, Jorim?"

Someone clutched a handful of her hair. "By God, she smells good."

Jorim pushed the man away. "She smells like smoke, you fool. She's come from the Canaanite camp."

Another man stuck his face into the back of her neck. "No, you can still smell the perfume on her." He grabbed her shoulders, tearing her away from Jorim. All the men gasped as they looked at her. The straps of the fine linen dress had fallen off her shoulders, exposing most of her breasts. The bottom fabric had been torn into shreds, so even her thighs could be seen. A dozen hands reached out to touch her, grabbing her hair, strok-

ing her arms and legs. They pushed her around the room, allowing different men to grope her.

"Enough!" The men stopped. Jorim strode forward. He
yanked Deborah to his side. "I found her. I get her first." He
thrust her onto the floor. "The rest of you can have a turn later."

Deborah rolled to her stomach and tried to crawl away.
Jorim easily flipped her to her back, slapping her face and
grinding her shoulders into the ground as she struggled to escape. He called behind him, "Deker! Come hold her arms."

Another man ran to her then pulled her bound hands over
her head. He ran his fingers through her hair as Jorim straddled
her body and tore the skirt of her dress open. Deborah thought
her heart would burst from terror as the huge man removed his
belt and lifted his tunic to his waist. *This can't be your will,
Lord! Help me!*

A thunderous voice echoed through the cave. "Stop!"

Jorim was too far along in his lusting to pay the voice any
heed. He pushed one of his knees between Deborah's legs and
forced them apart. He lowered himself onto her but was pulled
off by someone Deborah couldn't see. The man at her head let
go of her arms. She curled up into a ball, weeping.

She heard the sounds of a struggle over her own sobs. "You
said we could have her!"

"That's before I knew who she was."

"She's a whore. Anyone can see that."

"Not according to the girl." Someone approached her. "I
need to see her face."

A man knelt beside her. Deborah rolled away in panic.
"Deker, stop her." Hands reached out, lifting her by her shoulders so she sat up. The first man brushed her hair away from
her face. "Look at me."

Deborah couldn't lift her gaze. Humiliated. Shamed. She wanted nothing more than to die.

"Look at me!"

She looked at the man in front of her, filling her eyes with all the hatred and rage she could find within her soul.

He gasped. "Deborah?"

I know this man? She scanned his face. His red hair finally jogged her memory. *Lapidoth?*

He took a knife and cut the leather straps around her mouth and hands. When he finished, he backed away from her.

Deborah tore herself out of Deker's grasp then flung herself against the wall of the cave. No one moved. The only sound came from the snapping of the torch flames. Deborah opened her mouth to scream, but all that came forth was a pitiful whisper. Her grief welled up within her gut, she thought it would explode from her. She hit the wall with her fist and sucked in another breath. This time when she opened her mouth, she let out a small whimper that grew in volume until it reverberated off the cave walls. Lapidoth reached a hand toward her. She knocked it away.

"Don't touch me! Don't any of you touch me again!"

"Please," he begged. "We didn't know it was you."

Rage boiled through her blood. A righteous anger. She screamed again as she stood to face the men who'd attacked her. The spirit of God moved within her and she spoke with His authority. "This is why you fail! This is why God has turned his back on our people! You say you fight for Israel, to honor God, but you lie. You fight because you are filled with violence and hatred. You serve the gods of your own passions." She slapped Lapidoth across the face. "You didn't know it was me because you didn't seek God first when you saw the fire. The Canaanites treated me better than you. They at least sought the will of their gods before deciding my fate. They treated me with respect and honor.

"You all sought the will of your own lusts before the will of God!" She pulled the straps of her bodice up and covered her chest with her arms. "If you truly believed me to be a servant of Canaanite gods, you should have killed me before polluting your bodies with my wickedness. But instead you chose to wallow in decadence. Like pigs in mud. You disgust me."

Deborah crumbled to the ground. Jael ran from the tunnel toward her. She led Deborah away from the men and covered her with a blanket. Deborah pulled her knees into her chest, trying to make her body as small as possible. Again she wept. In rage. In humiliation.

Jael lay beside her, stroking her hair, murmuring softly, "Don't cry. All will be well. Please don't cry."

8 The Kishon Valley

The Following Morning

Sisera turned a piece of charred wood over with his sandal. The wind brushed his face and he lifted his head to scrutinize the camp. The mid-morning light made it easy to survey the damage. The foot soldiers had retrieved most of the horses. All the tents had been burned to ashes but only one of the wagons had been lost.

He could see the remains of two women lying among the smoldering tent, their bodies still letting off wisps of smoke. Sisera turned his head. What a horrible death.

Zuberi approached him. "Do you think we will find the other horses?"

Sisera shrugged. "I sent a patrol out to search the plains. I told them to look until mid-afternoon then join us outside of Jezreel."

The priest nodded, his eyes scanning the camp. "It is a shame about the prophet, but we need not tell Jabin about our plan. We will simply say he need not worry about her, now that she is dead."

"Are you sure?"

Zuberi's eyebrows lifted in surprise. "Nothing could have survived that inferno." He pointed to the skeletons. "Look at them."

"But how many women were in the tent? How many have we accounted for?"

The priest frowned as he thought. "We had five women with us, but Seria was with me."

Sisera kicked the smoking fabric of the tent. "There should be six bodies left, then. You put the girl in with the prophet, yes?"

"Yes." Zuberi pointed again to the skeletons. "These are the lucky ones, general. To have anything left at all. The others were probably buried under the tent until nothing was left but ashes."

Sisera called to one of the nearby soldiers. "You, come here." The man ran to his general's side. "I want you to gather as many men as you can and sift through this pile. I want any re-mains you find, human remains, uncovered. I want to know how many bodies were in this tent when it burned."

"Yes, sir." The man ran to a group of soldiers standing by the river and assembled them to help in the task.

Zuberi coughed as a breeze stirred up the ash. "What do you expect to find, General? The men and the horses have tracked through here as well."

Sisera ignored the priest and ordered the rest of the troops to pack in preparation for their departure in the afternoon. While the camp worked, the general stood watching the men sifting through the women's tent. It took an hour or so for them to uncover all remnants that survived the fire. Two whole skeletons and a collection of bones; several chalices and cooking pots; a few pieces of jewelry.

The general frowned. "I have never seen a fire burn so hot."

Zuberi's nose wrinkled up as Sisera poked at a skeleton with his sword. "What do you mean?"

"Fires are a common enough occurrence of battle." The skeleton pulverized into ash as he continued to poke it. "But I have never seen bodies destroyed like this."

The faces of the soldiers gathered around the tent looked fearful. They talked in low voices, but words like "punishment" and "the prophet" floated on the wind. Zuberi scowled. "Whatever the cause, there can be no doubt the girl is dead. The threat to our nation is gone."

Sisera paced around the pile the men had collected. Something caught his eye in a mass of bones. He bent down to brush away some ash and pulled up the turquoise necklace Deborah had worn.

A sharp pain knifed his stomach. He clutched the necklace to his chest. *No! She can't have burned!* Sisera stood with a growl and heaved the necklace away from him. Falling back to his knees he clawed at the pile of remains, searching for anything else of hers.

There was nothing.

He sat back, panting with exertion. The soldiers eyed him. He composed himself and brushed the dirt from his hands.

"Satisfied?" Zuberi stood near him.

Sisera frowned. "If the necklace survived, why not the bracelets?"

"Hmmm?"

"She wore golden bracelets on her wrists. Where are they?"

"Probably melted in the heat." He put a hand on the general's shoulder. "Come, my friend. It is time to go. There is nothing more we can do here."

Sisera rose, his gaze scanned the camp one more time then rested on the hills. *What was it she had said? Her god could part the Red Sea and cause the walls of Jericho to fall. Could he also cause a fire to free his prophet?*

9 The Hills South of Kishon

The Following Day

"Please." Jael pushed a piece of bread into Deborah's hands. "You must eat."

Deborah threw the bread over the girl's head. She saw the man, Jorim, pick it up. He cast a swift glance in her direction. His eyes filled with shame. *Good. I hope you choke on your guilt.* Deborah turned away to face the wall. Footsteps crunched hesitantly toward her. Jael backed up, covering Deborah with her body.

"Leave her alone."

"These are the prophet's." Something metallic clinked onto the ground, followed by a faltering sigh. "I'm sorry."

Jael showed Deborah the golden bracelets Zuberi had given her. "Here."

Deborah clutched them to her chest. *What do I do now, Lord?* Emptiness consumed her. She had no will. No thoughts except her sorrow. *What is to become of me?* She pulled the blanket up to her chin, trying to fend off the chill in her bones. Although she no longer sobbed uncontrollably, she couldn't stop single tears from escaping and running down her cheeks.

It had been a full day since she'd escaped from Sisera. She overheard Lapidoth and the men talking that the Canaanites had broken camp yesterday afternoon and moved north. Several men grumbled that they should follow them, but Lapidoth refused. "Not until the prophet is ready."

Deborah rested her head on the wall. Her soul cried out. *Oh, God . . . where are you?* Her heart longed for her father's arms. Azareel.

Go home, Deborah.

Deborah stiffened, unsure whether the voice was God's or her own desire. The familiar warmth of the Lord's presence stopped her shivering.

Go home. I have work for you in the hills of Ephraim.

She thought she was too dry to cry again, but tears of relief flowed freely. *Then you have not forsaken me? I am your servant?*

You are my beloved child. I will never forsake you.

But Lord, how can I face these men? To let them see my shame? How can I face my father?

The sin is not yours, Deborah. It is theirs.

But I feel so unclean. How can I ever serve you again?

You are innocent. Find your strength in me. I will make you whole again.

Deborah wept anew as God's peace flowed through her body, filling her with such a sense of joy she nearly laughed out loud.

Go home.

Deborah turned to the girl who sat like a sentry next to her. "Jael?"

"Yes?"

"Find Lapidoth. The red-haired man. Bring him here to me."

Jael ran off. Deborah looked around the cave. The men talked in hushed tones along the far wall. None looked in her direction. She wiped the tears from her face. As Jael approached with Lapidoth, Deborah pulled the blanket tighter around her shoulders.

Jael sat by her side while Lapidoth knelt down, several feet from her. "You sent for me?"

"The Lord has spoken."

Fear crossed Lapidoth's face.

"I am to go home."

He let his breath out slowly. "Of course."

"I cannot go in these clothes." She handed him the bracelets. "Take these into Jezreel and sell them. Take the money from one and buy me some decent clothes to wear. You're bound to have more money left. Buy supplies for our journey."

"What do I do with the money from the other?"

Deborah took Jael by the hand. "You will give it to the girl's family. To be her dowry."

Jael tried to pull away. "No! I want to stay with you!"

Deborah grabbed both of the girl's arms. "Listen to me, Jael. We have been brought together for a purpose. What it is exactly, I don't know. But now, for a time, we must be separated. My work lies in the South, but I feel certain you are to remain here. With your family in Jezreel."

"But I'm afraid."

Deborah cupped the girl's face with her hands. "Don't be, little one. The Lord's hand is upon you. You will do great things." The spirit within her affirmed her words. "I know this to be true. The God of Abraham will not forsake you, if you remember Him and remember me."

Now it was Jael's turn to weep. "I don't want to leave you."

Deborah smiled. "Be strong and courageous." She kissed Jael's forehead, then turned to Lapidoth. "You must take the girl into Jezreel with you. She has family there. Kenites. Find them and give them the money, but only on their oath that they will use it as her dowry. Understood?"

Lapidoth nodded. "Deker also has relatives in Jezreel who are Kenite. We'll have his wife accompany us, so there will be no scandal for the girl."

Not like my own disgrace. Deborah pushed the thought from her head. "Thank you."

"If we leave now, we can reach Jezreel by sundown."

Jael let out a soft moan. Deborah bit her lip to keep from crying. "That is for the best." She took Jael's wounded hand and gently kissed it. "Go, little one. And thank you for all you've done for me."

Jael fell into Deborah's arms. "I will never forget you."

Lapidoth called to the men in the cave and split them into three groups. He, Deker and Nathan would do Deborah's bidding in Jezreel. Jorim and the majority of the men would follow after the Canaanite army. Abiel, Neriah and Joseph would guard Deborah until Lapidoth returned. The men set about breaking camp and getting their provisions ready for their journeys.

Lapidoth approached Jael and Deborah. Cautiously, he put a hand on Jael's shoulder. "We must go."

Deborah pushed the girl from her chest. "Be brave."

Jael nodded.

Deborah forced a smile. "And help them to pick out a proper dress for me. Something a little more appropriate."

Jael lowered her eyes and hiccupped. She wiped away her tears then looked back at Deborah. "I will pick the finest dress the money can buy."

Deborah shook her head. "Don't do that. I have a long journey ahead of me. Look what happened to the fine linen of my last dress."

Jael sobbed and chuckled at the same time, causing her to end up in a fit of coughing. When she had gotten herself in control, she gave Deborah another hug, then stood up and walked to the entrance to the tunnel. A rock settled in the pit of Deborah's stomach as the girl turned back to look at her one last time. Deborah waved as Jael walked into the dark hallway. *Bless her Lord. Help Lapidoth to find her family. Keep her safe.*

Deborah slept through the rest of the day and night after the men left the cave. She awoke the next morning, famished and aching. She sat up, groaning from the pain in her arms and legs.

"Are you hungry?"

Deborah saw a man, Neriah, sitting at the back of the cave. His light brown hair and beard stood about his face like straw. She couldn't help but smile at his appearance. He lifted his hand up in her direction.

"Joseph has made some unleavened bread. Would you like some?"

"Yes, please."

He ran to the front cave. Deborah struggled to her feet. The room swayed so she sat back down. *Perhaps I should eat first.*

Neriah returned with a large piece of flat bread and a bowl of water. He stopped several feet away from her. Deborah reached out, but couldn't grasp the food.

"I'm afraid I'm a little weak. Can you bring it closer?"

Neriah ducked his head and shuffled closer to her. He held out the food again. This time Deborah was able to take it from his hands. He immediately backed away.

She took a bite of the dry bread. "Thank you."

His head bobbed, but his eyes stayed lowered. "You are welcome."

Deborah sipped some water to help her swallow. "You're Neriah, right?"

"Yes."

"I remember you from my uncle's house." She paused for a moment. "It seems so long ago now."

The man paled. "I wish you didn't."

"What?"

He let out a moan. "I wish you didn't remember me. I'm so sorry for what happened. For what we did. I never . . . we didn't mean . . . ." He sat on the ground and put his head in his hands.

Deborah didn't know what to say. She could not forgive the men yet, her pain too near the surface. She ate quietly while he wept.

After several minutes, Neriah lifted his head. "If it takes the rest of my days, Deborah, I will make right this insult against you. I will protect you with my very life."

"Thank you."

The young man stood. "Do you need anything else? Now, I mean? More to drink?"

"I would like to try standing up, but the last time I did, I found my legs a little weak." She held out her hand. "Do you mind helping me?"

He appeared terrified at the prospect of touching her. Deborah pushed herself up along the wall and took an unsteady step. She held the blanket around her shoulders with one hand and reached out to Neriah with the other. He sighed, whether in resignation or for strength, she couldn't tell. Together they walked to the front cave. A cool breeze blew through the entrance, bringing fresh air. Deborah breathed in deeply. Joseph and Abiel watched them from the floor.

Deborah swayed unsteadily. "Can I sit by the entrance? The air feels wonderful."

Neriah guided her to the plateau outside of the cave. The sun crested the horizon, blazing the sky in brilliant hues of orange and pink. Thin wisps of clouds hung low, still colored a deep purple from the night. Deborah squinted in the morning light and sat with the cave wall at her back for support. Shivering, she drew the blanket closer to fend off the wind.

"Would you like another blanket?" Neriah asked.

"No. It's refreshing." After the heat of the plains, the oppressive air in Zuberi's tent, and the musty smell of the cave, the mountain air was a welcome change. *Has it been only four days since I was in Shamir?* She reviewed her ordeal. One day of walking in the plains. The next in the tents of Zuberi and Sisera. The night of the fire and then a night in the cave. Four days. Three nights. *How my life has changed in such a short time. Why is it Lord that day to day minutes seem to stretch on forever, only to be broken up by sudden tragedy? In those moments, time seems as tenuous as leaves dancing on the wind. It floats, it spirals. Out of control and in no direction. I cling to you, Lord, for I know that you are good. I have heard your voice and know that you have a plan for me. Even in my despair, I will trust in you.*

Deborah prayed and meditated until the afternoon sun baked even the hills and the heat became unbearable. She napped in the front cave awaiting the return of Lapidoth and his men from Jezreel. They arrived well before sunset. A woman accompanied them.

Lapidoth glanced at Deborah as he put down the bundles he carried. "This is Deker's wife, Judith. She will travel with us."

Judith stepped forward. Although a brown cloth covered her hair, a long black braid hung over her shoulder. Her dark eyes looked at Deborah with compassion. "We have brought clothes for you to wear. Let me help you dress."

A sudden shyness overcame Deborah. She lowered her chin. *I have not sinned. I need not be ashamed.* She repeated the Lord's words to herself before speaking. "Thank you, Judith." She glanced toward Lapidoth. "Is there someplace I could wash first?"

He fiddled with a knot on his belt. "There's a stream, up the mountain a ways."

"I'll bring some water down," said Neriah. "It is too far for her to walk, Barak. She is still very weak." Lapidoth looked at him with curiosity, but nodded his head in agreement.

Deborah wondered at the name Barak that Neriah had used, but didn't have time to question it before Judith helped her stand. They walked to the back cave. "You rest here, and I'll start supper while we wait for the water."

Judith returned with Neriah a short time later. She laid Deborah's new clothes on one of the rugs. Next, she held out a bowl for Neriah to pour water in, then she shooed him into the front cave. A towel hung from the sash at her waist. Judith pulled it out and soaked it in the water. "Come." She waved to Deborah. "Let me help you."

Tears pooled in Deborah's eyes. *Why can't I stop crying? The Lord has taken my shame.* "I can do it myself."

Judith put the towel back in the water but didn't leave. Instead she moved closer to Deborah, her eyes staring intently. "This is the hardest part. The first time you shed the clothes you wore." She pointed to the blanket Deborah still held clutched around her body. "The first time you remove the covering." The woman dropped her gaze. "But you must. You must go on." When she looked up again, her own eyes were moist with tears. "Please. I have been where you are now. Let me help you."

Deborah caught her breath. "You?"

Judith nodded. "Canaanite soldiers. I was already married to Deker. Praise God he did not cast me away. Instead he swore vengeance. That is why he fights with Barak."

Deborah took the hand Judith offered and walked over to the bowl of water. Judith coaxed her to let go of the blanket. Deborah shivered as it fell to the ground. The dark-haired woman murmured soothing words as she helped Deborah strip off the remains of the Canaanite dress. Once naked, Deborah sank to her knees. Judith used the towel to gently scrub dirt and dried blood from Deborah's hands and arms.

"It will be all right," Judith crooned. "You will survive this. Cry now, but do not let this destroy you." She helped Deborah to sit back so she could clean the cuts on her knees and shins. All the while she kept speaking words of encouragement as Deborah wept. Judith scrubbed Deborah's calloused feet, then proceeded to wash her back. When she finished, she helped Deborah put on a new tunic of cream linen. Over this, she placed a dress of light blue wool. Judith wrapped a stripped woolen sash around Deborah's waist and tied it. Once Deborah had her new clothes on, her torrent of tears subsided.

Judith sat her back on the woolen rug. "Let me braid your hair."

Deborah relaxed under her new friend's ministrations. Judith pulled the brush carefully through Deborah's hair, trying to remove the tangles and dirt that had accumulated during her ordeal. Deborah closed her eyes. "May I ask you something?"

Judith tugged a particularly hard knot of hair. "Of course."

"If Deker knew what happened to you . . . why?" She struggled to put her thoughts into words. "How could he . . . ."

Judith put the brush down. "Men are different when they are with other men. Alone, they can be sweet and gentle. Most of them like little boys who long for us to comfort them." She picked up the brush again. "But when they are with other men.

It is like they're animals. They don't think the same. They don't act the same." She finished brushing Deborah's hair and began braiding it. "For what it is worth, this has shamed them all. I don't think they will ever take a woman in violence again. Even Barak has been subdued by all this."

"Why do you call him that?" Deborah tried to turn her head, but Judith pushed it forward so she could finish the braid.

"Barak? That's what Deker has always called him. Why?"

Deborah shrugged. "His name is Lapidoth. It means 'flame.' He's brother-in-law to my cousin Adara."

Judith tied the braid with a length of string then unfolded a piece of linen so Deborah could wrap her hair. "You'll have to ask Barak what it means."

Deborah bent at the waist as she fixed the scarf around her head and tied it. *"Barak" means lightning. Why change from flames to lightning?* Standing up, she straightened the scarf and her dress.

Judith smiled. "Much better. How do you feel?"

Deborah took a deep breath. "Like I will survive."

"Good." Judith put a hand on Deborah's shoulder.

"I've made some barley stew. Come and eat. I hear we have a journey ahead of us."

Deborah nodded. "Yes. A very long journey."

The six men and two women made a strained group around the fire. Only Lapidoth looked at Deborah, and then only with cautious glances when he thought she couldn't see him. Judith prattled on about family gossip with Deker, trying to put the rest of the group at ease. For Deborah's part, she reveled in the fresh bread and cheese the men had brought back from Jezreel, as well as the thick barley soup Judith had made. It had been days since she'd had a decent meal and both her body and soul were strengthened by it. She set her plate down reluctantly after she'd wiped it clean with a piece of bread.

Judith interrupted her chatter for an instant. "Would you like more?"

"Yes, please." Deborah kept her gaze down. "If there is enough."

"Of course there is." Judith scraped another serving from the bottom of the pot. She glanced over to Lapidoth and arched an eyebrow. "I'm sure she'd like more bread as well."

Lapidoth tore the piece of bread he held in two and passed one half to Deborah. She smiled briefly in thanks before tucking into her second meal. Lapidoth grinned.

"I guess you finally got hungry."

Deborah nodded. "Yes." She glanced at Judith. "The stew is wonderful."

"Thank you."

When Deborah finished her meal, she sat back contentedly and faced Lapidoth. "Did you find Jael's family?"

Lapidoth took a drink from a wine sack before passing it to Nathan on his right. "Yes. One of her uncles lives outside of Jezreel with his family. They're iron workers. They make plows and swords. She will be safe with them."

"Good." Deborah waited until his eyes caught her glance. "Thank you."

He held her gaze for a moment then tipped his head. "It was the least I could do."

Beside him, the black-haired Nathan took a drink. He chuckled before passing the sack on to Deker.

Lapidoth hit his friend's knee. "Why do you laugh?"

Nathan looked at Deborah with apology, but then ducked his head while laughing again. "I'm sorry. I'm just thinking of what

I heard in the market while I waited for you and Deker to return."

"What did you hear?" asked Lapidoth.

The man's dark eyes sparkled in amusement, glad to be the
center of attention, and having news to offer. "The Canaanite
army came through the town yesterday."

"We all know that." Deker smacked Nathan on the shoulder.
He passed the wine sack on to Judith.

"But the merchants were talking about the prophet." Nathan
lowered his head, but looked up at Deborah. "The soldiers told
them that the God of the Israelites burned his prophet, rather
than have her serve the Canaanite gods." He looked at the people gathered in the cave. "They are worried that now they will
be punished for capturing her in the first place."

Lapidoth smiled. "Good! Let them fear our God, whether he
caused the fire or not."

Deborah sat up. "But he did."

"Did what?" asked Neriah.

"He did start the fire. Or rather, He told me what to do."

They looked at her in amazement, so she told of how the
Lord had spoken to her while she prayed. When she finished,
the men again could not meet her gaze. All but Lapidoth soon
left the circle and settled on blankets to get ready for the night.
Deborah helped Judith wash and pack the utensils away for
their journey in the morning. Lapidoth waited until they completed their task before asking Deborah to step aside to the
cave entrance.

"It will take us take us a good three days to reach Shiloh. It
would be best if we stopped along the way in Shamir with
Michal."

Deborah shook her head. "No. I must not pass through Shamir again. And I'm not going home to Shiloh."

Lapidoth reached his hand out toward her shoulder, but placed it on the cave wall instead. "What do you mean?"

"Don't you see? The Canaanites think I'm dead. That is part of God's plan, I'm sure of it. If I am seen in Shamir, or even Shiloh, the news will get back to Sisera that I am alive."

"The general? Why would that matter?"

Deborah questioned her intuition but felt the Spirit affirm her belief. "If he knows I'm alive, he will not rest until he has hunted me down and brought me back to him."

Lapidoth pushed his hand away from the wall and stood back from her. The look on his face showed the disbelief he did not dare voice to "the prophet."

She frowned at his scrutiny. "Do not look at me that way. Sisera believes I have cast some kind of spell on him. I don't know why, but it's true." The Spirit moved her to speak without thought to her words. "The moment he finds out I'm alive will be the end. A battle such as that in Joshua's day will ensue. But it will not be until the Lord says it is time." Deborah trembled as the Spirit released her.

Lapidoth watched her with a sense of awe. She stood up straight. "We will not go through Shamir, but we may stop at Shiloh. I will enter veiled and in secret. I will need to see the high priest and tell him what has happened, and what needs happen now."

"And what is to happen, Prophet? What has the Lord decreed?"

Deborah held his gaze. "That I go home to the hills of Ephraim. To my father Azareel. There the Lord has new work for me to do."

Deborah and her companions stayed away from the main roads and traveled in the hills. The men tended to herd together in the lead, occasionally joking or arguing with each other. Judith and Deborah walked behind, with Neriah bringing up the rear. For the first day, Judith tried to draw Deborah into conversation, but when the prophet only answered in short, one word answers, she gave up. Deborah didn't mean to be rude, but her mind dwelled on the potential dangers of their journey as well as the questions that filled her heart. *Do I tell Azareel and Avram what has happened? Do they need to know? What if I am seen and captured by the Canaanites again? Can I resist Sisera and his desire for me?*

Her body had not yet recovered from the anxiety of her capture or from the night of her attack. Each new rise on the path made her muscles groan, but Deborah didn't complain. Neriah noted her slowing pace on the second day and offered to take the pack she'd been assigned to carry. At first she refused, but by mid-morning when he asked again, she let him take it. "Thank you."

Neriah frowned slightly. "I wish we didn't have to make this journey yet." He shifted her bundle onto his back. "You needed more rest."

"I will be fine." She looked out from the crest of the hill they stood on, the uninhabited land stretched out below them. Deborah sighed. "The Lord wants me to go home to Ephraim. He will see me safely there."

Judith waited for her to catch up, but Deborah hesitated by Neriah. "Can I ask you something?"

"Of course."

Her gaze wandered to Lapidoth and the other men. "Why do you call him Barak?"

Neriah indicated with his head that she should start walking again. "I was told one of the priests gave him the name when he sent him out to fight the Canaanites."

"But why Barak?" asked Deborah.

"Because he's unpredictable, like lightning. And because that is the way he attacks. Quick and deadly."

By late afternoon they neared Shiloh. Deborah and Judith fixed their veils to conceal their faces. Judith walked beside her husband while Lapidoth and Neriah took positions on either side of Deborah. The men had become strangely quiet during the course of the day. Deborah thought it might be their apprehension at entering the city, but suspected something more. All of them cast furtive glances her way, then at Lapidoth.

She looked at the position of the sun. "There is still plenty of time before sunset. I want to see Phinehas before I go to Leb's house."

Lines creased Lapidoth's forehead as he considered what she'd said, then he nodded. "You and the others go to the Tabernacle. Neriah and I will go to Leb's house and prepare him for your arrival."

"What do you mean, 'prepare him?'"

The soldier's face hardened. "You do what you must at the Tabernacle, Prophet. I will do what I must in the city."

Her voice quivered as she spoke. "My family doesn't have to know. Please."

Lapidoth put a hand on her shoulder, but pulled it away when she flinched. "I will do what is right. Do not fear. You will not be shamed again."

He stepped away from the group and looked to the men. "Neriah and I will go into Shiloh. The rest of you accompany the prophet to the Tabernacle. We'll meet at the house of Leb, the lamp maker, at sundown."

The Tabernacle soon came into view and the party split up. Deborah tried not to think about what Lapidoth would say to her family and instead prayed for the words to speak to the

High Priest. They fell in with another group of pilgrims making their way toward the holy tent. Joseph and Abiel engaged them in small talk, but the rest of their group remained quiet. Deborah could see Phinehas sitting outside of his tent. She caught up to Deker and Judith.

"Send the others ahead. Let them say they are just travelers who desire to pray at the holy Tabernacle. We will go to the High Priest's tent. Tell those that guard him you have a dispute between your wives that you need his council on."

Deborah's heart pounded as she approached Phinehas. The men who kept watch over the High Priest stopped them as they neared. Deker stepped forward and gave Deborah's story to them. The men smiled in sympathy, but shook their heads.

"That is not a matter for the High Priest. There are elders in Shiloh who can help judge their argument. Take your women there."

Deborah glanced around her to make sure no one else stood near. She stepped forward and lifted her veil. "Please, Phinehas. Forgive my deception, but I need to speak with you."

The old man frowned. "Who are . . . ." His face lit up with recognition. "Prophet!" He struggled to stand. The priests who served him ran to assist him.

Deborah took a few more steps toward him then knelt. "Please, Phinehas. Do not announce my return."

The old man stood before her. He took her face in his wrinkled hands. "Praise God that you are safe! We heard that you were taken by the Canaanites. There were rumors you'd been killed."

Deborah covered the priest's hands with her own. His thin skin barely covered the bones underneath. "I know. And for a while, I must remain as if dead."

Phinehas stared down at her. "But why? Surely we should rejoice at the Lord's mercy?"

"Indeed, but not publicly. It is not yet time. And the Lord has work for me to do in the hills of Ephraim."

"There is nothing in the hills." The old man shook his head. "What can you do for Him there?"

"He has not made that clear to me yet. But I am certain that is where I'm to go." She took his hands from her face but held them in front of her. "I needed to see you. To let you know that I still live. That YHWH has a plan." The Spirit within her moved, giving her words to speak. "When you hear news from the hills, you will know it is me. Listen for the Lord and act on his will. The final phase of His plan is unfolding, Phinehas. Remember as the turmoil increases, God has not forsaken us. He will defeat our enemies." Deborah let go of his hands and sat back on her knees. "Please." Her voice now sounded weak. "Don't tell anyone of my return until the Lord commands you."

"Of course, my child." He stared into her eyes with concern. Deborah's soul longed to confess all that had happened over the past week, but she held her tongue. Phinehas's gaze intensified. "You have been through much."

Deborah could only nod. If she spoke, the tears would fall again.

He watched her as she struggled with her emotions for a moment, then he reached out to cup her face. "The Lord passes His servant through trials like gold in the crucible. Refining it. Making it stronger." His hands moved to the top of her head. He pressed them down as he spoke. "Bless Your servant, Oh Lord. Do not let her be overcome by the trials she has seen or the trials that are to come. Fill her with Your strength. Fill her with Your peace. Fill her with Your joy." He kissed her forehead. "Amen."

They met back with Nathan, Abiel and Joseph then headed into Shiloh. The sun sat low on the horizon, causing them to quicken their pace, not wanting to be stuck outside the city when the gates closed at sunset. Deborah led them through the winding streets to her uncle's house. They arrived as dusk fell. Rachel stood at the door, waiting for them. The worried lines on her face slackened as she spied them coming down the alley.

"Thank the Lord! Lapidoth said you would be arriving." Neighbors looked out of their doors in curiosity. Rachel smiled in their direction. "Family from the north come to visit. I will tell you of their news tomorrow." She hurried the group into the house. Once inside, Deborah and Judith removed their veils. Rachel rushed to embrace her niece, her voice filled with emotion. "Thank God you are safe. When we heard you had been taken . . . ."

Deborah squeezed her back. "I'm fine, Aunt. I'm sorry you were worried."

"Come, come." Rachel ushered her guests to the center of the room and directed them to sit. Deborah introduced the others as Uri and Neriah came in from the courtyard. Katriel brought out a pitcher of water and a bowl for the guests to wash their feet, while Rachel served them a sack of diluted wine. She asked the men about the journey and chatted with Judith about the hardships of traveling through the hills.

Deborah looked around the room and out to the courtyard. "Where are Leb and Lapidoth?"

Her aunt's silence fell on the room like a hammer. She couldn't meet Deborah's eyes.

Uri finally answered her question. "They went into the market." He glanced at Neriah then dropped his gaze. "They should be here shortly."

A hush remained over the room. Deborah surveyed the faces around her. Strained, pale and worried. "What is going on?

What are Leb and Lapidoth doing?" Joseph coughed. Abiel and Nathan looked at their hands. "Rachel?" Deborah stood. "Neriah?" Her heart raced in her chest. "Tell me!"

"Deborah!" Her uncle's voice called from the doorway. He tried to hide the troubled look in his eyes with a grin, but Deborah could see it lurking behind the mask. He strode forward with his arms open, but hesitated before he embraced her.

Deborah glared over her uncle's shoulder to Lapidoth. "You told him."

The red-haired man stood silent in the doorway, his face set in stone. Deborah's heart sank when he gave a slight nod of his head. She backed away from Leb. "I should never have come here." His look of pity revolted her. She ran from the room, up the stairs to the roof. Coming to the ledge, she thought of throwing herself off. *It isn't high enough to kill me.*

"Deborah, please." Her uncle put a hand on her shoulder.

She shook it off. "I don't want your pity. I don't need anything from you."

"You need to show me respect. No matter what has happened." His round cheeks quivered as he spoke. "You owe me that much."

Deborah swallowed her anger. "I am sorry, Uncle." She glowered at Lapidoth, standing in the shadows. "I was hoping to forget what happened. To keep it to myself." She glanced back at Leb. "No one expects me to marry. No one else needed to know my shame."

Leb held her hand. "But he has asked my permission to marry you." A shocked gasp escaped her throat and she tried to pull her hand away. Her uncle held it tightly. "I told him he must speak first with Azareel, but that I thought he would agree." Deborah struggled against her uncle. He let go of her hand but grabbed her shoulders. "Listen to me. In this way you will avoid disgrace. Your shame will stay within the family. You can still have the honor of being God's chosen prophet!"

Deborah pointed a finger at Lapidoth. "I have that honor without marrying him!" She turned the finger back to her chest. "God still speaks to me. He has told me what to do next."

Lapidoth pushed Leb aside. "You would have this sin lay on my head, and my men's, before God? You would not let us do what is right and commanded by the Lord?"

Her chest grew tight. "What do you mean?"

Lapidoth shook with bridled rage. "God has commanded. If a virgin is raped outside of town, the man who violates her must marry her. Jorim already has a wife. It would only cause you more pain to marry him. Besides, it was on my order that he . . . did what he did. I may as well have taken you myself."

Leb groaned and sat on the ledge of the roof. He put his head in his hands. Tremors ran through Deborah's body, a combination of anger and grief. She willed herself not to let her emotions overtake her. "He didn't complete the act. I'm still a virgin in the eyes of God."

Lapidoth stepped forward. "It doesn't matter. Deborah, if what happened became known, it would ruin your reputation."

She crossed her arms around her waist. "Who would tell?"

"There were too many men present. It only takes one to confess his guilt to another in a drunken stupor and the story will spread."

The world spun around her. Deborah reached out her hand and balanced herself on Lapidoth's arm. He held himself still until she caught her breath. When she realized she leaned on him, she pushed herself away then walked to the far edge of the roof.

He came up beside her and spoke low. Deborah knew Leb wouldn't hear what was said between them. "There is something else I need to know before I ask your father."

Deborah bowed her head and hugged her arms across her chest. "Yes?" She waited for his question, but he remained silent. She peered at him from under her eyebrows. He concentrated on the early night sky. He took a deep breath as if he'd come to a great decision.

"Is it possible that you are with child?"

Her arms dropped to her side. "What?"

His eyes strayed to Leb then he grabbed her arm to pull her closer. She was too shocked by his question to react to his touch. "The girl . . . ."

"Jael?"

"Yes," he whispered. "She told us the Canaanite priest had drugged you one night. The next you were sent into Sisera's tent. Alone." He searched her face. "When you came back, you wore the Canaanite dress and your arms were bruised."

Deborah pulled away from his grasp. "And what would you do if I were? Would you forget your proposal since I'd already been ruined?"

Even in the gray light of twilight, she could see his hazel eyes fill with pain. He swallowed before he spoke. "Then we would forgo the betrothal period. I would marry you within the week and stay with you in your father's house."

Deborah sat down hard on the ledge. She didn't know whether to be pleased with Lapidoth's honor or angry at his practicality. She rubbed her face with her hands before looking up at him. "And if I am still a virgin?"

"Then I would leave you with your father after the betrothal while I continued to lead my men in the North. When . . . ." He glanced away, his eyes surveying the city below him. "When you felt you were ready, when the thought of marrying me didn't . . . ." He shrugged. "When it didn't repulse you so much. You could send for me and I would return and take you as my wife."

Deborah studied the man in front of her. He stood taller than Azareel. His body well-proportioned from his life as a soldier. A leader, as she was. His eyes stared down at her. She could read his concern for her in their depths. "I am not pregnant."

Lapidoth released his breath slowly then knelt in front of her. "You are sure? Were you drugged again?"

She shook her head. "No. The priest had bigger plans for me."

"What do you mean?"

Why not tell him everything, this man who wants to be my husband? "My virginity was of greater value to them than to your men. They intended to sacrifice my virtue on the altar of Baal. I'm sure it would have been quite a spectacle. Perhaps the crowds would have been allowed to watch."

She felt the rage pulsating from Lapidoth's body. He took her hands. "They told you this?"

Deborah nodded. "Sisera did. That night in his tent. It's why he wouldn't—"

His fingers tightened painfully around hers. "Why he did not rape you himself?"

"Do you see why marrying me is a foolish idea? I am not just Deborah. I am an instrument of God." She tore her gaze from his and stared at the lights from the house next door. "There are those who, if they found me, would try to use me for evil."

He placed his hand under her chin and turned her head to face him again. "That is why you need someone to protect you."

"I don't need you to protect me out of guilt."

"It isn't guilt alone."

Deborah blinked away the tears in her eyes as she focused on her hands, folded in her lap.

Lapidoth lowered his head so she could see his face. "I have only truly known you for a few days, but I have seen how strong you are. How courageous." He cupped her face, wiping the tears from her cheeks with his thumbs. "Deborah. I never thought to look for a wife, because I never thought I would find one strong enough for the kind of life I lead. Until I met you. Please. Let me make an agreement with your father." He glanced back at Leb, who still sat behind them on the ledge. "Your uncle and I will go to the market to buy gifts for the bride price. It will be a respectable betrothal ceremony. One befitting a woman of your honor. And virtue."

Oh Lord, what should I do? She waited to hear His command. *Is this your will for me?* When she heard it, it came as a whisper on the breeze.

Yes, Beloved.

She lifted her head to Lapidoth and nodded. "I will marry you."

10 Jezreel

The Following Morning

Sisera waited on the plains outside of Jezreel for a week until the rest of his army rendezvoused with his division. He sent spies into the city seeking any information on Deborah, but none could be found. If she'd survived, she hadn't come this way. Against Zuberi's advice, the general ordered the spies to Shamir to see if the prophet had returned to her home.

Once his army had convened, he inventoried their plunder. It took a full two days to assemble the various goods into separate areas where they could be counted and organized. The wagons of grain, those of pottery and jewelry, the livestock, the prisoners, all had to be recorded then distributed between the kings. Of course, Shaul of Megiddo and Jabin of Hazor would receive the largest portions, as they provided the most men, but every king would demand some of the campaign's profits.

Sisera called his officers together to his tent. "I have made a complete listing of all that was taken. Bela, you will be in charge of Shaul's portion. Magdiel, for the king of Carmel; Ezer for the chiefs of the pass and Alvah for the minor kings of the seacoast towns. I will take the rest to Jabin in Hazor."

Zuberi entered the tent, glowering. "General, why wasn't I asked to attend this council?"

Sisera clenched his teeth. "You are not one of my men, Priest. You have no say in how the goods are divided, nor can you see them safely transported to the various cities. I saw no reason to include you in this discussion."

The priest strode forward. "I am an emissary for King Shaul. I should be informed of all decisions that affect him."

"Bela will be leaving tomorrow with Megiddo's share. You can accompany him and see it safely brought to your master."

Zuberi's voice rose. "I am no man's slave, Sisera."

The general smiled. "I never said you were."

"You implied it," the priest spat.

The smile faded from Sisera's face. "I have business to discuss with my officers. If you wish to talk to me after my work is done, you may wait outside. But I have other matters to attend to now." He turned from the priest and focused on his officers. Zuberi made a grunt of discontent, but left the tent.

It took another hour to finalize the plans for the grain's distribution. Army divisions had to be reassigned to protect the caravans as they made their way throughout Canaan. The last order of business was to settle accounts with the soldiers. Sisera handed chests of coins to the leaders of each division.

"Pay the men when you reach your destinations," ordered Sisera. "We will lose too many along the way if we pay them now."

The officers nodded in agreement and, with a signal from their general, they disbursed from the tent. Zuberi strode in as the last man left.

"Why this insult, Sisera?" The priest's face was red. He pointed a finger at the general. "Do not think I won't tell Shaul of your behavior."

Sisera gestured to the low table. "Sit, my friend. Have some wine with me."

Zuberi stopped, his eyes reflecting his confusion. "What are you playing at?"

"I play no games." Instead of the irritated sigh he longed to voice, Sisera smiled graciously. He knew he must mollify the situation. He gestured again to the table in the center of the room. "Sit." He poured some wine and served a goblet to Zuberi. "I am a soldier first. When plans are being laid out and orders need to be given, I do not stand on courtly formalities."

The priest's eyes hardened. "It was not a mere formality that brought me here. I also had business to attend to on this campaign." He took a sip of wine as Sisera sat down opposite him.

"Yes. And what will we tell Jabin and Shaul of that business?"

Zuberi arched an eyebrow. "I thought we had already discussed that. The Israelite leader was killed in the fire. There is no need to fear them uniting against us."

Sisera shook his head. "I do not believe it. There were not enough bodies in the tent."

"It was impossible to tell how many died in there." The priest's voice rose. "You found her necklace, what other proof do you need?"

The general stood and paced the room. "A body."

Zuberi studied him. "Why?"

Sisera turned to his adversary. "To prove to myself that she is dead." He took a deep breath. "I want to be sure before I make any promises to Jabin."

"Is that the only reason?"

"What do you mean?"

Zuberi's fingers caressed the stem of his goblet. "I have to admit, I'm sorry she left us like she did. She cleaned up very nicely. I was rather looking forward to her services in the temple."

Years of training on the battlefield came to Sisera's aid and kept him from allowing his anger to overwhelm him. He took a drink before he spoke. "She was a tool to win us power, nothing more."

"Are you sure? You did not desire her for yourself?"

Sisera laughed. "What man does not desire a beautiful woman? But what I will miss is the opportunity to use her for our advancement."

Zuberi frowned and sipped his wine. "It is disappointing. But there is nothing to be done now."

"That is not true." Sisera strode toward the priest. "Jabin could send his spies throughout the southern lands."

Zuberi put his goblet on the table and stood to face Sisera. "We will not tell the kings that there is chance she lives."

"But it is a possibility."

The priest's face grew hard, his eyes glaring. "No, General. It is not a possibility. Shaul needs to know that I have rid him of his enemy."

Sisera drew himself up. "But Jabin needs to know that the threat may still exist." He waved a hand to cut off Zuberi's argument. "I am a military man. It is my duty to tell my lord the facts."

The priest's eyes narrowed. "Do not underestimate my power."

Sisera glanced at the dark man in front of him, noting the coldness with which Zuberi now watched him. "What do you mean?"

"I am a priest and oracle of the gods. They speak through me." Zuberi sat down. "The gods tell me many things, Sisera."

He picked up his goblet. "They tell me of their desires. They tell me of their will." He took a long sip of his drink then stared pointedly at the general. "And they tell me of those who would betray them."

"You would not dare."

Zuberi's chuckle was throaty and deep. "I would dare many things, to protect my standing with Shaul." He fixed his eyes on Sisera's. "The girl is dead. There is no threat. No need to send out any of Jabin's spies." The corner of his mouth lifted. "The gods have told me so. And anyone who defies their will is a traitor."

Sisera held the priest's gaze a moment longer before swallowing the rest of his wine. "Leave me. There is much to be done before the morning."

Zuberi took another sip from his cup then placed it on the table. "Of course. I am glad we could come to an understanding, General." He stood. "I look forward to seeing you again when you return to Harosheth."

Sisera watched Zuberi exit his tent. He kicked over the table and threw his cup across the room. *I must know for certain. I must have proof that she is dead.* Maybe the spies in Shamir will have word of her whereabouts. He would wait until then to make his plans.

11 Shiloh

The Same Morning

Deborah sat up from her pallet, gasping for air. *Where am I?* She looked around the darkened room, trying to make out the shapes surrounding her. Leb's house. She sighed in relief. *I'm in my uncle's house. There is nothing to fear.*

She had been dreaming of the Canaanites; the priest, with his tattoos and menacing smile. Of Sisera; his warm breath on her neck; his strong arms crushing her to his chest. Then his face had changed and Jorim held her. She relived the terror of his attack in the cave. *How long, Lord? How long will it be like this?*

She crept through the house and up the stairs to the roof. The sky had been full of stars when she'd been accepting Lapidoth's proposal. Now their brightness lay shrouded beneath thick clouds. Deborah shivered. *Can you really want me to marry him, Lord?*

"Are you well?" a man's voice asked.

Deborah jumped.

"Don't be afraid." A shadow spoke from the top of the stairs. "It's only me. Neriah." He took a few steps toward her.

She could just make out his face in the darkness. "What do you want?"

Neriah sat on the roof with the ledge against his back. "I heard you cry out."

She sat down on the ledge, a few feet away from the young soldier. "What did I say?"

Although she couldn't see it clearly in the blackness, Deborah sensed his shrug. "The same thing you've cried out every night since . . . ."

Will my humiliation ever end? "What do I say?"

"You call on the Lord. You cry out for Jorim to stop."

"Does everyone hear?"

Her eyes were adjusting to the lack of light. She could see Neriah shake his head. "Not tonight. Everyone is still asleep."

"But the men. Abiel, Deker . . . Lapidoth. They have heard me cry out in my sleep?"

Neriah nodded. Deborah hugged her arms across her chest. She walked to the opposite side of the roof. *I must be stronger than this. I cannot let them know how deeply I've been hurt. I can't let my father see my pain. Or Avram. I don't know what they'd do.*

Neriah approached her. "There is no shame in your dreams."

"Yes, there is." Deborah whirled around. "It means I am not trusting in God. He has said that I am innocent, and in the daylight I believe Him. But at night, in my dreams, I feel as though I've sinned."

"You did nothing wrong."

She turned away. "I should have been stronger. I should have kicked more. Something."

"It would have made no difference. Jorim and Deker would only have beaten you worse. There was nothing you could do."

Deborah sat down on the roof and hugged her legs to her chest. Neriah sat on the ledge behind her. Neither spoke. Deborah rested her forehead against her knees. Neriah placed a hand on her shoulder. Its warmth comforted her. *Why aren't I bothered by his touch? When Lapidoth's presence makes me nervous? Lapidoth. My betrothed.* Deborah pushed herself away from Neriah. "You shouldn't be here."

"What?"

Deborah fled across the roof. "We shouldn't be here. Alone."

Neriah remained sitting on the ledge. "I meant nothing by it." He shrugged. "I only wanted to help."

"I know. But the way things are . . . I have enough scandal to worry about without . . . ." She gestured with her hands, waving them between herself and Neriah. "Without adding to the rumors."

Neriah turned from her, taking a few steps toward the stairs. He paused and said something under his breath.

"What?" Deborah asked.

He faced her. The first gray light of dawn broke the horizon behind him. "I asked you if you love him."

"Who?" Deborah furrowed her eyebrows. "Lapidoth?"

"Yes."

A rooster crowed, signaling the start of a new day. Another answered in the distance. Deborah studied the young man in front of her, wishing she could see him better through the dim light.

Neriah met her stare. "I asked him first, you know."

"What?"

"I told him one of us needed to marry you. I asked if it could be me."

She took a step backward. Her heart skipped a beat. When it restarted, the sound pounded in her ears. A slow, deep drumming. "Why?"

He stepped toward her, even as she backed away again. "I have loved you since the first night I saw you at your cousin's wedding." He shrugged. "When I found out you were a prophet, I didn't think you would marry. But when all this happened, I thought it might be God's way of giving me the chance."

Deborah's legs brushed against the ledge and she sat down. Her head throbbed. "Why do you tell me this now?"

He knelt at her feet. "I thought you should know. If you don't love Lapidoth, there is another choice to save your honor."

She rubbed her face with her hands. *This is too much, Lord. Too many changes. Too many choices.* She looked at Neriah, worried by the hope she read in his eyes. She shook her head. "I don't love Lapidoth," she hurried on before he could interrupt her. "But I don't love you either. I'm sorry." A light in his brown eyes dimmed as he listened to her. "But I have asked the Lord, and it is His will that I accept Lapidoth's proposal." She reached out, wanting to touch Neriah's face, to try and comfort him, but pulled her hand back. "I'm honored, that you found favor in me. But my life is not my own. I must do as the Lord commands."

"I understand." Neriah rose. "I meant what I said in the cave." His gaze held hers. "I will protect you with my very life." He left her alone then, returning to the house below.

Deborah knelt on the roof. *Why did you have him tell me this? Why now? Was it to show me that Lapidoth spoke the truth? He did not have to be the one to marry me, but he has chosen to. Is that what this means?*

Her thoughts turned into prayers as she dwelled on the day ahead. *We leave for home today, Lord. Home. Azareel. What do I tell him, Lord? What do I say? Help me, Lord. Guide my actions. Give me words to speak to my father. Help me to know what to do.*

The city came to life around her as she continued to pray on the rooftop, the sun climbing upward in the sky, casting a warm pink blanket of light over the buildings around her. A shadow cooled the sun's heat. She looked up to see Lapidoth approaching her. A small gasp escaped her throat. Tall with broad shoulders, he was an imposing man, especially as he stood over her. He carried a cup of water and half a loaf of bread.

"We leave shortly." He sat down opposite her. "You didn't join us for dinner last night." He thrust the bread toward her. "You must eat now, or you won't have strength for the journey today."

Deborah ripped a piece of bread from the loaf. "I needed time to think."

"I know." He watched her eat several mouthfuls then chuckled softly. "You didn't hear me tell the others what happened at the market yesterday."

"No." She shook her head. "What?"

Lapidoth leaned back on his hands. "It seems the world already knows of our betrothal."

Deborah's shoulders tensed and she sat up straighter. "What? How?"

"Do not fear." His hazel eyes danced with amusement. "No one knows you're here, but they are calling you the 'Woman of Lapidoth'" He chuckled. "The woman of flames."

She smiled. The people may be calling her that because they believed she died in the fire, but she would take it as a sign. God seemed to be reinforcing His will, making her a little more confident in the decision she'd made to marry. But there were still things she needed to talk over with Lapidoth before they journeyed to the hill country. "I'm glad you came up here this morning. I have been praying since . . . ." Deborah tried to swallow, but found her mouth too dry. She took a drink from the cup Lapidoth had brought. "Since I agreed I would marry you." She tried to look at him, but couldn't meet his eyes.

"What worries you? You haven't spoken to any of us since that night."

Deborah twisted her hands in her lap. "I have been praying for guidance. I know the Lord wants me back in the hill country, but I don't know how best to speak with Azareel."

Lapidoth shifted his large frame. Deborah noted the tenseness in his body. "I will get him alone. I will ask to be allowed to marry you."

Deborah shook her head. "No. We must approach him together."

Deep wrinkles dug into Lapidoth's forehead. "That's not the way it is done."

She lifted her chin and squared her shoulders. "No, it's not. But then, you don't normally order the girl to be raped before you talk to her father either." Deborah forced herself not to raise her voice. "Azareel doesn't like you. He won't give his blessing unless I tell him that this is the Lord's will."

Lapidoth's lips tightened into thin lines. She didn't know which of her statements bothered him most, the reminder of his sin, or the fact that her father didn't like him. "And would you do this otherwise?"

"What do you mean?"

"I mean, is that the only reason you agreed to marry me?" He took hold of her hands. "Or is there hope that you could one day . . . care for me?"

The callused skin of his hands rubbed against hers. "I don't know." She discerned a kind of energy pulsating from him. *Perhaps it runs through his blood.* She trembled at the strength and power that radiated from him. *He could kill me. With his bare hands, he could break me.* Lapidoth's eyes searched hers, looking for something Deborah knew wasn't there. She respected him. She feared him. But she didn't love him. She read the pain her silence caused him. "I know it is God's will. That must be enough for now."

Deborah took a deep breath. "I'm sorry for my coldness. So much has happened." She looked away for a moment, watching thin wisps of clouds glide across the pale blue sky. She was grateful for Lapidoth's silence. *Maybe there is more to him than just the brute strength needed to be a soldier.* "I feel as though I've fallen off a cliff and haven't yet hit the ground. I am not sure I'll survive the fall, or what awaits me at the bottom." She focused back on Lapidoth. "I only know my life will never be the same."

Lapidoth nodded. The creases in his forehead relaxed. "I can wait for you."

She smiled weakly. "Thank you." She pulled her hands out from his grasp. "We should move on. The sooner we get there, the sooner Bithia can scold me for not warning her we were coming." She finished the last bite of bread, then brushed the crumbs from her lap as Lapidoth stood. He held out his hand. She took it and he helped to pull her up. He held onto her hand a moment longer than necessary, making Deborah keenly aware of how close they stood. Again, his size struck her. The top of her head just reached the bottom of his chin. She pulled away from him and went down the stairs to the house below.

Rachel *tsked* under her breath as she caught sight of Deborah. "Have you slept at all, Niece?"

Deborah gave a small smile. "A little. Don't fret. I don't have far to travel today."

Rachel finished wrapping a small bundle of bread and cheese for their journey. Katriel gave Lapidoth a skin of water. She carried another over to Leb.

Deborah frowned. "Uncle, you can't come with us."

Leb knit his brow. "Of course I am coming. You will need my help with Azareel."

"No." Deborah stood firm. "If you leave with us, it will cause suspicion. Your neighbors already wonder about our presence."

Leb scowled. "So what if they know you were here? What ill can happen?"

Deborah tried to push her anxiety away, but it clawed at her stomach. "You don't understand. The Canaanites believe I died in the fire. I cannot risk them learning so soon that I survived."

Lapidoth put a hand on Deborah's shoulder. "We will face Azareel together. God will soften his heart toward me."

Leb shifted his gaze between them both. "This is not right."

Deborah stepped toward him and away from Lapidoth's touch. "Trust me, Uncle. You must tell your neighbors that we brought news of the prophet's death near Jezreel. That we go now to inform Azareel." She held out her hand. Leb reluctantly gave her the skin of water. Rachel handed Judith the bundle of food. The family embraced each other and said their good-byes. Deborah and Judith draped their veils over their faces before they left the doorway.

They walked in silence through the city's streets and alleys. As they approached the city gate, Lapidoth paused. He gestured for the others to gather around him. "Abiel. You, Neriah and Joseph head north and meet up with the others." He glanced at Deker and Judith. "We will join you as soon as our business in the hill country is done."

The men all nodded, except for Neriah. "No."

Lapidoth's face darkened. "What?"

Neriah shook his head. "No, Barak. I have sworn to protect her. I will not leave until she is safe."

"She is safe with me." The two men glowered at each other while the others watched in tense silence.

Deborah placed a hand on Neriah's arm. "Go. You can better serve me by returning to the fight against the Canaanites. To stay here and argue will only make strangers curious." She gave his arm a gentle squeeze. "I will be safe."

Neriah's face looked downcast, but he followed Joseph and Abiel as they turned north out of the city gate. Deborah led the way south of the city, to the road that ran up through the hills to her home.

12 The Hills of Ephraim

The Following Day

Azareel stood, his eyes filled with anger. "I absolutely forbid this marriage!" His finger shook as he pointed it at Lapidoth. "You are a soldier. A fierce man. A man of blood with no home." Spittle flew from his mouth. "What can you give my daughter?"

Lapidoth rose, his face set in stone, his body rigid as granite. "I am an honorable man." His gaze flickered over to Avram as Deborah's brother stood up beside their father.

"What honor is there, living in caves?" Avram's voice ascended with barely suppressed fury. "Would you have my sister pick up the sword and fight the Canaanites with you?"

"Of course not." Lapidoth closed his eyes. Deborah watched as he willed himself under control. "I know this comes as a surprise, but I promise to make a good life for her."

"Never!" Avram sliced the air with his arms. "This will never happen."

Deborah's stomach tightened at the tension overflowing the small home. She had anticipated this reaction, but her body still recoiled from it. She placed her elbows on her knees and leaned her head against her hands. She was glad Azareel had asked the rest of the family to wait in Palti's house. She could not have handled the others' emotions in this drama. The men continued shouting above her, oblivious to her presence.

"You come here, asking to marry my daughter. I have no knowledge of you, only a little of your family. All I know is you are soldier. That you long to rebel against the Canaanites. That is not our life here."

"It will be soon enough," Lapidoth argued. "The hills will not save you from their persecution."

"Ha!" laughed Avram. "This from the man who claimed the prophet was wrong, that the Canaanites would not be moving south. Why do you believe her now?"

"Yes!" Azareel cried. "Why now? When you called her a . . . a ranting child just a few months ago?"

Deborah could hear the strain in Lapidoth's deep voice. "Much has changed since then. I was wrong about the Canaanites. I admit that. But I am not wrong about this."

"Yes, you are," Avram growled.

Azareel cut him off. "I will not allow it."

Deborah drew a breath to steady her nerves, then pushed herself off the floor. "You cannot forbid this, Father."

Azareel's eyes flashed. Avram stepped toward her, but Lapidoth took hold of her brother's shoulder and stopped him.

Her father's voice was firm. "You will not marry this man."

"It is God's will." She met Azareel's gaze and held it. "He has spoken. I am to be betrothed to Lapidoth."

Her father slumped, as if he carried a great weight. "I do not believe it."

Avram freed himself from Lapidoth's grasp. "I don't either." He put his hands on Lapidoth's chest and pushed him away. "How have you bewitched my sister? What have you done?" Deborah could see the anguish that crossed Lapidoth's face. She knew Avram saw it as well.

"How did you do it?" Avram shoved the bigger man again. "Tell me!"

"Enough!" Deborah called before Lapidoth could answer. "Leave him alone, Brother. I have not been bewitched. God has spoken."

Avram glared a moment longer at Lapidoth before turning toward his sister. "You are still a child, Deborah."

"I'm nearly seventeen."

"But you are an innocent." He squeezed her arm to stop her from interrupting him. "Remember, you told me your dreams on the roof. I know you desire to be married." He glowered toward Lapidoth. "But this is not the man to bind yourself with."

"I am no innocent." She could not look in her brother's eyes. "I have been a prisoner of the Canaanites. I have seen the cruelty of the soldiers first hand as they tortured their captives. I was threatened with death, with the humiliation of rape, if I would not bow down to their gods. I refused and the Lord protected me. Their own gods spoke to me. Offered me power and wealth, anything I desired, if I would serve them. I defied them." Inside her soul, she felt a subtle shift. As she spoke the words to her family, she sensed herself growing from the wounded child she had been, into the woman God desired her to be.

"I have been tested by the Lord. He has put me into the fire and removed the dross from my spirit. I have been refined and made stronger." The power of God's spirit filled her and caused her voice to ring out like a hammer on the anvil. "I am Deborah, God's prophet. I am Deborah, the woman of flames, the wife of Lapidoth."

Azareel appeared to shrink before her eyes. He steadied himself on Avram's arm. "I do not understand." His voice trembled. "Why would God ask this of you?"

"I don't know, Father. I only know it is His will."

Azareel's clouded gaze roamed between her and Lapidoth. "When will you marry?"

Lapidoth stepped forward. "We will be betrothed as soon as you deem possible. The wedding . . . ." He cleared his throat. "The wedding—"

"The Lord has not made it clear when we shall marry." Deborah took a deep breath. "Lapidoth must go back and lead his men."

Avram flinched. "What?"

"That is not the law of Moses," said Azareel. "A betrothed man must marry before he goes to war, and stay at home for a year with his new bride."

Deborah stood firm. "I don't question what the Lord has decreed. Lapidoth and I must be betrothed. It is essential the agreement be made, that he takes me for all purposes as his wife." She looked at all three men before she spoke again. "But we will not live as husband and wife until the Lord declares it is time."

Azareel shook his head. "Where will you live?"

"Here, Father. If you will allow it."

"Of course." He nodded slowly.

"And after the wedding," spat Avram. "Where will your home be? In the caves?"

"Here," Deborah answered, as Lapidoth said, "In Kedesh."

She glanced furtively at Lapidoth before turning to her brother. "We will do as the Lord commands. He has not spoken yet on where we will live."

She could see the frustration in her brother's eyes. "There is something you keep secret." He scowled at Lapidoth. "There is some madness behind this rash decision."

Lapidoth squared his shoulders and opened his mouth to speak, but Deborah put her hand on his arm. With the smallest shake of her head, she stopped his confession. She lifted her chin to address Azareel and Avram. "Believe me when I tell you this is not a rash decision. I have prayed." Her eyes filled with tears that she forced not to fall. "I have done nothing but pray for many days." She reached out and stroked Azareel's haggard face. "Do not fear for me, Father. This is the will of God. And if we are doing His work, we need not be afraid."

Tears spilled down her father's cheeks. "You were already taken from me too early." His breath caught in his chest. "You lived by the Tabernacle, doing the Lord's work. Speaking the words He gave you. I did not see you more than once a year, but at least I knew you were safe." He shook his head. "But to marry this man. To live as the wife of a soldier. What good can come of it? I am not a prophet, but I see only death in this union."

Azareel held Deborah's face in his hands. "My precious child, my Little Bee, it is as I saw at your birth. You bring me much sweetness." His voice broke. "But also much pain." He pulled her toward him and kissed her forehead. Azareel released her then looked up at Lapidoth. "Promise me something."

The red-haired man swallowed before he spoke. "What can I do?"

Azareel straightened his back. "Take care of my daughter. Do not let her come to harm."

A fierce determination flashed in Lapidoth's eyes. He looked first to Deborah then back to her father. "You have my word. I will do everything within my power to keep her safe." He put his hand on Azareel's shoulder. "I would give my life for her."

Azareel placed his hand along Lapidoth's neck. "Then I give you my blessing. May the Lord, in His infinite wisdom, keep you safe and give you many years of happiness."

The two men held the embrace for a moment longer before Azareel let go. He turned to Avram. "Go to Palti's home, fetch the others. We have time before the sun sets. We can have the ceremony tonight."

Deborah's heart jumped to her throat. *Tonight? So soon?* She shivered even in the overwhelming heat of the house. Lapidoth hurried over to his satchel and pulled out several objects wrapped in linen. Azareel poured a cup of wine then sat with it in the center of the floor. The rest of her family entered the house. Deborah scanned their eyes. Had Avram said anything to them? From the general lack of excitement or anger, she guessed not. Deker walked over to Lapidoth. The two men spoke in hushed tones. Deker glanced at Deborah, then back to his friend. He clasped his friend's shoulder and smiled.

Azareel ordered the others to sit. "Please. We must hurry before the Sabbath."

Bithia flitted to the stew bubbling over the cooking pot. "Yes! Tamar, run outside and get the bread from the oven."

"No, Wife. Sit first. Everyone sit."

"But, we don't have much time."

Azareel's voice rose. "I know. The other women will help when our business here is done."

"Business?" Bithia frowned. "What business?"

Azareel ignored her. "Come Daughter, sit next to me."

Deborah obeyed, sitting to her father's left. She watched as the rest of the family took their places around the floor. Avram sat on Azareel's right side, but left a space between them. Deborah lowered her head and focused on the threads in the rug.

Azareel squeezed her hand. He let go and gave a small cough. "Lapidoth has asked for permission to wed Deborah."

Deborah kept her head down, but could hear Palti and Bithia both cry out at once, "What?"

Nathan squealed, "My sister is going to marry a soldier?"

"Hush!" scolded Bithia. "Husband, you cannot seriously consider this?"

"I have given my blessing."

The room fell silent. Deborah lifted her head as Lapidoth stepped forward, the features on his face set in grim determination. "Azareel. I am Lapidoth bar Abinoam of Kedesh. I have seen your daughter overcome adversity. I have seen the power of our God move through her. More, I have come to revere her as a woman of virtue, strength and honor." Deker brought forth several items from the satchel. Lapidoth took them and approached Azareel. He knelt before Deborah's father. "I bring you these gifts, to honor you, the father of my bride." He held out a gift in each hand.

Azareel took the first, a small leather pouch. He opened it and poured out twelve gold coins. Nathan and Edin both gasped, their eyes wide with wonder. Azareel picked the second gift from Lapidoth's other hand. It was a large ring made of gold. A bright blue lapis was set in its middle. As he held the gift out for all to see, everyone in the room took a sharp intake of breath. Azareel slid the ring onto the middle finger of his left hand.

Deker retrieved another package from the floor by Lapidoth's satchel. Lapidoth turned to Bithia. "For the woman who was mother to my bride." Bithia unwrapped the linen and cried out. She lifted up two necklaces of gold and quickly hung them around her neck, admiring the way the firelight reflected off the bright metal.

Finally Deker sat the last three gifts by Lapidoth's side and sat down amid the circle. Lapidoth faced Deborah. "For my wife, I have these humble tokens of my devotion."

Deborah's hand shook as she reached for the smallest parcel. Inside she found four rings of braided gold. Lapidoth helped her put two on each hand. As his hands touched hers, they both trembled. She looked up at him and smiled. The corner of his mouth lifted slightly. Deborah laughed to herself, reading the near terror in his eyes. *He would rather be facing a hundred Canaanites in chariots than performing this ritual.* He was a man of action, not of ceremony.

Lapidoth handed her the next gift, two necklaces of round silver beads and one of turquoise beads. Deborah froze as she looked at it, remembering the turquoise necklace Zuberi had made her wear. She covered her trepidation with another smile and allowed Lapidoth to hang the necklaces around her neck. Where the priest had made her wear the jewels as a symbol of his power, she saw Lapidoth sit back and wait to see if she approved of his gift, his worry evident by the look in his eyes. "They are beautiful." She smiled as her fingers pressed the beads to her chest. "Thank you."

Finally Lapidoth unfolded the last package. Inside lay a beautiful robe made of fine cream wool. Purple, red and gold threads intertwined in a pattern of swirling semi-circles, almost like vines, running along the sleeves and hem of the garment. Around the neckline, the same colored threads shimmered, interspersed with beads of white, yellow, blue and green. Deborah had never seen a garment more lovely.

"When the Lord tells you it is time," Lapidoth said. "You will wear this at our wedding. I pray He makes it soon, for I long to take you into my home, and make you my wife." He draped the robe over Deborah's lap.

Her fingers caressed the soft fabric. *I will need your help, Lord. To forget all that happened and marry this soldier.*

Azareel motioned with his right hand. "Come, Lapidoth, husband of my daughter Deborah. Sit at my side and drink from the same cup, sealing the commitment you have made to each other."

Azareel handed the wine to Lapidoth. He took a drink then passed it in front of Azareel to Deborah. She took a sip and handed it to her father.

Azareel put the cup on the ground. "From this day on you are considered man and wife in every way but one. You are bound together by the laws of the Lord and cannot be separated. May the God of our fathers bless you and keep you safe until the time of your wedding ceremony and after." Azareel drained the last of the wine. "Come, let us eat the Sabbath meal together and celebrate the blessings that God has given us."

13 Hazor

One Week Later

It took several days for Sisera to finish his business with the King. Jabin had insisted on a royal parade through the streets of Hazor to honor the general and his men. The people had thrown garlands and palm branches down on the road before the soldiers. The priests made sacrifices in their honor. A week long feast for Sisera and his officers was held at the palace with wine and food overflowing the tables. For the first time in many years, Sisera drank in excess. The praises of the king, the adulation of the crowds, it all seemed hollow to him now. His spies had returned from Shamir. Deborah had not returned to that town either. No one had seen her since the night of the fire. *But I can't believe she's dead. Not without her body.* He convinced himself that the gods desired him to search for her. *Why else would I be consumed with thoughts of her?* Jabin noted his dark mood.

"What worries you, my friend?" The king called down from his table. "Your face is clouded like a storm on the Galilee."

Sisera forced a smile. "I am not a young man anymore, my king. The weeks out on the battlefield have worn me out. I am only weary."

"Ha!" Jabin took a swallow from his goblet. "Sisera tired? I never thought I'd see the day."

The general let out an exaggerated sigh. "It will pass, my lord. I only need the comfort of my own bed, not the rugged conditions of the campaign."

Jabin's eyes gleamed with delight. "I think it is time for my final gift. Perhaps that will spur you to celebrate with me awhile longer." He clapped his hands and whispered something to the servant who came and knelt before him. The king rose to speak to the men gathered about the room. "My friends, in honor of our final night of feasting, I've ordered my servants to bring in some of the finest treasures from the battles. In recognition of Sisera's success in this campaign, he will get first pick." Jabin smiled broadly at his friend. "Anything you desire, General, it shall be yours."

A parade of servants entered, carrying trays of gold coins and jewelry. Others pulled carts of beautiful pottery and fine cloth. The officers around the room cheered, praising the king as they ogled the wealth displayed before them.

Sisera groaned silently. *It is nothing. These baubles cannot give me the power I crave, nor stir my blood with the passion I felt with Deborah.* He forced himself to stand and clap with his men at the king's generosity.

"What do you think, Sisera?" The king's eyes bore into him. "Do you see anything you like?"

Sisera shrugged. "You have already given me much, my lord. Let my men pick first."

Jabin frowned. "Perhaps this is not the reward you desired?"

"I desired no reward," Sisera replied hurriedly, not wishing his mood to offend the king further. "My pleasure comes from serving you. My joy is on the battlefield."

Jabin nodded in acknowledgment of his friend's praise. He clapped his hands again. "Bring in the slaves." He smiled at Sisera. "Maybe one of these would be better suited for you. A strong back to aid you in Harosheth." Another servant led a group of bound Hebrew slaves into the room. Four muscled men and five beautiful women were roped together and marched around the room to the cat calls and jeers of the officers. The Hebrew men glared at their captors while the women hung their heads.

"What do you think, General? Do any of these please you?" asked the king.

Sisera glanced over the slaves, longing to be done with this ritual and go to his own home in the city for some rest. His gaze froze at the sight of the young woman at the end of the line. *Deborah?* Her hair shone with the same golden brown curls. *No. This girl is smaller. Younger.* Still, the resemblance made his pulse quicken.

Jabin stepped down from the dais, watching his friend's face. He quieted the other men with a wave of his hand. "I think you may have found something to your liking." He motioned to the servant standing next to him. "The girl at the end. Bring her to me."

The guards at the front of the line held their spears at the necks of the Hebrew men to keep them from resisting as the girl was untied and led to the king. Jabin brushed her hair away from her face. Terror filled her eyes. Her skin paled. She cried out softly as the king pulled her close and kissed her on the lips. Sisera clenched his jaw as the image of Jabin forcing himself on Deborah came to his mind. The king kissed the girl again then looked to the general. "She is indeed sweet, my friend. A good choice, though not what I would have expected you to pick." He thrust the girl to a servant and gestured for her to be brought to Sisera. "I would have thought you had your fill of women on the battlefield."

The servant led the girl to the general's side. "There are some things a man never tires of, my lord."

Jabin laughed. "Do you want her now? I could arrange for her to be brought to one of the rooms."

His officers applauded this idea, but Sisera shook his head. He forced himself to play along with the sexual innuendos around him. He pulled the girl toward his chest and fondled her breast as the men shouted their approval. "I think I would rather savor this morsel alone." The men groaned their disappointment. "I feel like being selfish."

Jabin smiled. "Bring the girl to the general's house. Keep a guard on her until Sisera arrives home."

Sisera tipped his head. "Thank you for your generosity."

"And now, gentlemen. Feel free to take whatever you desire." The king opened his arms as if he could encompass the entire room in his grasp. "I give this treasure to you, my faithful friends." He returned to his seat on the dais. Both he and Sisera watched as the rest of the men divided the spoils among themselves.

Sisera's mother greeted him when he arrived at his house later that afternoon. "My son. The gods have answered my prayers and brought you safely home." Visnia kissed him on the cheek.

"It is good to see you, Mother." He turned to receive a kiss on the other side of his face.

Visnia placed a hand along his neck. She stared into his eyes. "Come and have some refreshment. Tell me about the campaign."

Sisera groaned. "I have done nothing but feast, drink and talk for the past three days. I want only to rest."

A shout rang out from courtyard. His sons ran in and hugged his legs. A young Egyptian woman followed behind them.

"Father! You're back!"

He patted his sons' heads. "Yes." He pushed them away so he could look at them. "E-Saum, you have grown!"

The youngster grinned. "Look at my muscles!" He flexed his arm.

His older son frowned. "What about me, Father? Have I grown too?"

Sisera squinted and pursed his lips. Finally he nodded. "Most definitely, Khenti. And how are your arms? Have you been practicing with the bow and arrow I gave you?"

"Yes, Father! Come and see!"

Sisera put a hand on each boy's shoulder. "Later. I have only just come from the campaigns." He pushed his sons toward their servant. "Go with your nurse. In the morning you must show me your skills with the bow."

The boys' eyes pleaded to stay with their father, but they both answered, "Yes, sir."

"Come, masters," plied the Egyptian woman. "We will go to the kitchen and see if the cook will give us a morsel before dinner tonight."

The general grinned as he watched his sons. "They are fine boys."

Visnia nodded. "We have done well."

Sisera bristled at his mother's comment, but said nothing.

"Come and sit for a moment before you retire." Visnia led him into the dining area. "Tell me about the campaign."

A low table sat in the middle of the expansive room. Pillows sat along both sides of it. Two doorways opened onto the court-yard. A stone altar occupied one corner, a collection of idols displayed upon it. In the opposite corner, a tiered fountain bub-bled. Sisera lowered himself onto a pillow. "There is not much to tell. The battles are all the same." He took the goblet of wine a servant offered him. "Where is my wife?"

"The queen has been holding her own festival."

Sisera sipped his wine. "You did not attend?"

"Of course I went." Visnia sat opposite her son. "But when my servant told me Jabin had presented the officers with gifts, I knew you would be returning home." She refused the wine the servant offered. "I came home to see you first."

"So Miu is still at the palace?"

Visnia's lips curled up slightly. "Yes, my son. Your wife will be there another evening, I am sure."

Sisera relaxed into the pillows at his back. "Good."

His mother's eyes narrowed. "A guard brought a young slave girl to the house just before you arrived. I thought you accepted her as a housemaid for Miu." She scrutinized him further. "But perhaps she is for your own amusement?"

Sisera stared at Visnia a moment longer before he broke her gaze. He took a sip from his goblet. "I do not know who she is for."

"What is it, my son? What has happened?"

He stared out into the courtyard. The grass looked yellow and hard. "Something . . . something I do not understand."

"I knew it."

He turned back to her. "What?"

His mother leaned toward him. "I presented an offering to Asherah and had the priest read the signs. He warned me."

Sisera was tired of talking. He lifted his eyebrows to indicate his mother should continue.

Visnia stroked his cheek. "He said a cloud darkened your path. Trouble, power and magic were all seen in your future."

Sisera grabbed her hand. "Yes. All of it." He released her and hit the table with his fist. "I do not know what to do."

"Tell me." She stroked his arm. "Let me help you."

Sisera walked to the open doorway that opened to the inner courtyard. "I found a girl. Woman, actually. In Shamir. A prophet."

His mother let out a short snort of air to show her disbelief. "Prophet?"

He turned sharply toward her. "She knew the army came for the grain. She had the town bring in half the harvest and leave half for us. She said her god had told her it was the only way I would let them live."

Lines creased Visnia's brow. "Impressive."

"Yes." He stepped toward his mother. "Later, I saw . . . I heard . . . ." He struggled to put his thoughts into words.

"What?"

He knelt in front of Visnia. "Our gods spoke through her. Her voice changed. Even her face was different. The gods told us things."

"Who else was there?"

"Zuberi, the priest. He heard her too." Sisera sat back on his heels. "The gods told us we could use the girl. We could seduce her into serving them. She would become more powerful than Jabin." Sisera's breath quickened. "They said that the girl would rule over all of Canaan and that I, as her lover, would rule over her." He leaned toward Visnia and whispered. "I could be more powerful than all the kings, combined."

His mother's eyes gleamed. "Where is this prophet now? Does Jabin have her?"

Sisera shook his head and sat back slowly. "She is gone."

Visnia frowned. "What? Where?"

He stared past her, out into the darkening courtyard. "There was a fire. In the tent where she slept."

"She is dead?"

He turned his focus back to his mother. "That is what Zuberi thinks."

Visnia tilted her head. "But you do not?"

"She told me she had faith her god would save her. And there was no way to be sure her body was one of the ones we found in the tent."

His mother's mouth hardened into a straight line as she considered what he'd told her. "Is there more?"

"Only that I am convinced she lives. Why else would the gods keep her face in my mind? They are willing me to search for her."

Visnia nodded. "Then you must search."

"But Zuberi won't let me tell Jabin that she lives. He has threatened to discredit me if I pursue her."

The older woman again snorted in disgust. "So? Who says you must tell Jabin of your plans?" Her mouth formed a sly smile. "No, I think it is best you search for her alone, my son."

"What?"

Visnia stood and paced about the room. "Yes. Seek her quietly and on your own. When she is found, you can take her as your lover, marry her, even."

"What of Zuberi?"

"Once she is proven to be alive, do you think it matters what that idiot priest says?" She gave a dismissive wave with her arm. "No. Once you have her, you will have all the power. No one will be able to stop you."

Sisera rubbed his chin. "But it will take months, years to find her without the king's resources at my command."

Visnia stood over him. "Do not worry about how long it will take." She ran her hand through his hair and rested it on his neck. "It is better to seek her quietly and alone. The gods will deem when the time is right for her to return." His mother grinned. "Then, my son, their plan will be fulfilled, and you will rule Canaan."

Part Three

Woman of Flames

1 Southern Jordan River Valley

Several Months Later

J ael sat on the hard earth, flexing her palm. It pained her to move, but she knew if she didn't, the muscles would seize up and she would be crippled. Her aunt, Rivka, had examined the wound closely when Jael had first come to live with them, several months ago.

"You were lucky, child." The old woman's brow had lifted, causing even more wrinkles to form on her forehead. "The knife pierced straight through the hand without breaking the bone."

Jael didn't feel lucky. She felt lost. She had only met Rivka and her husband, Pallu, once before, but it had been many years ago. She hadn't remembered their faces, only their names. Pallu and Rivka, father's relatives from the north. Ironworkers and tent dwellers as her own family had been. *I shouldn't feel so lost. My life is much the same as it had been.*

But not quite.

Her father was dead. Strong and tall, her father had seemed invincible. The muscles in his arms alone were like mountains. Thick and strong from wielding the hammer to pound the hot metal into sickles, wheels and swords.

Her sister was dead. Orpa had been in love with one of the Hebrew boys that lived in the nearby village. They were going to get married. No more.

Hanan, her brother. Always teasing, pulling her hair. Grabbing her hand to show her some new animal or plant that he'd found. *Where was Hanan? Did he manage to escape in the chaos of the fire, or was he being led to some Canaanite city to be sold as a slave. Would his new masters treat him kindly or would they beat him? Was he already dead somewhere? Stabbed through the chest with a Canaanite spear as her father had been?*

Her mother; beautiful; overflowing with love for her family. Her arms always ready to embrace her daughter, to kiss her head and stroke her hair.

Jael blinked away the tears that trickled down her cheeks. She made a fist with her wounded hand. She gasped at the bolt of pain that shot up her arm then smiled to herself. She'd learned, soon after coming to live with Rivka and Pallu, that the best way to fight her sorrow was to give herself over to the pain. She wriggled her fingers, relishing the throbbing ache that radiated from her palm. This physical agony cut through her grief. It sliced through her anguish much as the priest's knife had sliced through her hand.

I will never forget. I will never forget my parents and the way the Canaanites killed them like dogs. I will never forget the priest and his eyes as he drove the blade into my palm. I will never forget Deborah. How she held me close and sang to me to ease my fear. I will never forget.

"Is anything wrong?" Rivka's voice pulled Jael from her thoughts. "Do you need ointment for your hand this morning?"

Jael grasped a wooden spike in her left hand. "No. I am fine." She positioned the large peg within a rope loop and picked the mallet up in her right hand. She raised the hammer above her head, then swung it against the head of the spike. Her arm vibrated with the force of the blow and the nail sank into the hard ground.

Rivka came up beside her. "I am so glad you are with us. I don't have the strength to set up the tent anymore."

Jael whacked the spike again. "I don't understand why we had to come south. Why not stay near Jezreel?"

"Pallu is a nomad at heart. We've always moved with the seasons." Rivka let out a long sigh. "And he hates the rain in the north. It is drier here."

Jael's uncle had walked to the nearby village to let the people know he was available to repair their plows before the winter planting season began in earnest. Once that work was finished, he would begin making knives that he could sell when they moved back north in the spring.

Jael finished staking the tent ropes and helped her aunt lift the fabric into place on its wooden frame. She couldn't stop her thoughts from spinning. *But I liked Jezreel. And now I know no one and no one knows where I am. Not even Deborah.* Their short time together had bonded her closer to Deborah than to her own sister. She had hoped her friend would try to find her one day. But with this move, her dream had faded. One more disappointment to add to her life.

Her aunt must have sensed Jael's unspoken depression. "Do not fret. We have wintered here often. We know many families." She beat a straw broom against a striped woolen rug. "You will have friends in no time."

Pallu returned home with the purple clouds of dusk. He grinned and rubbed his hands together as he entered the tent. His small dark eyes sat deep within his face, peering out at his surroundings with the furtive movements of a mouse. Jael appreciated that he and Rivka had agreed to take her in, but even after living with them for several months, she did not feel at home. Her uncle's constant shifting gaze unnerved her. He always seemed to be watching her, watching everyone around him, looking for a way to make a profit. Sometimes, if she caught a glimpse of his face from the corner of her vision, her heart would stop, for it was then she could see the resemblance to his brother, her father. For a moment she would remember how her life had been before the Canaanites had destroyed her family. But then the pain would come and fill her soul with bitterness again.

Pallu lowered himself to the rug, still rubbing his hands. "This may be our most profitable year yet, Rivka."

Jael's aunt scooped the fragrant garlic spiced couscous onto a wooden plate and sat it in front of her husband. "Why is that?"

He waited to answer until he had ripped a portion of bread from the loaf Jael offered him. He waved the piece in the air to punctuate his excitement. "The Canaanites came even this far south. They destroyed a lot of the plows, and of course they took any weapons they could find." He plunged the bread into the couscous then stuffed the food into his mouth. "Who would have thought the Canaanites would be the key to our wealth?"

Jael picked at the bread on her plate, no longer hungry. *They killed your brother, and yet you praise them? What kind of monster are you?*

Her aunt smiled weakly. "You mustn't let the Israelites in town hear you say that. We have a treaty with them."

Pallu took another mouthful. "Of course, not." His beady eyes glanced toward Jael. "And I meant no disrespect, Niece."

Jael bit her cheek to keep from speaking out in anger. Rivka hurried to fill in the silence. "What other families have arrived? Yishai and his wife?"

Her uncle shook his head, his bushy dark hair bouncing with the movement. "No. But Achida and his sons are here."

"Achida? He has returned from Egypt?"

"Finally. After so many years. Has it been three?"

Rivka served her husband more couscous. "I think it has been five."

Pallu stopped chewing but left his mouth open for a moment. "Five? Are you sure it's been five years?"

"Perhaps four."

Her uncle nodded. "Yes, four. That seems right." He finished chewing. "He has remarried. And his youngest son has brought home an Egyptian bride as well."

Rivka raised her eyebrows. "Really? Egyptians? What are they like?"

Pallu glowered at her. "How would I know? I didn't talk with them. I spoke only with Achida. I invited them to dine with us tomorrow."

"Tomorrow?" Rivka sat up. Her gaze darted around the tent as if taking inventory of what food they had to serve. "So soon?"

"Why not? I will slaughter a lamb in the morning. We should celebrate that we made it through this difficult season with our lives." He tore off another piece of bread. "We are safe another year and should see much profit besides."

Jael knelt beside her aunt before an assortment of wooden idols. Rivka placed an offering of grain in a bowl and presented it to the tiny gods in the corner of their tent. Her aunt then recited a prayer under her breath.

Jael shuddered. *I have seen what a real god can do. These dolls are nothing compared to the God of the Israelites. I have seen his power.*

Rivka patted Jael's knee. "Do not fret. The gods will answer your prayers."

Jael stifled a laugh. *She thinks I asked these gods for something?*

Her aunt's kind face regarded her. "Perhaps tomorrow you would like to make the offering?"

"No." Jael regretted the harsh tone of her voice. "I don't feel worthy."

"Who is worthy? That is why we have the gods." Rivka groaned as she stood to her feet. "Come, we must prepare a feast for our guests tonight. Knowing Pallu he is inviting even more to our tent."

They sat outside together and ground wheat to make fine flour. Rivka tried to make conversation. "Your uncle likes the bread from wheat better than that of barley."

Jael forced herself to smile. *That's because it makes him feel like a rich man to eat the softer bread. Only poor people have to eat barley bread at every meal.* "I rarely ate wheat flour at home."

Rivka stopped pouring the grain. "When will you start thinking of this as your home?"

Jael lowered her head. "I'm sorry."

"It is nothing to be sorry about." She placed a hand on Jael's knee. "I only hoped you would feel more comfortable by now."

Jael made a fist with her left hand. "I am still getting used to life here. Everything is so different."

"Perhaps, now that we're settled for a while." Rivka smiled as she patted Jael's knee. She poured more wheat kernels into the hand mill. "I know it is hard."

After the grinding, they prepared the meat for the dinner. Jael and her aunt placed the lamb on a spit then lit a fire beneath it. Jael scraped the hide then set it out to soak in a vat of water and urine while Rivka made the bread. They worked throughout the day, cleaning the camp then making hummus and couscous to serve alongside the meal. In the afternoon, they set about getting themselves ready for the arrival of their company. They washed in a nearby stream before returning to the tent.

Jael sat in the corner, braiding her black hair. Once finished, she draped a linen cloth over her head.

Rivka brought a veil over to her. "Let me fix this about your face."

"Why?"

"We've never entertained an unmarried man before. Your face should be covered with him in the house."

"I thought Pallu said the son was married?"

"His youngest son. But there is another. An older boy. A man now. Heber must be well into his twenties." Rivka knelt behind Jael. She placed the veil so it sat along the bridge of her niece's nose, covering the lower half of her face. "There. Let me see."

Jael turned and Rivka appraised her handiwork. She shifted the veil so it sat a little higher on one side. "Perfect. Now we can see your beautiful eyes, but the rest remains a mystery."

"I am not pretty. Why should it matter if a man sees me?"

Rivka stared at her with disbelief. "Who told you that?"

Jael shrugged. "No one. But I know I'm not."

Her aunt grasped Jael's hands. "You have not seen yourself then. In just the few months you have been with us, you have bloomed." Rivka's eyes glistened with tears. "I know we have not spoken of things since you came, but you are of a marriage-able age."

Jael squirmed under her aunt's perusal.

"Your courses are regular; you should be able to have a child."

Jael backed away from the older woman. "Please. I'm not ready to be married."

"No?" Her aunt looked puzzled. "You would be a worthy prize for any man."

"Me?"

"Of course. With your beauty and your dowry?" Rivka smiled. "Any man would be honored to have you for his wife."

My dowry . . . I had forgotten. Lapidoth had gotten a hefty price for Deborah's gold bracelets. As he promised, he had given the value of one of them to her uncle, to serve as her dowry. She had never seen so many coins in one purse. Not even when her father had come from town after selling the blades he had made.

Shouts and laughter broke into her thoughts. Her uncle called out in greeting and various voices answered him. Rivka hurried to the entrance. She motioned to Jael. "Come meet our company. Remember what is expected of you when they are seated?"

Jael nodded. Her uncle enjoyed entertaining visitors often and he liked having his niece available to serve them.

Pallu entered the tent. He seated his guests around the wool-en rug in the center. He brought a pillow over to someone Jael could only assume was Achida. The man placed it by his side so he could recline against it. His silver hair and beard were cut short. His hazel eyes surveyed the contents of the tent.

"The years have been good to you, Pallu."

Two younger men sat to Achida's right. Their golden hair startled Jael. She had never seen hair that color before. It was almost as strange as the deep green of their eyes. Two women entered next. They removed their veils and bowed their heads toward Rivka and Jael. Their dark skin and exotic features denoted their Egyptian heritage.

Her aunt spread out her arms. "Welcome. May you find refreshment and peace within our home."

"Thank you," the older of the two women answered. They sat opposite the men. Jael walked to the back of the tent. She tucked a towel into the sash of her robe then picked up a pitcher of water and a bowl. She approached Achida and knelt before him.

"Excuse me, my lord. Would you like me to wash the dust from your feet?"

The handsome man raised an eyebrow before turning to Pallu. "A servant? You have done well."

Her uncle swelled with pride, but then chuckled. "This is my niece, Jael. I have adopted her since her parents died."

Her knees hurt from kneeling on the hard floor and she longed to shift her weight. She remained still however as Achida scrutinized her. "It would please me to have my feet washed." He moved the pillow so he could rest his back against it as he swung his feet toward her. When she finished with Achida, she washed the feet of his sons. She tried to focus on her task, but couldn't resist looking up at those beautiful green eyes. When she did, she noted both men watching her. Her face grew hot and she quickly lowered her gaze.

It is the veil. They wonder who hides behind it. Jael dried the younger son's feet and then her hands. *I am sure they would be disappointed if they truly saw me.* Bitterness so scarred her heart, she could only imagine it marred her face as well.

2 The Hills of Ephraim

Several weeks later

"Hurry, Deborah!" Edin tugged on her robe. "Hurry!"

Deborah chuckled before hardening her face and turning to the boy. "I cannot get my work done with you pulling on me."

Edin's brown eyes filled with tears. His lips pouted. Deborah placed a gentle hand on his head. "Now, now. Don't cry. I'm not angry, but there is work to be done before we can go up to the olive grove." She patted his hair. "Go on. Run to Asher's house and say hello to your brother." Edin wiped his tears on her sleeve then ran off.

Deborah sighed. In the months she'd been home the boy had come to see her as his mother. She pounded the dough in front of her. *That will change soon enough.* A surprising ache filled her heart. The rest of the family had made their way to Shiloh this morning to celebrate the Feast of the Tabernacles. While there, Avram would make arrangements to bring Adara's cousin, Daliyah, back as his wife. Another woman in the home. Already sensitive to Bithia's many moods, Deborah wondered how her new sister-in-law would affect the dynamics of the household.

Please, Lord. I pray your blessing on this union. Let her be a good mother to Edin and the baby, Ben-onni. Perhaps, God willing, Daliyah would bear her own child soon and could nurse Avram's son, too. *It would be a good thing for Avram to have his whole family under one roof. As crowded as that would be.*

Deborah left the dough to rise in a wooden bowl then set about making cheese for the evening meal. With most of the family in Shiloh, the extra milk from the goat could be used for such an extravagance. For dinner she would pair it with couscous made from the cracked wheat of the recent harvest.

She looked forward to spending some time with her sister-in-law, Tamar, over the evening meal. She and Palti had stayed in the village to finish pressing the late olive harvest into oil. Azareel's anger toward Palti had lessened over the years, especially as Bithia often called on Tamar for help caring for Edin and Nathan. Even so, Palti and his wife rarely joined them for dinner, eating in their own home instead. *It will be nice to talk to another woman my age for more than a minute at the well.*

Deborah frowned. Most of the friends from her youth were married and living in neighboring villages. She hadn't spent much time with the young wives of the men in the village. They didn't know her as anything other than "the prophet," and so were hesitant and respectful around her. Besides, as she was still unmarried, they had little in common.

Lord. I am lonely. Perhaps you could send a friend my way? Maybe Daliyah? Someone, Lord, to talk to.

Avram no longer sought her confidence. Deborah had hoped his anger at her betrothal would pass, but it hadn't. He would only shake his head whenever he caught her looking at him. He could tell she held something secret from him, and he refused to talk to her until she shared it. *Please, Lord. Help Avram to forgive me. Please let him speak with me again.*

Despite the ache she felt for a friend, Deborah found great pleasure in the time alone as she worked. Azareel had tried to persuade her to journey to Shiloh for the Feast of Tabernacles, but she refused. It wasn't fear that kept her from Shiloh, but this desire for some peace. Although Edin stayed behind, she knew there would be time like this morning, where she could be alone with her thoughts. *I've missed this as well, Lord.* Shiloh had been a busy, crowded city, but Deborah had spent many hours alone on the roof carding the flax and making the wicks for the oil lamps. Here in her little village, she may not have a friend, but there was always someone around to interrupt her thoughts. She prayed while she continued making the cheese and then formed the risen dough into a loaf of bread. Edin arrived as she placed it into the oven to bake. He followed her back into the house.

Deborah wiped her hands on a cloth tucked at her waist. She removed it and put it in a niche in the wall. "How is Ben-onni this morning?"

Edin sat on the floor. "He is getting bigger. He took a step across the floor to me today!"

Deborah raised her eyebrows in exaggerated surprise. "Really? He must know that you're his brother."

The boy puffed out his cheeks. "Do you think so? Or will he think Samuel is his brother, since they live together?"

Deborah sat beside the youngster and put an arm around his shoulders. "It won't be long and Ben-onni can live with you. But right now, he needs your cousin Martha to feed him."

"I know." Edin kicked his heels into the floor. "I don't like it though."

She gave the boy a squeeze. "Would you like to walk to the olive grove?"

He jumped up. "Yes! I'm ready!"

Deborah laughed as she stood. "Let's go then. We can sit in the shade of the trees and I will tell you stories."

"Won't we get in trouble for not working?"

Deborah shook her head. "There is no one here but us and I say it is fine. We've done our chores for the morning and with only our mouths to feed tonight, we don't have to worry about making a big meal. The others are celebrating in Shiloh. Let us celebrate in the olive grove."

Edin grinned as he grabbed Deborah's hand. Together they walked through the town and up into the hills. They lay on their backs for the rest of the morning, looking at the clouds, watching birds flit about the branches of the trees.

Deborah told Edin stories of their faith— about Moses and the Israelites leaving Egypt, about Abraham and his journey to the Promised Land. Edin snuggled up against her as the sun passed its high mark.

A cool breeze brought with it the gray clouds of impending rain. Deborah eyed them suspiciously, but determined the rain wouldn't come until later that afternoon. She put her arm around her nephew. He soon drifted off to sleep. At first, Deborah prayed while Edin napped, but she soon slipped into a dream.

She sat in Zuberi's tent, wearing the clothes he had bought for her.

From the corner of the room, the idol of Baal called out, "Come to us, Deborah. Come and serve us. We could give you anything you desired."

An invisible hand drew her toward the bull-headed figure. "Power. Food. Riches. It can all be yours if you serve us!"

Deborah stood before the statue, her knees and close to surrender. "God, help me." Her hand thrust forward, hurling the idol to the ground.

A scream of agony reverberated through her head. Her legs regained their strength. She turned to run from the tent.

Sisera stood in the entryway. He grabbed her by her shoulders. "Do not run from me, Prophet." He pulled her close, his breath warm, eyes burning with passion. "You refuse my gods, but do not deny me."

She fought against his hold, but could not loosen his grasp. His eyes burned with passion. "I too, can give you anything you desire. But you would not have to serve me, Deborah. I would serve you. What do you dream of? In your tiny home made of dirt? You could live in a palace, with fine linen on your bed, a pillow for your head. Meat and choice wine for your table."

The dream Sisera knelt at her feet and kissed her hands. "Return to me. Give yourself to me and I will give you all of Canaan to rule."

Deborah's heart beat like the pounding of a war drum in her ears. "No!"

She pulled her hands free from Sisera and stumbled away from the general. "No! I escaped from you. I will never return." She ran toward the back of the tent, it burst into flame as she touched it. The fire surrounded her. I am Deborah, the woman of Lapidoth. These flames cannot harm me." She stepped into the fire and woke up.

3 Southern Jordan River Valley

The Same Day

"Zahra, it's beautiful!" Jael reached out to touch the fabric on the loom. "I've never seen this quality before."

The petite Egyptian woman blushed, her black eyes lowering. "I was trained in the temple of Amsi. I use to weave the cloth for the priestesses."

Rivka looked up from where she sat sewing, cross-legged on the ground next to Achida's wife, Sanura. "You wove for the priestesses?"

Zahra nodded as she pulled the bar on her loom and pushed another row of thread down into the fabric. "Since I was eight, I lived at the temple."

"What was it like?" Jael watched her new friend with awe. "What does Egypt look like?"

"The temple is . . . beyond explanation." Zahra took the spindle and wove it through the threads of the loom as she spoke. "I've seen nothing in your land to compare it to."

Jael noted Zahra didn't speak with pride, more with a tone of wistfulness. "Was it big?"

"Very big." The young woman nodded. "With thirty stone steps, all polished so they shone in the sunlight." She sighed as worked the thread. "From the temple itself we could see the Nile."

A breeze tugged at the veil she wore to cover her hair and face. "Did it look like this?" Jael surveyed the Jordan River valley. Lush green grass lined the river's banks. Bushes and trees dotted the landscape. Hills and mountains sat purple along the horizon

Zahra looked up from her loom. "Egypt does not have the hills that this land does. And the ground away from the Nile is only sand." She focused back on her work.

Sanura stood and stretched her back. Her hand rubbed her swollen belly. "I think this baby will burst through my skin! And I still have many weeks before I am to be delivered."

"Send for me, when your time is near." Rivka brushed a gray hair from her eyes. "I have been a midwife at many a birth."

Sanura continued to rub her belly. "Did you have many children of your own?"

"Three. Two boys and a girl." Rivka sighed. "But only Anna survived past a year. She's married now."

Worry creased Sanura's forehead. "Achida wants another son. He married off his only daughter before we left Egypt." Her deep red lips tightened into a hard line. "I don't know what he'd do with a girl."

Rivka paused with her sewing. "You don't think he'd kill it, do you?"

Jael watched as her friend forced a smile, her white teeth in shocking contrast to her black skin. "No, of course not." The wrinkles on her brow lessened, but did not disappear entirely. "But I will be praying for a boy."

Rivka nodded. "As will we all."

The four sat working in companionable silence. Sanura and Zahra had visited Pallu's tent the week before and the women had forged a tentative friendship. Jael hoped that their visit today would further the women's trust. She longed to have a friend. After some time, Zahra asked if Jael would like to help her make locust cakes.

"What are they?"

The young woman laughed. "You've never had them?"

Jael shook her head.

"Then come with me. I'll show you." Zahra walked across the camp toward one of three tents. A large tent, in the center of the compound, was for the men and company. Zahra and Sanura cooked and slept in a smaller one to the right. Heber and his younger brother stood in front of the third tent, stoking a fire in order to heat up the metal plow blade they worked on. The clang of the hammer against the iron rang through the air. The harsh smell of hot metal left a bitter taste in Jael's mouth. She paused, envisioning her father at work. Heber swung the hammer down again, then lifted his head and caught sight of her. He wiped the back of his arm across his brow. His brother whispered something to him and he chuckled deeply. Jael tore her gaze away.

"Wife!" The younger brother called. "Bring us some water."

Zahra gestured to Jael. "You can go into the tent. I'll be right back."

Jael swept aside the flap and surveyed the room. A pallet with several pillows lay along the back wall. In a corner opposite sat a low table with three wooden idols. Jael could only guess at what the various sized jars set about the room held. Leather and fabric sacks hung from a bar next to the tent entrance. She let the tent flap fall and approached the back wall where panels of cloth were suspended. She placed her hand behind some cream colored fabric with golden threads woven through it, marveling at its sheerness. *Zahra is truly gifted.*

"We'll sell them when we return to the cities in the spring," Zahara said when she returned.

Jael dropped her hand from the cloth. "I've never seen their equal. How do you get the thread so fine?"

Zahra shrugged. "It is the flax from the Nile. It is different from what is grown here." She motioned for Jael to sit while she took a sack down from one of the rods and picked up a jar from the floor. She placed them next to Jael and picked up a bowl. She threw in a few pinches of spices from other jars then sat down. Opening up the sack, she poured some into the bowl. "This is the locust flour. We bought it before we left Egypt."

Jael wrinkled her nose at the fine, speckled substance. "Is it really made from locusts?"

Zahra chuckled. "Yes. And they're very good. We eat them whole, drizzled with honey and cooked. They're delicious."

"I've heard of such a thing, but never tried one."

Zahra set about making the dough for the cakes. "Hand me the jar next to you."

Jael picked it up with both hands, careful not to drop it. Zahra paused before taking the jar from Jael. "What happened to your hand?"

Jael held it out in front of her, looking at the scar. Pallu had told her not to say she'd been a prisoner of the Canaanites. *"No one will believe you escaped with your virtue."*

"My brother accidentally struck me with a knife."

Zahra took the jar, but held onto Jael's hand, her thumb rubbing softly over the mottled flesh. "The scar is still healing, I think."

Jael pulled her hand away, tucking it under a fold of her dress. "It happened just before he was killed."

Her friend watched her. "Killed?"

Jael wished her veil covered her eyes, so she wouldn't have to worry that her friend would see her nervousness. Pallu had wanted her say her family died of some disease, but she couldn't. She wouldn't dishonor their memory that way. "Canaanites raided our village. I escaped."

Her friend's dark eyes clouded. "I'm sorry."

"Thank you."

Zahra poured honey into the bowl and mixed the ingredients with her fingers. "So you were left with nothing?"

"No. I have a dowry."

The young Egyptian cocked her head. "Really? From Pallu?"

Jael fidgeted. Pallu had not given her a story to tell regarding her dowry. "No. Not from my uncle." She put the lid back onto the honey jar. "My father sent me to Pallu before the Canaanites arrived. He didn't want me to be a burden to my new family."

Zahra formed the dough into balls. "Is it large?"

"What?"

"Your dowry. Did your father send you with goods or coins?"

"I . . ." Jael twisted her hands in her lap.

Her friend smiled. "I'm just curious. I had no dowry when I married. Other than my skill with the loom."

"And that is priceless."

"Yes." Zahra sighed. "For a man who can afford to buy the tools necessary, I am worth the investment."

"I was given a purse." Jael hesitated. "A purse filled with coins."

"Then you are lucky, my friend." Zahra finished rolling the dough into balls. "Now you won't have to rely on the gods to bring you a good husband." She placed the last ball into the bowl. "Could you bring me a pan?" She gestured with her head. "The one hanging there?"

Jael took down the pan.

"Now, take the oil." Again she indicated with a nod of her head. "And pour some in the pan." Jael did as she was asked, while Zahra wiped her hands clean of the dough. The Egyptian brought the pan outside to hang over the cooking fire. Jael followed behind with the bowl of dough balls. They sat by the fire, the wind whipping the smoke around their heads like a snake.

Jael took note of the graying sky. "The rains will start soon. Within the week, I think."

"Taavi has told me little of the weather here. What are the winter months like?"

Jael shook her head. "I've never been this far south before, but I think it will be almost the same as where I've come from. It will get cold, but Rivka says we do not get as much rain here."

The dark-skinned woman shivered as the breeze blew stronger. "We will have to move the loom inside. I will miss the sun."

Jael smiled to comfort her friend, forgetting that the veil would hide the gesture. "The season only lasts a little while. Then it will be warm again."

Zahra picked up a dough ball and flattened it between her palms. She threw the cake into the pan. The hot oil sizzled and popped as she threw in the rest of the dough. After a few minutes, Zahra flipped them over. She didn't wear a veil and Jael noticed her chew on her lower lip.

"What's the matter?"

Zahra surveyed her. "I'm trying to figure out how old you are. You are very small, like a child, but your eyes tell me you're older."

"How old are you?"

Zahra sat up straight. "How old do you think I am?"

Jael looked at her new friend. Her teeth were still bright, as were her eyes. The strands of hair Jael could see peeking from her head wrap were black in color, with no sign of gray. But Zahra had a confidence and maturity about her that made her seem old. "I think you are about twenty years?"

Zahra laughed, a musical sound that delighted Jael. "I'm only sixteen."

"You seem older."

The Egyptian woman smiled. "That's because the priestesses taught us at a young age how to behave." Again she stared at Jael. "Let me see your face so I can have a better guess at your age.

Jael's gaze darted around the camp, looking for signs of Taavi and Heber. The constant clang of the hammer told her that they still stood over the fire, working. From where she sat, they would be unable to see her.

"Come on," coaxed Zahra. "Only for a moment."

Jael reached behind her head and unfastened one end of her veil. She pulled it from her face.

Zahra smiled, then chewed her lip again. "I cannot say!" She laughed. "You are a puzzle."

Jael refastened her veil. "Make a guess."

"Maybe . . . eleven?"

"I am thirteen. I will be fourteen during the winter rains."

"You are so small!"

Jael grinned. "My mother was tiny too. Father called her his date blossom." Her heart grew heavy at the memory. She lowered her head so her friend wouldn't see her eyes welling with tears. She flexed her left hand and drew a sharp breath.

"Are you well?"

Jael nodded. "Sometimes, it hurts to remember all that I've lost."

Zahra put a hand on Jael's knee. "I know." She pulled the golden cakes from the pan, placing them into a basket. Then she put another batch of dough in to cook. She told Jael about the family in Egypt that she'd not seen since being taken to serve at the temple.

"You've had no family since you were eight?"

Zahra shrugged. "The other girls became my family. But now I don't have them either. Just Sanura."

"How long have you known her?"

Zahra turned the cakes. "Since I was married to Taavi. A year ago now."

"She seems nice."

"She is. Most of the time. The baby has made her irritable. It has made Taavi irritable as well. He wonders when I will become pregnant."

"It has not been that long."

Zahra focused on the clouds rushing across the sky. "I know. And there has been so much change. I hoped we would stay in Egypt, but Achida told his sons they must move back to this land with him."

"Why is the older one not married?"

"Heber?"

Jael nodded.

"His wife died from fever." Zahra pulled the cakes from the pan and put them with the others in the basket. She took the hot pan from the fire and sat it in the dirt next to her. "Achida wants him to marry again though. I've heard them talking."

She leaned in close to Jael, her voice soft. "Something happened many years ago. Something that forced them to flee to Egypt."

Jael shuddered in the cool wind. "What?"

"I do not know. But they prospered in Egypt, so the gods couldn't have been that angry with them. They learned a great deal from our craftsmen. Heber, in particular, has become a master sword maker. Whatever caused them to leave, Achida felt the danger was past and made us all return with him."

"Jael!" Rivka called. "It is time for us to go."

Jael stood. "Thank you for showing me how to make the locust cakes."

"You must take some with you. Wait here." Zahra scurried into the tent.

The steady pounding of the hammer stopped ringing. Rivka called again. "Niece! Your uncle will be angry if we are not home before he wants his dinner."

"I'll be right there."

Zahra came out of the tent and handed Jael some cakes wrapped in linen. "Here. See if you like them." She leaned in close to Jael. "If you tell Pallu they're Achida's favorites, I know he'll love them!"

Jael let out a short, loud laugh. Her friend was very perceptive. "Thank you. You and Sanura must come visit us later this week. Before Sanura gets too big!"

"We will."

Jael walked away and stepped into the path of Heber. He stopped short, cursing under his breath, before they collided.

"I'm sorry, m-my lord." Jael bowed her head low. "I should have looked where I was going."

He took a deep breath. "I should also have been more careful."

She glanced up, becoming entranced at once by his deep green eyes. His lips curled in a soft smile. "Tell me your name again?"

She had to think before answering. "Jael, my lord."

"Jael. *Little gazelle.* Is that what it means?"

She nodded.

"It suits you."

Rivka rounded the tent. "Jael! We must leave-" She stopped when she saw Heber. "I'm sorry, my lord."

He shook his head. "I apologize for delaying your niece." He took a step then paused. "Feel free to visit us again. I know my sister-in-law and Sanura are most pleased to have your company."

Rivka nodded. "Thank you." She grabbed Jael's hand as Heber strode toward the river. "Come. We must hurry home." She smiled as her gaze followed the handsome man. "But I do not think Pallu will mind if I tell him why we were late."

4 The Hills of Ephraim

A Week Later

The week spent with Edin had not been as peaceful as Deborah had hoped. The dream of Sisera and the idol repeated until the night before her family was due to come home. On that night she knelt in the corner while Edin slept. She prayed to be delivered from the dream. *I will not serve another god, Lord. I will not return to Sisera. Free me from this nightmare. You know my heart. Is this dream because I fear to do your will and marry Lapidoth? I will obey you. I pray you soften my heart toward him. Grant me peace, Lord.*

She fell asleep on her knees, head pressed to the floor, her arms stretched out before her. Conscious that she dreamt, she was relieved to see that this time the nightmare did not return. Instead, she saw a line of people standing under a grove of palm trees.

Old men spoke with younger ones as they waited. Women, too, stood in line. Some of the people wore the simple tunics of peasants, but others dressed in linen or wool robes. As she watched, more people arrived and stood. Deborah's view of the crowd broadened, as if she now flew above them. The line of people grew and grew until it stretched through the hills and down to the plains. And still the people kept coming. She heard their voices.

"Justice, I ask for justice."

"Have mercy, Lord. Please, help me."

"Wisdom. Who is wise enough to discern the will of our God?"

The scene shifted again. Now she sat in a tent. At first she feared she would dream again of Sisera, but as she looked around, she realized the tent was not one of the Canaanites. The clothes she wore were her own, simple and modest. Remiel appeared before her.

She knelt before the angel. "What is it the Lord desires?"

"The Lord seeks a willing and contrite heart." Remiel's voice filled her soul with joy. "He has found it in you, Deborah. You have resisted the call of the gods of Canaan and the Lord is pleased. Look on me, servant of the Most High."

She raised her head. Light glowed around the angel, illuminating the tent with such brilliance that she squinted to protect her eyes.

"Prepare yourself now for what the Lord will do. Power and honor are yours, Deborah. More than any woman has been given."

Deborah shuddered. "No. I desire only to serve. I don't wish for power."

Remiel smiled down at her. "That is why it shall be yours. Seek the Lord in all you do, and you need not fear what will happen. Rest now, Deborah, for the work will be hard. Wait upon the Lord and see how He blesses those who serve Him."

The angel reached out toward her and Deborah fell into a dreamless sleep.

"Wake up!"

Deborah stirred and opened her eyes, closing them in pain from the bright sunshine pouring in through the doorway.

Edin rocked her shoulder. "I'm hungry."

Deborah rolled away from the light and tried again to open her eyes. "Why is the door open?"

"I had to make water."

She struggled to sit up. "How long have you been awake?"

"Not long. But I'm hungry." He tugged on Deborah's linen shift. "Father and Grandfather are coming home today."

"God willing, they will be home before supper." She rubbed her face then stretched, trying to loosen the knots in her muscles. "Go next door and see if Tamar has some bread made." Edin jumped up and ran for the door. "Ask nicely, little one."

Deborah poured water into a bowl to wash her face and hands. She pulled her blue woolen tunic over her head then tied the striped sash about her waist. She sat braiding her hair as Edin came back, chewing a hunk of bread. Tamar followed him in.

"What's wrong?" She asked. "I didn't see you at the well. I thought you must have gotten up earlier."

Deborah tied the braid into a knot before wrapping a piece of cream linen around her head. "I am well. I overslept is all." She chuckled. "Don't tell Bithia!"

Tamar smiled. "I won't. What are you making for their supper?"

Deborah scratched her arm. "I don't want to make anything that will not keep, in case they are delayed."

"If you make a lentil soup, I'll prepare some hummus."

Deborah glanced up at her sister-in-law. "Perhaps you could teach me how to make honey cakes? Bithia has told me how good they are."

Tamar blushed. "We will make the dough this afternoon while Edin sleeps."

Deborah stood. "Wonderful. It will be a meal fit to celebrate our family's return."

She and Edin spent the morning sweeping the house and making bread. They beat the rugs outside. Deborah had cleaned the bed linens the day before, wanting to make everything as clean and fresh as possible for Daliyah. *It will be hard enough to start life with a new husband and family. I want her to be pleased with her new home.* Some months before, Deborah had picked wild roses on the hillside. She'd dried the petals and now put some in a bowl. She placed the fragrant flowers on a shelf in the wall that separated Avram's section of the house.

Tamar pulled the delicate cakes from the clay oven and dropped them into the cloth Deborah held open between her hands. Edin ran toward them from the center of town, his feet kicking up miniature dust storms.

"They're back! Father and Grandfather! Grandmother too!"

Tamar removed the last cakes from the oven as Edin approached. He went to grab Deborah's hand, but she backed away, arms filled with honey cakes. He turned to Tamar.

"Come with me! Come and see!"

Tamar brushed the crumbs from her hands and the front of her tunic. "Can you finish preparing the dinner?"

Deborah nodded. She took the cakes into the house and placed them into a basket, making sure the cloth covered them to keep their warmth. The aroma of garlic permeated the house.

Deborah gave the lentil soup a final stir and seasoned it with a pinch of coriander. She grabbed a bucket and ran out to the pen at the side of the house to milk the goat. She retrieved enough for several cups. Standing, she caught sight of a group of people walking down the center of the village. Many families had gone to Shiloh, traveling together for safety. She couldn't yet see her father and Avram, but knew they were in the crowd.

She placed the milk on a shelf then hurried to the oven to pull out the loaves of bread she'd made. By this time, the various families headed to their own homes. Deborah saw Edin running ahead of the group along with Nathan. She brought the loaves inside and placed them in baskets. She looked around the house. *It will be crowded with all the family.*

Edin flew into the room, his round face lit with excitement. "They brought a donkey! We have a donkey!"

Nathan grinned behind his nephew. "It's true!"

"What do we need a donkey for?" Deborah wiped her hands on the cloth at her waist. She pulled it out and set it in a niche in the wall.

"It carries a surprise!" Nathan's smile grew wider. "For you!" He clapped his hand over his mouth.

"What?" Deborah shook her head as the boys bounded outside again. Through the open doorway she could see Avram and Daliyah, as well as Palti and Tamar. Others followed close behind them, but she couldn't see their faces.

Strange. Who else has come besides my family? "Nathan!"

Her brother didn't hear her, or perhaps he ignored her call, as he proceeded to scurry up to the crowd coming toward the house. Deborah sighed and turned back to her duties within; she would know soon enough who else came and what they brought. She pulled a sack of wine from the storage area, as well as several more cups. She only hoped they had enough for everyone.

Nathan and Edin scampered in, squealing with laughter. Avram and Daliyah followed. Avram cast a stern glare. "Boys! Quiet down!"

Deborah stepped forward. "Brother, it is good to have you home." Nathan and Edin scurried behind her. Edin grabbed onto her tunic, pulling the fabric to cover his face.

Avram put his arm around the woman next to him. "You remember Daliyah? She is now my wife." She stood as tall as his shoulder. Linen wrapped her head, but Deborah could see light brown hair peeking out along her forehead.

"Welcome, Daliyah. Sister." Deborah moved toward them, but was stopped by Edin who grabbed her leg and yanked her back. "Edin? Let go!"

Palti and Tamar entered the room, forcing Avram and Daliyah to step to the corner. Behind them came Bithia. "Do you have supper ready?" She hurried to the pot and frowned. "What else is prepared?"

"We have two loaves of bread, hummus and honey cakes that Tamar made."

Bithia's hands flew to the front of her tunic and she pulled on her sash. "I do not think that will be enough."

"I have olives," Tamar offered. "I will go and fetch a bowl."

Bithia nodded, distracted. "Good, good."

"Daughter!" Azareel called from the doorway. Her uncle, Leb, stood next to him. Deborah ran to greet them.

She embraced her father first. "I am so glad you are home. The journey was not too difficult?"

"No." Azareel patted her back. He separated himself from her, holding her at arm's length and piercing her with his look.

"What is it?" She worried at what hid behind his eyes. "What has happened?"

Leb put a hand on her shoulder. "All in good time. First, do you have a welcome for me, Niece?"

She smiled at the chubby man's round face and broke from her father's embrace to give her uncle a hug. "Of course. How is Rachel? Did she come with you?"

"No, no." Leb chortled under his breath. He pulled Deborah further into the house. "She is preparing for yet another grandchild."

Deborah beamed. "Katriel?"

Leb squeezed her shoulder. "Yes! Due in a month or so, but Rachel worries the baby might come early."

"I will pray for the mother and child both."

"Good." Leb's eyes flickered over to the doorway.

Deborah followed his glance. A tall man with red hair stood at the entrance. Her heart skipped a beat. "Lapidoth?"

Avram scowled. "He insisted on coming with us."

Deborah broke away from Leb and took a step toward the soldier. Her hands fluttered to straighten the linen wrapping her hair and to flatten the wrinkles in her dress. "I am surprised to see you."

The rest of the family stepped back to watch their reunion. Lapidoth remained in the doorway, his imposing frame obscuring the evening light. He stared at her.

Deborah could only guess at the coldness her betrothed had to endure from her family on this journey. She longed to put him at ease.

Leb coughed. "There is a matter we need to discuss."

Fear and confusion pulsated through Deborah's thoughts with each beat of her heart. *Has something happened? Has someone told Azareel of my disgrace?* She struggled to keep herself calm. "Let us eat first." She hurried to the soup. "You all must be famished."

Avram left Daliyah's side and strode over to her. "No. We discuss this now."

Deborah surveyed the room. Daliyah stood with her head bowed, obviously uncomfortable with the situation. Bithia, Nathan and Edin huddled together in the far corner of the house, while the men in the room all scrutinized Deborah. *Is this a trial? Have I been accused of some wrongdoing?* "What is it?"

Azareel gestured with his hands. "Sit." He motioned again to Lapidoth who remained in the doorway. "Come."

Deborah sat in the center of the room between Avram and Azareel. Lapidoth sat opposite her, his face showing no expression. Azareel looked to Leb, still standing near the doorway. "Show her."

The portly man shuffled outside. Deborah was sure the men could hear the pounding of her heart in the silence that permeated the room. Leb returned, struggling with the weight of the wooden chest he carried. He lowered it to the floor in front of Deborah then wiped the sweat from his forehead before sitting down near Lapidoth.

No one spoke.

Deborah looked around at the men around her. *What do they want me to do?*

Avram sat to her far right, where he could easily see her face, as well as Lapidoth's. "Open it."

She reached out and removed a wooden peg that fastened through a leather loop on the front of box. Glancing up at Lapidoth, she glimpsed the flash of some emotion racing across his eyes. Anguish? Fear? Her hand froze over the chest as she watched him. His eyes focused on hers. He settled his face into a neutral attitude before giving her a small nod. She lifted the wooden lid.

Deborah gasped as she jerked her hand away from the chest. The box, which stood about a foot in height and two feet in length, was filled with gold and silver coins. "What is this?"

Leb smiled. "It is your dowry."

Deborah furrowed her eyebrows. "What?"

Her uncle shrugged. "It is your dowry."

She could see Lapidoth's jaw tighten as he sought to keep his emotions in control. *He's angry. But why?* "Where did this come from?"

Leb shifted his weight and rubbed his knees. "When you worked for me, making wicks. Did you never wonder what I did with the money we received from their sale?"

Deborah shook her head. "I worked to help you. To help Rachel. Not for money."

"It would not have been right, to make you work for free. But I knew you lacked for nothing in our home." He shrugged again. "I invested the money you earned, hoping to create a dowry worthy of the Lord's prophet."

"Invested? How?"

"Merchants. Traders in spices from Egypt." Leb grinned. "This past year, with the Canaanites cutting off the routes, the price for any rare commodity has risen by a hundred fold."

Deborah studied the men around her. Leb's face reflected his pleasure. Lapidoth remained strained. Azareel sat with his head bowed, while Avram's eyes fairly danced with anticipation. Her brother leaned toward her.

"Don't you see? With this wealth you will lack for nothing. If you feared being a burden on your family, you needn't worry now."

"What do you mean?"

His gaze flickered over to Lapidoth and Deborah saw the hatred her brother held for the red-haired man. "You need not marry. You can be an independent woman, free from the ties of a husband."

A hush fell throughout the house. Her flesh rose with goose pimples as she weighed the implications of her brother's announcement. *I don't have to marry this man. This brute who ordered my rape. I don't have to obey any man. With this wealth, I could forever live in my own home. Serving no one.* She stared at the coins in the box. An image from her nightmares intruded on her thoughts. The voices she heard call from the idol of Baal called to her now from the chest. *Serve us, Deborah. We can give you anything you desire.*

She stifled a scream and pushed herself away from the coins. She tried to catch her breath, but her lungs wouldn't cooperate.

"Daughter?" Azareel placed a hand on her shoulder. "Are you well?"

Her body shaking, Deborah lifted her face to Lapidoth. His shoulders straightened. He seemed to steel himself against whatever she would say to him. "Have you found fault in me?"

He looked puzzled. "What?"

She inhaled deeply, hoping the act would still her trembling. She rose to her feet and walked around the chest to stand before her betrothed. "Have you found fault in me? Do you wish to write out a divorce decree and put me aside?"

Lapidoth stood, his face etched with emotion. "No. I still desire to have you for my wife

"Then this money will be yours."

Avram moaned in frustration while the rest of the family let out a gasp. The warmth of God's spirit flooded Deborah's body. **Well done, Beloved.** She basked in the Lord's pleasure, His love overflowing her spirit.

Lapidoth tensed again before reaching his hand out to grasp hers. "No. The money is the Lord's. He will instruct you."

Tears sprang to her eyes as the Lord melted the coldness of her heart toward the man in front of her. She tightened her grip on Lapidoth's hand. "God's will be done. He has made me glad this day, to be betrothed to a man such as you."

The lines of his face deepened as Lapidoth searched her eyes, as if seeking validation of her statement. "I will strive to serve the Lord, and you, with all the strength I have."

Deborah turned to her family. "Come. Tamar and I have prepared a dinner to celebrate your safe return." She opened her arms to Daliyah. "Sister, welcome. I am sorry, on this, your first night here, our thoughts should have been on making you feel at home." She pulled Daliyah to the center of the room and sat her down next to Avram.

Tamar stepped forward and placed a bowl of olives on the rug before Azareel while Deborah went to the soup. Lapidoth sat next to Leb. The younger boys fought to sit next to the soldier. The rest of the family crowded in on the rug as Deborah and Tamar served the food. Once Azareel said the blessing, Deborah did her best to lighten the mood of the house by drawing Daliyah into conversation. Soon Bithia joined in, telling Deborah and Tamar about the news in Shiloh. All the while, Deborah caught her brother's cold stare from the corner of her vision. The only thing that lessened the sadness of her heart at his anger was the glow she could see in Lapidoth's eyes when she glanced his way.

Deborah laid out her blanket for Leb and Lapidoth in the far corner of the house. Her father and Bithia had already fallen asleep, Nathan next to them. Edin too, had crept in by Bithia, too nervous of Daliyah to want her near him. Avram whispered to his wife before she lay down behind the half wall. He and Daliyah were the only others awake in the house. Leb and Lapidoth had stepped outside to take care of the donkey that had born the burden of Deborah's dowry.

Avram motioned to his sister. His cold eyes softened as she neared him. "You are determined, then? To marry that man?"

Deborah put a hand on his shoulder. "I have not wavered since the betrothal ceremony. God has decreed this, and I am happy to do His will."

Avram snorted. "Happy?"

She rubbed his shoulder. "Yes. God has planted a seed in my heart for Lapidoth." She leaned forward and whispered. "It isn't the same love that you and Eglah shared. But it is a kind of love. And I know it will grow, if I allow it to." She took her brother's face in her hands. "Please, Avram. Soften your heart toward my husband. He is doing what the Lord demands as well."

Avram gave her a slight nod. "I will try."

She stood on her tip toes and gave him a kiss on the forehead. "That is all I ask."

Avram stiffened. Deborah turned to see Lapidoth and Leb in the doorway. She smiled at her brother. "Goodnight. Don't keep your new wife waiting any longer."

Avram looked to the others. "Goodnight, Uncle." He took a deep breath. "Lapidoth. Good night."

She grinned at the surprise on the Lapidoth's face. "Good night."

Deborah grabbed her traveling cloak from the corner of the house. She would use it to wrap herself at Palti's house.

Lapidoth stepped in front of the doorway. "Did you mean what you said? That you are glad about our betrothal?"

A ripple of anxiety ran down her spine as she approached him. *Help me Lord, to forget the past and remember the feelings you gave me this evening for this man.* She searched his face and read again his fear. Fear that she would reject him, now that her family no longer observed them. "I am glad, Lapidoth. Glad the Lord has chosen such a good man to be my husband."

"I promise. . . ." Color rose to his cheeks. "I swear to you, I will never harm you."

She glanced furtively around the room. "I know," she murmured.

He leaned his head toward hers and matched her low tone. "I'll leave tomorrow and winter in Kedesh with my men. I will repair the house my father built there."

Her response froze on her lips. *Kedesh? So close to Jabin in Hazor?*

He placed a hand on her arm. "What is it?"

"Nothing." She offered him a slight smile. "When will you return so we can marry?"

He squeezed her elbow before letting his hand drop to his side. "It may not be until the following spring. I will come for you when I have built a house worthy of God's prophet."

"I will be waiting."

5 Harosheth

Late Winter, Several Months Later

"Your Hebrew whore is pregnant."

Sisera looked up from the table where he studied his maps and made plans for this summer's campaigns. Miu stood in the doorway, her small frame trembling with anger, her black eyes rimmed red from crying.

"Did you hear me?" She strode into the room. His slave, Iabi, took a step toward her, but Sisera stopped him with a wave.

"Leave us."

The dark man nodded before exiting to the courtyard.

"Come, Wife." He pointed to a chair across from him. "Would you like some wine?"

"No! I do not want wine!" Her arm swept across the table. Sheets of papyrus flew into the air, fluttering down like autumn leaves. "I want to know what you will do with this bastard!"

Her arm stretched toward the table again, but Sisera stood and grabbed it. He turned it until she cried out. "Do not. Touch. My things." He twisted her arm again. "Understand?"

Miu screamed.

"Understand?"

"Yes!" She sobbed. "Yes."

He let her go and strode around the table. He pushed her down into a chair. "Now. Tell me what has upset you."

Her dark face paled under his scrutiny. "The whore you have been rutting with is pregnant."

His hand stung with the force of his slap against her face. Her head snapped backward. "Be careful how you speak to me."

"How can you do this to me? Humiliate me in this fashion?"

"In all the years you have been with me I have had hundreds of women. Why does this one bother you?"

"I never saw them." Her body crumpled against the chair. "She is under my roof. My servant."

"Jabin gave her to me. She was my reward for my service to the king." He rested his hands on the wooden arms of the chair and leaned down close to her face. "This is my house. Everything in it is mine. I have given you two sons. They will inherit all my wealth. What more do you want?"

A tear fell from her eye. "I want your respect. Your love."

He brushed the tear away. "That is the one thing you cannot have."

Miu struck his hand. "Why? What have I done to displease you?"

Sisera laughed. "You never did please me. You were the person my mother and the king chose for me to marry. I have done my duty by them and to you. The king has his soldiers, you have your sons."

Her eyes grew hard under his stare. "And what does that whore give you that I cannot?"

Deborah. She reminds me of Deborah. "Nothing."

"Then send her away."

"You dare order me?" He raised his arm as if to strike her again. She covered her face. He let his hand come to within an inch of her cheek. "You will never speak to me again the way you have today. You will not come into my presence, unless I summon you. If I am in residence here, you are to take your meals in your room, away from the children and out of my sight." He turned from her and strode back to his seat at the opposite side of the table. "Iabi!"

The large Egyptian stepped through the courtyard entrance.

"Take her to her room." His wife sat quaking in the chair. "Inform the other servants that she is to stay there until I leave for Hazor next week."

Iabi nodded to Sisera then dragged the sobbing woman from the chair and out of the room.

He sent for the girl when he retired to his quarters that night. Iabi poured him a goblet of wine and brought a robe of soft wool for him to change into while he waited.

Sisera took the wine and paced to the window. He looked out over the land below, the oil lamps of Harosheth twinkled like faraway stars. He turned back to Iabi. "Leave me."

The Egyptian bowed and left the room as the girl entered. The tension in Sisera's shoulders melted away at the sight of her. Her golden brown curls framed her heart-shaped face. Her brown eyes danced in the candlelight. One corner of her pink lips lifted in a smile.

"You sent for me, my lord?"

He studied her more intently and took note of the slight roundness of her belly, the soft glow of her cheeks. "You are with child?"

Her smile became tentative. "Yes."

"Why do you look so frightened?"

She looked toward the floor. "Are you pleased?"

"Come here."

The girl took a hesitant step toward him.

"Come, come."

She kept her head bowed as she crossed the floor, her bare feet making no sound on the stones. He lifted her head and grinned. "I am very pleased." His fingertips traced along her cheekbone and down her neck. The girl shivered with delight. Her eyes, the color of ripe dates, looked up at him in anticipation. She lifted herself onto her toes and drew her lips together. He brushed them with his thumb, excited by the flush of pink that colored her cheeks. He lowered his head and pressed his lips to hers. She squeezed herself next to him, her arms wrapping around his waist and pulling him even closer. He scooped up her petite body, carrying her to his bed without ever breaking the kiss.

After their lovemaking, the girl lay with her head on Sisera's chest. His fingers played with her hair while she slept. *What is her name?* He frowned as he struggled to remember it. Letting out a soft snort of laughter, he ran his fingers down her arm. *What does it matter? She satisfies me. That is enough.*

He had not approached the girl for the first months after she'd arrived. Consumed with thoughts of finding the prophet, he'd secretly pooled together a handful of the best spies and sent them out. Meanwhile there had been more rebellions to put down, and the distribution of the grain to guard.

But when he'd returned to Harosheth in the autumn months, he had found himself drawn to the slave. Instead of forcing himself on her, as was his right, he'd decided to make a game of seducing her. To practice, as it were, for the time Deborah would be returned to him. It hadn't been easy. The girl had trembled like a frightened rabbit the first few times she'd been brought to him. But Sisera kept his distance. He had her brought to his study and asked her questions about herself, about her faith, about her god. Once he saw her fear had abated, he allowed himself to glance at her with longing.

At first she shied away, her eyes darting to the floor. But as the weeks went on, she would hold his gaze longer, studying him herself. That led to conversations between them over shared cups of wine and then, a lingering touch of his hand on hers as he took the goblet from her and sent her away, always with a heavy sigh and a look of regret in his eyes.

She had given herself to him willingly. She had taken his hand one night as he reached for the wine. Her face, flushed with passion, her whole body quivering with it. "Please," she'd whispered. "Do not send me away."

Sisera chuckled to himself as remembered how he'd acted surprise at her offer. He knew it would delight her to think that she seduced him. That she controlled the situation. He'd taken her to bed that night and enjoyed himself more than he had with any woman before. But he knew it paled next to how it would be with Deborah.

Deborah.

Still the spies found no sign of her, but he would not relent. He would find her. She would be his.

6 The Hills of Ephraim

Several Weeks Later

A late spring rain had drizzled through the night. Deborah breathed in the smell of damp earth as she made her way to the well. Daliyah and Tamar walked beside her.

Daliyah's free hand jerked to her stomach. "I felt it! The baby moves!"

Deborah took her sister-in-law's jug. "Already? Are you sure?"

Daliyah's face glowed with happiness. "Yes! It flutters inside me. Like a moth against my stomach!"

Tamar's eyes showed her disappointment. "That's wonderful. Now you know the baby will be strong, if it is moving so young."

Tamar tried to hide her humiliation, but Deborah could see the pain behind her smile. Tamar had been a wife for four years and still had no child, while Daliyah had become pregnant the month after she arrived in their village.

"You should let Avram know," said Deborah. "Go on. I'll carry your jug as well."

Daliyah glanced back toward the house. "Are you sure?"

"Yes." Deborah chuckled. "Go!"

Daliyah sprinted toward home. Deborah longed to give Tamar a hug, but couldn't with the two jugs in her arms. Her sister-in-law shuffled toward the well.

Deborah caught up to her. "Don't worry. Your time will come."

Tamar searched her face. "Are you sure? Or do you just hope?"

"It is more than a hope. I can't believe the Lord would not grant you a child of your own."

Tamar looked crestfallen. "But you have not seen anything?"

"No."

They walked in silence. A crowd gathered around the well. Not just of women, but men also. Deborah slowed her pace. "What's going on?"

One of the men turned as they approached. "There she is."

The group split apart and a boy, perhaps twelve or thirteen approached her. "You are the prophet?"

Deborah's blood froze. No one outside her village had called her prophet for almost a year. She studied the boy as he neared her. He had not reached his full height, but still stood tall for his age, only slightly shorter than Deborah herself. His clothes were of the Israelite style, but made of finer linen than a peasant.

"Are you the prophet?" he asked again.

Lord, protect me. "I am." *Is this a trick of the Canaanites?*

"My grandfather did not say the prophet was a woman."

Deborah shrugged. "Perhaps he didn't know."

The boy drew himself up. "My grandfather is a wise man. If the prophet he seeks is a woman, he would know it."

She shifted the jugs she carried onto her hips. "Then maybe I am not the prophet he seeks."

A gust of wind tossed the boy's straight black hair into his dark eyes. As he brushed it aside Deborah could see him chew on his lower lip. A deep crease in his forehead made her laugh under her breath. *Poor boy, to be so confused.*

She took a step toward him. "Why don't you tell me what your grandfather desires and I'll seek the Lord's guidance as to whether I'm the one to help."

The worry lines in the boy's brow smoothed out. "My grandfather and I set out from Jerusalem two days ago. He said the Lord called him to the hills to teach the prophet."

Deborah's stomach rolled with guilt. She had to admit to herself that she'd enjoyed the months of peace. "Teach the prophet what?"

The boy shook his head. "All I know was he needed to come into the hills. He said the angel would tell him where to find the prophet."

Deborah dropped the jugs she carried. They fell to the ground with a heavy thunk and rolled. "What angel? What was his name?"

"He did not give his name."

"Did he say what the angel looked like?"

The boy's eyes sparkled with excitement. "He was tall, with white hair and no beard. And his eyes were the deep blue of a fall sky."

Her heart beat like a rabbit's. "Remiel!" She rushed to the boy's side. "Take me to your grandfather!"

Tamar ran to her. "Sister, you cannot go alone with him!"

Deborah stopped, frustrated at the laws of decorum that governed her life. She turned to the boy. "What is your name?"

"I am Jude bar Lael of the tribe of Levi."

"Jude, where is your grandfather?"

"He waits for the prophet in the palm grove on the road between here and Bethel."

Deborah placed her hand on his arm. "Go to him. Ask him to come here and stay with my family."

Jude backed away. "My grandfather was told to set up his tent in the grove. The angel said to wait there for the prophet." The dark haired boy shook his head. "He will not leave."

Deborah shivered remembering her dream of sitting in a tent in the grove of trees. "A low tent? Brown with a deep red roof?"

Jude's eyes widened. "When did you see it?"

"The angel showed it to me, many months ago." Deborah hurried over to the fallen jugs. "I must bring water to my family. Then I will ask my father to accompany me to where your grandfather waits." She ran to the well, the villagers making a clear path for her. They whispered questions to her as she filled the containers with water.

"What does it mean?"

"What did you see, Deborah?"

A young woman, with a baby on her hip, touched Deborah's shoulder. "Is there trouble? Are the Canaanites coming?"

Deborah finished her task then faced the people. "Do not fear. God has not told me of any impending attack or disaster." The crowd seemed to let out their breath as one. "I do not know what this stranger wants, but I know it is only for our good."

She hoisted the jugs against her hips and waited for Tamar to fill her containers. Deborah nodded toward Jude. "Go now. Tell your grandfather that my father and I will come directly." The boy sped off, his brown tunic flapping behind him.

Deborah and her father approached the grove of trees.

Azareel hesitated. "What have you seen? What does this man want?"

"I'm not sure. I didn't see the man, just this place." She tried to sound more confident than she felt. "This is a good thing, Father. Somehow I will be able to help many people here."

Azareel nodded. "Then let us see what this man wants to teach you."

The dark red cloth of the tent's roof appeared through the trees. Jude sat outside its entrance at the feet of his grandfather. The old man rested on a short wooden stool. The breeze picked up strands of his fine gray hair and lifted them around his head, as if his skull burned with white fire. He sat with his elbows on his knees, his body moving in a slight rocking motion. Jude spotted Deborah and placed his hand on his grandfather's back, leaning in to speak to him.

"The woman I told you about is here."

The old man raised his head. Eyes, clouded milky white, blindly sought Deborah. She drew near to him and knelt. "I am Deborah bat Azareel."

"I am Obed of the tribe of Levi." As old as he seemed, his voice still had strength. Authority.

"What do you need of me?"

The man struggled to straighten his back. "I was a priest of the Lord. I served Him with all my heart at His Tabernacle for most of my life." His shoulders slumped forward. "Until my eyes dimmed. I could not bear to be so close to the Holy of Holies and know I could never enter His presence again. I went home to my family in Jerusalem and prayed the Lord would allow me to die." His dead eyes filled with tears. "What was my life if I could not serve Him?" He sighed. "For many years I despaired that God kept me alive. Until I quieted my spirit before Him and He showed me new work I could do."

His deep, gravel-filled voice moved Deborah's spirit. *I could listen to him for days and never tire.* "What did the Lord desire?"

"He told me to teach the sons of Abraham. And so I have done. In Jerusalem, in Micmash, and Bethlehem, I have gone out and taught the young men about our God, so that they can teach their families."

An elderly woman came out of the tent, carrying a flat loaf of bread. She stopped when she spotted Deborah and her father. "Why didn't you tell me that guests were here, Jude?"

The boy stood. "I'm sorry, Grandmother. They only just arrived."

The woman placed the matzo in the pan sitting over a fire next to the tent. Obed grinned a nearly toothless smile. "This is my beloved wife, Elisheba. She is truly my helpmate and saver of my life."

Elisheba wiped her hands on a stained cloth hanging from her belt. "And you are my life, Husband." Even at her advanced age, she moved with grace and energy. She looked to Azareel. "Are you the prophet my husband is seeking?"

Azareel shook his head. "No. It is my daughter."

Elisheba's focused her sight on Deborah. "A woman?" Her eyes brightened after a moment. "You were the girl who called for the fasting. Five years ago?"

Deborah nodded.

Elisheba moved to Obed's side. "That was the year after we left for Jerusalem." She stood behind him and placed her hands beside his neck. "Do you remember, Husband? How we longed to travel to Shiloh to hear the new prophet, but couldn't because I was so ill?"

Obed covered her hand with one of his own. "Yes. Praise God that you were delivered from death."

Elisheba beamed. "Blessed be His name." She squeezed her husband's shoulders. "Well, Obed. What do you think about teaching a woman the laws of the Lord?"

Deborah's gaze flickered from Elisheba's amused face to Obed's more serious one. The old man patted his wife's hand. "I think the Lord has quite the sense of humor." Again, his toothless grin flashed. "But if the Lord has taught me anything, it is that anyone can serve Him." He slapped his hands on his knees. "And so a blind old priest will teach a woman the laws of their God."

The breeze that had been blowing gently throughout the grove intensified. The Lord's Spirit spoke to Deborah as the wind swirled around them.

Listen and learn, Deborah. Prepare yourself for my work.

I will Lord.

You will lead my people. Through you, I will save Israel.

She prostrated herself under the weight of His words. *I am only a woman, Lord. I cannot do this.*

The wind continued to move around her, wrapping her in its energy. **On your own, you can do nothing. Through me, you will become greater than any woman before you.**

She raised her head and spoke into the zephyr. "I am afraid!" The others stood, faces filled with awe at the whirlwind that surrounded them.

Do not fear. The air stilled. **Lean on me. I will give you strength.**

Deborah remained kneeling. The boy, Jude, stared at her as if she were some kind of animal he'd never seen. Obed rose to his feet, leaning on Elisheba for support. "Glory to God in the highest. He has given a blind man new life and allowed him to see the salvation of his people." His wife led him over to the prophet.

Deborah took the old man's hands. "I am the Lord's servant. I will do all that He asks of me."

7 Southern Jordan River Valley

The Same Day

"**A**chida, my friend, what brings you here?" Pallu put down his hammer and the blade he'd been working on. "Is all well?"

The distinguished older man strode into their camp as if on a mission of importance, accompanied by his older son, Heber. They wore robes of fine Egyptian linen, striped in deep reds and browns. Jael noted that Achida had trimmed his thick silver hair and beard. Heber's golden curls had also been tamed, his darker beard cut close to his chin.

"Jael," hissed Rivka. "Fetch your veil before they see you!"

Jael rose and hurried toward the tent. She cast a glance over her shoulder and met Heber's eyes. His stare froze her step. She had never seen him, or any man, look at her with such frank curiosity. She turned away and ducked into the tent. *What does he want with Pallu?* She knew Achida lacked for nothing, being one of the wealthiest men of the Kenites. She found her veil and secured it in place. She stepped to the doorway just as Pallu swept the curtain aside.

"Niece, fetch us some wine." Pallu allowed his guests to pass him as he held the curtain open. Achida and Heber sat on the woolen rug in the center of the room. Jael took the wine jug out from the back of the tent and found three goblets. She served Achida first, then Heber. Again, his piercing eyes stared at her, causing her hand to shake as she handed him the cup.

He nodded at her. "Thank you."

"It is my pleasure, my lord." Jael turned and filled Pallu's cup.

"Now tend to the fire. See it doesn't go out before our business here is done." Her uncle dismissed her with a wave of his hand.

Jael bowed and exited the tent. Rivka stood outside the doorway. The gray-haired woman wrung her hands. "What do they want?"

Jael shrugged. "I don't know." She left her aunt to eavesdrop by the tent, while she picked up the bellows and flamed the fire under Pallu's work station. The heat warmed her chilled hands. She and Rivka had spent the afternoon washing rugs and bed linens, getting ready for the move back north for the summer months. The Jordan's waters were still cold from the winter rains and the snow from the mountains. Jael rubbed her red, chapped hands over the glowing coals.

Rivka stepped back from the tent as Pallu stuck his head out through the flap. "Rivka. Jael. Come here."

Jael noted the flash of excitement in his eyes, the one that only came when he smelled a profit from some business deal.

"Come! Hurry now!" His head disappeared into the tent as she and Rivka ran to hear the news. They stepped inside together. Achida and Heber still sat, but Pallu stood and waved them inside. "Sit down, sit down."

Jael sat with her aunt across from their visitors. Pallu re-clined to Jael's right. "Niece, I have good news for you."

She lifted her eyes to his face. "What is it, Uncle?"

He could barely contain his happiness. "Achida has come on behalf of his son. He wishes you to be Heber's bride."

Her mind seemed to float outside of her body for a moment. As if her spirit watched the proceedings from outside of herself. She could see Pallu, fairly bursting with the knowledge that he would now be related to the likes of Achida. Rivka, too, looked on with delight. Achida surveyed her with the stern appraisal of a man buying a horse. Heber watched her as one also de-tached. She wondered whether he desired this match or wheth-er it had been made for him.

Pallu spoke again. "I, of course, have agreed. May the gods bless you both." He glanced to Heber.

The young man cleared his throat. "We will be married when your family returns here next autumn."

Everyone turned their gaze toward Jael. *What am I supposed to say?* No one had prepared her for this. Pallu nodded his head in encouragement toward her. She found her voice, soft at first, but gaining in confidence as she spoke. "I thank you, my lord, that I have found favor in your eyes. I am honored and will await our union with much happiness." *At least I will be with friends. Sanura and Zahra. And Heber is a handsome man. Even if a little frightening.*

"Good! Good!" Pallu clapped his hands together. "Let us drink on the arrangement!" Heber drank from his goblet and passed it on to Jael. She lifted her veil from her mouth and took a sip.

"We should have a celebration, before we leave." Pallu turned to the men. "What do you think, Achida?"

"I leave for business in Egypt in three days."

"Well, then," Pallu gestured to Rivka, "We must get busy, Wife. We will invite all we know to attend a dinner here the day after tomorrow. To announce the agreement made between our families."

Only Rivka's eyes betrayed the panic she felt at hosting a feast in two days. "Of course, Husband. Jael and I will prepare a wonderful meal."

Pallu nodded. "I will go to our friends tomorrow and extend the invitation."

"I'm sure Zahra will help as well," offered Heber. "I will ask my brother to send her over tomorrow to assist you."

"Thank you." Rivka bowed her head.

Achida finished his wine and put a hand on Heber's knee. "It is time for us leave." Everyone rose as he did. "We will see you at sunset in two days. I will bring the bride price to you then."

Pallu shrugged and placed his hand on the shoulder of his guest. "You are a man of honor, Achida. I know you will keep our bargain."

Jael shivered. *That's what I am? A bargain?* She studied Heber as he exited the tent. He never smiled, but his eyes remained focused on her the entire time. *What has brought this about? What does he want from me?*

Rivka squealed with delight and ran to hug her niece as Pallu walked his guests outside. Jael could barely breathe from the tightness of her aunt's embrace.

"Heber! I can't believe it!" Rivka squeezed tighter still. "Such a handsome man, and he's to inherit his father's wealth!"

Jael twisted out of her aunt's arms. "But why? Why does he want me?"

Rivka pinched her niece's cheeks. "I told you. You are beautiful! And strong." She released Jael's face and patted the girl's hips. "Anyone can see that you will bear many children. Not like those frail Egyptian women they brought back with them."

Pallu reentered the tent, his hands rubbing together in excitement. "Well, done!" He patted Jael on the back. "I knew taking you in would bring a reward."

Jael's eyes narrowed. "What do you mean?"

Her uncle walked to the back of the tent to pick up the wine jug. He poured a cup and laughed. "I mean nothing. Only that the gods must be pleased with my generosity toward you. To marry into such a family."

"What have you told him about me?"

Pallu shook his head. "I have said nothing, other than to extol your virtues." He tipped his cup to her in a kind of salute. "It is you who have done the work."

"Me?"

He took a swallow of wine. "Your talks with Zahra have proved fruitful, as I knew they would."

Jael clutched at her stomach, trying to stop the sickening feeling as it churned in her abdomen. "I don't understand."

"You told her of your dowry. It seems that Heber wishes to expand their trade to the northern territories. Achida's fortune is in animals and linen. He doesn't want to sell any of it in order for Heber to buy the tools he needs." Again Pallu offered her a toast. "Your dowry will allow him to do that. He has promised me a third of the sheep born this lambing season in return." His eyes shone with excitement. "My own flock!"

Rivka put a hand on her niece's shoulder. "We must discuss our plans for the celebration." She sat Jael down on the woolen rug. "We only have a day and a half to prepare."

Jael tried to focus on the plans Rivka made, but could not help watching Pallu as he paced the room, drinking wine and smiling a cunning grin. She had known a man would be chosen for her, but her parents had allowed her sister to have some say in the decision. Jael's heart cried out in frustration. *You've sold me to a man I hardly know for a flock of sheep?*

Zahra arrived the following morning to help prepare for the feast. She brought locust flour and raisins, as well as jars of honey and olive oil. Jael helped her friend unburden her donkey with the gifts and bring them to the tent. Once inside, they removed their veils.

"Congratulations." Zahra embraced Jael. "I am glad we will be sisters."

"Thank you," said Jael.

Rivka covered her head and fixed a veil around her face. "I'm going with Pallu into town. We'll need more wine. And spices for the meal . . . ." Her aunt continued to mumble to herself as she made her way from the tent.

Jael took the hand mill from the shelf then turned to Zahra. "Would you help me grind some wheat?"

"Of course."

The two women worked in silence, Zahra pouring the grain and Jael grinding the wheel.

"You seem deep in thought," the Egyptian noted. "Are you troubled?"

Jael kept her focus on the grinding stone.

"Are you unhappy with the betrothal?" Zahra stopped pouring the kernels.

Jael shook her head and waited for more grain.

"Then what troubles you?"

"I don't like this feeling." Jael shifted her legs, trying to find a more comfortable position on the hard ground.

"What feeling?"

"That I am nothing but a thing. Property to be bought and sold." She lifted her head. "I would like to have some say in my life. Some control."

Zahra let out a sharp laugh. "Women have no control. We are at the whims of men."

Jael curled her hands into fists. "It doesn't have to be this way."

Her friend sighed. "Of course it does."

"No!" Jael punched her knees. "I believe otherwise."

Zahra sat back and rested on her elbows. "Even the priestesses of the temple answered to the priest."

"I know of a woman, a Hebrew, whose God gave her power."

"Power to do what?"

"She escaped from a priest. And from the commander of the whole Canaanite army."

Zahra raised her eyebrows. "She escaped, but was she free? She had to hide, didn't she?"

"For a while." Jael leaned forward. "This same woman gave orders to the Hebrew soldiers."

"I don't believe you."

"It's true." Her voice rose in excitement. "They tried to rape her, but her God wouldn't allow it. At first, she cowered, as any woman would, but then her God filled her with strength again."

The Egyptian's black eyes narrowed. "How?"

"The Hebrew God speaks to her."

"Through signs? In the sacrifices?"

Jael shook her head. "He speaks to her. She hears his voice."

Zahra sat back, a stunned expression on her face.

"She told the soldiers what to do. The same men who tried to subdue her sat at her feet and accepted her commands." Jael stared at her friend. "I would like to have that power. Or any power. Just to have the ability to say 'this is my desire.' Or 'no, I do not want that.'"

"Where did you meet her?"

Jael's thoughts froze. "What?"

Zahra sat forward and rested her elbows on her knees. "This woman, where did you meet her?"

Jael knew her uncle would be angry if he knew she admitted to being a prisoner. "I didn't meet her. I was told about her."

Her friend shrugged. "It probably never happened."

Jael struck the ground with her hands. "It did. I trust the one who told me."

"It makes no difference. It is not your fate or mine. We are trapped in the roles the gods have placed us in."

"But what if I want more?"

Zahra took hold of Jael's hands. "Do not. Be satisfied with what you have."

Jael stared into her friend's eyes, seeing the sadness behind them. "As you are satisfied?"

Zahra looked away.

Jael squeezed her hand. "Are you happy with Taavi?"

Her friend shrugged. "He is a good man, for the most part." Zahra's lower lip trembled. "The three of them--Achida, Heber, and Taavi are angry men. Men who are hungry for respect and power. They demand it from those around them." She placed her other hand over Jael's. "Put away these thoughts of being in control. It will only bring you pain."

Anxiety rippled through Jael's body. "Pain? How?"

Zahra collected herself and sat back. "Nothing. I meant nothing." She picked up the grain sack. "Come. We have much work to do."

8 The Hills of Ephraim

Several Months Later

Deborah and Jude sat at Obed's feet while Elisheba puttered about the camp, sweeping out the tent, grinding barley kernels into flour. By the third hour, men from the surrounding hillside were lined up by the edge of the grove. Their voices hummed on the morning breeze.

"Should you start hearing their complaints, Grandfather?" asked Jude.

Since setting his tent up between the towns of Ramah and Bethel, Obed's reputation as a priest in God's Tabernacle had spread throughout the hill country. Because of his wisdom, the people came to him to be the judge of any disputes arising between them and their neighbors.

"Not until Deborah has repeated the passage I taught her from yesterday."

Deborah focused her sight past Obed's shoulder and out into the palm trees. "'I will give you peace in the land, and you will be able to sleep without fear. I will remove the wild animals from your land and protect you from your enemies.'" She watched a large frond dance in the wind as she tried to remember the rest of the passage. "'In fact, you will chase down all your enemies and slaughter them with your swords. Five of you will chase a hundred, and a hundred of you will chase ten thousand! All your enemies will fall beneath the blows of your weapons.'"

The old man nodded. "Good." He reached out toward her and Deborah took his hand. "I have never taught one as bright as you." He gave her hand a forceful squeeze. "Truly the Lord is with you."

She smiled at Obed's praise. "He has sent me the finest of teachers."

The old man chortled, his laugh resonating deep within his chest. "You speak words like honey. It is the gift of women to flatter men and make them feel important."

Deborah shook her head. "It isn't flattery. I speak the truth."

"Don't say anymore," Elisheba scolded. "It will only go to his head. I have trouble enough keeping him humble."

Obed chuckled again. "But you do your job well, Wife." He let go of Deborah's hand. "Come, sit beside me. Listen to what the Lord will teach you through the cases of the day." His head tilted toward Jude. "You must go and help Deborah's family in the fields."

Deborah sighed. She wished Obed would allow her to pay him from the money Leb had given her, but he insisted Jude earn the food they bought from the neighboring villages by working in Azareel's fields. As Jude left the camp, he sent the first of the men in line toward his grandfather.

Two men approached Obed. Their gazes flickered to Deborah for a moment before returning to her teacher. The taller man took a step forward.

"I bought a goat from Abner, and three weeks later, it was dead."

Abner, a stocky man with thick brown hair, glowered. "It died because you didn't feed it! You can't expect an animal to live on just a handful of grain."

The tall man sprayed spittle as he argued, "I fed him more than a handful of grain! You sold me a sick goat!"

Obed and Deborah sat in front of the tent throughout the late summer day, not even resting for lunch. Elisheba served them bread and milk, which they ate as they waited for another case to come forward. Deborah nibbled on the snack and thought about the months of learning she'd spent at Obed's feet. It had only taken a few weeks for the surrounding villages to learn that a priest had set up a tent nearby. They came to him seeking counsel for their various disagreements and questions. From the beginning, he'd allowed Deborah to sit and listen to the cases brought before him to judge.

She noted with pleasure the change in the people who came to them. At first, the men would not even look in Deborah's direction, even though she kept her face hidden by a veil so there would be no impropriety. But the more Obed referred to her and asked for her advice, the more tolerant people became of her position, until now it was common for those that came to make their complaints to address both she and Obed.

On the rare occasion that she and her teacher disagreed on a verdict, the two would pray together before Obed gave the final judgment. Sometimes he would take the time to clarify a point of law that she was not yet familiar. But there had been times when, after prayer, Obed had turned to those who waited and said, "The prophet is correct. This is what the Lord says in this matter," and he would proceed to pass the verdict that Deborah had recommended. In those moments, Deborah tried not to fall into the sin of pride, but she did feel a sense of great satisfaction that she had learned so much from the priest in such a short time.

The men even accepted her presence as they came to discuss politics with Obed. Often elders from various towns made their way to the grove to seek the priest's intercession to God on their behalf. The Canaanites had increased the level of attacks throughout the land until all of God's people felt the heavy hand of servitude. The men begged Deborah, as the prophet, for news of God's word. "When will the Lord save us from this oppression?" She had no answer for them, for the Lord's voice had been silent for almost a year.

Deborah and Obed held court in the grove until Jude returned from the fields at dusk. The enticing sent of garlic and onions wafted on the evening breeze as Elisheba opened the flap to their tent to let in her grandson.

"It's time for Deborah to head home to her family, Obed."

The old man nodded. Deborah helped him to his feet. His lips brushed her cheek in a light kiss. "Bless you, Prophet. Go now in peace."

"Thank you. I'll see you tomorrow." She made her way through the grove and up the well-worn path to her village.

Since she spent her days now with Obed, it would be her duty to see to the cleaning of the evening meal in her own home. She also enjoyed taking care of Avram and Daliyah's new baby, a girl they named Sarah. Deborah would often find a moment to steal the baby from her mother and sit with her in the corner of the small mud house. There, with Edin and Nathan at her feet, she would tell the stories of their forefathers that Azareel had shared with her when she was a girl.

The gentle rhythm of the days reminded Deborah of her childhood, before God had entrusted her with the responsibility of speaking to his people. He had not given her another vision, not since Remiel had shown her the palm grove and Obed's tent almost a year ago. But His spirit stirred within her daily as the old priest taught her more of God's law and His words to their forefathers. She reveled in the peace that surrounded her days as she trudged up the hill toward her village. The sun slid behind the horizon, casting the sky in iridescent purples and pinks. Deborah stood for a moment and offered a prayer of thanksgiving for all the Lord had given her.

9 Southern Jordan River Valley

Winter

Jael sat by the river and rinsed the dishes off from the evening meal. The frigid water chapped her skin. She finished the job quickly, so she could return to the women's tent and warm her hands by the fire. She pushed the tent flap aside with her shoulder. Zahra looked up from the corner.

"Heber wants you. In the small tent." She gave Jael a worried look. "He argued with Achida again. I think he's been drinking."

Jael sighed as she put the dishes down. She stopped for a moment to hold her fingers over the fire.

Sanura nursed her son. "Why don't you bring some wine with you?" She gave Jael a knowing look. "Perhaps have a cup before you go to him?"

Zahra retrieved a sack from the back of the tent and poured Jael a cup. "Is it any better with him?"

Jael shrugged. "It is not so bad." She glanced at Zahra. "How is it with you and Taavi?"

"Taavi does his business and falls asleep."

Sanura raised an eyebrow. "Achida is like a bear in bed. I wish he would do his business with a little less enthusiasm."

Jael's cheeks burned at their talk. The other women chuckled at her embarrassment. She stared into the flames of the fire. "It isn't just a physical love I desire. Am I foolish to want love? Respect? Someone to truly know me and still care for me?"

Sanura pulled her baby from her breast then burped him against her chest. "You will never find that with Heber. He is too much like his father." When the babe fussed, she gave him the other breast to suck. "Be satisfied that you live in relative comfort. That your husband does not beat you. You could have it much worse."

Jael finished her wine. "You are right." She brushed her hair, rubbing oil scented with cassia through it. She lined her eyes with kohl then rubbed her cheeks to bring some pink to them. When she finished, she picked up the wine sack and grabbed a clean cup. "Goodnight."

The other women bid her goodnight as Jael left to make her way to the smaller tent. She had married Heber three months ago and settled into life within his father's compound. She worked through the days with Sanura and Zahra. Little tension simmered between the women as each was gifted in different ways, each had an important role to play within the camp. Sanura, as the eldest and the wife of Achida, oversaw the running of the camp. Achida not only had the metal working business, but had accumulated flocks of sheep and goats while in Egypt. With her new son on her hip, Sanura made sure the servants did as they were instructed with regard to those flocks. Zahra, as a gifted weaver, spent most of her time at the loom. Her cloth could be sold for a high price in the city markets and traded with merchants from Egypt and other foreign lands. Jael, as the youngest, did most of the meal preparation and other basic domestic chores. The three women shared a tent, unless requested by one of their husbands, as Heber had Jael.

She arrived at the small tent and called out, "My lord? May I enter?"

"Come in."

Heber smiled when she entered the tent. For a moment she thought it was at her. She felt heat rush to her cheeks, but then he reached out to grab the wine from her hand. "You must have read my mind." He didn't wait for her to give him the cup, instead he threw back his head to drink from the sack. She noted the empty goblet already by his side. He'd begun his drinking much earlier, as Zahra had intimated.

Heber reclined against some pillows on a pallet of linen and woolen blankets. Jael sat by his feet. When he put the wine down, she poured herself a cup. "Is something wrong, my lord?"

His gaze fixed vacantly on the striped wall of the tent. The soft glow of the oil lamps reflected in his green eyes, turning their color almost gold. "I need to move, Wife. To get away from my father and his control." He picked up the wine and took another long swallow. "I have a plan."

Jael's heart beat rapidly. She knew Heber was only thinking aloud. He didn't want her opinion. But if she remained quiet, she would know his desire.

"I have more talent at metal working than my father and brother combined." He waved his arms in a furious gesture. "Achida is satisfied selling plows and knives to Israelites, but I want more." He turned to Jael, his eyes ablaze with fury. "I want to see the Israelites destroyed for what happened. Do you understand me?"

Jael sat still, convinced if she moved, Heber might snap in his anger and strike her. "But the treaty," she whispered, hoping to remind her husband of his obligations.

"Damn the treaty and damn the Hebrews!" His red face came within an inch of hers. "I don't care what the Kenite chiefs have said. I want revenge for my brother." He took hold of Jael's face with one hand and squeezed.

Tears sprang to her eyes from the pain. "Please, my lord."

He didn't loosen his grip. "I will unite myself with the Canaanites. Once the spring comes, you and I will leave my father's camp and move to Kedesh. There, I will present King Jabin with a sword of such craftsmanship that he will take me into his confidence." Heber's face glowed with manic enthusiasm. He released Jael's chin and ran his hands through her hair. He pulled her close and pressed his lips against hers in a painful kiss. When she whimpered, it seemed to excite him more. He forced his mouth against hers even harder.

"I will become the chief weapon maker to the Canaanites. My swords will draw Israelite blood. In that way, I will be revenged." He forced her to lie on the ground. Jael closed her eyes, making herself limp, as he satiated his anger with her body. When he finished, he rolled away to pick up the wine sack. He drank himself into a drunken sleep. Jael lay where he'd left her. He had not dismissed her from the tent, so she would stay there until the morning.

Jael thrashed against the foul smelling guard as he dragged her across the compound. She gained no ground with her weak attempts to escape his grasp. He only dug his fingers deeper into her arms. He pulled aside the flap to a tent and threw her inside. She didn't look around at her surroundings before sidestepping the soldier to make a run for the exit. He caught her

again, wrapped his arms around her chest, then carried her to a low table. Deborah sat across from her. The tall priest, with the dark skin and frightening tattoos, strode toward her. He drew a knife from his belt. Jael felt the blade drive through her hand, but before she could wake, the scene shifted. She stood in front of the tent she shared with Heber. A large man approached her. The air around him vibrated with energy, like the wind during a storm. His white hair was cut short and he wore no beard. The skin on Jael's arms prickled as she gazed at the man before her.

"Do you remember the pain, Jael?" The man's voice echoed in her ears.

She fell to her knees. "Yes, my lord."

"Do you remember the one who gave herself to those men so that you would not suffer?" His deep blue eyes blazed with intensity.

"Deborah. I will remember her always."

"Remember the faces of those who enjoyed your pain. Those who sought to use the Lord's servant against Him."

"I will never forget them."

The man smiled. "And the Lord has not forgotten you, Jael. He will use you in a mighty way. Prepare yourself."

The sound of rushing wind surrounded her as a blinding flash of light consumed the man.

Jael sat up on her mat, panting. Heber stirred beside her. He rubbed his hand over his face.

"What is it? A dream?"

Jael nodded in the muted, pre-dawn light of the tent. "Yes."

Heber rolled away from her and pulled the blanket up to his chin. "Go back to sleep."

Jael rested on her mat, but knew sleep would elude her for the rest of the morning. Instead, she lay awake thinking about what the man of white had told her. *Prepare yourself. The Lord will use you in a mighty way.* Jael shivered with anticipation. She glanced at Heber, knowing instinctively that the man in white was from the Hebrew God. She knew that whatever was coming would go against Heber's desires, but she didn't care. She had longed for this opportunity and she would not fail when it presented itself.

10 The Hills of Ephraim

The Same Day

Deborah rubbed her hands together to try and warm them before picking up the jug of water she'd bring to Obed's tent. Puffy clouds formed with every breath she exhaled as she walked the path. Her thoughts turned to prayers as the early morning sun struggled to break through the gray clouds. *Please, Lord. Send the rain. The winter planting needs to start soon. We need the rain to soften the ground. Have mercy, Lord. Bring the rain.*

An eerie quiet welcomed her at the palm grove. No one waited to greet her outside the tent. A racking cough split through the early morning silence. A low murmur drifted out into the grove.

"Obed?" She called. "Elisheba?"

The gray-haired woman flung back the tent flap. "Come in. Come in."

The dark circles under Elisheba's eyes made Deborah's chest tighten. "What's wrong?" She stepped inside the tent. Obed lie on his pallet, his face the color of ash. Deborah ran to kneel at his side. "What happened?"

Obed's body answered with a fit of coughing. The priest appeared to have aged twenty years. Deborah looked to Elisheba. "When did this come upon him?"

The older woman placed a hand on Deborah's shoulder. "The evening of the Sabbath. He came in after the day with you, complaining he felt tired. He barely made it through prayers before he fell asleep." Deep lines of worry etched Elisheba's face. "The cough began by morning."

"Why did you not come to me?"

"Nothing could be done during the Sabbath. I have already sent Jude to Ramah to talk to the healer there. Maybe some herbs can be found to ease his cough."

With that, Obed's chest heaved again in another fit of hacking. Deborah touched his forehead. "He has a fever."

Elisheba fetched a bowl of water and a cloth. Deborah saw how her friend moved without her usual speed and grace.

"Give me the water. I will tend to him while you rest."

The old woman frowned. "I will see to him."

Deborah took the bowl from her friend's hands. "It will do no good for you to become weakened and sick as well. You rest now, so you are ready for when Jude returns with the herbs."

Elisheba glanced down at her husband, anxiety written across her face. Deborah gently pushed her toward Jude's pallet in the opposite corner. "Go and sleep. I will take care of him."

Deborah knelt back at Obed's side. She wrung out the cloth and held it against her teacher's forehead. He coughed again. Deborah had to move the bowl to keep him from spilling the water. *Please, Lord, heal my master. Strengthen him. Cleanse him from the illness that has taken over his frail body.* As she prayed, Deborah could sense a dark feeling of dread sinking into her bones. *Do not take him. Please don't take him from me, Lord. There's still so much I need to learn.* She continued to pray as Obed's cough, and Elisheba's soft snores, filled the tent. Several hours later, Jude returned carrying a leather pouch filled with herbs. He glanced at his grandmother still sleeping in the corner before sitting by Deborah.

"How is he?"

Deborah hoped her worry wouldn't show in her eyes. "Did you bring medicine?"

Jude held up the pouch. "The healer said to brew a tea from the leaves. She also said to make a plaster of mustard and garlic to place on his chest."

Deborah took the medicine from the boy's hand. "I will get the tea started. You run to my home. Ask Bithia to make the plaster. I know she has done it before."

Jude stood.

Deborah reached out to stop him. "Ask her to send some bread as well. I will make a soup later, once I've made the tea."

"What should I tell the others?"

"What others?"

"There are people waiting for Grandfather to hear their complaints. What should I tell them?"

"Tell them he is sick. They should pray for his healing and come back in a few days."

Jude nodded and ran outside. Deborah placed the last of the morning's water over the cooking fire to boil. She ground the herbs and leaves in a mortar, then put the powder into a square of linen and tied it with a thin piece of leather. Throwing the bundle into the boiling water, she took the pot off the fire and allowed it to steep. *We will need more water for the stew.* It would be a long walk to the well in her village, but it had to be done. She went to Elisheba and gently shook her awake.

The old woman sat up and clutched Deborah's arm. "What has happened?"

"Nothing," Deborah soothed. "I need to get you more water. I did not want you to wake and think I left you."

Elisheba took a deep breath. "Has Jude returned?"

"Yes. I sent Jude for help from Bithia. I made a tea from the herbs he brought. Let it cool, then give it to Obed." She rose and grabbed the water jug. "I will be back as quickly as I can."

Elisheba groaned as she stood. "Thank you."

Deborah embraced her friend. "He will get better."

The old woman sighed. "He is in God's hands."

Deborah exited the tent. Bright beams of sunlight filtered down through the palm fronds and danced about the grove. *How can you shine with such life when death hangs so close?* She wiped the thought from her mind as she hurried toward the path. Several villagers waited along the edge of the grove. A young man stepped forward.

"Deborah! May we speak with you?"

She stopped, aware that she had not put on her veil in her rush to leave the tent. She lowered her gaze to the ground. "I'm sorry, but Obed is sick and cannot hear your cases this morning."

"Please, Prophet," said another man. "Could you hear our complaint?"

She clutched the jar to her chest. "Me?"

"Yes," the first man said. "You sat with Obed when my father brought his case last month. I saw how he consulted you and took your advice. I heard him praise your wisdom."

A great weight pressed down on her, making it difficult to breath. *Me? Judge alone without Obed? Can it be done, Lord? A woman discerning your will in the matters of men?* She took a step away from the group. "I need to bring water to my teacher and minister to him today. I will pray about what you asked of me. Come back tomorrow for my answer." She turned away and ran up the path toward home, not waiting to hear their response.

She spent the day with Elisheba and Bithia, nursing Obed as he drifted in and out of a feverish stupor. At sunset, she and her stepmother returned home. Daliyah had prepared the evening meal. Deborah gratefully sat down to eat.

Azareel said the blessing then tore off a piece of bread to dip in his soup. "How is the priest?"

Bithia frowned. "He is not well. It is a hard illness for one so old to bear."

Her father sighed. "It will be a great loss if he dies. His wisdom has been a blessing throughout the hill country."

The others murmured their agreement. Deborah poked at her food. "Father, there were men today who asked if I would judge their case."

All around her, the household grew still. She felt the stares of her family as she kept her head down. Her father cleared his throat. "What did you tell these men?"

"I told them I would pray about it." She lifted her gaze so she could scan her family's reaction. Avram looked angry. Bithia and Daliyah appeared scandalized. Azareel bowed his head as though in prayer. Deborah stared back down at her soup. "When the angel first showed me the tent, months before Obed arrived, I was alone. I heard the people praying for guidance and I was the only one who could help them."

Avram slapped his legs. "A woman cannot judge the matters of men."

A thought pierced through Deborah's doubt. She lifted her head and faced her brother. "A woman can't, but a prophet may."

Her brother's voice rose in anger. "It would be a sacrilege! Who do you think you are?"

"I think I am God's prophet. I think He has told me that He will use me to save our people."

Avram stood. "Be careful, Sister, how you speak of the Lord. It is one thing to be given visions; it is another to claim the kind of power you are claiming."

Deborah shook her head. "I claim no power. I am only the tool God will use to bring about the salvation of Israel."

Her brother pointed a finger at her. "It has gone too far. All this teaching of Obed's has warped your thoughts."

Azareel placed a hand on his son's leg. "Sit. You are too angry."

Avram pulled himself away. "You have always coddled her. Always she was your favorite. And now look what is happening!" He whirled around to face Deborah again. "A woman should never have been allowed such knowledge and freedom! My sister is insane."

Deborah rose to confront him. "That is your problem, Avram. You have never been able to see me as anything but your sister, the little girl who longed for your attention and love." She gestured with her hands. "I am no longer that girl. I am God's chosen servant. I do His will no matter what the consequence to me."

Avram fumed a moment longer before striding out the door. Deborah growled in frustration. "Why is he so stubborn?"

From his seat, Azareel chuckled. "Perhaps it is a flaw in both my children?"

Her muscles relaxed as she looked at her father. She sat back down. "I have been in prayer about this. And I believe God is leading me to stand in Obed's place."

Bithia's face grew red. "You cannot be serious?"

Azareel placed a restraining hand on her knee. "We will speak no more of it tonight. We will each pray and see how God leads you in the morning."

Deborah nodded. Although her body ached in exhaustion from the work and worry of the day, she knew she would get little sleep tonight.

It was well past the third watch when someone knocked at the door.

"Deborah?" Again a fist pounded against the heavy wood. "Deborah!"

Azareel struggled to get to his feet, but Avram already stood at the entrance. "Who is it?"

Deborah sat up in her corner as the rest of the family stirred. Edin whimpered. Daliyah's voice soothed him back to sleep.

"It is Jude. My grandfather is awake and asking for the prophet. Please, let her come."

"It's the middle of the night! She will come in the morning."

Deborah stood and grabbed her traveling cloak.

"Please." Jude's voice cracked. "I think the end is near. He cries out for Deborah . . . please."

She put her hand on Avram's shoulder. "I need to go to him."

Her brother gave her an irritated glance before shaking off her touch. He opened the door a crack. "We will be there short-ly."

Jude's footsteps pounded in retreat as he ran back to the tent. Avram shut the door. "Wait for me to get my cloak. You can't be walking along that path with just the boy at this time of night."

Deborah picked up an oil lamp and lit the wick while she waited for Avram to retrieve his coat. The muted light cast an eerie glow on the packed earth as they walked through the village. All around, the houses sat as dark sentinels. Deborah pulled her cloak tighter around her neck to fend off the chill. They had to slow their pace along the path to the palm grove, their eyes having difficulty navigating the way, even with the lamp. Jude met them at the edge of the grove and hurried them to the tent.

Inside, Elisheba knelt by her husband's frail body, holding his hand. Her face, glistening with tears in the light of the tent, settled into a look of relief when Deborah entered. She bent closer to Obed. "The prophet is here. Wake up."

Deborah sat by the priest and took up his other hand. "I'm here, Master. What do you need of me?"

"Deborah?"

"Yes, Master."

Thick mucus scratched his throat as he spoke, giving his voice the sound of dry branches snapping in the wind. "You must lead our people, Deborah. You."

From behind her, Avram grunted with discontent. Obed closed his eyes. "Who else is here?"

"It is my brother, Avram."

"The Lord does not look with the eyes of men, Avram. The Lord's eyes roam this world and seek out the hearts of those who would serve Him." Another coughing fit forced him to sit up. His body bent at the waist as Elisheba pounded against his back. Once his breath loosened again, his blind eyes sought the place where Avram stood. "The Lord has chosen Deborah. Do not dismiss His servant because of your own prejudice." He motioned for Deborah to come closer to him. He placed his hands on her head. "Deborah bat Azareel of the tribe of Ephraim, you are the one to guide the sheep of Israel. You will lead them out of slaughter and bring them to a place of peace and prosperity.

Israel is like iron in the hands of the Lord. When He places the metal into the flame, it bends to His will and fulfills His desire. But when He removes the rod from the flame, Israel's heart hardens. They no longer seek their Lord and their deliverer."

Obed's voice rang out strong and clear through the tent. "Deborah, you will be like a mother to Israel. You will be her judge and her guide. By your love and your direction, Israel will be free of Canaanite chains and will return once more to the God of Abraham."

With this final proclamation, the priest weakened. He collapsed onto his pallet; his body wracked with coughing. Elisheba drew her husband to her chest, and rocked him as his breath quieted. His eyes opened again, still clouded over with their milky film. Obed's hand clutched onto Elisheba's tunic; his mouth moving as if he spoke.

Elisheba leaned closer to his lips, her face contorted with desperation. "What is it, my lord?"

Deborah couldn't make out the old man's whisperings, but Elisheba's face lit up with joy. "Praise God." New tears streamed down her face.

Obed's body shuddered, then went limp. Deborah reached out to stroke her teacher's wrinkled face and lower the lids over his eyes. She looked up at Elisheba, who still rocked her husband like a newborn baby in her arms. "What did he say?"

"He said 'I see!'" She kissed her husband's head. "'I see!'"

11 Harosheth

Early Spring

The prophet struggled against his grasp. Her chest pressed against his as she fought to free herself. Sisera groaned. He loved the feel of her next to him. She radiated power. It flowed from her and into his body. His blood pulsed with renewed energy as he bent his head to hers and kissed her lips. The girl moaned. She clung to him; her eyes filled with desire and fear.

He caressed her cheek. "Do not be afraid, Deborah."

"But my life is not my own. What of the priest? What of the king?"

Sisera kissed her again. "You are mine. No other will touch you."

Her warm breath inflamed his passion as she whispered into his ear. "What would you do, General? To have me?"

"Anything." He knelt down before her. "Anything you desire."

She ran her hands over his head, entwining the braid he wore around one of her wrists. "And yet you do not search for me."

Sisera shook his head. "For two years I have searched. Zuberi was right. You burned in the fire."

He shivered at the girl's cackling laugh. "You believe that idiot priest? Do you think mere fire could destroy me? I live."

He grabbed her forearms. "Truly?"

Deborah bent toward him; her eyes pulling him into their depths. "I live, Sisera. But soon I will be given to another."

Anger pulsated through his body. "No! You are mine!"

Her eyes held him. "Then find me. Find me and make me yours."

Sisera opened his eyes. The dream had been so real. He could feel her body; smell the lavender in her hair. The scent still lingered in the air of his room. He sat up and let his legs hang over the sides of his bed while he caught his breath. *She lives.* He would renew his efforts to find her before the spring campaigns were upon him. His spies had roamed throughout the major cities and religious sites looking for her, but had come up with nothing. Only the repeated stories of her death in the fire that had consumed the Canaanite camp.

Sisera threw on a robe and made his way to the lower level of his house. The cold stone floor helped to clear the fog from his mind. He strode into the main living room and approached the altar in the corner. Kneeling, he rested his hands on the edge of the stone table. *You have sent me this dream. You have called me again to find this prophet. Now help me. Guide me. What is it I have overlooked? Give me discernment. Give me your wisdom.* He stood and poured some wine into the bowl that sat before one of the figures. He knelt again. *Accept this sacrifice. Look favorably on your servant. Give me what I lack!*

Sisera remained before the altar until a thought rose in his mind with such clarity, he knew it was from the gods.

It is not enough.

The thought was not his own. It came from someplace outside of him. His hands reached out again to clutch the corners of the altar. *What is not enough?* Sisera's eyes lifted to the stone table and rested on the bowl of wine. *The offering? What do you want? What do I have to do to find her?*

A sacrifice. A sacrifice of blood.

Sisera pushed himself from the altar and stood. *So be it.*

Sisera waited three excruciating weeks until the priests declared the moment right for his sacrifice. Finally, he stood with his household before the great stone altar in the temple of El. The god's statue looked out over them in silent observation. Two priests stood above them on the platform that held the altar. Their linen robes were trimmed with golden thread and jewels. Swirling tattoos patterned their arms and faces.

The priests lit several sticks of incense. The sweet-smelling smoke drifted down from the altar; circling around those that had gathered. Sisera's sons, Khenti and E-Saum, knelt at his right. His trusted slave, Iabi, was to his left. Next to his children knelt Visnia and Miu. Beside Iabi knelt the Hebrew concubine and her son. The rest of his servants gathered behind them.

The sun broke the horizon behind the Eastern columns, bathing the sky in bright red. As its rays stretched into the open temple, the priests began to chant. One lifted a shining golden bowl up toward the sky before setting it on the altar. The second priest pulled a gleaming silver dagger from its sheath. He too, lifted it toward the sky, but he kept his hands raised as the other priest walked down the steps of the altar. He stood before Sisera.

"Do you know what you want of our father, El?"

"I do."

"And you have a sacrifice worthy of his answer?"

"Yes."

The rising sun reflected in the priest's eyes. A small shiver of anticipation ran up Sisera's spine as the priest took another step toward him.

"Bring it to me."

Sisera got up from his knees. He turned and nodded to Iabi. The slave took hold of the Hebrew girl's shoulders. She let out a cry of surprise, then caught sight of Sisera's face. She clutched her son to her chest.

"No!" She struggled against Iabi's grip to no avail. "No! No! No!" The baby wailed as his mother squeezed him tighter in a vain attempt to save him.

Sisera watched her with disgust. Her once luxurious hair had straightened after childbirth. Her hips now spread wide. Her breasts hung large and swollen. She no longer resembled Deborah in any way, and so he had no need for her. *But I do have need of her child.* He grabbed hold of the baby she protected and ripped it from her arms. She clawed at the air, trying to retrieve her son, but Iabi held her back. Her screams echoed off the stone columns and reverberated through the early morning quiet before Iabi covered her mouth with his hand.

Sisera carried the squalling child up the stone steps. Once at the top of the platform, he stripped the baby, and placed it on the altar. With one hand Sisera held the baby's head while the other hand stilled its feet. The child's red face turned toward his father. Its brown eyes wide with shock at being naked in the cold spring air. Sisera asked his question to El as his son wailed.

Where is Deborah? How do I find her?

He nodded and the priest plunged the dagger into the baby's chest. Sisera took the tiny, bloody corpse and carried it to the fire burning beneath the statue of El. He placed his son into the flames and knelt prostrate before the silent stone. *Is the child enough?*

Shamir.

Sisera stiffened. *But my spies have searched Shamir.*

Shamir.

He had first encountered Deborah in Shamir. Even if his spies had found no clue of her, she had lived there at one time. Someone there had knowledge of her. She must have family there. And if she had family, then he had a way to her. He remembered how she had been willing to submit to almost anything to save a girl she hardly knew from torture. He grinned as hope sparked within him. *How much more will she do to save someone from her own family?*

12 Shiloh

A Week Later

Deborah stood high above the plains on a mount that rose like the hump of a camel from the surrounding land. Above her, the stars shone fiercely in the midnight sky. As she watched, their fire grew and grew, until all the heavens appeared to burn. A great battle cry sounded. Deborah fell to her knees and covered her ears trying to block the blaring noise. One of the stars plunged from the sky. Closer and closer it fell as the noise of war surrounded her. The flaming orb took the shape of a man as it slowed its descent. Deborah recognized Remiel as his feet touched the ground near her. The angel approached, the star's light still radiating from his body. She lowered her gaze.

"The time is coming." The angel's voice boomed like thunder in her head. "The Lord has heard the cries of his people. Their hearts are almost ripe to return to him."

He took a step toward her. "Lean upon the Lord. Great will be the trials ahead before God's salvation comes. Be strong and courageous, and do not be discouraged. The Lord is with you."

Deborah woke with a start and surveyed the house around her as she tried to subdue her thoughts. She'd been summoned by Lapidoth to meet him in Shiloh for the Passover. The time had come to discuss their wedding. She had arrived at her Uncle Leb's home the evening before, with her family. She had thought to have seen Lapidoth by now, but there had been no word. Her cousins had not come yet either, and Adara and Michal had been expected yesterday afternoon. Passover began at sundown and Deborah prayed the others would make it to Shiloh in time to celebrate.

She rolled onto her back and stared at the ceiling. *What new trial is coming, Lord? What more must we endure?* A more immediate worry pressed on her heart. *What am I to tell Lapidoth?*

In the months since Obed's death, Deborah had accepted the role of Israel's civil, and moral, leader. She knew, with certainty, God wanted her to judge the people from the hills in Ephraim. Could she convince Lapidoth to move south to be with her? Although her name and reputation were known in the northern tribes, she knew she would be overshadowed by Lapidoth's role as Barak, the military leader of Israel. She questioned her motives for not going to Kedesh with him. *Is it pride, Lord? Have I gotten so accustomed to authority that I cannot give it up to be a wife?* She searched her heart and remained convinced that her role as judge was God's will. *Clear a path, Lord. Help Lapidoth and me to come to an agreement.*

Sighing, she pulled the blanket up under her chin and turned to her side. Sleep, when it did come, was not restful. Although she didn't dream again, she heard Lapidoth's voice calling to her from the darkness.

Deborah pulled bundles of flax up the stairs and dropped them on the roof of Leb's house. Tamar followed behind her with her own arms full of the heavy stalks. Deborah brushed rogue strings of plant life from her dress. "We'll lay them out on the western side of the roof to let the sun dry them quicker."

Tamar nodded and scratched her arms. "How long will it take?"

Deborah grabbed a bundle and pulled it to the far side of the roof. "Several weeks."

The women worked through the late morning, pulling the flax about the roof and spreading it out so the stalks could dry before they were separated into strands and carded into thread. They hurried to get the work done so that they could then help Rachel prepare the Passover meal. The sun stood past its high mark when Leb's voice called up to them.

"Deborah?"

She ran to the top of the stairs. "Yes, Uncle?" She kept her voice calm, but the fact that he'd left his workshop to come home during the day meant he had news of some kind.

"Come down." His stocky body shuffled nervously. She could make out her father's form by his side.

Deborah made her way down the stairs. Azareel drew her into a tight embrace. Dread seeped from his pores and into her heart. She broke away. "What has happened?"

He put his arm around her shoulders and led her out into the bright courtyard. Adara and Michal sat on the stone bench in the center of the yard. Deborah's smile at seeing them faded when she noticed Neriah walking toward her. His face, his demeanor, everything about him, bode of ill news. Her knees weakened and she swooned to ground. Azareel and Leb struggled to keep her from falling as Michal and Neriah rushed to her side. Neriah swept her up into his arms, lowering her to the bench next to Adara.

Deborah gripped his tunic. "What has happened?"

Neriah and her cousin exchanged glances.

Her voice sounded harsh to her own ears. "Where is Lapidoth?"

Neriah took hold of her shoulders. His touch steadied her quaking. "We'd stopped in Shamir—Barak, Abiel, Joseph and myself. He wanted to journey to Shiloh with his brother and Adara."

Deborah tried to focus on the words the young soldier spoke, but they swam about her head in a frantic dance, not making any sense. "So where is he?"

Neriah looked to Michal before going on. "There were Canaanite soldiers in the town. A small battalion. At first we thought they were there to demand tribute, but they were asking questions . . . about you."

Her body trembled as fear gripped her. "Me?"

Neriah nodded. "They asked about your family. If any relatives lived in the area."

Deborah turned to Adara; her cousin's face grew pale. Deborah looked back at Neriah.

Neriah continued. "Barak set off for Michal's house before any of us could stop him. He knew someone would eventually tell the soldiers of the link between Michal and your family."

Deborah tried to stop the frenetic rush of emotions and images flashing through her mind. *I'm going mad. God help me.*

Adara took up the story. "Lapidoth arrived as we finished packing for our journey here. He told us to flee. He ran to the neighbor's homes and told them to escape as well. We had no idea what the soldiers were going to do. We thought he would follow us into the hills once he'd warned everyone. You know our home. We lived outside the city; there weren't many houses near us."

The madness in Deborah's brain quieted as her whole body numbed. She didn't recognize her voice when she spoke, its tone flat and dead. "But he didn't follow, did he?"

Adara shook her head.

Neriah took hold of Deborah's hands. "He went back to Michal's house and waited for the soldiers. He had Abiel and Joseph wait in other houses nearby." The young man lowered his head. "He ordered me to hide in the fields so I would not be found. He wanted me to . . . to be the one—" His shoulders heaved as he fought a sob. "He wanted me to come to you. To tell you what had happened."

"What did the soldiers do?"

"They dragged him from the house and asked him his name. He told them he was Michal."

Deborah's stomach tightened as she envisioned the scene.

"They beat him, asked him about his family. Barak told them they had gone to celebrate the Passover in Shiloh. Other soldiers questioned Abiel and Joseph, believing them to be neighbors. They were brought to Michal's house. They told the soldiers that Barak was Michal. That he told the truth. Their families had gone to celebrate the Passover together."

Deborah reached out and lifted Neriah's face. "Then what happened?"

Tears ran freely down the young man's cheeks. "Two soldiers grabbed Barak's arms and held him while a third soldier beat him with the staff end of his spear. They kept asking him where you were. They did the same to Abiel and Joseph. They wouldn't speak of you. The soldier's beat them until they were unconscious." Neriah's voice cracked with a sob. "Then they stabbed Abiel and Joseph with their spears and dragged Barak to one of the chariots. I heard one say, 'maybe Sisera can loosen his tongue.'"

Deborah's body shivered as if she had been thrown into an icy river. Neriah rubbed her arms to try and warm her, but it did nothing to stop her quaking. She thought of the red haired soldier, bruised and bloodied, standing in front of Sisera. She thought of the priest, Zuberi, and the enjoyment he had taken when stabbing Jael's hand. *Will Sisera call for the priest and use him to question Lapidoth? What new tortures will they devise to force my betrothed to betray me?*

Deborah shut her eyes and cut off the insanity that threatened to overtake her. She remembered her dream. *Be strong and courageous. Do not be discouraged. Lean upon the Lord.* Deborah lifted her head. "Leave me now. I must pray. The Lord is God and His hand is in all things. I will pray for His guidance as I decide what I should do next."

She brushed away the hands that tried to comfort her and walked to the corner of the courtyard. She knelt, lifting her arms and her prayers to the only one who could save her husband.

13 Harosheth

The Same Day

Sisera stifled a gag as he breathed the fetid air of the jail cell. The dark stone walls let in no heat and a torch was the room's only light. He observed the bloodied pulp of a man in front of him. Two soldiers held the man between them, their support the only thing keeping the prisoner upright.

"Who are you?"

The man's head remained limp on his neck. Sisera gestured to a guard nearby. The soldier walked outside the cell to a trough of water. He filled a jug and poured it over the prisoner's head. The man sputtered, coughed and came alive.

"Who are you?" Sisera asked again.

"I am Michal, son of Abinoam, of the tribe of Naphtali."

The general nodded. "And who is Deborah?"

The prisoner remained silent. The guard who had thrown the water punched him in the face. The man slumped forward, unconscious again. The two guards at his side shook him until he woke. "My name is Michal, son of -"

Sisera waved a dismissive hand. "Yes, yes. Michal son of whomever. Do you know who I am?"

Michal studied his face. The prisoner shook his head.

"I am Sisera, commander of the entire Canaanite army." He noted with satisfaction that the man stiffened at the mention of his name. "You have heard of me?"

Michal nodded.

"What have you heard?"

The man coughed then spat a wad of bloody phlegm on the floor. "I know you have attacked my people, raped our women, and enslaved our children." He lifted his head to stare at Sisera. "You are a monster."

Sisera grinned. "Then you are aware of my power, Michal, son of Abinoam, of the tribe of Naphtali. If you tell me what I need to know, you will live. If you do not tell me what I need to know, you will live, but wish you were dead. Do you understand?"

The man glared at him. Sisera gestured to one of the guards who slapped Michal across the face.

"Do you understand?"

The prisoner nodded.

"Who is Deborah?"

Michal fixed him with an icy stare. "She was cousin to my wife."

"And where is she now?"

The prisoner's head lolled down to his chest but he didn't answer.

Sisera walked toward him. "Where is she hiding?"

"She is in Sheol."

The general's heart beat with excitement. "Where is Sheol?"

Michal let out a snort of air, almost a laugh. "I would be glad to take you there."

"And so you shall." Sisera stopped a few feet from the prisoner. "Where is it?"

The man lifted his head, his swollen lips shifting into a shape more grimace than smile. "It is not far. Only a heartbeat away."

"What do you mean?"

The man's eyes gleamed with hatred. "It is where we go when we die."

Sisera punched the prisoner in the stomach, enjoying Michal's grunt of pain. "Do not think you can mock me, Israelite. You will tell me what I want to know."

"Deborah is dead."

"Do not lie to me!" Sisera struggled to control his voice. It would not do to let the guards see their commander so agitated. "I know she lives."

Michal shook his head. "Our God killed her. Burned her in a fire to prevent you from using her."

Sisera bent his face close to the prisoner's, ignoring the man's stale breath and the odor of urine that hung on him. "Do you know that I am half Egyptian?" The general spoke as if relating a story to an old friend. "My father married a cousin of the pharaoh himself. When he died, my mother sent me to live with my uncles in Egypt for a few years. The Egyptians are much more advanced than we Canaanites. I learned many things there. Swordsmanship, strategy, hand-to-hand combat." He paused and lifted the prisoner's head to face him. "And torture. I learned many ways to interrogate someone who is reluctant to reveal needed information."

Michal's eyes darkened as Sisera went on. "I will use every technique I know to find out where Deborah is. In the end, you will beg to talk to me. And I will listen, Michal." He smiled at the man. "I will listen as you tell me all you know about Deborah."

14 Kedesh

A Month Later

"Tale," Jael called to the tall Moabite woman. "Where's Ebo?"

The dark skinned slave fairly glided across the camp as she walked toward Jael. "He took the sheep to graze. He'll be back this afternoon." A few deep lines on her face were the only hint at her age.

Heber had bought the Moabite and her husband in Jezreel two months ago. Tale served as Jael's helper. The woman was pregnant with her own child and would hopefully serve as nursemaid to any children Jael would bear. Ebo watched over the small herd Achida had given his son before Heber had moved north. They settled a few miles outside of Kedesh, near the Oak of Zaanannim. Jael missed the companionship of Sanura and Zahra, but found being the mistress of her own small camp satisfying, especially when Heber left to trade his swords in the city.

His mood had brightened since leaving his father's camp, but he was still prone to fierce bouts of anger. He'd set off for Hazor the day before to present his gift to King Jabin. Jael had to admit, the sword he'd crafted was magnificent. Although she dreaded the thought of Heber being united with the Canaanites, she did not see how Jabin could refuse such a fine gift, nor deny Heber's request to be a weapons maker for the Canaanite army.

Tale interrupted Jael's thoughts. "Did you need Ebo for something, mistress?"

Jael stood from the bowl of chickpeas she mashed and pointed to the distance. "I see strangers coming. Run and fetch him, in case they stop here."

Tale scrutinized the horizon. "Do you fear them?"

"Heber would not like us to receive any men without Ebo present."

Tale nodded. "He shouldn't be too far off."

Jael entered the main tent and fastened her veil so the lower half of her face was covered. While inside she found the olive oil and garlic she would mix in with the chickpeas to make hummus. When she stepped outside, the strangers were closer, definitely on a path that would bring them into her camp. Jael stifled the fear that stirred in her belly. *It is a small group, probably travelers seeking food.*

She sat in front of the tent and continued to make the hummus. She studied the strangers as they approached. *Four men? No, just three. Tall.* They walked toward the camp with assurance, but not exhibiting any threatening behavior. She finished mixing the chickpeas, oil and spices, wiping her hands on a cloth at her waist and rising to greet them as they stood at the edge of the camp. The men wore traveling cloaks, even though heat had come in early spring. The leather bands that lay diagonally across their chests suggested weapons strapped across their backs and hidden by the cloaks.

"Gentlemen." Jael nodded toward them. "Greetings. May I offer you something to refresh you from your journey?"

One of the men stepped forward. "We would be most grateful. My name is Nathan. These are my friends, Neriah and Lazar."

"Please. Come. Sit." Jael turned and fetched a pitcher of water and a bowl for the men to share. She approached them with confidence she did not feel, trying not to let them see her nervousness. She placed the pitcher and bowl before them.

Nathan's dark eyes danced as he smiled. "May our God bless you for your kindness."

Jael made a closer study of the three men's clothes and relief spread through her. "You are Hebrews, are you not?"

"Yes," answered Nathan.

"What are you doing here?"

"We are looking for a Kenite named Heber. We heard he has weapons to sell."

Jael stepped back, startled. "You seek my husband, but he is not here at the present."

Nathan stood. "When will he be back?"

Jael shrugged. "I don't know."

The other men groaned and shared a bowl of water while Nathan scratched his bearded chin.

"I must warn you," said Jael. "Although I have no prejudice against you, my husband will not sell you weapons."

Nathan's eyes narrowed. "Why not?"

"He nurses a wound from his youth." Jael shook her head. "He has sworn the Hebrew people are his enemy."

Nathan motioned to the other men on the ground. "Come. We will trouble this woman no further."

Jael watched the men as they gathered themselves to leave. Something about them seemed familiar. What were their names? Nathan, Lazar and Neriah. Lazar was older and stockier than the others. Neriah's hair was wild and his brown eyes seemed filled with worry.

"We thank you again for your hospitality," said Nathan. "I hope our visit does not bring you trouble with your husband."

Jael studied the man who stood before her. He was tall, his black hair and beard thick with little gray. She stared intently into his eyes, trying to remember where she'd seen him before. He seemed surprised at the frankness of her stare.

"Is something wrong?"

Jael furrowed her brow. "I know you."

"What?"

"I know you." The memory of her time spent with Deborah and the Israelite soldiers flashed before her. "You were in the cave."

The soldiers' hands went to the hilts of daggers strapped to the sandals on their legs.

Jael raised her hands to her sides. "No, please. I mean no harm. I am just surprised to see you."

The men watched her with suspicion. "Who are you?" asked Lazar.

"I am Jael, friend of Deborah, your prophet."

The men let out a collective sigh and Neriah smiled. "You were the little girl. The one we found with Deborah."

Jael beamed. "Yes." She motioned with her hands. "Please, come sit and tell me what has happened since we last met."

Neriah shifted nervously while Lazar scanned the horizon. Nathan again rubbed his beard.

"Do not fear my husband's return; he will not be back for at least a day." Jael no longer feared the men, knowing they would not harm a friend of their prophet.

The soldiers relaxed as Jael ran to fetch a bowl of dates to offer them. "Tell me about Deborah." She sat down across from them. "I have heard nothing of her since we parted."

The men exchanged glances before Neriah spoke. "Whatever we speak of must remain with you, Jael. It would be dangerous if the Canaanites knew the truth."

"Deborah saved my life. I would never betray her."

Neriah nodded. "She is well. She lives in the hills of Ephraim."

Jael smiled at the news. "And is she married? Does she have a family?"

Neriah frowned.

"What?" Jael leaned forward. "What has happened?"

Neriah's face revealed a maturity gained by trials. "She is betrothed to our leader, Barak."

Jael searched her memories of her time with the men. "You mean the one Deborah called Lapidoth. The one who brought me to my uncle?"

"Yes." Neriah's eyes filled with pain. "He has been captured by Sisera."

She placed her hand on the ground to steady herself. "How long has Sisera had him?"

"About three weeks," said Lazar. "We think they may be in Hazor."

"But we've had no word of Barak," finished Nathan.

"Does Sisera know of their betrothal?" asked Jael.

Neriah shook his head. "Barak pretended to be his brother, Michal. Married to Deborah's cousin."

Jael thought of the dream she'd had months before and the man of white who had told her to be prepared. "What can I do? How can I help?"

Nathan shrugged. "We hoped to buy weapons from Heber to better arm our men, in case we can find Barak and need to raid the prison to free him."

Jael stood. "I will give you what weapons we have here."

Neriah faced her. "You should not break faith with your husband. If he would not sell to us neither should you."

Jael sat up straight. "I have been given a vision from your God. He told me a time would come when my family would be avenged. A time when I could help Deborah as she helped me in the Canaanite camp."

Lazar and Nathan rose. All three men looked at something behind her. She turned to see Ebo and Tale running down the small rise toward the camp. Ebo's eyes flashed brightly against his black skin.

"Mistress?" He called as he ran to her side.

"All is well, Ebo." She touched his shoulder. "No need to worry. These men are friends."

"Friends?" The older man panted.

"They knew my family, back in Jezreel." Jael sought to convince the man of her need to give the Hebrews hospitality, without fearing his telling Heber about them. "I owe them my life. They saw me safely to my uncle after the Canaanites killed my family."

Tale bowed toward them. "A debt like that takes a lifetime to repay."

Ebo nodded, but his face reflected his distrust.

Nathan lifted his hands to his side, his palms facing upward. "We are pleased to see you again, Jael, and glad to know you are safe. But we should be going. We will visit again when your husband is here."

"Tale, fetch them the sack of wine from my tent and the bread from last night." She turned to the men. "It isn't much, but perhaps it will ease your journey. Ebo?"

"Yes, Mistress?"

"Bring them to Heber's work tent. Let them each pick a weapon from inside."

"But, mistress-"

"That isn't necessary," said Neriah.

Jael squared her shoulders. "But it is. You men saved my life. I must do what I can to help you now. My husband would be angry if I did not try and repay my debt."

Ebo bowed and headed toward the smaller tent near the edge of the camp. Jael stopped Neriah as he passed by her. "What else can I do?"

"You have done much already."

She gave her head a slight shake. "I only obey the will of your God. Heber seeks an audience with the Canaanite king, Jabin. If he should tell me any news regarding Sisera or Barak, how can I contact you again?"

"There is a woman in Jezreel. Judith."

"Yes, I remember her."

"Try and get word to her. She'll know how to reach us."

"I will do what I can."

Neriah's dark eyes held her gaze. "Be careful, Jael. These are dangerous men."

"Do not fear." Jael smiled broadly. "I know your God and I know He has a plan for me. He will protect me."

15 The Hills of Ephraim

Several Weeks Later

A cold breeze seeped in through the cracks of the shelter built by Azareel and Nathan. Made of palm fronds and branches, it offered Deborah shade from the summer sun and protection from the winter rains, but it did little to keep out the chilled winds that often whipped through the hill country, even in these late summer evenings. Still, she was grateful for the comfort it did offer as she daily sat beneath it and helped to govern the people of Israel.

They came from all areas of the land now to seek her council, not just the hill country. They traveled from Jerusalem and Bethlehem in the south. They journeyed from Jezreel, Kedesh and Miram in the north. Old and young; peasants and rich merchants; all trekked up the hills of Ephraim following the road between Ramah and Bethel until they came to the Palm of Deborah. There, under the watchful eye of Elisheba and sometimes her father Azareel, Deborah would sit and listen to the needs of those that sought her. Veiled and robed in simple homespun cloth, the prophet led God's chosen people.

Another gust of wind whipped through the shelter and Deborah trembled. Elisheba stepped inside the tent she used to share with Obed and brought out a woolen blanket. She waited until Deborah had pronounced judgment on the case before her, then placed the blanket on the prophet's legs.

The old woman fussed as she ministered to Deborah. "It will do none of us good if you fall ill."

Deborah smiled at her friend. Elisheba still moved with a grace belying her age, but slower, since Obed's death. Her friend's hair had grown grayer and lines of deep sadness etched her face. Deborah touched the older woman's arm. "Thank you."

Elisheba's smile faded as another group of men entered the grove. "I would have thought the coming barley harvest would keep the crowds away, yet still they come."

Deborah sighed. "They are hungry for a word from the Lord."

The gray haired woman nodded and stepped aside to her cooking fire as three men approached Deborah. Dressed in heavy woolen robes and wearing leather sandals, she could see that these were not simple peasants. They wore gold rings on their hands and servants with packed donkeys waited behind them. The two older men had long brown beards streaked with gray. The youngest of the three kept his beard closely cropped about his face. The shorter of the elder men stepped forward.

"Mother of Israel, we need your help."

"Please my friends," Deborah gestured to a woolen blanket that lay on the ground before her. "Sit. What is your problem?"

The men sat down. Again the shorter one spoke. "We come from Tyre, along the northern coast, my lady. We come to plead with you to intercede on our behalf. I am Dumah," he gestured to his two companions. "This is my son, Caleb, and my friend Shomer. We are merchants. We come at the request of the elders of the tribes of Asher and Naphtali."

Deborah rested her hands on knees. "How can I help?"

"Plead for us," begged Dumah. "Pray to the Lord our God to free us from the clutches of the Canaanites."

Shomer now leaned forward. "They have cut off all the trade roads. Their soldiers line the plains so that no Israelite may travel. We are forced up into the hills."

"Those that try and remain in the villages are attacked," said Dumah. He lifted his arms toward Deborah. "Tell us what to do! What does the Lord require?"

Tears fell down Shomer's cheeks. "My only son was murdered before my eyes. I watched my daughter dragged off screaming by Canaanite soldiers, and there was nothing I could do. Nothing." He lowered his head into his hands and sobbed.

Deborah grieved for the older man's sorrow, yet her heart hardened. She had heard similar stories over the past months from many of those that sought her council. God's Spirit moved within her. "Are you ready now, my lords?"

Shomer lifted his head. All three men looked at her questioningly. Dumah's son spoke. "What do you mean?"

"Will you repent now and call your tribes to repentance as well?"

"I don't understand," said Shomer.

Deborah growled in her frustration, God's righteous anger swelling up inside her. "Why are you so thick and slow? For how long have I called His people to repentance?"

She threw off the blanket at her legs and stood up. "For six years, I have been crying out to you. Six years, I have told you of the Lord's anger with us. Have I been crying out only to the wind?"

She glared at the men, their confusion only inflaming her rage. "Do you think you can mock Him? Do you think you can give sacrifices to the gods of the Canaanites? That you can worship at their temples, and dance at their festivals, and then call on the God of Abraham to save you when it is convenient for you? When the false gods fail you?"

The men cowered before her. All three prostrated themselves on the woolen rug. Deborah regarded them with contempt. "Do not bow to me! I am not God!"

They lifted their heads. "Tell us what to do!" begged Dumah. "Is there no hope?"

She stepped toward the men. "Go to Shiloh. Sacrifice an offering to the Lord for your transgressions."

"We will do as you command." said Dumah's son, Caleb.

She stared at him. "It is not my command, but the Lord's."

The men nodded.

"Speak to the High Priest—Phinehas. Tell him the Lord demands the prayers of his people. He demands their repentance. He longs to fulfill His covenant with us but we must be found worthy. Tell Phinehas that the time of our deliverance approaches."

The prophet's anger lessened as she gazed into their eyes. "Go back to your tribes. Spread the message throughout the country as you make your way home. The Lord is ready to redeem His people. He will move in a mighty way, but only when all of Israel cries out as one for Him." Her knees weakened and she sank to the ground. Elisheba rushed forward, but Deborah waved her away. She kept her gaze on the men before her. "It is up to us, my friends. The Lord waits now only for us to return to Him."

Shomer reached forward and took her hands. He bent down and kissed them. "We will do all that God commands."

Dumah repeated the gesture. "Thank you."

Dumah's son also kissed Deborah's hand. "You are truly God's chosen. A mother for all Israel. Bless you."

The men stood and walked back toward their servants. Dumah and Shomer undid bundles from their donkeys and brought them to Deborah. They laid them on the ground in front of her.

Dumah bowed. "Accept these gifts as an offering to the Lord, in thanks for your service to Him." The men bowed again as they walked backwards out of the grove.

Elisheba waited until the men were out of sight before she gave her hand to help Deborah up. Both women groaned as Deborah rose. Fatigue slid its fingers into every one of the prophet's joints. She longed to make her way home and fall to sleep on her pallet in her father's house.

Elisheba eyed the bundles at their feet. "What did they bring you?"

Deborah shrugged. "I don't know." She surveyed the grove for more petitioners but saw no one. "Let's bring it inside your tent before anyone else comes."

The women grunted as each picked up a bag. "They are heavier than I thought," said Elisheba.

Deborah nodded, but said nothing. They carried the gifts inside and sat down to inspect their contents. One held a marble jar of myrrh, its rich fragrance filling the tent when the Deborah lifted the lid. The bag also contained a wooden box filled with necklaces of silver and stone beads. The other satchel contained gold and silver coins. Elisheba gasped at the sight.

"What will you do with all this money?"

Deborah sighed. "The same thing I have done with all the rest the people have offered me. I will give it to those in need who come seeking my help." Many who made their way to the grove had lost everything. They came seeking only the comfort of God's prophet and the reassurance that He still held control of their lives. It gave Deborah great pleasure to not only give them the spiritual peace they craved, but a physical gift that represented God's tender care. She lacked for nothing in her father's house, and the few coins she offered these pilgrims could mean the difference between life and death. Between hope and despair.

"Deborah?" A voice called from the grove. "Deborah, are you there?"

She stood and opened the tent flap. "I am here." She caught her breath when she saw Neriah and Deker standing by the cooking fire. She clutched a tent pole for support. "Is there news of Lapodith?"

Neriah stepped toward her. "We have not found Barak yet, but there is reason to hope."

Deborah kept the tent flap open and motioned for her friends to come inside. "What has happened?"

"We thought you'd want to know." said Deker. "We have a spy now among the Canaanites. One close to Sisera. We hope for news soon."

Deborah marveled at the Lord's provision, even as she feared for the man who dared to betray Sisera. "Who is it?"

Neriah smiled. "An old friend of yours."

"What?"

"The girl who escaped from the Canaanites with you. Jael."

Deborah gasped. "Jael? I don't understand . . . how?"

"About three weeks ago, Nathan, Lazar and I sought out a man named Heber. We'd heard this Kenite was a master sword maker. We needed to arm ourselves with better weapons if we hoped to help Barak escape."

The tent seemed to swim at the mention of Heber's name. Deborah lowered herself to the ground.

Elisheba rubbed her back. "Prophet? What is wrong?"

The vision of Heber, straddling her body in the meadow as he tried to kill her, flashed before Deborah's eyes. Then came her dream of him standing in the moonlight with Seff's blood on his hands. She choked down a sob. Perhaps it wasn't the same man. "Did you meet him? This Kenite?"

Neriah's eyebrows furrowed. "No. But we talked to Jael. Heber's wife."

Deborah looked up. "Jael is married to this man?"

Confusion clouded Neriah's eyes. "Why does this trouble you?"

"Did she say anything about him? Did he help you?"

"She said her husband held no love for the Hebrews. Something had happened in his past. He considered us his enemies."

Deborah groaned as she folded her arms across her stomach. "It is him."

Deker studied her face. "How do you know this man?"

She looked away from his scrutiny. "It is too long a story to tell now. Please. What did she know of Barak?"

Neriah watched her with a worried gaze as he spoke. "When she said her husband wouldn't help us, we went to leave. But it was then that she recognized us and revealed who she was. She asked about you. She said our God had given her a dream, and she would help us anyway she could."

"The Lord spoke to her?"

Neriah nodded. "She gave us weapons and food. She said Heb—her husband had gone to speak with King Jabin. We asked her to send word to Judith if she heard any news of Barak or Sisera."

"And has she heard anything?" asked Deborah.

"A message came last week saying that Sisera would be passing soon to inspect her husband's weapons," said Deker. "I am hopeful. Wherever Sisera is keeping him, he has gone to great pains to keep Barak hidden. Maybe Jael can learn something."

Deborah's stomach sank. "Perhaps he is already dead. That is why there has been no news."

Neriah took hold of her hand. "You must not think like that. I know Barak would never betray you, and I don't think Sisera would give up his only link to finding you so quickly."

"Quickly?" Deborah snorted. "It's been two months!"

"But he has searched for two years. He has shown himself patient and cunning when it comes to tracking you."

Elisheba again rubbed Deborah's back. "Do not give up hope. You told me yourself that the Lord chose Lapidoth for your husband, did you not?"

Deborah nodded.

The old woman knelt beside her. "Then believe that He will deliver Barak when it fulfills His purpose."

Deborah leaned against her friend's chest and squeezed eriah's hand. "I will believe."

A pale halo glowed around a silver moon as Deborah made her way to Palti's home. She would sleep there for the night. Neriah stood in the doorway of Azareel's house and watched her go. She stopped and walked back to him.

"Is something wrong, Prophet?" He asked.

She pulled her wool cloak around her neck to fend of the cold. "It is Jael."

"What about her?"

Deborah tried to read his eyes in the full moon's light. "Is she well? Does she seem happy?"

Neriah shrugged. "I only saw her the one time."

Deborah sensed his hesitation. "Go on."

"She did not seem happy with Heber's treaty with the Canaanites. She insisted on helping us although it went against his wishes."

Deborah stepped closer to her friend. "I fear for her if Heber should find out she's helped us in any way. He is an evil man."

Neriah's eyes grew wide. "You have met him before?"

"A long time ago. He has killed before and I don't believe he would hesitate to harm Jael. I will pray the Lord protects her."

Neriah nodded. "I will pray for her as well."

Deborah smiled. "I knew when we parted that God had a plan for her. I knew someday she would come back into my life."

The young soldier placed his hand on Deborah's shoulder. "Then I promise you to do all I can to keep her safe."

Deborah placed her hand over Neriah's. "Thank you." She bowed her head. "Good night, Neriah."

"Good night, Prophet."

Deborah turned toward Palti's house. She paused to look up at the bright, full moon. *Perhaps Lapidoth can see this moon where he is? Help him, Lord. Let him know I am thinking of him. Help him know you are with him. Bring him safely home to me.*

16 Harosheth

The Same Day

The prisoner lay on the dirt floor, his arms splayed out to the side of his body. His hands, already bearing the scars of torture, grasped futilely at the ground. Hemp ropes bit into his ankles and secured them to a wooden board that suspended his legs. A soldier stood and beat the soles of the prisoner's feet repeatedly with a thin, whip-like stick. Sisera watched the proceedings with a grudging sense of admiration for the peasant. The man had proven stronger than the general would have believed.

Michal had been scourged. The skin from his back barely healed before he was whipped again. It took a full three weeks for him to recover enough strength before they tried pushing reeds up under his fingernails. Unlike when he'd been scourged, Michal could not remain quiet during those sessions. His screams of agony had echoed down the dark prison corridors and off the damp stone walls. In the few moments of quiet, as he lay gasping on the cell floor, he still revealed nothing. Only the same chant, over and over again. "I am Michal, son of Abinoam of the tribe of Naphtali. I am husband to Adara, cousin of Deborah. Deborah, the woman of Lapidoth." One of the guards had explained to Sisera that "Lapidoth" was the Hebrew word for "flame."

Michal writhed on the floor; crying out as the whip slashed his feet again and again. When Sisera had first learned of this torture, years ago in Egypt, he'd not considered it particularly affective. That is, until he'd had it explained to him by the Master of the Egyptian prison.

"The soles of the feet are more sensitive than any other appendage. The pain is nominal at first, but by inflicting it repeatedly, it soon consumes the entire body. I've seen it reduce the strongest man to tears in less than an hour."

Sisera had only watched it administered once before now and had been amazed by the results.

Michal's back arched completely off the floor and he let out an inhuman cry. Sisera held up his hand to stop the beating. The prisoner collapsed, his body heaving with sobs. The man mumbled something as he lay gasping. Sisera leaned closer.

"I am Michal, son of Abinoam of the tribe of Naphtali. Husband of Adara, cousin of Deborah. The woman of Lapodith."

"Leave us," Sisera commanded the guard. Once alone with the prisoner, the general lowered himself to one knee by Michal's head. "I am running out of time and patience." The king had ordered his armies to battle. Sisera left for Hazor the following day. He stared down at the crying man.

"I know she lives, Michal. I have been given a dream."

The prisoner continued to mutter his litany.

Sisera gritted his teeth. "I know she is to marry. The gods have shown me this."

The man's body stilled. Only his hands continued to move, clenching and unclenching the dirt around him.

Sisera smiled. "You seem surprised to hear that my gods speak to me. That is a failing of you Hebrews, thinking there is only one god. There are many and they are powerful." He bowed his head closer to the prisoner. "She is mine, Michal. Our gods spoke through her and promised her to me. Did she ever tell you that?"

Michal's focus shifted from behind his swollen eyelids to stare at Sisera. The general could see the curiosity behind the man's pain. "She was my prisoner for a short time. Mine and Zuberi's." Sisera shrugged. "A priest of limited ability and too much power. But it was Zuberi who had the means that opened your prophet up to the influences of our gods. And it was then that she was promised to me."

Sisera felt a sudden kinship for the shell of humanity that lay in front of him. He reached out and wiped some of the dirt from the man's cheek. "She is beautiful, I know. And she is powerful. You probably love her yourself, even though she is not your wife."

A strange look flickered across Michal's face. Sisera picked up the prisoner's hand and held it. "Have I hit upon the truth? Do you love her also?"

The man's gaze went cold under Sisera's stare. "Do not fear for her. If you give her to me, she will come to no harm."

Amazingly, the prisoner snorted out a laugh.

Sisera hardened his grasp on Michal's hand. "You do not believe me?

Michal shook his head.

"But it is true. She would be honored by our people. Practically a goddess herself."

The man mumbled something under a strained breath.

Sisera leaned closer still. "What did you say?"

"She told me."

Sisera's heart pounded, hard. "Told you what?"

"Take her to Jabin . . . ." Michal grunted. He sucked in a deep breath before speaking again through clenched teeth. "Rape her at the altar."

"That was the priest's plan, not mine." Sisera watched the man struggle to deal with the agony in his body before the realization of what Michal had said sank in. "If you knew that, then you have spoken with her since she was our prisoner." A slow smile crept across his face even as the knowledge of his betrayal registered on Michal's.

Sisera patted the man's hand. "You have revealed nothing I did not already know. I swear to you, she will come to no harm if you tell me where she is. Jabin will not touch her. Neither will the priest."

The prisoner's hand went slack. He stared up at the ceiling.

Sisera dropped the man's arm. "If Zuberi becomes aware that she lives, he will kill her to avoid reprimand from King Shaul. Do you want that? I can give her life! A life of riches and honor!"

"I am Michal, son of Abinoam of the tribe of Naphtali."

Sisera stood up and kicked him in frustration. "Tell me where she is you fool! She is mine!" He kicked the man again.

"Husband to Adara, cousin of Deborah. . . ."

Sisera growled in fury. "Guard!"

Two soldiers rushed into the cell.

"Beat his feet until he passes out from pain. Then lock him in the solitary cell. In the morning, I want him bound and ready for travel." He bent down to whisper in Michal's ear. "If you will not tell me where she is, then I will use you as bait to draw her out."

The prisoner stopped chanting.

"She will come. When she hears how you have been tortured. When I let it be known that you will be executed in Hazor. I know she will come."

He turned to the guards. "You have my orders." Michal's screams accompanied him down the halls and out into the night.

Iabi removed Sisera's cloak and offered him a goblet of water when he returned to his home.

"Your mother wished to see you, my lord."

Sisera growled under his breath. "I have much to do before I leave for Hazor tomorrow. What does she need?"

The dark slave shook his head. "I do not know, my lord. But she insisted that it was important."

Sisera swallowed the water and thrust the cup back at his servant. "Where is she?"

"I am here." Visnia glided down the hallway toward him. From a distance, she still seemed a young and beautiful woman. But upon closer inspection, Sisera noticed the signs of age. Her rich, dark skin no longer glowed. A few deep wrinkles now etched lines around her eyes and mouth. He could not be certain, but he believed her luxurious black hair was a wig. Visnia approached him and lightly kissed his cheeks.

"How can I help you, Mother?"

Her eyes narrowed and she took his arm. "Do not patronize me, my son. I know you are busy, but there is something we need to discuss before you leave." She pulled him into the main room. She glared at the servants hovering along the limestone walls. "Leave us."

The slaves scurried away as Visnia lowered herself to the woolen carpet and reclined against several pillows. Sisera sighed and sat opposite her.

Visnia's eyes, though somewhat clouded with age, burned with intensity. "There is trouble brewing in your household, and you need to deal with it."

"What is it?"

"Your Hebrew concubine."

"Is Miu still harping about her?" Sisera waved his hand dismissively. "You can assure my wife I no longer use her."

Visnia frowned. "Believe me, Miu already knows."

Sisera ran his hands across his face. "Stop being obtuse, Mother. Tell me what the problem is."

"The two of them have become extremely close since you sacrificed the Hebrew's son. Miu does not leave her room, as you ordered, but the Hebrew spends many hours up there with her."

"Is she neglectful of her household duties?" Sisera couldn't decipher his mother's angry look. "Do you have need of her?"

Visnia nailed her son with her gaze. "Do not underestimate them because they are women. Do you not think them capable of plotting together for your demise?"

"Miu?" the general laughed. "She doesn't have the backbone for betrayal."

His mother's voice rose. "You have taken away her position, her children, her dignity. You have given her that backbone. And the Hebrew girl only incites her more."

Sisera leaned forward. "You know this?"

"I have guessed it from the change I have seen in Miu, and from what my servants have gleaned for me."

Sisera sat back against the pillows. "I will have the Hebrew killed then. For disobedience."

"I do not think that wise."

Sisera started to object, but his mother continued. "The slave was a gift from Jabin. If he asks about her, what will you say? His spies are bound to know you had a child by her. He will think you cannot control your mistresses."

The general rubbed his chin. "What do you suggest I do?

"Give Miu back her place at the table. Give her back her pride."

Sisera sighed. "And the Hebrew?"

"Bring her to Hazor with you. Put her to work at the residence there. In a few weeks, while you are away on Jabin's campaign, she could meet with an unfortunate accident."

"Why not kill her here? A lesson for Miu?"

His mother shook her head. "They are too close. Here, it would feed Miu's hatred of you. But if the girl is sent away and Miu is already re-established as the head of your household, she will not see the connection as readily. And if the slave turns up beaten in an alley, Jabin will think her a random victim of crime. In fact, he may seek to reimburse you for her loss."

Sisera nodded. "It will be done." He stood and made his way toward the door.

"My son," Visnia called. "One more thing."

He stopped and turned back to her. "What?"

"Take your wife to your bed tonight."

Sisera knew his contempt for the idea could be read on his face.

"Do it," his mother demanded. "Speak gently to her. Convince her of your shame about this whole affair."

He clenched his hands into fists at his side.

Visnia smiled demurely. "Lie to her, my son. But convince her of your sincerity. A scorned woman is like as adder waiting to strike. And she will strike, mark my words. She will strike when you least suspect it."

17 Kedesh

Two Days Later

Jael held her breath as the Canaanite general came into the tent. *Sisera.*

She had hoped to never see the man again. He took off his helmet. Sweat glistened from his shaved head. Jael's gaze was transfixed by his black eyes. *Empty and cold like the pit of death he dwells in.* She forced herself to look away, lest she draw attention to herself.

Heber bowed. "I have completed over twenty swords, and have the blades finished on twenty more."

"Can you have the rest finished by the end of the summer, Heber? Jabin wishes to give them as rewards to his officers at the end of the campaigns."

"Of course, my lord." He gestured to Tale. "Fetch some wine for our guest. Wife, bring him something to eat."

Tale rushed to pick up the jug of wine that had been saved for the general's visit. Although older, she had an exotic beauty

that Jael could see Sisera appreciated. The slave moved gracefully. She knelt before the general and poured him a cup of the
deep purple liquid. He smiled as he took the wine from her
hand. If Tale's dark skin could show a blush, Jael was certain
the slave's cheeks would be red. Tale backed away then offered
Heber a cup.

Jael clamped her jaw tight as she presented a plate of almonds to Sisera. She kept her gaze downward and retreated,
motioning to Tale to bring the basket of fresh bread and hummus she'd made earlier.

"I have a goat roasting outside," Heber said. "A feast for you
and your men."

Sisera nodded. "We will rest here for the night before making
our way to Hazor." He threw an almond into his mouth. "The
king wants a full report of your progress."

"I am sure he will be pleased." Heber reclined against a pillow. "After your refreshment, I will show you all I've done."

Jael excused herself to tend to the dinner preparations. She
let out a deep sigh of relief as she breathed the fresh air. *He
does not remember me.* Her stomach knotted. *Yet.* She had
spent the last few days in torment, reviewing the time she had
spent as Zuberi's prisoner. *Had they ever asked my name? No.
Only Deborah spoke to me. Zuberi and Sisera used me as a tool
to bend Deborah to their will.*

Jael made her way over to the fire where a goat hung on a
spit. A young slave boy turned the carcass to keep it from burning. Jael took a brush of goat hair and dipped it in a sauce of
garlic, cumin and olive oil. She let the marinade drip over the
meat. "You are doing well, Hakim. Not much longer then you'll
be able to rest your arms."

The boy gave her a weary smile while turning the spit. Jael
spied a group of soldiers setting up a large tent. Several others
made lean-tos with branches from the oak trees. Two ox drawn

carts pulled into the camp escorted by three chariots. The charioteers yelled out greetings to their comrades. Several older men
dressed in tunics jumped down from the wagons. They ran
around to the front of the chariots as they came to a stop. Un-
hooking the oxen, they led the animals down to the river to
drink while other servants disembarked from the carts. The last
to exit was a young woman. Jael took a second look.

Deborah?

No. The girl was heavier than Deborah, and although the
same color, her hair didn't curl as much as the prophet's. The
face was similar, however, and that's what had made Jael look
twice. The girl stopped by the second cart, peering inside. Animal skins covering the sides of the wagon blocked Jael's view.
The girl leaned forward, as if trying to remove some cargo. Two
soldiers approached and spoke harshly to her. She scurried
away. One of the soldiers thrust his spear into the wagon and
laughed.

The girl walked toward a separate grove of oak trees. Jael
noticed the hardness in the woman's countenance, as well as the
deep sadness in her eyes.

"Welcome to our camp," Jael said as she approached the
young woman.

The girl appeared startled. She made an awkward bow. "Mistress."

"What is your name?"

"I am called Hadassah."

"A beautiful name."

"Thank you."

"Would you like to sit?" Jael gestured to the ground.

A look of distress passed her eyes. "I'd prefer to stand, if you
don't mind.

Jael looked back at the wagons where the servants now un-
loaded several baskets. The two soldiers still stood guard at the

back of the other cart. "Of course. You've had a long journey. Would you like to walk to the river to get a drink?"

Hadassah nodded. "Thank you." The two women passed by the servants tending to the oxen. They greeted Hadassah and lowered their heads toward Jael.

Jael watched as the woman knelt and cupped her hands to drink from the river. "You remind me of someone I knew. Many years ago."

Hadassah drank again before speaking. "I am the only one of my family who has come this far north." She gazed off toward the horizon. "My people live at the base of the southern hills."

"You are Hebrew, are you not?"

Hadassah nodded.

"My friend was also Hebrew." Jael looked around to make sure they were alone. "She was a prophet of your people."

The woman's eyes grew round. "Do you speak of Deborah?"

Jael took the veil from her face. "Yes." She sat down next to the slave. "Do you know her?"

"Only by reputation. I heard her speak once when I was younger. It was at the feast of the Tabernacles." Her eyes clouded with suspicion. "Why do you ask about her?"

"Do not be afraid. I am a friend." She took the girl's hand. "She saved me from the Canaanites. From the general, Sisera."

Hadassah pulled her hand from Jael's. Her face hardened into a mask. "The same general who has come to your camp?"

Jael tried to let some of the venom she held inside come out in her voice. "He comes to my husband, not to me."

Hadassah studied her. "How did the prophet save you?"

Now it was Jael's turn to scan the horizon, seeing the Canaanite camp; remembering her terror and the pain. "It was several years ago. Two rainy seasons have come and gone. Sisera and his army had destroyed my village, killed my family. Only my brother and I were saved. Taken prisoner. We were forced to harvest the fields of those the Canaanites conquered. On the fourth day, a young woman was tied with me before we set off on our long march back to the main camp. It was Deborah."

Jael turned to Hadassah. "There was a priest in the camp. He used Deborah's compassion for me to force her to take a drug."

Hadassah shook her head. "I don't understand."

"He wanted to use her. To have his own gods speak through her. When she resisted him, they brought me in." Jael held out her hand, allowing the girl to see the red puckered skin of her scar. "The priest stabbed me, then threatened to do more if Deborah didn't take his drugs." Her hand ached at the memory. Jael flexed her fingers to loosen the tension in her palm.

"Did she do it?"

Jael nodded. "Another god did speak through her." She shivered. "It was terrifying to hear. Even Sisera was frightened. But your God saved her. The following night he caused a fire to burn down the Canaanite camp so she could escape." Jael smiled. "Deborah could have left me behind, but she woke me and insisted I run with her to the hills. Later she gave Hebrew soldiers a dowry to give to my family. They saw me safely to my relatives in Jezreel."

Hadassah's eye again grew round. "You were there? Truly? When God helped her escape?"

Jael nodded. "We went through much together, she and I. I owe her my life."

Hadassah was silent a moment. "And you say I remind you of her?"

"Yes. Your face is similar and the color of your hair. Although Deborah's eyes are unique. Almost golden."

The girl thought for a moment then cast her glance toward the camp. "This explains much."

"I don't understand."

"I was taken captive and brought before King Jabin's court. It is there Sisera chose me for his slave; a prize for a successful campaign." The girl let out a frustrated sigh. "For the first months I served in the kitchen. But then the general seemed to take an interest in me. I felt his eyes upon me as I served at the table. Even when I was alone, I seemed to feel his presence."

Hadassah looked up at Jael. The girl's eyes revealed her despair. "He took me as his concubine. For over a year he treated me with care and concern." A tear fell from her eye. "Until our son was born. Then his love withered. He looked at me with disgust." She wiped her eyes. "He murdered our son on the altar of El. An offering to the god."

Jael gasped. "For what reason?"

"He didn't reveal it to me, but one of the servant's told me he wanted to know if Deborah still lived."

"Did the god speak?"

"Yes," Hadassah glanced at the wagons. "Sisera sent his elite guards to Shiloh. They came home with him."

Jael followed her gaze. "Him?"

"The one in the wagon, under guard. He is a relative of the prophet. Sisera has had him tortured for the past two months, but as far as I know, the man won't speak."

Jael could barely hold in her excitement. "Lapidoth is here?"

"No." The girl shook her head. "His name is Michal. He is married to her cousin, I think."

Jael clutched Hadassah's hands. "He pretends to be Michal, but it is Deborah's betrothed, Lapidoth."

"How do you know this?"

"His men stopped by our camp last month."

"Sisera has given up on torturing him. He's taking the man to Hazor to try and lure Deborah."

"What do you mean?"

"He's going to put Michal on trial in Hazor as a spy. Once convicted, he will be executed. Sisera hopes Deborah will offer herself to save him."

"As she once offered her life for me."

Hadassah nodded.

"I must get word to Jezreel. Tell his men where they can find him." She growled in frustration. "It will be difficult to fight the guards to free him."

The sun sank down behind the horizon blazing the sky in sharp orange streaks. A frog called from the river, his cry breaking the quiet of the dusk.

Jael bit her lip. "I must go and serve the meal." She turned to Hadassah. "Thank you for all you've told me. Now pray to your God that I can get word to Lapidoth's men."

"I will." Hadassah stood. "And, Mistress?"

"Yes?"

"Send word to Harosheth, to Miu, Sisera's wife. Mention my name and she will help. I am sure of it."

Jael's brows furrowed. "Why?"

The Hebrew's lips curled in a sad smile. "Anything to cause him pain would bring her joy."

Jael replaced her veil. "We must both return to the camp before we are missed." They walked up the rise together, Hadassah heading toward the other servants, while Jael hurried to where the lamb still roasted.

"Hakim! You can stop turning now. Let's douse the fire and let the meat cool a bit before we serve it."

The boy nodded. Jael studied him from behind her veil. *How old is he? Ten, maybe twelve years? Could he be trusted with such an important task?* One thing was certain, Heber would not miss him. The boy helped her and Ebo. She could easily make up a story to explain his absence to the slave.

"Mistress? Do you need something?" asked Hakim.

"Yes. Something important." She squatted down by the goat and motioned for him to sit beside her. "Something that must be kept secret."

18 Hills South of Hazor

Two Days Later

Sisera surveyed the hills around him with a keen eye, knowing bandits often hid behind the rocky terrain. The setting sun cast long shadows for outlaws to hide among as well. If he travelled with his army, the pass would not have given him second thought, but now . . .

Curse Miu and her fears. His wife had sent a runner to Heber's camp the day before, requesting Sisera send soldiers back to Harosheth. "A threat from the Hebrews," the messenger had told him. "Against your sons." If it had been against Miu, he would have waited to order his best men's return until he'd reached Hazor but, for his sons, he couldn't take the risk.

Sisera looked over the contingent that travelled with him. Still enough in number to repel any thieves. He swore under his breath. The trouble was the wagon that carried his prisoner. He'd had Michal moved to a smaller, uncovered cart, but it still slowed their pace to a crawl. Sisera growled as he held up his arm. "Halt."

The three chariots accompanying him drew to a stop. Sisera waited until the wagon caught up to the others before he spoke. "We'll camp here for the night. Be ready to start at the first break of day."

Hadassah ran up to the chariot. She held out a skin of wine. "Here, my lord."

He snatched it from her grasp, continuing to scan the hills as he drank his fill. "Light no fires," he called to his men. "We do not want to alert anyone to our presence." He handed the skin back to Hadassah. "We will eat bread and cheese tonight."

The Hebrew slave curtseyed before running to the donkey carrying supplies. Sisera jumped down to converse with his soldiers. Eleven men, he counted. Thirteen, if he included the two young men driving the prisoner's wagon. *Thirteen swords, plus my own, to fend off any marauders. That should be enough.* Still, he couldn't shake the strange chill in his blood warning him of some danger.

At his signal, the soldiers gathered around their general. "I want at least four on watch throughout the night." He separated the men into three groups. He pointed to the youngest soldiers. "I will sit with you on the third watch." He gestured to his most seasoned guards. "I will wake you for the last watch. The moon will be full tonight. Use its light. Watch the shadows."

The sky turned violet as the sun sank behind the hills. The men broke into their groups to eat the meager meal, and refresh themselves with the watered wine Hadassah served among them. The Hebrew girl pulled a hunk of bread off one of the loaves. She scurried toward the wagon. Sisera smiled to himself as he stood to follow her. *Perhaps some sport would lighten my mood.*

Hadassah jumped onto the back of the wagon. "I have brought you some bread."

The prisoner groaned.

"You have to eat something. To gain your strength."

Sisera peered into the cart. Michal struggled to push himself up, but his arm collapsed beneath him. The beaten man cried out as his body hit the wood.

Hadassah crawled to Michal's side. "Here." She put the piece of bread in his hand.

The prisoner stuffed the bread into his mouth, seeming to swallow it whole.

Sisera chuckled.

Hadassah turned at the sound, eyes wide. "I should have asked first, my lord, but I thought you'd want him to make it to Hazor alive."

The general nodded. "You were right." He called over his shoulder. "Iabi, bring the wine here."

The large Egyptian obeyed. Sisera gestured with his head toward Hadassah. "Give it to the girl."

Michal watched the Hebrew slave, with rapt attention, as she lowered the skin of wine to his lips. Sisera smiled. He knew what the prisoner was thinking.

"You see it too, don't you?" Sisera asked. "How much she looks like your prophet."

Michal let out a sputtering cough. Hadassah backed away.

The general hopped up into the wagon. He squatted between Hadassah and Michal, but his eyes stayed on the prisoner's face. "I have had her, you know. This girl. Taken her to my bed, as I will take Deborah." It pleased him to see Michal's body tremble. "Does it bother you to know that your life has been reduced to this? That you will be used as bait to draw Deborah to me?"

He grabbed Hadassah's wrist and pulled her to his side. The girl whimpered in protest as Sisera ran his fingers along her cheek. He glanced down at Michal. "I will lie with Deborah. My lips will taste her sweetness." He yanked Hadassah closer, kissed her roughly, then pushed her away. The girl squeaked as she scrambled from him. Michal tried to push himself up.

"Amar. Hopni." Sisera called. "Come here."

Two soldiers hurried to the wagon.

"Our friend would like to sit up." Sisera's blood pounded within his chest; warming his body and chasing away whatever worries had earlier tried to dampen his spirits. "Make sure he has a good view of the . . . festivities."

The general threw Hadassah off the wagon as the soldiers climbed up. He watched her try to get to her feet. "Iabi. Stop her."

The huge Egyptian crossed to her in three long strides. He took hold of her arms and pinned them behind her back.

Sisera waited until his soldiers had Michal upright on his knees before he spoke again. "Why imagine what I will do to Deborah, when I can show you?"

An inhuman noise escaped from the prisoner's mouth, but he was helpless against the men holding him. Hadassah struggled in Iabi's arms, but the Egyptian barely moved with her thrashing.

Sisera jumped from the wagon. The girl stopped her flailing.

"Please, my lord." Her voice whimpered in the gray of twilight. "Please, my lord, do not do this."

He tore her linen tunic from her in one violent movement. "I would not want our guest to have any doubts as to what will happen to the woman he loves." He pulled her from Iabi and thrust the naked girl in front of Michal. His soldiers held the prisoner's head so he had to face the quaking slave. She cried out as Sisera's hands groped her breasts then moved down her body.

Sisera pushed her to the ground. He straddled her before she could scoot away. He looked up at Michal. "Remember this, Michal, son of Abinoam of the tribe of Naphtali." He undid his belt and lifted his tunic. "Let this be the picture in your mind when your prophet offers her life for yours. Only know that it will be Deborah who lies beneath me, not this whore."

Several soldiers took their turn with the Hebrew slave before night fell. When they'd finished with her, Sisera ordered her put in the wagon. He wanted Michal to sense the girl's humiliation, even if the night kept him from seeing it clearly.

Although he had assigned himself the second watch, Sisera sat up with the first as well. Four soldiers sat in the center of camp with their backs to each other so that no direction was left unobserved. Sisera patrolled the perimeter of the camp with Iabi. The hills glowed silver around them, but nothing moved, not even the wind.

"It is too quiet, Iabi."

His Egyptian slave said nothing.

One of the soldiers yawned as Sisera circled past him.

"Sorry, General."

"If you cannot keep alert, I will wake another to take your place."

The young man shifted position so he sat up straighter. "No sir. I'm awake."

By the time the moon had crept halfway across the sky, Sisera knew he had to get some sleep. *We have a full day's journey through the hills tomorrow.* He shook his most trusted soldiers awake for the last watch before laying down himself. Iabi lay close by, a dagger clutched in his hand, ready to defend his master.

"Attack!"

Sisera's body jerked awake at the cry. His brain struggled to make sense of the scene around him. Clouds covered the moon so his eyes couldn't focus. Footsteps pounded toward the camp. *More than four men, I think.* He drew his sword; sweeping it in an arc around him as he came more awake.

Someone let out a grunt. Sisera had heard the sound enough times on the battlefield to know one of his men had been stabbed in the back. Next came the thud of the victim's body as it fell to the ground.

"Over here," called an accented voice. "In the wagon."

Sisera cursed. *Hebrews.*

A strong hand gripped his shoulder. "Stay with me, my lord," Iabi whispered. "I will protect you."

The sound of clanging swords rang through the night. At least three of his men were engaged in battle. *Where are the others?* As he moved forward with Iabi by his side, he stumbled over the body of the youngest soldier. A spear pinned the boy to the ground. Now that his eyes had adjusted, Sisera could make out the bodies of four others. Iabi moved behind him and thrust his dagger, catching the enemy that stalked them in the stomach. The Hebrew cried out, before collapsing in a heap.

Men shouted to each other. Sisera couldn't distinguish between the Hebrew attackers and his men. He'd inflicted enough pain on Michal, however, to recognize that man's screams above the sound of battle.

"Hold on," a voice called. "It's me. Deker."

Michal groaned in response.

"Stop them, Iabi," Sisera ordered. "They're freeing the prisoner."

The Egyptian advanced slowly.

From the cart came an inhuman cry. A man's voice shouted in surprise.

A screeching demon leapt from the wagon and swung a sword toward Iabi. The crazed figure swung again at the big man. He dodged the attack. As the clouds parted, Sisera could see Hadassah's face, insane with hatred. She shrieked as she hacked the sword at the air. Iabi circled her, then, in a sudden move, slashed her arm with his dagger.

The sword fell from Hadassah's grip, but instead of stopping her attack, she turned on Sisera. She leapt toward him, her nails clawing at his eyes. He raised his weapon, but the girl grabbed the blade with her hands. Sisera let it drop, amazed the wounds didn't stop the demon. She punched at his chest, scratched at his face, showered him with her warm blood.

Hadassah's screams cut off sharply. Her rabid eyes dimmed. Iabi pulled his blade from her back. She fell forward. Sisera instinctively grabbed her to keep her from falling. Blood spurted from her mouth as he threw her to the ground.

Sisera let out a stream of curses when he looked up. Through the inky blackness he could see only two of his soldiers remained standing. The Hebrews had fled into the hills, taking Michal with them.

19 The Hills of Ephraim

Three Months Later

Deborah stood trembling in Elisheba's tent. Adara and Tamar helped her remove her headdress and heavy bridal robe. Next they took off the multitude of bracelets and necklaces she wore and set them aside. The scent of incense only caused Deborah's stomach to churn more. She'd been too nervous to eat both before and after the ceremony.

I'm married. She shivered in the thin gauze shift she'd worn under the bridal robe.

Adara smiled gently. "It will be all right. It will be over in a moment. It doesn't hurt too badly, if you relax."

Tamar nodded. "It is true, Sister. Let him do what needs to be done. Then you can sleep."

Deborah swallowed with difficulty. "Were you scared?"

"Palti was more nervous than me, I think," admitted Tamar. "He wasn't very sure of what needed to be done. It made it easier."

"I was terrified." Adara chuckled. "I'd only met Michal the one time, at our betrothal. And he was so much bigger than me."

"Lapidoth is big, too." Deborah eyed her cousin nervously. "And I know he knows what to do."

Adara hugged her. "Don't worry, Deborah. I'm sure he will be gentle."

Tamar embraced her as well. "May it go well with you, Sister. And may you be blessed with many children for your patience."

Deborah sat down on the pallet they'd made for her and Lapidoth in Elisheba's tent. The older woman and her grandson would stay with Azareel during this week of the wedding celebration. Adara gave Deborah's hair a final brushing while Tamar spread dried rose petals on the floor.

When they finished their tasks, Adara stood up and snuffed out the oil lamps, leaving only the glow of one lamp burning in the corner, as well as the flame of the incense. Pulling back the tent flap she turned and smiled at Deborah. "Blessings, Cousin." Then she and Tamar stepped outside.

Deborah waited in the soft light; heart pounding, mind racing. A loud cheer went up from the crowd gathered outside as the women left the tent. Deborah blocked her ears from the comments the men shouted. *So much for respecting your prophet, Lord.* She thought back over all that had occurred in the past twelve weeks.

After freeing Lapidoth from Sisera, Deker and his men had carried their leader to the hills of Naptali. Judith had nursed him back to health. Neriah had been sent to make sure Deborah stayed in Ephraim.

She could still feel Neriah's hands on her shoulders as he forced her to listen to reason. *"There are soldiers searching for him still. And for you. Sisera knows you will want to be with him. Besides, Barak refuses to let you see him until he is healed. Until he can come to you healthy. Strong. And take you as his wife."*

Lapidoth had come to her two weeks ago. His body scarred deeply from his torture, but he himself remained strong. Plans had commenced immediately for the wedding.

The curtain in the doorway pulled aside and broke her out of her thoughts. Lapidoth stood like a statue, his eyes fixed on her.

"Come in. Husband."

He blinked as if surprised to hear her voice then stepped inside the room, letting the flap fall behind him.

She watched him for a moment, marveling. For a man so full of confidence and strength, he appeared to be uncomfortable in his own body. "What's wrong?"

Lapidoth shook his head. "Nothing." He remained standing in the middle of the room, the low ceiling forcing him to hunch his shoulders. His eyes burned with an intensity she'd not seen before. She guessed they shone like that when he went into battle. She shuddered.

Lapidoth took a step forward. "Please, don't be afraid of me." The fire left his eyes, replaced with a look of grief. "I . . . ." He lowered his head. "I won't hurt you."

He knelt down at the foot of the bed. "We don't have to do anything, if you're still afraid."

Deborah lowered her gaze. "They will look for proof of our consummation in the morning."

"There are ways to fool them." He sighed. "I want only to please you, Deborah."

She rose to her knees and crawled over to him. She drew her hand through his hair, then lightly traced the shape of his jaw. "I am not of afraid of you." She felt heat rush to her cheeks and sat back on her heels. "It is natural for a bride to be a little frightened on her wedding night."

"You are sure?"

Deborah nodded shyly.

"Perhaps a drink would help us both." Lapidoth stood and poured them each a cup of wine. He sat down on the pallet across from Deborah so their knees almost touched and passed her a drink. He lifted his cup to hers. "May God bless our union. May we live long in happiness and with many children."

Deborah smiled and took a large mouthful of wine. Its warmth spread from her stomach to her muscles, freeing her from some of the tension she'd felt for the past week.

Lapidoth stared at her before finishing his wine with a large gulp and putting his cup down. "I would like very much to touch your hair. May I?"

She couldn't answer with any more than a whisper. "Yes."

Lapidoth's strong, scarred arm reached across the space between them. Deborah's heart filled with emotion as his hand trembled before he finally rested it against her head. His fingers played with a lock of her hair, pulling it gently so that the curl straightened and then he let it go. Lapidoth's smile grew larger still as he did the same thing with another curl. "It's so soft. I dreamed it would feel like this, but I wasn't sure."

Deborah's heart pounded within her chest. She realized she'd forgotten to breathe. It took her a moment to remember how. She inhaled deeply, her breath coming out in tiny gasps.

Lapidoth's forehead creased. "Are you all right?"

Deborah nodded.

His hand stroked her cheek. His skin was calloused and dry, but Deborah didn't mind. His touch sent sparks of heat through her body.

"You are so beautiful." His eyes filled with tears. "I can't believe you're mine."

Deborah turned her face and kissed the palm of his hand. Lapidoth let out a soft groan. He dropped his hand to his knee.

For a moment they sat, not speaking. Not touching. Finally Lapidoth whispered, "May I kiss you?"

"Please," Deborah gasped.

He leaned forward and gently covered her lips with his own. Deborah pulled him closer to her. She had not felt such passion, even with Seff. That had been a kind of wild current of emotions. She'd been young. What filled her now was the desire of love. God had given her this man. A man to protect her; to comfort her; but most of all; a man to love her.

Lapidoth's hands reached out and grabbed fistfuls of her hair, his kiss becoming more urgent as he pressed himself closer to her. She shifted her body so she could recline onto the blanket beneath her. Lapidoth pulled away, his eyes questioning. "Are you sure, Beloved?"

She pulled him down on top of her. "I am sure."

She rested against her husband's chest, her head lifting with the rise of his breath. She wanted to stay like this forever. Warm. Loved. Protected. Safe. Her heart filled with joy for the man the Lord had given her.

Lapidoth stroked her hair. "Are you asleep?"

"No."

"Are you . . . did I hurt you?"

She smiled at his concern. "No."

"You are sure?"

She lifted her head and turned to meet his gaze. "I am sure."

He touched her lips with his fingertips. "You needn't lie to me."

Deborah furrowed her brows. "If there is one thing you should know about me by now, it's that I tell the truth. I have always told you what I was thinking. Even in the beginning."

Lapidoth traced her eyebrows then ran his hand down to her neck. "I remember."

She leaned over and kissed him. "I am very happy." She nestled her back against his chest, pulling his arm around her. "Sleep now."

His hand caressed her arm. "I cannot sleep. I'm afraid I'll wake up and find that I was dreaming again."

"You dreamed of this?"

His fingers drew tiny circles on her shoulder. "It is what kept me alive. In Sisera's prison."

Deborah rolled over to face him. She put her fingers on Lapidoth's mouth. "Please. Don't speak that name in our bed. Never again."

He pulled her hand away and kissed her roughly. "I need to prove to myself this isn't a dream. Always before, I would wake at this moment." He rolled on top of her. "Now that I have been with you, I cannot imagine my life without you." His eyes burned with desire and intensity. "I want you again. Tonight. Please, my love?"

Deborah smiled. "Tonight. And always. I am yours."

She stood on the plains, looking up at a lone mountain rising up in front of her. Deborah shuddered as she recognized it from her previous dream. "No, Lord! Not yet. Let me stay with Lapidoth. Let me be just a woman. For only a moment." From above her, a great cry sounded. The very stars moved and thrashed about in their orbits against some unseen force. The ground below her shook. She struggled to keep her footing as it quaked underneath her.

Wake up, Deborah. Wake up and strike the call for war.

"Not yet, Lord. Please."

Wake up, Deborah. Tell Barak to arise! He must call the tribes of Naphtali and Zebulon to Mount Tabor. You will lure Sisera to the Kishon River. There, I will deliver the Canaanites into the hands of the Israelites. I will deliver my chosen people.

The shouts from the heavens above her joined with the roar of the ground beneath her. Surrounded by the deafening noise Deborah could not hear her own voice as she pleaded with God. "I beg you! Not now! Why must you take everything just when I have tasted joy?"

The earth and stars engaged in battle around her. The tumult reverberated throughout Deborah's body. She screamed and fell to her knees, fearing the very noise would tear her body apart. Then all went silent.

Wake up, Deborah.

She couldn't answer the Lord through her weeping.

A gentle breeze swept around her, lifting wisps of her hair, caressing her face. **Who am I?**

"You are 'I AM.' You are the Lord."

What am I?

"You are good. You are merciful."

Wake up, Deborah. All your life has been for this moment. The time is now.

"What?" Lapidoth threw the covering off and sat up in the bed. "What are you saying?"

Deborah lay on her back, staring up at the deep red cloth that made the ceiling. *Red. Like the battlefield I've seen covered in blood.* Lapidoth reached down and caressed her cheek. She grabbed his hand. "The time is now. You must call the men of Naphtali and Zebulon to war. Lead them to Mount Tabor."

"Now?" His hand squeezed hers. "Today?"

She pulled herself up, covering her body with the blanket he'd cast aside. "Yes. The time is now."

He grabbed his tunic from the floor and slipped it over his head. Standing, he paced the cramped tent. "What is this? What have I done?'

"Nothing." Her voice broke. "I swear to you, Lapidoth, I have heard the will of God. He has told me to strike the call for war."

Anger pulsated from his body. His feet slapped against the packed earth as he circled around her. "What kind of trickery is this? You wed me and send me off to my death? Is it His will that I leave you here to become a widow after one night in my bed?"

She rose to her knees and reached toward him. "No." She missed his leg and he strode to the farthest corner of the tent, unable to meet her eyes. "I will not stay here. I will lead the men of the South. I am to lure Sisera to the Kishon Valley. Once we are there, you will lead the attack from Mount Tabor."

At this, Lapidoth's head jerked up. "No!" His eyes grew dark. "I know that man, Deborah. I have seen his obsession with you. You cannot face him alone."

"I won't be alone. God will protect me. I'll have the men of Ephraim and Benjamin behind me."

He shook his head. "No."

The familiar stirring of God's Spirit moved within her. "Barak! Listen to me. You must take with you ten thousand men from Naphtali and Zebulon and lead the way to Mount Tabor. There the Lord will deliver Sisera to your hands."

He covered the space between them in two strides and knelt before her. He took her face in his hands. "If you go with me, I will go. But if you don't go with me, I won't go." His eyes pleaded to her in desperation.

Lord! What do I do? Convince him, Lord. The Spirit spoke through her. "Very well. But the honor of the victory will not be yours. The Lord has handed Sisera over to a woman."

Lapidoth clutched her to his chest. "I don't care. Take the honor, as long as you are safe. As long as he does not touch you again." He kissed the top of her head. "I couldn't bear to think of you in his arms. His bed."

"The time is now, Barak. We must call your men to war."

A cry of celebration erupted from those who waited outside the tent as Lapidoth emerged from the doorway.

"Awake already, Barak?" called Deker. "I'd have thought you might stay in bed a little longer!" The men around him laughed until they took note of their leader's dark countenance.

"Deker, assemble all our officers. Quickly." He motioned to Neriah. "Run into the village and gather the elders. Ask them to meet us here. The prophet has heard from God."

20 Harosheth

Late Winter

Sisera looked up from the papyrus he studied. "Who is here?"

"Heber. A Kenite." answered the soldier. "He says he has a gift for you."

"Ah," Sisera sighed happily, rubbing his hands together. "He must have finished my sword. Send him in." He clapped his hands and Iabi stepped forward. "Fetch a servant to bring us some wine." He paused for a moment. "And bring a purse of coins down from my room. If Heber's workmanship on my sword is half of what I saw him do with Jabin's I want to see him nicely compensated."

The large Egyptian nodded and left the room without a sound. Moments later a young woman entered with a jug of wine and another carried two goblets. They poured the wine and stepped to the side of the room to wait for another command. Two guards escorted Heber to the doorway. Sisera motioned him forward.

"Come in." He gestured to the cup on the table. "Sit and have a drink after your journey."

Heber haltingly stepped forward. His eyes darted about the room, taking in the limestone walls and heavy cloth that covered the windows cut into the stone. Sisera smiled at the man's awe, knowing that his home rivaled that of King Jabin. Heber did not go to the wine; instead he unfastened the leather strap from his chest and lifted a sword from his back.

"I have finished it, my lord." Heber knelt and held the scabbard in front of him. Sisera strode over and lifted the gift from Heber's hands. The sun's light, streaming through the courtyard doorway, reflected off the polished hilt made of gold. Vines of silver twisted around until they met with the thick leather-covered handle. *Beautiful.* Sisera placed his hand on the grip and pulled the sword from its sheath. The reflection off the steel blade sent sparks of light dancing about the room. He held his arm straight out and felt its perfect balance. He sliced at unseen enemies, reveling in the way the blade seemed to be an extension of his arm. *Perfect.*

Heber lifted his head. "You are pleased?"

Sisera nodded and turned the sword in the air again. "Very pleased."

"I am glad."

The general placed his hand on the man's shoulder. "You have done exceedingly well, Heber the Kenite."

"Thank you, my lord."

Sisera patted his back. "Now, come and join me in a drink."

The Kenite rose and shuffled to the table. Sisera could see the blisters on his feet from the long walk to Harosheth. Heber pulled out a stool and sat. Sisera sheathed the blade and placed it on the long wooden table.

• *418* •

Heber smiled as he took a sip of the wine. The general knew the man had never tasted anything as good. Sisera lifted his own cup to his mouth.

"How was your journey?"

"Good," Heber sputtered, wiping his hand across his mouth. "The roads are dry since the rains stopped early again this year."

"And our soldiers? Did you notice their presence along the way?"

"Yes," Heber nodded. "There is no doubt who controls travel along the trade routes, my lord."

Sisera smiled. "Good." He lifted his goblet to the Kenite. "It is important to hear the opinion of the everyday traveler. What I see when the army goes out and what you see can be entirely different."

"Which brings me to the reason for my journey, my lord."

Sisera frowned. "Was it not to bring the sword I commissioned?"

"Not entirely." Heber leaned forward on his elbows. "The Israelites are mobilizing."

Sisera was caught off guard by the intensity in the Kenite's green eyes. "What?"

"I have heard it from their own lips, my lord. Their leaders are even now calling for the tribes in the north and south to join together to fight against us."

"Who?" Sisera could hear his heart drumming in his ears. "The tribes have had no one to lead them in years."

"A man named Barak is calling on the men of the north." A look of loathing crossed Heber's face, as if he held a bit of rancid meat in his mouth. "And their prophet seeks to lead the men of the south."

Sisera rested his hands on the table. He rubbed them against the polished wood trying to ground himself into the present moment. He kept his voice calm. "Their prophet?"

"Yes. A woman named Deborah."

Sisera pounded his fists on the table as he stood. He strode over to where Heber sat. "Where did you hear this?"

"Several Hebrews came to my camp, looking for weapons. They did not know of my allegiance to you and King Jabin."

"Did you give them these weapons?"

"Only a few swords, General. Enough to fool them into giving me their trust."

"Tell me everything they said."

Heber stared ahead as if remembering the scene. "They said that Deborah had called Barak to her in the hills of Ephraim. She said the Hebrew god had told her to attack the Canaanites. Barak was to gather the northern armies and wait for you at Mount Tabor. Deborah would lead the southern armies to the Kishon Valley nearby."

Sisera ran his hands along his bald head. He paced away from Heber and clapped. Iabi entered and, with a nod from his master, presented the leather purse he carried to the Kenite.

The general turned to him. "You have done well, Heber. Both with my sword and your news. Accept this token of my gratitude."

Heber gasped as he took hold of the purse and felt its weight. "I long to see the destruction of the Hebrews as you do, my lord."

"Then join with my army." Sisera raised a clenched fist. "This is my moment. I will crush the Israelites with my bare hands and send them back to the wilderness they came from." He voiced his true desires only to himself. *And Deborah?* He thought of her power and her beauty. *Deborah will be mine.*

21 Mount Tabor

Early Spring

Neriah approached.

"What is it?" Barak used a stick to poke the embers of the fire at his feet.

The young soldier's gaze flickered to Deborah before returning to his commander. "The Canaanites have ridden out into the field. It looks like they want to hold a summit."

Barak's stern face nodded. "Can you see who waits?"

Again Neriah's eyes glanced to Deborah before he spoke. "It is Sisera."

The Israelite leader glowered. "Good. It is time I face him as an equal, not a prisoner." He rose.

Deborah reached for his arm. "This battle is not yours. It is the Lord's."

Her husband hesitated. "I know whom I serve. But there are things this Canaanite dog must know before we fight."

She squeezed his arm. "Be careful, Barak."

He leaned down and kissed her forehead. "I will." He gestured to the men around the circle. "Nathan, Jorim and Lazar come with me. Neriah?"

Neriah stepped forward. "Yes?"

"Stay here with the prophet. If it is a trick of some kind and the Canaanites attack, I am trusting you to see her to safety."

The young soldier stood tall. "You have my word. She will come to no harm."

Deborah said nothing as Barak and the others fastened their swords to their belts and put on their cloaks. She stared after them as they made their way out of the encampment, disappearing into the forest surrounding the summit. Neriah sat beside her.

"They will be safe."

"I know." Deborah's gaze focused on the trees "The time for the battle has not yet come. But I fear for Barak.

Sisera waited on the plain north of the Kishon River. Mount Tabor loomed over him like a crouching lion, its forested round hump darkening the horizon. The Canaanite army had sat ready for battle for two days. And still, the Israelites did not attack. *They cower on the mountain, trembling at the sight of my army and the iron chariots that will grind them into the dirt.*

Above, the sky shown a bright blue. A breeze carried the smell of acacia tree blossoms and the stink of two thousand horses. Sisera narrowed his eyes. A group of men emerged from the trees around Mount Tabor. They walked toward the general and his two officers without fear. Sisera did not dismount. *Let them look up at me. Let them see the power of the full Canaanite army.* His camp lay only a mile behind him. The sight would impress even the most hardened of warriors, and these Israelite vermin were not seasoned soldiers; just an assortment of farmers and laborers playing at war.

The four Israelites stood before him. They wore their beards long, their hair touched their shoulders. Not one of them wore armor, and only three carried swords. The fourth held a wooden spear.

Sisera looked down at them. "I offer you the chance to surrender. It is the only time you will be given such an opportunity." He studied the faces before him. Grim. Steely eyes. Determined. "Do not seek to be martyrs. You cannot win this battle. We outnumber you both in men and weapons."

A black haired man stepped forward. "Why should we surrender? God has promised us the victory."

Sisera gripped the side of his chariot as the horses strained at their bridles. "Do not listen to foolish priests and magicians who convince you falsely. I too, have been promised victory by my gods. Who is right?"

The Israelites glanced between them. Another man stepped forward, this one with long reddish hair. The man seemed familiar.

"Do you know me, Sisera?"

The general frowned. "Who are you?"

The man grinned. "You knew me by my brother's name, Michal."

The air left Sisera's lungs as if he'd been punched in the stomach. He squinted toward the Israelite. "It can't be."

"I survived your torture. I defied your determination to break me. And know this; I am not Michal, but Barak, leader of the Israelite army."

Sisera growled and jumped off the chariot. He strode to the red-haired man. "You may have escaped me once, but not again." His hand grasped the hilt of his sword, but the three men surrounding Barak drew weapons as well.

The red-haired man tossed his head back and laughed. "You know nothing, General. You have already lost the battle."

Sisera's officers ran to his side with their weapons ready. An archer stood in one of the chariots with his bow strung. Sisera took his hand from his sword. The others relaxed and lowered their weapons.

"I have lost nothing. You will lose it all, Barak. All I want is your prophet, Deborah. Give her to me and you, and your men, can leave. I will have my revenge on you another time."

Barak's eyes darkened, even as the man smiled. "You have lost her as well, Sisera."

"I know you lied! I know she lives!"

"I told the truth when I said she was the 'woman of Lapidoth.' For before I was Barak, I was Lapidoth, son of Abinoam. Deborah is my wife, Sisera. She is mine and you will never lay a hand on her again."

Sisera lunged for the red-haired man, but the tip of the wooden spear pointed at his chest stopped his forward motion. Rage boiled through Sisera's body. He spoke low, refusing to let his anger erupt. "You will die, Lapidoth, son of Abinoam. I will cut off your head myself and present it to the prophet. She will know who it is who can protect her. Who can give her everything she desires."

Barak's voice matched his in intensity, but Sisera could see the strain of his anger in his neck. "She desires me, General. I have laid with her. Even now, she could be carrying my son."

Sisera roared. "There will be no mercy. No prisoners will be taken." His arm chopped through the air. "Your men will be buried on the plains beneath the feet of my horses. Your bodies will be left to rot and be torn apart by the lions and the vultures." Sisera leapt onto his chariot. "The gods have promised her to me, man of flames. She will be mine!" He grabbed the reins from the driver and whipped the horses forward. The Israelites and the Canaanite soldiers scattered as Sisera ran the chariot at them before turning back toward the camp.

22 Mount Tabor

The Next Morning

Deborah woke before dawn. She left the tent she shared with Elisheba and made her way through the mass of humanity that lay about the mountain summit. Ten thousand men rested, their lungs seeming to inhale and exhale as one large beast. Deborah trod around the sleeping soldiers, careful not to step on one, or wake them with her movement. She came to the edge of the mountain and knelt by an old pine tree. She had come every day to this spot to await the sign from God that the battle should begin. She faced the north, not daring to look at the southern plain thick with Canaanite soldiers. She prayed for God's mercy and strength. For His protection for her soldiers. For victory over their enemy.

The sun broke the horizon and Deborah's heart skipped a beat. The crimson orb rose and bathed the overhanging clouds in its blood red hue. Fingers of scarlet spread across the valley floor as if the very sky bled out onto the plain. *It is today!*

Gather your army. The time is now.

Deborah ran back to the camp and found Barak already awake. He spoke around a cooking fire with Nathan, Lazar and Neriah. He lifted his head as she hurried through the still sleeping bodies that surrounded him.

She could not suppress her excitement. "Arise, Barak! Wake up, men of Israel! For today is the day the Lord will give you victory!"

Barak stood. "Are you certain?"

Deborah rushed to face him. "Yes! The sun rises with blood. It is the sign I've been waiting for."

Lazar shook his head. "But that means rain. We cannot fight in the rain."

The prophet whirled to face him. "Do you not understand what I have told you? Again and again I've said that the battle will not be yours, it is the Lord's! The very stars in heaven, the earth itself will win this battle today, not you."

The dark-haired man scowled. "But Deborah-"

She turned to Barak. "Do not dismiss my orders. If you do not battle today, all will be lost."

Barak hesitated only a moment to look at the faces of the friends around him. "God has spoken through the prophet. Wake the men." He slapped his hand against Neriah's shoulder. "Sound the shofar! We go to battle today!"

Neriah ran to his pack and brought out the curved ram's horn. Pressing his lips against one end he blew. The note reverberated throughout the camp, sending a chill down Deborah's spine. Neriah blew again. The soldiers jumped up in alarm.

Barak strode throughout the camp. "Arm yourselves! This is the day!" He patted young men on their backs and gripped older men by the arm. "The Lord has spoken! Today is the day we free ourselves from the oppressor! Wake up!"

Above the camp, the ruby sky of sunrise grew dark and gray. A cold wind whipped across the summit, causing the men to shiver and tighten their cloaks about them. The soldiers rushed to arm themselves, grabbing what weapons they had; swords, wooden spears, pitch forks and scythes. All the while Barak moved among them, encouraging and commanding.

Neriah brought out a crate and placed it at the center of the camp. As the men finished their preparations they gathered to hear Deborah's final admonition. She stepped onto the box, unable to see over the heads of many of the men, but knowing the Lord would carry her words to them.

"Men of Israel! I sense a wariness in your hearts as you prepare to face the enemy below us. Do not fear! For the victory is the Lord's! As He led our people out from slavery in Egypt, so He will lead us from the yoke of the Canaanites." Deborah looked at the men, trying to catch each one's glance. "Was it Moses who called forth the frogs and the locusts and the darkness into Egypt?" The soldiers only murmured their reply.

Deborah's voice rose in volume as she sought to fill the men with her passion. "Who killed the first born of Egypt? Who parted the Red Sea so our people could walk across dry land?"

"The Lord!" shouted Barak, Neriah and some of the older men.

"Who caused the walls of Jericho to crumble, was it Joshua?"

"No!"

"No!" Deborah cried. "It was the Lord! Who stopped the sun in the sky so that Joshua could defeat the Amorites in the desert?"

"The Lord!" called even more men.

"Yes! If the Lord is for us, than who can defeat us?"

"No one!"

"If the Lord is for us, who can defeat us?" she asked again.

"No one!" cried the soldiers, their eyes now alight with the intensity of the coming battle.

"There is no enemy so great that they can overcome the Lord our God. There is no army, no matter how many chariots, or swords, or arrows, they send at us, that can cause the will of YHWH to fail! Hear O Israel, the Lord our God, the Lord is one! It is He alone who will win this battle! To Him be all the glory and honor!"

As one voice, ten thousand men called out, "Praise God!" The sound echoed among the trees surrounding the camp. Above, lightening flashed and a deep roll of thunder pealed in answer to their cry.

Deborah threw her hands up to the sky. "The plans have been laid. Go now, soldiers of the Most High! Fight for Israel! Victory for our God!"

The huge mass of bodies swarmed down the hill toward the Canaanites with a great roar. Deborah remained with her arms raised toward heaven until the last man left the camp, then she knelt on the ground, prostrate, and prayed to God to protect the soldiers and fulfill His promise.

Sisera's army had moved like a finely tuned machine at the first call of the Israelite's shofar. The battle horn alerted the Canaanite watch, who then sounded their own alarm. Nine hundred chariots, manned by twenty-seven hundred warriors, stood at the front of the line. Each chariot carried a driver, an archer and a spearman. Behind this colossal front came an army of fifty thousand foot soldiers, armed with swords and spears.

Sisera stood in his chariot and smiled at the horde of Israelites swarming from Mount Tabor like ants. *And we will crush them under our feet like the bugs they are.* He longed to meet Michal, *Barak, Lapidoth* and drive his spear through the man's heart. He would throw it on the fire of the altar to Baal as a sacrifice for their victory today. And he would lay the head of his enemy at the feet of Deborah. She would know that only Sisera could protect her. Only he was worthy of her devotion. His knuckles whitened as he gripped the sides of the chariot. *Tonight I will have her. There will be no seduction, only the force of my will over her. Later, she will come to love me. Now, she must pay for betraying me.*

Sisera lifted his arm to ready the chariots to charge. The Israelite horde now teemed across the plain. As he brought his arm down to signal the advance, a great crash of thunder vibrated through the air. The horses rushed forward and the ground trembled under the weight of the surging army. A flash of lightening cut across the sky and the clouds opened. The wind, which had been still throughout the night, pushed down from the north, driving the rain into the Canaanite army. Shards of cold water and pellets of hail battered the faces of the horses, causing them to falter in their advance and strain at their reigns. Driver's sought to control the animals, but because of their close positions, they ran into each other. Wheels locked. Men were thrown from the backs of the open chariots as they came to a sudden stop.

"Forward!" Sisera cried over the roar of the storm. "Kill them all!"

The chariots again lurched toward the opposing army, but the sleeting rain slowed their progress. The hard-packed dirt of spring soon bogged down with mud. Iron wheels sank into the muck and, no matter how hard the horses pulled, could not loosen the earth's hold on the chariots.

Sisera held his hand over his eyes, trying to shield them from the ice that cut into his skin. The Israelite army, with the wind and rain at their backs, moved unhindered across the open ground. Sisera called to the *maryannu*, "Hold fast! Do not try and advance from here! Archers, take your aim!"

At his signal, the archers let loose their own rain of arrows upon the Hebrews, but the pelting ice drove most of them down before they reached their marks. Sisera swore under his breath. He ordered the spearmen from the chariots to press forward on foot. He then yelled to the infantry to come around the chariots and engage the Israelites.

As the two armies rushed forward, the bombarding hail melted to rain, easing some of the burden on the Canaanite army. Still they advanced into the storm, which lashed into their faces and arms with stinging bites. Thunder roared and the wind howled, drowning out Sisera's orders to his men. Chaos ensued. The flailing Canaanite army turned on itself, foot soldiers hacking members of their own troops, as the rain continued to blind them.

"Baal!" Sisera screamed as a finger of lightening split the sky and exploded a tree at the base of Mount Tabor. "Stop this storm! Give us dry land and a chance to defeat your enemies!"

Sisera leapt from his chariot, sinking ankle deep into the mud. Someone yelled above him. His side burst with pain from the kick of a horse. He fell into the sludge as his breath exploded from his lungs. He rolled onto his back, gasping for air. One of his officers thrust a spear toward him.

"Grab hold, General! I'll pull you up!"

Sisera clutched the weapon. The other man pulled, but the earth gripped the general harder. The two men strained against the mud's hold until it finally released Sisera with a sucking sound. As he stood, he saw another army of Israelites coming in from the Southeastern hills.

"Get the chariots out of here!" He ordered. "They are only in the way. Retreat to Harosheth!"

By now, the first wave of infantry had slogged up to where the chariots stood mired in mud. The *maryannu* struggled to free their wheels and retreat as their general had commanded. The main thrust of the Israelite army from Mount Tabor stayed away from the chaos of the Canaanite soldiers, horses and chariots. The soil below the Hebrews still held firm, as if the great storm had loosened the earth only beneath the feet of the Canaanites.

As Sisera watched, the Israelite army split and a figure emerged. Dressed in a long blue robe, the figure wore a leather breast plate and helmet. Sisera felt his heart burst within his chest. *Deborah!* She removed her helmet and threw it to the ground. Her brown hair flew about her head as the wind whipped around her.

Her voice pierced through the storm. "Sisera!"

He stood straight and took a step toward her. Although too far away to see her eyes, he knew when she'd seen him.

She stretched out her arm toward him. "The Lord has heard the cry of his people, Sisera! He has heard and He has promised to free us from the heavy yoke of bondage you have placed upon us."

He couldn't take his eyes from her. *Come to me! Come to me Deborah, prophet of God.*

She lifted her arms toward the sky. "Even now the Lord our God calls upon the forces of his earth and sky to defeat you. You do not fight the forces of man Sisera, but it is the God of Israel you battle against! Behold!"

Even through the muck, Sisera felt the ground beneath him vibrate. All around, men fell over, unable to maintain their balance. Something other than thunder rumbled through the air. The horses, already in a frenzy, foamed at the mouth, their eyes rolling in panic. Sisera pulled his legs free of the mud. He pushed himself to the drier ground between himself and the Israelites. Other soldiers tried in vain to follow him as a tremendous roar echoed throughout the valley. From the south, a vast wall of water pounded down the banks of the Kishon River toward the Canaanite army. The wave overflowed the banks of the river, wiping out the rear flank of Sisera's men. Soldiers were flung like pebbles in an ocean wave and crushed upon the valley floor. Even the wind, thunder and water, could not drown out the screams of those swept away by the flood.

Sisera watched in growing terror at the carnage around him. The water rose from the river, continuing to drown those caught in its path. His own men cut each other down in the desperate attempt to get to dry land. He could see the victorious glint in the eyes of the approaching Israelites as they drew their weapons to kill any who were lucky enough to escape death by the storm.

He caught a glimpse of blue as the opposing army swarmed on top of the Canaanites. Deborah stood within twenty feet of him.

"Prophet!" he called. "Come to me!"

She searched through the crowd at the sound of his voice.

"Here, Deborah! I am here!"

She spied him. Someone fell against his back, knocking him to his knees. Deborah fought her way through the crowd until she stood over him. He reached out for her but she stepped back from his grasp. A young soldier with wild hair ran to her side. He took her arm, pulling her away from the battle. She wrenched herself from him and ran back to Sisera.

"Listen to me General, for this is the last time you and I will meet. Hear my words. Your army is destroyed. Canaan will be ours." She stared down at him. Sisera could see the hatred in her eyes. "And now is the hour of your death!"

His blood turned cold.

The young Hebrew soldier called to her. Deborah turned and walked back through the battle toward Mount Tabor.

"Retreat!" The general called to his men, but none could hear him over the noise of battle and storm. "Retreat!"

And Sisera ran. Fled on foot to dry land and the hope of salvation from the death that surrounded him.

23 Kedesh

The Following Day

J ael stood alone on the edge of the camp, scanning the gray horizon. She'd pretended concern over the fate of her husband, sending Ebo to Jezreel for news of the army. Tale and her baby watched the flocks in the nearby fields. Jael had awakened this morning knowing that this would be the day. Somehow, in some way; large or small; she would be used by the Hebrew God.

A damp breeze blew as Jael wandered back to her tent. Inside, she took the veil from her face and set it down. She sat on a short stool then picked up a skin of milk. She meditated while she churned the skin, curdling the milk inside into a kind of yogurt. She had not been one to pray—the Kenite gods of her family had done little to protect them. She did not desire to worship the Canaanite gods—lusting, angry deities who sought only blood or sexual gratification. Since her dream, she found herself talking to the Hebrew God. She didn't know His name or what He looked like, but she knew He was powerful. And she knew He understood her pain. Jael wondered what would be asked of her. *Anything. Anything you ask, I will do. Let my life have purpose. Let me have a reason to have survived.*

Her mind drifted as her hands worked the skin of milk. She fell into a dream. The shining man from her vision appeared before her. His breath came in short pants, as if he'd run a great distance.

"The enemy approaches, Jael."

She fell to her knees before the messenger. "What am I to do?"

Sweat covered his face and his blue eyes flashed with excitement. "Be as gentle as the lamb, but cunning as the wolf. Do not fear. The Lord is with you."

A swirling wind blew open the flap of her tent, waking Jael from her trance. She ran to tie it down. She looked over her shoulder, expecting to see the shining man behind her, but she stood alone. Instead of refastening the flap she replaced her veil then stepped outside. Above, the sky rumbled with the thunder of a spring storm. She walked to the hill at the edge of camp and looked out. Far in the distance, a figure ran. She waved to make her presence known. The figure stopped, staggered, and changed direction to run toward her. Jael's stomach lurched as the person approached. For now she could see it was a man, a soldier. An officer by the glint of his armor.

Sisera ran toward the woman. He had fled from the battle, hiding in the forested hills and watching as the Israelites pursued his retreating army. Slaughtering them. When he could no longer stand to watch, he turned east, and headed toward the Jordan River Valley. He stumbled throughout the dark night, desperate to put his failure behind him. With the glow of the dawn on the horizon, Sisera had turned north. *How far have I traveled?* He recognized the trees as he stumbled onward. *I must be near Kedesh.*

"Come, sir," the woman called. "Come to my camp and I will give you rest."

He took off his helmet as he drew closer to her. The woman gasped. He scrutinized the figure on the hill. Although veiled, she seemed familiar.

"Do I know you?"

She nodded. "I am Heber the Kenite's, wife."

Sisera's jaws clenched. He knew Heber was dead, swept away by the torrent of water. He would not tell her now. He didn't want to deal with her tears.

She held out her hand. "Come into our camp."

He lowered his head and forced his legs to move up the hill. He walked until he came to the cooking fire outside her tent. There his knees buckled. He sank to the ground. His mind went blank as he stared into the flames. The woman remained quiet. He barely noticed her take a seat across from him. *What do I do now? How do I tell Jabin that I have lost everything?*

The woman spoke.

Sisera lifted his head. "What did you say?"

"I asked if there was news."

He snorted and closed his eyes. "News?"

"Of the battle."

"There was no battle." His stomach tightened. Anger soon overwhelmed the exhaustion in his body. He slammed his hands onto the ground then pushed himself up. "A battle is man against man. Swords and arrows and spears. That is a battle!" His arm cut through the air in front of him. "This was not a battle. This was the god of the Hebrews sending the very elements of nature against us."

Jael rose. "I do not understand."

"Neither do I." He whirled to face her. "We outnumbered them by tens of thousands. We had better weapons, better soldiers." He grabbed her shoulders. "But who can battle against a raging river or the stones from heaven?" He shut his eyes and dropped his hands. "Forgive me. I have lost much."

Dark clouds obscured the pale yellow sun. Sisera shivered in the damp wind. He surveyed the camp. Only one tent stood, but a simple shelter of palm fronds and branches sat between some trees a few yards away. He had not seen a servant, although he remembered seeing them when he'd visited the camp before. "Is there someplace I could rest? Before I continue to Hazor?"

Jael hesitated for a moment. "Come into my tent."

He frowned.

The veil hid her mouth, but Sisera could see the smile in her eyes. "Do not be afraid. Come in." She pulled the flap aside and he entered.

He was surprised to see no servants inside. As a married woman, she was forbidden to let another man into her private quarters, especially without supervision. He stood, unsure for once, as to what he should do.

"Please, sit." Jael gestured to the cooking fire. "Warm yourself." She brought him a pillow to recline on as he stretched out on the ground.

"What is your name?" He asked.

A look of fear crossed her face before she answered him. "Jael."

He studied her more closely, analyzing why him knowing her name would cause her such fright. He could think of nothing. "Jael. Please bring me some water." He sighed. "I am very thirsty."

"Of course, General." She hurried to the back of the tent. When she returned, she handed him a beautifully carved wooden goblet filled with a creamy liquid. He looked at her with a raised eyebrow.

"It is curdled milk, my lord. My mother used to give it to me when I needed comfort."

He watched her over the rim of the cup as he took a sip. The rich drink soothed his parched throat, and eased the pain in his gut. "It is very good."

"It always brought me peace when I was young." Jael knelt in front of him.

He drank again, not taking his eyes from her face. "You are still young."

Her head shook slightly. "I am older than I seem."

Sisera drained the milk then placed the goblet on the floor. Although his muscles ached with the stress of the day, he couldn't help the surge of heat that flowed through him as he studied her. Thick black lashes rimmed her round, brown eyes. A strand of black hair broke free of the linen covering her head and fell across her face. He reached across to gently brush it aside. The woman shivered.

The air inside the tent grew heavy with the tension between them. Jael seemed to him as a deer, which hearing a noise, stands ready to flee. He could see her hands trembling in her lap. The familiar rush of passion consumed his body and mind.

He wanted her.

He had survived the onslaught of the Hebrew god. He had lost the prophet, his single obsession for the last two years. He needed this woman. He needed to release the frustration from the battle. To subdue the rage within him by conquering the woman before him.

He took the veil from Jael's face.

She let out a soft gasp. "Please." Her voice broke. "I am married."

"No." His fingertips whispered across her cheek. "You are a widow." He grabbed the back of her head so he could pull her toward him. He pressed his lips onto hers. Her arms pushed against his shoulders, trying to force him away, but he only kissed her harder. She resisted for a moment longer, then melted into him.

He pulled back. The fear had left her eyes. Now all he saw was a fierce determination behind her gaze. She ran her hands up his neck. They kissed again. He moaned at her touch, his muscles trying to remind him of their exhaustion, even as he longed to experience more of this woman. Jael pressed her body into his. He could not fight the excruciating pain that engulfed him. She backed away as he cried out.

"What is it?"

Sisera clutched his side. "A horse kicked me as I fought to get out of the mud."

She watched him, firelight dancing in her eyes. "You should rest tonight, my lord. There will be time for more when you have healed."

The pain from his injury stole whatever energy his passion had given him. He fell back onto his knees, struggling to catch his breath. Jael stood over him and helped him out of his armor. She brought him another pillow then rinsed the mud from his body with a towel and a bowl of water. When she was finished, she poured him another goblet of milk.

"Drink this and rest, General."

His eyelids grew heavy as he finished the drink. She pressed him to lie down, but he struggled against her. "You must stand at the door. Wake me if anyone should come."

"Do not fear." She covered him with a thick, woolen blanket. "You are safe."

He reclined onto the pillows and was asleep in a matter of moments.

Jael wiped her hands on her dress as she stood. She longed to run to the river and wash Sisera's touch from her body. *What do I do now? I have invited him into my tent. The laws of hospitality demand that my family and I protect him with our very lives.* She stared back at the sleeping man. *But he has killed my family. Their blood cries out for justice.* Jael wandered to the back of the tent. *Do I run to Jezreel and find Judith? No. He will be gone before I get back.* She wrung her hands. *Do I strive to keep him here until the Hebrew God sends someone for him?* She rejected this idea as well. *I cannot hide my hatred any longer. It must be done now. But what?*

Her gaze fell upon the basket that held the tent pegs. Her body moved on its own. She reached down and took a metal spike in her left hand then grabbed the hammer from the floor. She treaded silently across the woolen rugs toward Sisera. He murmured. Jael paused while he rolled to his side. She didn't move until she was certain he still slept, then she crept forward and knelt beside his head. She stared down at him, waiting while visions of the past two years raced through her mind. She saw her father pinned to the ground with the Canaanite spear. She saw her mother's chest ripped open, her eyes staring lifelessly at the sky. She felt the pain of Zuberi's dagger through her palm while Sisera held Deborah prisoner in his arms.

As her anger boiled within her she lowered the spike above Sisera's head. She raised the hammer and steeled herself against the impact before swinging it down toward the nail. The sound of the blow rang out through the tent as the spike pierced Sisera's temple. His eyes flew open. His whole body rose in a rigid spasm of death. Jael lifted the hammer, ignoring the blood that sprayed her face, hands and clothes. She pounded the tent peg again and again until she felt it take root into the ground. Only then did she hear her screams.

Jael stripped off her bloody clothes and submersed herself in the frigid river. Picking up handfuls of sand and pebbles, she scrubbed her skin raw trying to remove the blood from her fingers, arms and face. When her body could take no more of the icy water, she stumbled to the shore. Her muscles trembled violently from shock as well as cold. Jael could barely walk the distance to her tent. She closed her eyes before pulling aside the flap to enter. She refused to look at the mangled corpse in the center of the room. Instead, she skirted around the edge of the tent in order to find a clean tunic and robe to wear. Still shivering, she grabbed a blanket and a head wrap before leaving.

She had no concept of how long she'd waited outside before Tale returned from the fields with the sheep. The Moabite approached her.

"Mistress? Are you well?"

Jael sat with the blanket wrapped tightly around her. She lifted her eyes and tried to focus on the woman in front of her. She swallowed what little spit her mouth held. "You must go to Jezreel. Find the woman Judith."

"What?"

Jael's voice hardened. "Find Judith. Tell her to get word to the Israelites that I know where Sisera hides."

Tale knelt in front of her. "How?"

"You need only deliver that message. After that, find Heber's father, Achida. You are his now."

"I don't understand, Mistress."

"Heber is dead. I will not return to my father-in-law's camp. I will go to my own people." She held Tale's gaze. "You and

Ebo belong to him now. I am sorry." She looked around the camp at the sheep and tent. "All this belongs to Achida now."

The slave's eyes searched hers. "How do you know these things?"

"A messenger, while you were in the fields." Jael pointed to the provisions she'd put aside earlier. "Take bread and water. Go now. Find Judith."

"But where will you go?"

"I will wait here for the Israelites."

"But you shouldn't be here alone, Mistress."

Jael smiled weakly. "Do not worry. Nothing can harm me."

Tale reached out a dark hand. "What has happened?"

Jael took a deep breath. "I have fulfilled my purpose, Tale." Strength returned to her body as she spoke. "The Israelite God has avenged my family, and I know He will protect me until I am home again." She took the slave's hand. "Go now. Do not fear for me."

Tale took the water, but left half the loaf of bread for Jael. The storm clouds lightened by mid-afternoon, allowing the sun to break through and warm the young woman who still sat outside her tent. She lifted her face to the light and saw three Israelite soldiers making their way into her camp. She stood to meet them, letting the blanket drop to the ground. They hesitated as they approached. She took a step toward them. Although covered in mud and blood, she recognized them. Barak, Neriah and Lazar.

Barak nodded his head in greeting. "You are Jael, are you not?"

"Yes, my lord."

"We met your servant on the road from Jezreel. She said you had word of Sisera."

Jael lifted her arm toward him. "Come. I will show you the man you are looking for."

Barak frowned.

"Do not fear." She turned away from the men and walked to her tent. She pulled aside the flap that covered the entrance. "Come."

The soldiers drew their weapons, stepping cautiously toward the tent. Barak thrust his sword before him as he swept inside. The other two followed close behind. Jael remained outside, holding the doorway open.

Lazar retreated from the tent, his eyes wide. He stared at Jael, but said nothing. Barak and Neriah came out a few moments later. Jael let the flap drop.

"He came seeking shelter." She tried to read the look on Barak's face, but couldn't fathom it. "The blood of my family and the will of your God over rode the laws of hospitality. He had to die."

"You?" Barak's eyebrows furrowed. "You killed him?"

Jael nodded.

He let out a short laugh. "She said Sisera would be handed over to a woman. I thought she meant her."

Jael shook her head. "What?"

"Deborah," Barak explained. "She said the honor of the victory would be given to a woman. I assumed she meant herself."

"Honor, my lord?"

Barak placed his hand on her shoulder. "Do you not understand what you've done, Jael? You have killed the enemy of Israel. Your name will be remembered forever."

She shivered as her muscles released the tension they'd been holding. "You mean you are not angry with me? For breaking the law? For denying you the right to kill him?"

Barak laughed. A deep, rich chortle from his gut. "Angry? That the mighty Sisera fell at the hands of a woman? I delight in this news!"

She had not realized how much she had feared his reaction before this moment. Tears flowed down her cheeks in gratefulness that she would not be punished. Those tears soon mingled with the grief and anxiety she had held within her for the past two years.

Barak stepped back from her, confusion written on his face as her sobs grew louder. "What is wrong?"

Neriah grabbed the blanket she'd dropped, then wrapped her in it. He led her over to the fire and helped her to sit down. He looked up at the Israelite leader. "Do you not remember your first battle?"

Barak nodded. Jael's chest heaved with the force of her grief. Neriah placed his arm around her. She fell against him.

Barak entered the tent, returning a moment later with a skin of wine. "Here. Make her drink some this."

Neriah held the wine to her lips. Jael struggled through her sobs to swallow. "All will be well. You are safe now." He spoke softly into her ear. "You need not fear. You are safe."

The warmth of his breath against her cheek, and the strength in his arm that supported her body, brought Jael peace. Her weeping lessened as he continued to whisper reassuring words to her. Her body relaxed. Her head dropped against his chest. The soft, but strong, beat of his heart comforted her further. She soon drifted off to sleep.

24 Shiloh

Three Days Later

The armies of Nephtali, Zebulon, Asher and Issachar returned to their homes in the north, ready to fight with Barak when he returned to Kedesh to crush the remnants of the Canaanite army near Hazor. Deborah traveled toward Shiloh with Deker and the armies of Benjamin and Ephraim. She would wait there for news of her husband's quest to find Sisera. The small army grew during the two day trek toward the Tabernacle. Women and children rushed out from villages along the way, shouting praises to God, and playing tambourines and pipes. By the time they reached Shiloh, the plains teamed with Israelites celebrating God's victory.

Deborah walked at the head of the army with Deker by her side. Her brothers, Avram and Palti, followed somewhere behind her. Elisheba had found Jude after the battle, and the two of them made their way south somewhere in the multitude. As they approached the Tabernacle, Deborah could see the smoke of the altar being lifted on the wind toward heaven. She fought the desire to gag when the breeze shifted, carrying the aroma of the burning meat and incense to her. She clutched her stomach. Deker stopped.

"Are you well, Prophet?"

She swallowed the bile that rose to her throat. "I'm fine. I only need to rest soon." She smiled at his concern and indicated they should continue walking. As she approached the Tabernacle gateway, the crowds parted. Azareel stood waiting for her, with Bithia, Leb and Rachel close behind. She ran forward to meet them.

"Father! The Lord has answered our prayers."

Azareel placed his hands on her shoulders then kissed both of her cheeks. "He brought you back safely. That was my prayer."

She stood tall and strong in front of him, even though her body was exhausted from the weeks of travel. Her stomach still churned. "We are free, Father." She turned to speak to the crowds behind her. "We are free!" She lifted her arms toward heaven. "Praise the Lord!"

The people roared their joy and thanksgiving to God. Deborah entered the Tabernacle courtyard and knelt before Phinehas, the high priest. The old man's hands pressed against the top of her head.

His ancient voice called out strong and clear. "Deborah, bat Azareel of the tribe of Ephraim. You are truly a prophet of the most high. You are filled with the power of our Lord. You are a mother for Israel. Guide the Lord's people. May you lead all of Israel for many years!"

He lifted his hands and Deborah stood. All around the Tabernacle courtyard, the priests lifted their arms and praised her and the Lord. Behind her, the voice of the assembly rose as one in a shout of thanksgiving. Above her, rays of sunlight burst through the clouds as if God himself celebrated their victory.

I do, Beloved. I do rejoice with you.

Then you are pleased, Lord?

You have served me well. Be at peace.

The warmth of God's spirit flooded Deborah's body. Tears poured over her cheeks as she lifted her hands in her own silent hymn of gratitude.

Deborah returned to Leb's house that night to rest while the celebrations continued on the plains surrounding the Tabernacle, spilling into the city of Shiloh itself. Even in her exhaustion, she did not sleep easily, as she still feared for Barak and his encounter with Sisera. She awoke at dawn. After fetching water from the well for Rachel, she spent the morning in prayer in Leb's courtyard.

At about the sixth hour she sensed a shadow over her. She looked up, but could only make out a silhouette against the sun's glare. She lifted her arm to shield her eyes, but someone grabbed it and pulled her to her feet. She found herself in Barak's embrace. He smelled strongly of sweat and blood, but Deborah didn't care. She circled her arms around him tightly, burying her head against his chest.

"You are alive," she whispered.

With one arm he gripped her waist. His free hand rested on the back of her head. "Of course I'm alive. Nothing could keep me from you." He turned her face toward his and lowered his lips against hers. Passionate, strong and full of love. Barak crushed her even closer to his body as their kiss continued. She brought her hands to his face and pushed him away with a gentle laugh.

"You must let me breathe, Husband!"

His hazel eyes stared into hers. "It is over."

Deborah knew he spoke of Sisera, but she couldn't say his name. "He is dead?"

"Yes." Barak kissed her again. "You need not fear anymore." He swept her up off the ground, spinning her around like a child. "We are free, Beloved!"

Deborah threw her head back and laughed as her husband danced her around the courtyard. They whirled together, their happiness mingled with tears, for what seemed to her to be an eternity, before she caught sight of someone standing in the shadows. Deborah whispered, "We have an audience."

Barak placed her back on the ground. Deborah held onto his arm, still dizzy from twirling, and tried to see who watched them.

"Neriah!"

The young soldier grinned. "Yes, Prophet." A veiled woman stood beside him. He placed a hand on the woman's shoulder. "I have brought a friend to see you."

Deborah studied the figure at his side. She was dressed in a robe of fine wool. The veil that covered the lower half of her face was of expensive Egyptian gauze. The woman stepped forward after a gentle push from Neriah. Deborah could see the dark eyes that peered out from above the veil.

"Jael?" She gasped.

The woman nodded.

Deborah ran forward to embrace her. "Praise God you are safe!" She squeezed her friend even tighter. "I've been so worried since I learned you were Heber's wife." Jael stiffened under her arms. Deborah stepped away. "Are you all right? Did he learn you'd helped us? Did he hurt you?"

The small figure shook her head. "No. Your God protected me."

Deborah put her hand on Jael's shoulder, marveling at how petite she was. *She still seems like a child to me, although she is a married woman.* "But now?" Deborah glanced at Neriah and Barak. "Will he not be angry that you are here now?"

Jael lowered her gaze as Neriah stepped beside her. "Heber is dead. He fought with the Canaanites."

Relief and grief both warred within Deborah's mind. Relief that she needn't fear Heber's reprisal for Jael's betrayal, and grief that her friend was now a widow with no husband to care for her. Deborah looked to Barak. "Can you not take her back to her kin? Surely they did not all perish in the battle?"

Jael spoke before Barak could answer. "Please." Her eyes brimmed with tears. "Please do not send me back to them."

"My friend, what's wrong?" Deborah's heart broke with the pain written across Jael's face. "Were they cruel to you?"

"No." Jael shook her head slightly. A single tear escaped to roll down her face. "It is only . . . ."

"What?"

The young woman knelt at Deborah's feet. "Please, Prophet. I will do anything. It would be my honor to serve you in any way you deem possible. I long to be with you. To learn more of your God."

Deborah's mind raced with a myriad of thoughts. *Serve me? No, she's my friend. Learn of our God? But she's a Kenite. What is she asking?*

Barak helped Jael to her feet. He turned the girl to face him. "You will serve no Israelite, Jael. Do you understand?"

The girl trembled, her eyes filled with fear. Deborah tried to decipher what was going on between them. Barak place his hands on Jael's shoulders. He stood so much taller than the girl, Deborah was afraid he would accidentally crush her in his desire to reassure her. "You are a hero, Jael. As Rahab hid Joshua's spies in Jericho and helped them to escape, so you helped our people to win against the Canaanites. More, you freed us from the wrath of Sisera."

Deborah felt the blood drain from her face. "What?"

Barak nodded. "On a command from our God she lured him into her tent and killed him while he slept."

Deborah stepped toward the girl. "My husband speaks the truth. You will serve no one."

Jael took Deborah's hands. "But how can I stay with you? I have nothing. I have no place in any of your tribes."

"You will live with us," Barak said. "Not as a servant, but as an honored guest in our house."

Deborah saw the flush in the girl's cheeks. *She is young yet. She does not want to live her life as a widow in the house of a married couple.* Deborah caught a movement behind Jael. Neriah shuffled his feet, his eyes focused on the ground. She remembered how he had stood next to the girl, waiting for Deborah to notice them. His hand had gone protectively to Jael's shoulder. He had watched her with tenderness.

"There is another way, Husband."

Lines furrowed his forehead. "How is that?"

Deborah tried to sound as if she did not already have Jael's wedding planned. "If a man would come forward from one of the tribes . . . ." She caught Barak's gaze and directed her own toward Neriah. She saw the understanding cross her husband's face.

"It would have to be a man worthy of such a great honor."

Jael looked up, hope and fear in her eyes. "But I am a widow. I have no dowry."

Barak shrugged. "You have saved our people, Jael. Your courage is your dowry."

"I would insist on someone who would treat her with kindness," Deborah added. "She has suffered much in her life and deserves happiness."

She and Barak turned expectantly toward Neriah. The young soldier lifted his head, his unruly brown hair blowing wildly in the spring breeze. "I. . . . I." Neriah's gaze pleaded to Deborah for help. She couldn't help but smile at his awkwardness.

"Have you thought of someone, Neriah?" She saw the look of frustration that flashed across his face, and laughed out loud. "Jael, I can speak for the man who stands behind you. He is a man of great courage and honor. But he is also a man who will treat you with the respect and love you deserve."

Neriah drew strength from Deborah's words. He touched Jael's arm. She turned to face him. Taking her hands, he took a deep breath. "Deborah speaks the truth. I am not a wealthy man, but I do have a brother near Kedesh. Now that there will be peace, I am sure I can go back and help him farm. It will be a hard life, but a good one."

Barak placed a hand on each one's shoulder. "I can vouch for him as well, Jael. He is one of my most trusted officers and a good friend." He looked down at the young woman. "Would you consider taking him as your husband and truly becoming one with our people?"

Jael's large brown eyes gleamed with joy. "It would be my honor to be his wife." Her eyes darkened. "But only if he does so of his own free will. Not out of a sense of duty to his commander, or the prophet."

Neriah glanced at Deborah. "The Lord knows the pain of my heart. I thought I would never love another woman." He cast an apologetic glimpse toward Barak before looking down at Jael. His face glowed in the courtyard sunlight. "But now I know that God has given me a great gift. By making me wait to find a love of my own, He knows I will cherish and protect it with my every breath." He cupped Jael's face in his hands. "Truly, I do this of my own free will, full of hope for our future together."

Barak clapped his hands on their backs. "Let us go inside and make this betrothal official. I am sure Leb has some wine to make your pledge with and then we will join the crowds outside in celebration."

Barak led the way, followed by Neriah. Deborah took Jael's hand, and together they walked into the crowded house. Barak's commanding voice echoed through the rooms.

"Everyone! We have an announcement! Please!"

From the various corners of the house, family members scurried to hear what Barak had to say. The red-haired man whispered something to Leb while the others gathered around. Her uncle leaned over to Rachel and spoke to her. Deborah's aunt clapped her hands in delight then ran to fetch a skin of wine and a goblet. Barak arranged the family in a circle with Neriah and Jael in the center.

As the simple oaths of intention were spoken Deborah gazed about the room. Tears came to her eyes as she looked at the faces of all those she loved. Azareel and Avram. Tamar, Daliyah and Adara. Deborah's heart was even full at seeing Bithia and Palti in attendance. Many of her friends had taken Leb's offer of hospitality as well, and they too stood about watching the ceremony. Judith and Deker. Nathan and Lazar. Even Elisheba and Jude had stayed overnight in Shiloh so they could celebrate God's victory.

When the new couple drank from the same goblet the crowd let out a cheer. Jael blushed and hurried over to Deborah's side. Barak pulled Neriah up and slapped him on the back. Deker, Nathan and Lazar joined in gently teasing their friend at his new status as a married man.

Elisheba made her way through the crowd toward Deborah. The old woman's eyes sparkled. "When Barak called out, I thought you had told him your news."

Deborah frowned. "What news?"

A look of surprise crossed Elisheba's face. "Why, that you're carrying a child."

A hush fell over the room. "But . . . ." Deborah shook her head. "I am not."

Elisheba pulled her into a corner. The other women all rushed to gather around them while the men stood back. "I am an old woman, but I'm observant. We have seen each other every day for the past year and a half. I know you, Deborah. You have not had your courses since we left the hills of Ephraim ten weeks ago."

Deborah thought hard. Her friend was right. She had her last flow two weeks before her wedding. In the stress of recruitment and battle she had not even given it thought. She looked at the women around her. "Surely it is from all the changes." Adara and Daliyah smiled. Rachel and Elisheba fairly glowed with amusement. Bithia stepped forward.

"Have you any other signs? Have you been tired?"

Deborah laughed. "Of course I have been tired. I have helped to lead an army of ten thousand men to war!"

Her stepmother pursed her lips together. "How about smells? Has your stomach turned at any smells lately?"

The smile on Deborah's face faded as she remembered the aroma of the sacrifice the day before. The others saw her expression and giggled amongst themselves. Rachel took Deborah's face in her hands and kissed her cheeks. "Congratulations, Niece. Praise God he has seen to make you fruitful."

She looked up to see Barak and Azareel standing next to each other, their eyes focused intently in her direction. She turned back to the women. "Is it possible?"

Adara pushed her gently toward Barak. "Of course it is possible. Now tell your husband he is going to be a father!"

Barak's face lit with happiness. "Is it true?"

"I think so," Deborah nodded. "Yes."

He crossed the room and threw his arms around her. "Oh, Beloved." His voice caught in his throat and Deborah knew he choked back tears.

"I pray God grants us a son as brave and honest as his father."

To her great surprise, Barak kissed her in front of all the family. His eyes glistened as he placed his forehead against hers. "And I pray He blesses us with a daughter as faithful and strong as her mother. A true servant of the Lord most high."

Azareel's voice called out, "Amen!"

And all God's people gathered around Deborah and answered, "Amen."

AUTHOR'S NOTE

This work of fiction is based on the Biblical account found in Judges 4&5. I also took information based on Jewish Midrash, the oral traditions and teachings of rabbis, to further enhance the novel. These were the first stories suggesting the Biblical citation that Deborah was the "wife" of Lapidoth could also be translated as the "woman" of Lapidoth. This slight variance in translation could be interpreted as she was either from a town named Lapidoth, or she was a "woman of flame." Some traditions surmised Deborah earned her title by weaving the wicks for the oil lamps in the Tabernacle. I chose to incorporate this idea, along with that of her being married to Lapidoth. Her escape from Sisera through supernatural fire was not from any research, but my imagination. Another total fabrication was Deborah's possession in Zuberi's tent. The inspiration came from 1 Samuel 16:14 in which God's spirit leaves King Saul and an evil spirit is allowed to torment him.

Another story from the Midrash claimed that Barak and Lapidoth were the same man, with still another tradition asserting that he had also been known as "Michal." This nugget of information led me to imagine Lapidoth as having taken his brother's name while Sisera's prisoner. It wasn't a direction I'd originally planned on traveling, but I liked the twist.

Among all the research I did for the book, I never found an answer as to why Jael was led to betray her husband, and the strict code of hospitality that existed, to kill Sisera. That her family had been killed by Canaanites and she had been rescued by Deborah is this author's attempt to give her motivation to commit such a brutal act.

ABOUT THE AUTHOR

Since their two children moved out, Kim and her husband
have filled their house with three crazy fur babies,
numerous stringed instruments, and tons of books.

For more information about Kim, her novels and her
performances check out:
www.kimstokely.com
www.facebook.com/kimstokelyauthor/
Twitter: @KStokelyWrites

CHECK OUT KIM'S OTHER BOOKS ON AMAZON
Contemporary Christian Fiction
Winter Trees
Spring Rains

Young Adult Fantasy
A Shattered Moon
Where Shadows Lie

Biblical Fiction
In the Shadow of the Queen (To be released October 2018)

SPECIAL ADDITION

A Sneak Peek at Kim's next novel

In the Shadow of the Queen

Jerusalem, 76 B.C.

For the first time in history, a woman rightfully reigns over Israel.

The queen's rule gives Anna, a gifted young seamstress, opportunities for work and education she never thought possible. But to achieve her dreams, Anna must enter a world festering with intrigue and deceit. Those living within the queen's shadow already plot to seize the throne when she is dead. Even Lev, Anna's first love, is drawn into this underlying world of power, pleasure and political maneuvering.

Torn between her own desires and the traditions of her people, Anna's story is one of enduring courage and her inspired belief in God's love and faithfulness in all circumstances.

CHAPTER 1

At thirteen, Anna had seen a royal parade before, but never one this grand. The dry, arid wind from the east did little to cool her as she stood in awe, shoulder to shoulder, with all of Jerusalem to watch the procession. Sunlight gleamed off the polished breast plates of the palace guards. The bright light burned her eyes, but she could not turn away. The sound of the horses' hooves clopping on the stone road, the jangling of their bridles, and the cries of those that followed behind, all had her transfixed. All of this because Alexander Jannai, the king and high priest of Judea, was dead.

The king's body rested on the bier being pulled by six chestnut horses. Soldiers surrounded it as the entourage made its way to the royal tomb. As they marched solemnly by, Anna's mind kept wandering to how this man, who had caused so much pain to so many in the past, would rot away to bone and dust. Then those bones would be placed in a box to rest with those of his fathers. All that power. All that wealth. And what would be left?

Her older brother, Daniel, whispered under his breath as the soldiers passed, "Praise Elohim, the monster is dead."

"Quiet, you fool," their father chastised. "We may yet be in danger."

Anna shivered at the fear she saw in her father's eyes. The king had ordered eight hundred Pharisees, including two of her uncles, crucified. She had only been a baby when it happened, but her parents still wept when they recounted the story.

The wind blew Daniel's dark hair across his face. "They say his wife Salome will be his successor, and she has been far more reasonable to us than her husband."

"She reigns now as a Hasmonean. She will side with the Sadducees," Father argued. His brown eyes flashed. "Just as Alexander did."

"Have faith, Father." Daniel smiled even as a group of paid mourners passed by, wailing and tearing at their clothes. "God has not forgotten us." He reached out to pull Anna to him. "Perhaps Queen Salome will have a heart like our Anna, pure and honest."

She wrapped her arms around her brother's waist, hoping her embrace would show him how much she appreciated his words.

Father placed his hand on her head. "If only I could believe it to be true." He glanced over at Daniel. "Will you come to the house?"

"Malachi will be expecting all his students back tonight."

Anna frowned. "Can you come home for a little while? To see Mother?"

A wave of sadness passed over Daniel's face. "How is she?"

Father put his arm around his shoulder. "Some days good. Some days bad. We take each as a blessing from the Lord."

Anna walked ahead of the men as they wove through the swarming streets of Jerusalem, up the hillside and toward their home near the base of the Temple Mount. The bleached clay and stone of the houses rose around her like a maze, but one she easily navigated. Weaving through the still milling crowds, she thought about what Daniel had said. Salome Alexandra, widow of the last two kings, would be their successor. A woman would rule Judea.

Her heart raced with excitement. She had never known any woman to be more than a wife and mother. Yet Salome would speak and be heard. She would enact laws and edicts that men would follow. The idea was totally foreign even though Anna's father often told her of the powerful women God had used in the past. Deborah, who helped lead an army against the Canaanites, was to be emulated. Athaliah, who had usurped the throne from her grandson, was to be cursed. *What kind of queen will Salome be? And what will it mean for me?*

A haze of dust and dirt, kicked up by the throng of people, settled over the streets as Anna continued to push toward home. She wiped sweat off her forehead and coughed lightly to clear her throat. The world was changing, and first to change would be Jerusalem, the center of their faith. What future would she have here?

"Anna!" Her friend Tova ran up and embraced her. The mantle she wore on her head could not contain the mass of light brown curls that fell down her back. Anna often wished such curls would appear in her hair. "Did you see the king's bier? Was it not magnificent?"

"I saw."

Although shorter than her, Tova was older by half a year. They turned off the main road and down a narrower street bordered on both sides by the smaller, one-story clay houses of the laborers and merchants. She and Tova had lived on this same road all their lives, playing together with sticks and leather balls as some younger children did now, while mothers and grandmothers gathered in their doorways to discuss the funeral procession. Older men stood off to themselves, arguing about the upheaval Alexander's death would cause throughout the land.

Anna would have liked to eavesdrop on those conversations, but Tova continued to prattle. "Did you see the size of the mourning party? Do you think they were all from his family, or did the queen pay for them all?"

"My father says they were paid."

"And the finery on the cart," the shorter girl mused with wonder. "All that gold? It must have cost a fortune!"

Anna agreed. "Money that could better have been spent on refurnishing the temple."

Tova's full lips pouted. "Why must you be so practical? Can you not appreciate the beauty of the spectacle?"

"I am sorry." Anna sighed. "It is the curse of being the daughter and the sister of scribes. It is all my father and Daniel can talk about lately." She pulled her friend closer to her side. "I have learned something else today, something you may not know."

Tova's eyes sparkled. "What is that?"

"Queen Salome plans to rule in her husband's place."

Tova stopped. "But what of her sons?"

"I do not know." Anna shrugged. "Perhaps she feels they are too inexperienced to rule." She pulled her friend along. "Come, I must get home to Mother."

"A queen over Judea . . . ." Tova's face mirrored Anna's thoughts.

"It is an exciting time to be alive, is it not?" *If a woman could rule men, what could she and Tova accomplish in their lifetimes?* Anna stopped in front of her house. "I must tell my mother all about the procession before Father and Daniel get home."

Tova's face lit up. "Daniel is coming?"

"Only for a moment, to see our mother."

Her friend's shoulders sagged.

"He is only concerned with his studies for now. He notices only what is written in a scroll or spoken by his teacher."

"I know." Tova sighed. "Perhaps I should pay someone to draw my likeness on parchment. Maybe then he'd realize he should marry me."

Anna laughed as she gave her friend a hug. "I am sorry he cannot see what a prize you are."

Tova's thin arms squeezed her hard. "Tell him you saw me today. Remind him that I exist!"

"I will." Anna pushed open the wooden door to her home. Her eyes struggled to see in the dim light.

"Ahhhhh," her mother wailed from the corner where she lay. "Shut it!"

Anna took one last breath of dusty air before stepping inside and closing the door behind her. She crossed the cool dirt floor and knelt down to where her mother lay in the corner. "Your head still hurts?"

"A knife between my eyes." She whimpered. "Will it never end?"

"Should I go to the well and fetch you some cool water?"

She groaned. "There is no need. It will only be warm by the time you bring it back."

Anna poured her a cup of watered wine and brought it to her pallet. "Here, Mother. Perhaps this will help."

She sat up to sip the drink Anna held to her lips. "Nothing will help."

"Even the news that Daniel is coming?"

She laid a frail hand on Anna's arm. "Truly?"

"Yes. He found Father and me among the crowd. They should be here any moment."

Mother's cheeks flushed. "Perhaps I feel better after all. I could make us dinner."

"He cannot stay. He is only coming to see you." Anna placed the cup on the floor then stood to grab the comb from the niche in the stone wall. "Let me fix your hair before he arrives."

"Yes, yes." Mother nodded. "I cannot have him seeing me like this."

Anna pulled the ivory-toothed comb gently through her mother's graying wisps. The comb had been a wedding gift from a wealthy aunt, and it was her mother's prized possession. "The funeral bier was something to behold, Mother. Gold and fine linens covered it. There must have been a hundred soldiers on horseback." She spoke softly as she worked, hoping her story would help her mother forget the pain in her head even more than her brother's visit.

Sunlight poured in as her father opened the door. He stepped aside to let Daniel inside. "Look who has come to visit us, Miriam."

Her mother shielded her eyes from the brightness and swatted Anna's hand to make her stop combing. "My son!"

Daniel lowered his tall frame and knelt at her side. "How are you, Mother?"

Anna put the treasured comb back on its shelf then set about making dinner. It would be a light meal, as the priests had called for a fast in honor of the high priest's death. Though her father refused to mourn the evil man, the markets were closed and any cooking fire might be spotted by the palace guards and reported. In preparation, she had made two loaves of bread the previous day, as well as goat cheese and hummus. They would not be feasting tonight, but they would not be fasting either. She sliced the bread as Daniel talked with their mother, telling her all about his studies with Malachi, one of the chief Pharisees.

"The rabbi has said I am one of his brightest students." Daniel stuck out his chest in exaggerated bravado.

"Of course you are." Her mother beamed, her face showing the first signs of health in several days. "You were always a smart child."

Someone knocked on the door and Anna quickly hid the bread and cheese beneath a cloth in the corner. She sat down in front of it as her father opened the door.

"Shalom, Phanuel." A deep, resonate voice spoke in greeting. "Is Daniel here?"

"Shalom, Lev." Father stood aside. "Come in. Come in."

Lev, taller than her father, ducked his head as he came through the doorway. Anna tried to keep her eyes downcast, as any modest girl would do, but her gaze strayed up several times. Lev was a beautiful man. Eyes the color of honey. Brown hair, thick with curls. As he was not much older than Daniel's twenty years, his beard was not as full as an older man's, but it framed his strong chin well. She felt heat rush to her cheeks as Lev smiled at her frank stare. She quickly looked to the dirt floor.

"Shalom, Anna."

"Sh-Sh-Shalom," she answered, humiliated by her stuttering.

"Miriam." Lev stepped toward her mother's pallet. "It is good to see you sitting up. Did the herbs my mother send help you?"

Miriam nodded. "They were a blessing."

"She will be glad to hear it. I am sure she will make you more." He gestured toward Anna. "Send your daughter to our house sometime this week to pick them up."

Anna tried to hide the smile that threatened to explode across her face.

Phanuel *hrumphed.* "We would not want to be a bother to your family."

Her happiness faded as rapidly as it had appeared. But then Lev spoke again. "Anna is never a bother. And it makes my mother happy to help others."

Daniel leaned forward and kissed his mother on the cheek. "I will pray for your health. As I always do."

The flush of her cheeks paled as Daniel stood. "It was good to see you, my son."

"I will be home again, on the Sabbath."

Lev chuckled. A musical sound that thrilled Anna's ears. "My father is a hard task master. Only the death of the king and the command of God can give us more than an hour away from our studies."

"Send him our best regards," Phanuel said as he opened the door.

"I shall." Anna lifted her eyes in time to see Lev smile at her. "Good night, Anna. I will tell my mother to expect your visit."

Happiness filled her, especially when her voice did not stammer as she answered, "Thank you."

Mother laid down as soon as the door shut behind them. Her father sighed, glancing between the two of them. His gaze rested on Anna. "Do not set your heart on Lev."

Her hands trembled as she picked up the tray of food behind her. "You are both Pharisees."

"His father is one of the finest rabbis at the temple." He stroked his full beard. "I am a mere scribe."

Her mouth went dry.

"I am sorry, Anna. No matter how much attention he gives you, Malachi will not allow his son to marry beneath him."

"Perhaps you think too little of yourself, Father. Too little of Malachi." The tray rattled as she set it down on the table. "And Daniel is certainly in the rabbi's favor."

He placed his hand over hers. "You have many fine qualities. I will find a good husband for you. Soon."

Her eyes filled. She could feel the tears wanting to spill down her cheeks. She turned away to retrieve the wine sack and wooden cups then passed them to her father. He waited until she sat to say the blessing. They ate in silence.

When they were finished, she sliced bread for her mother and mixed it with a little goat's milk to soften it. She sat next to her and lifted her head. "Eat, Mother."

"I am not hungry." She turned her face to the wall.

Anna sighed. "And what if Daniel comes again? Do you not want him to see you well?"

It took a moment, but Miriam shifted herself toward her daughter. Anna placed a morsel on her mother's tongue. Her nose wrinkled, but she dutifully chewed a few times before swallowing. She finished about half her meal before shooing Anna away. Anna cleared the remains of their meal to the courtyard to clean, while Phanuel sat down near his wife. He began to recite a song of David. The words soothed Anna's aching heart like a balm. Under her breath, she sang the words her father spoke, "The Lord is my strength and my shield; my heart trusts in Him, and He helps me."

Later, as she lay awake on her pallet, staring at the ceiling, Anna prayed, "El-Shaddai, please. Give me the desire of my heart. Soften Malachi's heart toward me. Let me be betrothed to Lev." For she knew, in her soul, she would never love anyone the way she loved the rabbi's son.

Made in the USA
Las Vegas, NV
30 January 2022